Born in Glasgow and now a dual US/UK citizen, **T.F. Muir** is one of Scotland's most popular crime novelists, with nine books in his gripping DCI Andy Gilchrist series published. The first in the series – *Eye for an Eye* – won the Pitlochry Award for the best crime novel by an unpublished writer, and the entire series continues to garner great reviews. Although T.F. Muir makes his home in the outskirts of Glasgow, he can be seen often in the streets of St. Andrews carrying out some serious research in the old grey town's many pubs and restaurants. T.F. Muir is working hard on his next novel, another brutal crime story suffused with windswept alleys and cobbled streets and some things gruesome.

Also by T. F. Muir

(DCI Gilchrist series)
Eye for an Eye
Hand for a Hand
Tooth for a Tooth
Life for a Life
The Meating Room
Blood Torment
The Killing Connection
Dead Catch
The Murder List

(DCI Gilchrist Short Story)
A Christmas Tail

DEAD STILL

T. F. MUIR

CONSTABLE

CONSTABLE

First published in hardback in Great Britain in 2020 by Constable

This paperback edition published in 2021 by Constable

A CIP catalogue record for this book is available from the British Library.

ISBN: 978-1-47213-107-2

Typeset in Dante MT by Hewer Text UK Ltd, Edinburgh
Printed and bound in Great Britain by Clays Ltd, Elcograf S.p.A.

Papers used by Constable are from well-managed forests
and other responsible sources.

Constable
An imprint of
Little, Brown Book Group
Carmelite House
50 Victoria Embankment
London EC4Y 0DZ

An Hachette UK Company
www.hachette.co.uk

www.littlebrown.co.uk

For Anna

AUTHOR'S NOTE

First and foremost, this book is a work of fiction. Those readers familiar with St Andrews and the East Neuk may notice that I have taken creative licence with respect to some local geography and history, and with the names of some police forces, which have now changed. Sadly, too, the North Street Police Station in which DCI Gilchrist is based has not only been closed but demolished – I still struggle to believe it – but its past proximity to the town centre with its many pubs and restaurants would have been too sorely missed by Gilchrist for me to abandon it. Any resemblance to real persons, living or dead, is unintentional and purely coincidental.

Any and all mistakes are mine.

www.frankmuir.com

CHAPTER 1

10.35 a.m., Monday
Gleneden Distillery, Outskirts of
St Andrews, Fife, Scotland

Detective Chief Inspector Andy Gilchrist switched off his car's engine. Rain battered the roof in a hard drum roll, and streamed down the windscreen in sheets. He leaned forward to peer up at the thunder clouds, but it looked as if the downpour was on for the rest of the day, maybe even the month.

From the passenger seat, Detective Sergeant Jessie Janes said, 'Not halfway through the month yet, and the Met Office is saying this could be the wettest January on record.'

'*Could* be. Which at least gives us some hope.'

'The way it's pissing down, I'd say it gives us *no* hope.'

Then . . . just like that . . . the rain slackened.

'Looks like the sun's trying to break through,' Gilchrist said.

'Oh that's really going to make a difference.'

'You got an umbrella?'

'Just the suntan lotion.' Jessie tutted, and opened the door to an icy January wind. 'Let's get on with it,' she said. 'At least it'll be dry where the body is.'

Gilchrist beeped his remote as Jessie scurried along a concrete path – head low, collar up – and into the entrance foyer of Gleneden Distillery. Glass-encased shelves, brightened by soft lighting, glowed with an array of golden malts that stood to attention on tartan-covered plinths. Padded velvet-like boxes lay opened to display sets of nosing glasses engraved with *Gleneden Distillery*. Pocket flasks, tops unscrewed as if to entice a quick toast for the road, stood amongst sets of sterling silver stirrup cups shaped as stag antlers, fox heads, howling hounds, wing-spread eagles.

His attention was drawn to the centrepiece, a metal-rimmed glass case that looked strong enough to withstand a hammer blow, and which housed a dark, bulbous bottle with a Victorian scroll proclaiming it to be a fifty-year-old single malt. A black tag lay next to it, with a gold-flaked inscription that priced it at £15,000. It looked inviting, he had to confess, but you would have to be filthy rich or stoned drunk – maybe both – to spend that on a bottle. Of course, at that price you wouldn't drink it, just store it some place safe, knowing that with each passing year it would rise in price. Gilchrist wasn't a whisky drinker *per se*, more of an eclectic drinker, preferring the thirst-quenching satisfaction of real ales, even the occasional mass-bottled beer if the mood took him, and now and again the odd whisky when he had one too many last ones for the road, often to his own detriment.

When he caught up with Jessie, she had her warrant card out and was challenging the receptionist, a young blonde-haired woman whose tartan outfit seemed two sizes too small and several years too old. He had a sense that she was someone who never looked polished no matter what she wore. Or maybe her bitten fingernails and a messy tattoo that peeked from the throat of her blouse in red and yellow swirls gave that impression.

'Mrs Dunmore rarely visits the distillery,' the receptionist was explaining to Jessie.

'What is it about *expecting us* that you don't understand?'

'There's nothing noted in her appointments' diary.'

'Get her on the phone.'

'She's not in her office.'

'I don't care where she isn't. Phone her mobile.'

'I don't have her mobile number.'

Gilchrist stepped in with, 'Is the distillery manager around?'

'That would be Robbie Marsh.'

'Now we know his name, is he available?'

'I haven't seen him this morning.'

Gilchrist smiled. 'That's all right. We'll make our own way to the ageing sheds, then.'

'You're not allowed to go there without—'

'Inspector Gilchrist?'

All three turned towards the voice, which came from a middle-aged woman who had entered the foyer through a door in the back wall and was now walking towards them, hand outstretched. A belted wax jacket, which matched green wellington boots, glistened with water droplets, as if she'd just stepped in from a light shower.

'Katherine Dunmore,' she said. 'I own Gleneden.' Her grip was dry and firm, and her lips twitched in a half-hearted smile.

'Detective Chief Inspector Gilchrist. St Andrews CID.' He held out his warrant card, then introduced Jessie. 'Detective Sergeant Janes, who'll be assisting in our investigation.'

Jessie nodded in response, but Dunmore's gaze darted to the receptionist, while her hand took hold of Gilchrist's arm and steered him towards the door. 'We'll be with Robbie,' she said over her shoulder. 'In number one warehouse.'

Outside, the rain had picked up again, but Dunmore seemed not to care as she strode down a gravel pathway alongside a black wooden building that reeked of creosote and tar, splashing through puddles in her wellington boots like a child heading to school.

Inside the warehouse, silence reigned, as if the rain had stopped. A fousty smell that reminded Gilchrist of dusty dampness swamped his senses. He scanned the warehouse. Every square inch, it seemed, was taken up by wooden casks of various sizes lying on their sides on rails of wood – larger casks stacked two high, smaller casks three high.

Dunmore pulled back her hood, tucked strands of dark brown hair behind both ears, and shouted out, 'Robbie?'

'Yes, Mrs Dunmore.' The voice came from behind rows of large wooden casks off to Gilchrist's right.

'That's the police here,' she said. 'Can you show them the . . .'

Her voice tailed off as a man emerged from between a lane of casks, removing a pair of heavy-duty gloves. He approached Gilchrist as if intent on tackling him, then shook his hand with a steel grip. 'Robbie Marsh,' he said, then nodded to Jessie.

'I believe you called it in, Mr Marsh,' Jessie said.

'I did, aye,' and without further prompting said, 'It's over here.'

Gilchrist walked after Marsh's slim figure, aware of Dunmore trailing behind. When they reached the open cask, Marsh stood back to let them look inside. That close to the cask, the air was redolent of an enticing whisky aroma that teased Gilchrist's taste buds – well, for a beer drinker, who would ever have thought?

4

The wooden cask stood upright, metal hoops slackened, lid off – some four feet tall, three feet in diameter. When Gilchrist leaned forward, he saw that it was drained of whisky, with a fully clothed body crammed inside. He didn't have to see the face to know it was the body of a man: checked shirt rolled up at the sleeves to reveal strong arms and an expensive watch with a man-sized face still fastened to the wrist; shirt collar up at the back to reveal a woollen tie, presumably still knotted; thick corduroy trousers the colour of whisky.

'Okay,' he said to Marsh. 'Run it past me. How you found him.'

Marsh glanced at Dunmore, and Gilchrist had a sense that permission to speak had been sought, and granted. 'We're one of a handful of distillers that have their own bottling plant.'

'That's unusual, is it?'

'Most use one of the major bottling plants in Edinburgh or Glasgow.'

'Okay. Keep going.'

'We were getting ready for our bottling run this morning, but when we rolled out this cask we could tell right away that something was wrong.' He raised his eyebrows, puffed out his cheeks. 'So we popped the bung to nose it, and that was that. It was off.'

'In what way?' Gilchrist said.

'Just didn't smell the way it should.'

'So then what?'

'We tried to insert the dog—'

'The what?'

'The dog. It's a copper tube, like an oversized test tube, on a bit of string, that we use to take samples through the bunghole. But we couldn't get it in. Something was blocking it.'

5

'Did you not think of calling the police then?' Gilchrist said.

'What for? We thought it was a bung cloth that had worked its way in, that's all.'

'Does that happen a lot?'

'Almost never, but when we tried to dislodge it with the bung puller, that's when we knew we had a problem and that we needed to open it.'

Gilchrist nodded. 'Keep going.'

'Well, we rolled it out and stood it up—'

'Bung in or out?'

'We put the bung back in, of course.'

Jessie said, 'It helps if you don't miss out bits. Okay?'

'Okay.' Marsh scratched his head. 'Well, we put the bung back in, and rolled it from over there to here. Then we stood it up, and drove off the top hoops so we could remove the lid. And that's when we discovered what the problem was.' He nodded to the body.

Gilchrist eyed the warehouse floor. Bone dry. 'What did you do with the whisky that was already in the cask?'

'Nothing. It's still in there.'

Gilchrist looked into the cask again, and in the dim light saw that the lower half of the body was actually submerged. 'You didn't drain any off?' he asked.

'No need to.'

'I don't understand.'

'Over the years,' Marsh said, 'the cask absorbs some distillate. And the wood's porous, so some evaporates. We lose about two per cent on average a year. That's what Customs and Excise allow you, anyway.'

'The angel's share?' Jessie said.

6

'It is, aye. But the older the whisky, the higher the percentage lost.'

'How high?'

'After twenty-five years, we would expect it to be about half full.'

'Jesus,' Jessie said, 'the angels should be bouncing off heaven's walls.'

Gilchrist coughed an interruption. 'What did you do after you found the body?'

'I phoned Mrs Dunmore—'

'Why do that?'

'What d'you mean?'

'You'd just discovered a body. Why not phone the police?'

'Well, I . . .' Marsh scratched his head again. 'I . . . I wanted to know what to do.'

Gilchrist glanced at Dunmore, whose gaze seemed focused on some spot on the warehouse floor. 'And what did Mrs Dunmore say?'

'She told me to phone the police. Which I did. And now you're here.' Marsh seemed pleased to have that part of the conversation over. But Gilchrist had a sense of not being told the truth, the whole truth, and nothing but the truth.

He faced Dunmore. 'Is that your recollection of events?' he said.

She looked at him, wide-eyed. 'Yes, it is.'

But Gilchrist was having none of it. 'So your manager phones you up and tells you he's found a body, and you tell him to phone the police?'

'Yes.' A tad uncertain.

He looked at Marsh, who seemed more interested in the condition of the opened cask than in Gilchrist's questions. Back to Dunmore. 'You didn't think to ask anything else?'

Dunmore's resolve seemed to surrender under Gilchrist's hard gaze. She grimaced for a moment, then edged closer to the cask. Without looking inside, she said, 'I did ask Robbie if he thought the body could be Hector.'

But even as Gilchrist said, 'Hector who?' the vaguest of memories stirred – a missing person, back in the eighties, maybe nineties, the man's name appearing before him—

'Hector Dunmore,' she said. 'My brother.'

'Who disappeared twenty-five years ago,' he added, the logic tumbling into place.

Dunmore closed her eyes and nodded.

'And what did you say, Robbie?' Jessie said. 'When she asked you?'

Marsh shrugged. 'I told her I couldn't say.'

Of course he couldn't, Gilchrist thought. Marsh would've been in primary school when Hector Dunmore vanished. And twenty-five years ago, Gilchrist had less than half a dozen years on the force under his belt. But even though he knew the answer, he said, 'Mrs Dunmore, can you positively identify the body as that of your missing brother?'

She pursed her lips, then said, 'I can, yes. It's Hector.'

'Did you touch the body in any way?'

Her gaze shot at him.

'To identify him, I mean.'

'No. I knew from his clothes and his hair. And his watch.'

Gilchrist waited.

'I bought that watch for his twenty-first. A Seiko. Hector liked the black face, and the date-window thingy. It was all I could afford back then.'

'And the clothes?'

8

'That's what he was wearing when he disappeared.'

'You remember what he was wearing?' Jessie said.

Dunmore's back straightened. 'Why wouldn't I?'

'Clothes are clothes,' Jessie said. 'What month did he disappear?'

'December. The twelfth.'

'That's the middle of winter. And he wasn't wearing a jacket?'

Dunmore seemed taken aback by the question. 'Well . . . I . . . No. He wasn't.'

'So when and where did you last see him?'

'The night he disappeared.'

'Keep going,' Gilchrist said again.

'As best I remember, George and I went round to Hector's to drop off some shopping – fresh cuts of meat that we buy in bulk from a local farmer.'

'And George is . . .?'

'My husband.'

Gilchrist caught Jessie's eye. They would need to talk to George, too. 'And what time would that have been?'

'We didn't stay long. Got there about six-ish. Stayed less than an hour.'

'And Hector was wearing then what he's wearing now?'

'Yes.'

'What about shoes?'

'Shoes . . .? I . . .' She shook her head. 'Slippers, maybe.'

If the body of Hector Dunmore was wearing the same clothes as when his sister and brother-in-law had last visited, then it seemed logical to conclude that he hadn't gone outside that evening after they'd delivered his shopping – in the middle of winter, no jacket or cold-weather garments – and must have been killed indoors. Were the Dunmores the last people to have seen Hector alive? Rather than voice conjecture, he made a mental note to obtain the records of Hector's misper investigation.

With that in mind, he said, 'We're going to have to seal off this area while we carry out our investigation.' He looked at Marsh. 'Can you show me exactly where the cask was stored for twenty-five years? We'll have to seal that area off, too.'

Marsh nodded to a wall about six feet away. 'Just over there.'

Gilchrist followed Marsh to a pair of wooden rails on the warehouse floor, nothing more than lengths of four by two on which casks could be rolled, then wedged into place.

'It was the last one in,' Marsh said, pointing to a spot near the wall.

Gilchrist tried to imagine the layout before the casks were moved. Rows of casks ran either side of him, stacked two high. 'I thought you stored them bung up so you can sample them over the years.'

'We do, aye.'

'So how do you sample these on the lower level, if there's a row of casks stacked on top of them?'

'You don't,' Marsh said. 'Once the top row's stored and wedged, you're only able to sample those on the top. Unless you started shifting the top row. Which is a lot of work for not a lot of return.'

'So not every cask in this warehouse is sampled?'

'No. There's loads of casks left untouched from start to finish.'

Gilchrist frowned. 'So whoever put the body into *that* cask twenty-five years ago, also knew that if they stowed it here,' he said, and tapped the ground with his foot, 'then it would likely never be sampled at all in twenty-five years.'

'That's correct, aye.'

He let his thoughts drift for a moment, as he walked back to Jessie and Dunmore. 'So who first moved the cask?' he asked Marsh.

'Jimmy Mitchell. He's the assistant manager. And that's when he got hold of me.'

'Where's Jimmy now?'

'Probably in the canteen.'

'Take DS Janes to talk to him. We'll need his statement. And yours, too.' He turned to Dunmore. 'And a statement from yourself.'

'Of course.'

Gilchrist looked around. 'How many doors to this warehouse?'

'Two.'

'Lock them both,' he said to Marsh, 'and make sure none of your staff can access this area until our Scenes of Crime Officers have completed their forensic examination.' Then to Dunmore, 'Some place warm and dry where we can have a chat?'

'My office.'

As he followed her, he was struck by how unmoved she appeared, as if discovering the whisky-preserved body of your long-lost brother after twenty-five years was an everyday occurrence. No tears. No parting look. No backward glance. No whispered prayer for a rediscovered soul. Nothing.

Over the years Gilchrist had interviewed hundreds of bereaved individuals, and one thing he'd learned was you could never predict how someone would react when confronted with the news of the death of a family member. Most cried, some inconsolably. Many held it together in stoic silence. Others sat there with glazed eyes, as if incapable of understanding what they were being told. But one – and Gilchrist remembered the moment well – actually laughed, jumped up from her chair, and offered to open a bottle of champagne in celebration.

He'd seen how cold Katherine Dunmore could be, and wondered how she would respond to deeper questioning.

Well, he was about to find out.

CHAPTER 2

Dunmore's office was on the second floor, at the back of the distillery, with a corner window that overlooked an expanse of windswept meadow, grasses brown and flattened from the winter rain and lack of sun. Talking of which, whiter clouds on the horizon seemed to be thinning to a bright blue. For all anyone knew in Scotland, it could be the start of spring.

'Can I get you anything?' Dunmore said. 'Tea? Coffee? Something stronger?'

'I'm fine, thank you. I don't intend to take up much of your time.'

'You don't mind if I do.' Not a question, he knew, as she opened her desk drawer and removed a crystal tumbler and a half-bottle of whisky. 'Gleneden Reserve,' she said. 'One of my favourite blends.' She proceeded to pour herself a measure – close to a treble, as best he could guess – then dribbled in no more than a few drops from a jug of water. 'You sure I can't persuade you?'

Gilchrist raised his hand. 'Positive.'

She nodded then took a sip that barely wet her lips. 'God,' she said. 'That's good.' She reclined in her high-backed swivel chair and narrowed her eyes. 'That's one of the good things about owning a distillery. You're allowed to sip whisky for lunch.'

'Or breakfast,' he said.

'You don't look like a whisky drinker, I have to say.'

'And what does a whisky drinker look like?'

She tapped the side of her nose. 'Trade secret.' Then she opened another drawer and removed a couple of miniatures. 'Here.' She pushed them across her desk. 'Try them. I think you'll find them palatable, maybe even enjoyable.'

'That's very kind of you. But no thank you.'

'On duty?'

'At the start of a murder investigation.'

The mention of murder seemed to wipe all pleasure from her face. Then, as if in the huff, she leaned forward and pushed the miniatures across her desk so that Gilchrist had to catch them as they toppled off the edge. 'I insist,' she said.

He returned both miniatures to the corner of the desk, beyond her reach. 'So when did Robbie Marsh call you this morning?'

'Some time after nine.'

'Quarter past? Five past?'

'About that.'

'Which is it?'

'Quarter past. Give or take ten minutes. I mean, it's not like I was timing him.'

'And what did he say? Verbatim, if possible.'

'Hah. Now you're asking. Memory's not as good as it used to be.'

'Give it a try.'

She raised her eyes to the ceiling. 'He said, Good morning, Mrs Dunmore. But I could tell from the tone of his voice that something was wrong.'

'In what way?'

'He sounded slightly off. Nothing much. Nothing I could put a finger to.'

'He might not've been feeling well. A frog in his throat. That sort of thing.'

'No, it wasn't that, it was just . . . I wished him good morning in response, then asked if anything was the matter.'

'You asked him that, after just four words – Good morning, Mrs Dunmore?'

'Yes.'

Silent, Gilchrist waited.

'Then Robbie said he had some disturbing news, that they'd discovered a body, and would I like him to call the police?'

'Exact words?'

'Yes.'

'To which you said?'

'Is it Hector? And he said that he couldn't say.'

'How long has Robbie worked at the distillery?'

'Oh, I don't know. Ten, twelve years, maybe.'

'So how did he know Hector?'

'He didn't know him. Hector had disappeared long before Robbie joined us.'

'Which is why I'm puzzled that he said he couldn't say it was Hector, rather than ask who Hector was.'

'Oh, everybody who works in Gleneden knows about Hector.'

Gilchrist let several seconds pass, but Dunmore seemed content in her answer. 'Did Robbie tell you *where* he'd found the body?'

'No.'

'So you didn't know he'd found it in a cask?'

'I assumed that's where it was.'

'Why would you assume that?'

'Because I knew they were doing a bottling run, and that's where Robbie had been. I mean . . .' She rolled her eyes. 'Where else would it have been found?'

'It could've been found by the roadside,' he said, 'before they started the bottling run. A hit and run, perhaps. Or in one of the fields. An elderly person who'd gone for a walk, collapsed, and died from hypothermia. I can think of other possibilities, but I'm intrigued as to why you presumed the body might be Hector.' He held her gaze, and waited.

She reached for her tumbler, took a sip that drained it to the halfway mark that time, then returned the glass to her desk with slow deliberation. 'Well . . . I . . .' She shook her head. 'I don't know what else to tell you. That's the first thing that came to mind. Was it Hector? He'd been missing for so long. And there's never a day goes by that I don't think about him.' She dabbed a hand at the corner of her eye. 'He was my brother, after all. The owner of the distillery until . . . well . . . until he . . . he disappeared.'

Crocodiles had shed more convincing tears, he thought. 'I understand you don't visit the distillery very often.'

'Who told you that?'

'Don't you?'

'Not as often as I used to. No.'

'Once a day, a week, a month, what?'

'At least several times a month, I'd say.'

'So how did you know they were doing a bottling run?'

'It's Monday. They always do bottling runs on a Monday.'

'How did you know they were bottling a twenty-five-year-old cask this morning? And not a ten-year-old?'

16

'I . . . eh . . . Robbie must have told me.'

'When he phoned you this morning?'

'Yes.'

'You didn't say that.'

'As I said, memory's a bit dodgy now.' She hid her gaze behind another sip.

Gilchrist waited until she returned the glass to the desk. 'How old was Hector when he disappeared?'

'Twenty-six.'

'And he ran the distillery until then?'

'Not only ran it. He owned it.'

'Lock, stock and barrel, one hundred per cent?'

'Mummy had a small share in it at the time.'

'Tell me about the watch,' he said.

'I bought it for his twenty-first,' she said, unfazed by his sudden change in tack. 'He'd wanted a Rolex, but I couldn't afford that, not then, anyway.'

'And how old were you then?'

'Nineteen. Hector was two years older. One year and nine months to be exact.'

'Were your parents alive?'

'Mummy only. Daddy died the year before. Mummy was so upset. She cried for days and days, poor soul.' Another sip gave Gilchrist the sense that she had no fond memories of her father, and might have been toasting the memory of his passing.

'He must have been young when he died, your father.'

'He was, yes. Forty-something. Five, I think. Maybe six. About that.'

'And his name?'

'Edwin.'

'Your mother's name?'

'Alice.'

'Is she still alive?'

'Oh, dear goodness, no. After Hector disappeared, she went to pieces. She was never the same. I ended up having to put her in a nursing home. I couldn't look after her. Best place for her, as it turned out. But she never settled there. She shrank into herself, would be a good way to describe it. The poor soul then had a series of mini-strokes, micro infarctions of the brain, is the medical term. Then she passed away one night in her sleep.'

'I'm sorry to hear that.' But he could have been talking to a cardboard image for all the emotion being shown. 'Any other brothers and sisters?' he asked.

'No. Just me.'

'So,' he said, measuring his words. 'When Hector disappeared, and your mother fell to pieces, who took over the distillery?'

'I did.'

'All by yourself?'

'George helped.'

'Are you and George still involved in the running of the business?'

'Very much so. You can't find good help any more. It's a generational thing. In my day, you worked the hours you needed to get the job done. Nowadays, it's all mobile phones, and minimum hours for maximum wages. Free handouts is what they're looking for.'

'All from only several days at the distillery a month?'

A momentary pause, as if to recalibrate her thinking, then, 'Most of our work's done by email these days. Or phone. Business is handled perfectly well from home.'

'What about Robbie and Jimmy?'

'What about them?'

'Do they expect free handouts?'

'No. Robbie's one of the best managers we've had. Jimmy's still on probation.'

Probation seemed an odd word to use about an employee. But that aside, he did a quick mental calculation. 'So when Hector disappeared, you would've been twenty-four?'

'Yes.'

'Were you and George married then?'

'Yes. We got married the year before.'

'What did your father think of George?' he said, just to throw it out there.

'He never met him, but I'm sure he wouldn't have liked him. He never liked anyone I brought home.'

'Why is that?'

'Over-possessive of his only daughter, I assume. My relationship with Daddy was ... how should I say it? ... *fraught*. He wasn't a pleasant man at times.'

Gilchrist pulled his questions back on track. 'Where can I find George?'

'At home.'

'Which is where?'

She rattled off an address, and he scribbled it down – Hepburn Gardens, St Andrews. 'If he's not there,' she said, 'he'll be at his office. GC Publicity.' Another address, followed by a couple of phone numbers.

'What does GC stand for?' he asked.

'George Caithness. I never took his surname when we married. For business reasons.'

He mouthed an Ah, then said, 'Did Hector attend your wedding?'

'Of course. Why wouldn't he?' Irritation seemed to creep behind her eyes. She took another sip, lips tight, as if his question had soured the whisky. Then she returned her glass to her desk with a firm thud of finality. 'I don't particularly care for what you're suggesting, Mr Gilchrist, that Hector and I didn't get on with each other. On the contrary, I loved Hector more than any sister could love her brother.'

'And your husband, George,' Gilchrist said, just to keep the pot simmering, 'how did he and Hector get on?'

'Like the best of friends. How else would you expect them to?' She slid her chair away from her desk, swivelled it around so she faced the meadows, and Gilchrist the back of her chair. 'You're beginning to annoy me, Mr Gilchrist. I don't feel inclined to continue with this . . . this *chat*. I'll be talking to my lawyer. You'll probably hear from her before close of business. Good day.'

Gilchrist was surprised by Dunmore's needless threat, and pushed to his feet, his eyes on her reflection in the window. But she seemed more interested on something in the distance than in a DCI preparing to leave her office. The manner in which she'd talked to him irked, and he found himself unable to resist stamping his authority. 'When you do call your lawyer,' he said to her reflection, 'it would be in your best interests to tell her that you're expected at St Andrews North Street Police Station at 8 a.m. tomorrow for a formal interview.'

'I'm not sure I can fit that in.'

'Change whatever plans you have,' he ordered. 'And be there. At eight.'

'And if I don't?'

20

'I'll consider that a wilful attempt to obstruct a criminal investigation, and I'll have a warrant issued for your arrest.'

Dunmore swivelled her chair around. Her hands, tight and sinewed, gripped the arms of her chair like eagle's claws. Her eyes blazed with a sheen of anger, maybe madness. 'How *dare* you,' she said. 'How *dare* you come into my office and threaten me with arrest when the body of my dear brother has only just been found.'

Gilchrist slipped his hand into his pocket and removed a business card. He laid it face-up on her desk. 'Tomorrow morning,' he said.

He let himself out, conscious of Dunmore's eyes on him all the way.

CHAPTER 3

As Jessie strode after Robbie Marsh on the hunt for Jimmy, she struggled to keep up with him, his long stride more suited to someone seven feet tall than the short-arse Scotsman he was. They crossed a gravel road, passed the entrance to the distillery, rounded the back of the building to a paved area that seemed to double up as a smoking area and barbecue slash picnic spot. A group of three people – two women, one man – huddled beneath an overhead canopy fixed to the wall. The rain had turned to drizzle as fine as haar. In the cold air a grey fug of cigarette smoke hung around them like personal fog.

Marsh shouted, 'Jimmy,' then gave a sideways nod with his chin – over there, by the fence. Jimmy pulled on his cigarette as if his life depended on it, taking it down to his thumb and middle finger. Then he dropped the dout and stomped it into the slabbed paving.

With just that action, Jessie took an instant dislike to him. She no longer smoked – how long had it been? Eight years? – and the sight of discarded fag ends littering the ground pissed her off. Maybe it had to do with the fact that she had a son, Robert, from whom she'd managed to keep the sin of smoking. But not only was smoking a filthy habit, smokers were filthy, too. What would the world look like if everyone who ate or drank cast their left-overs onto the ground for others to clean up? Same difference as douts, as far as she could tell—

'This is Jimmy Mitchell,' Marsh said.

Jessie flashed her warrant card, and wrinkled her nose at the acrid fragrance that clung to Mitchell's clothing. 'Right,' she said, 'tell me about it.'

Mitchell seemed confused, until Marsh said, 'When we opened the cask—'

'I'm not talking to you,' Jessie said. 'I'm talking to him.'

'Oh, aye, right,' Mitchell said. 'We were getting ready for the bottling run, when I rolled out that last puncheon—'

'What?'

Jimmy looked at her, puzzled.

'Rolled out that last what?' she said.

'Puncheon. It's the largest of our whisky casks. Five hundred litres.'

Well, it would have to be that size to stuff a body inside, she thought. She scribbled on her notepad, then said, 'You were saying . . .?'

'Aye, right.' He coughed, cleared his throat. 'So, when I rolled it out, the way it kind of wobbled, I could tell something was inside. I told Robbie, and after he'd checked it out, he said we had to open it. And when we took the lid off, there he was, stuffed inside, soaked all the way through with whisky.'

'Did you not think of wringing him out?'

'Naw, we wouldnae . . .' He stopped when he realised Jessie was being sarcastic.

'Then what?' she said.

'Robbie ran off to phone the boss, like. And I carried on with the bottling run.'

'All by yourself?'

'Naw, me and the girls.' He glanced at the two other smokers, and Jessie tutted as she turned on Marsh.

'Only you and Jimmy, you said. Now we've got another two.'

Marsh shrugged. 'Thought you were only asking about opening the cask.'

'Anyone else?' Jessie said. 'Did you phone the rest of the staff to come and have a look? Any family members, friends, neighbours?'

'Only Mrs Dunmore.'

'And did she have a look inside the cask?'

'She did, yes.'

'Before or after you reported it to the police?'

'Does it matter?'

Jessie turned the full heat of her ice-cold stare on him. 'What I'm trying to establish here, and what you seem to be trying to avoid telling me, is how long did it take you to phone it in after finding the body?'

Marsh glanced at the ground, shuffled his feet, as if deciding whether or not to tell the truth. In the end, he said, 'About an hour, I guess.'

'I'm not interested in guesses. How long, exactly?'

'I can't say exactly for sure.'

'How about you, Jimmy?'

'I don't know nothing about phoning the cops.'

Back to Marsh. 'Okay, Robbie. You're it. And you'd better stop pissing me around, or I may have to check you out in greater

24

detail. And before you try to slip me another porky, be advised that we can and will check phone records.'

Marsh puffed out his cheeks. 'Maybe an hour and a half?'

'Maybe an hour and three-quarters?'

'Maybe.'

Jessie glanced over Marsh's shoulder. 'Is that the canteen?'

'It is, aye.'

'Right, let's go. I want written statements from the pair of you, the girls, too.'

Gilchrist had just returned to the warehouse when he noticed a Range Rover bumping alongside the gravel path. It pulled to a gentle halt. The engine died. The vehicle was angled such that he couldn't see the driver through the windscreen, although he did recognise the personal registration number plate as Cooper's.

The door opened, and Dr Rebecca Cooper – police pathologist – stepped to the ground. He caught his breath at the sight of her hair. What he had always seen as one of her most attractive features – thick strawberry-blonde waves that folded over her shoulders in a sensuous mass – was now cut in a styled bob that hugged her cheeks. And where she used to rake it back from her forehead with her fingers, a fringe cut as straight as a ruler ran through her eyebrows. The change was so dramatic he could have been looking at a stranger, rather than a past lover.

'You look surprised,' she said.

'Does it show?'

She removed a packet of coveralls from the boot, and tore it open. 'I've always been able to read you like a book, Andy.'

'I take it Mr Cooper approves?'

'Mr Cooper's no longer around to approve of anything.'

Which was a surprise, although with Cooper he had learned never to be surprised by anything she said or did. 'Nothing serious, I hope.'

'Regrettably.'

'Hence the new look?'

'For attracting a new man, you mean?'

Cooper had this way of diverting his most innocent of comments down a path that led him deeper into trouble. So he decided not to respond, even though he wondered if Maxwell Cooper's absence was permanent, or just another period of separation until he returned to continue where he'd left off. Instead, he said, 'Not quite what I was suggesting.'

'And what were you suggesting?'

'New situation, new look?'

'The body's in there, is it?'

She walked off towards the warehouse, and for a moment he almost followed.

Cooper was one of Scotland's most respected forensic pathologists, and had worked with Gilchrist on a number of major cases. He would regret – probably to his dying day – that they'd had more than a professional relationship which at one time he'd hoped, maybe even expected, would progress to something more permanent. In the end, he found out he was not Cooper's kind of man; world-travelled, knowledgeable epicure, CEO of own company. But even so, he couldn't shift an irresistible sense of attraction, and an unsettling longing that stirred in his groin.

He shoved his hands deep into his pockets, and went looking for Jessie.

What Marsh had called the canteen was more small café slash shop where visitors to the distillery could have tea, coffee, cakes, and purchase any number of bottles of Gleneden whisky. He found Jessie seated at a corner table with two women and Robbie Marsh. Jessie was gathering her notes, as the others pushed to their feet.

'Thanks, girls,' she said. 'I'll be in touch if I've any more questions.'

As the women walked past him, Gilchrist caught Marsh's eye. 'Another question?'

Marsh looked at him. 'Sure.'

'When you phoned Mrs Dunmore this morning, did you mention anything about the bottling run?'

'Told her we were bottling a twenty-five-year-old.'

He thought the answer too quick, as if Marsh had been primed. 'And what did she say to that?'

'Nothing, really.'

'Was it important that she knew?'

'Not really.'

'So why did you tell her?'

'It's . . .' He shrugged. 'I don't know. I just did.'

He waited a couple of beats before saying, 'Anything else?'

Marsh shook his head. 'That's about it, I think.'

Gilchrist handed him a business card. 'Call, if you think of anything.'

Marsh walked away, mobile phone already in his hand.

Gilchrist sat opposite Jessie. 'Any luck?' he asked.

'Don't know if you'd call it luck, but that Robbie boy didn't call it in as quickly as he said he did.' She sifted through her notes. 'Best I'd say, an hour and forty-five minutes from the time they discovered the body, and him calling it in.'

'The reason being?'

'Had to wait for Lady Gleneden to put on her make-up.'

'That's a bit weak.'

'As water.'

'What do you make of Dunmore? Do you believe her?'

Jessie shook her head. 'We've found a body, Mrs Dunmore. Oh, is it Hector?' She scoffed. 'No, I don't bloody believe her. And what's this about her and her husband visiting Hector the night he disappeared? If she remembered him wearing the clothes he's still got on, then he must have been murdered that night at home.'

'My thoughts, too.'

'I think she's being economical with the truth, the lying trollop.'

'You'll have a chance to tackle her again. She's bringing her lawyer to the Office tomorrow first thing. So get hold of Jackie and get her to dig out the misper files for Hector Dunmore's investigation.'

'What about her husband, George? Will he be with her tomorrow?'

'You and I are going to have a chat with him later.'

'Why not right now?'

'I want to see how Cooper's getting on. You interested?'

'Do I have a choice?'

'Try to keep it friendly for once.'

'How d'you expect me to do that?'

'Pin that tongue of yours to the roof of your mouth.'

CHAPTER 4

The area outside warehouse number 1 was no longer deserted. Two white SOCO Transit vans were parked close to the wooden building, their side and rear doors wide open. Crime scene tape across the doorway flapped in the wind.

Inside, Gilchrist could tell all was not well. Cooper stood with her back to them, voice raised, her frustration clear. Three SOCOs kneeled on the ground by her feet, and it took him several seconds to realise they were struggling to lay Hector Dunmore's whisky-soaked body into a body bag without damaging it. Despite their professional expertise, human flesh – any flesh, for that matter – soaked in alcohol for twenty-five years was unforgiving to the touch. Skin sloughed off bare arms like overcooked meat, to expose sinewed musculature. Dunmore might have had a fine head of hair as a twenty-six-year-old, but the body on the bag looked as if it was wearing an ill-fitting topper complete with crumpled left ear. One of the SOCOs swore as her hand slipped free, taking with it the skin of a bony right foot.

So, no winter shoes, no slippers, no socks.

Gilchrist interrupted the scene with, 'Anything obvious to explain cause of death?'

'Christ, Andy,' Cooper snapped. 'But if we're ever able to get the body back to the lab intact, I'll have an answer for you in a day or two.'

'You couldn't have something for me by tomorrow, could you?'

'No, I couldn't,' she said. 'And what's the rush? One day longer in a twenty-five-year-old murder enquiry isn't going to make one iota of difference.'

Well, he supposed she had a point.

'Don't let that slip,' Cooper said.

But the belt buckle on Dunmore's trousers had already pierced the skin, and a roll of bloated intestine squeezed out from under his shirt and into the SOCO's hands like purple sausage meat.

'Chrissake,' someone hissed.

Body bags were made of non-porous material and, once zipped up, nothing escaped. Although Gilchrist saw that the problem was not something slipping out, but that everything was zipped up in the first place.

'No shoes?' he said.

'Nor socks.'

A glance into the emptied cask confirmed that Dunmore hadn't been wearing slippers either, or anything else on his feet that might have slipped off in the decanting. With checked shirt and corduroy trousers, Dunmore should have had something on his feet to walk about his house. At least, that's what Gilchrist would have worn. But did it matter if he was barefooted before or after he was murdered?

Probably not, came the answer.

'We'll leave you to it,' he said. But he could have been talking to a mannequin for all the response Cooper gave him.

Outside, walking back to his car, Jessie said, 'She's a cold one.'

'She can be difficult to communicate with at times. I'll give you that.'

Jessie chuckled. 'Something tells me that you're still hankering after her.'

Gilchrist pressed his remote fob and his car beeped at him. 'Did Jackie get back to you with Dunmore's misper file?'

'It's early days.'

'Get onto it.'

The drive from Gleneden Distillery to Dunmore's home in Hepburn Gardens took less than fifteen minutes – a short commute that did nothing to explain why it had taken Dunmore so long to arrive at the distillery after Marsh phoned her. Gilchrist pulled onto a red-paved driveway that led to a two-storey house with a circular turret, and freshly painted roughcast that must have cost three months of a DCI's salary to paint. An expansive lawn, green and manicured despite it being winter, filled one corner of the property. A ten-foot-high hedge, which must have been trimmed with the help of a spirit level, lined the boundary.

He parked next to a black Range Rover Sport, and stepped into the cold January air.

Jessie blew into her hands and sniffed the air. 'Just stinks of money, doesn't it?'

'It's well maintained, that's for sure.'

'Master of the understatement. How much does a distillery owner earn anyway?'

'More than you and me.'

31

'Yeah, added together. You ever think you're in the wrong business?'

'Often.'

She eyed the front door. 'Come on, let's knock this punter up, and get back to the Office for a cuppa.' But after five minutes of Jessie cursing and pressing the bell, rattling the knocker, the door remained unanswered. 'Don't think anybody's in,' she said.

'I'm the master of what, did you say?'

'You got a number you can reach him?'

Gilchrist called the number Dunmore had given him for GC Publicity. On the third ring a woman's voice said, 'Hello?'

Gilchrist introduced himself, then said, 'I'm looking for George Caithness?'

'I'm sorry, but Mr Caithness isn't here.'

'Do you know when he's expected?'

'No, I'm sorry, I don't.'

'You got another number I can reach him?'

'Give me a second.' The line clattered, then silenced, clattered again, and a mobile number was rattled off. Gilchrist assigned it to memory, and when he ended the call, tapped it in. He cursed when he got through to a dead line. 'It's disconnected.'

'Maybe your memory's not as good as you think it is,' Jessie said. 'I don't know how you can remember numbers like that. I've got to write them down.'

Gilchrist did indeed have a memory for numbers, but just in case he'd got it wrong, he handed his mobile to Jessie. 'Phone Caithness's office again and check it out, will you?'

While Jessie located the number and redialled it, Gilchrist walked along the side of the house. He unlatched a wooden gate at the corner of the garage, which opened up to a back garden as well maintained as the front, private, too, despite the adjacent homes. A twelve-foot-high leylandii hedge, trimmed as flat as a wall and squared at the top like topiary, ran around the entire boundary. Stone slabs inset into the lawn formed a path that led to a gazebo in the corner, which looked trapped by winter-bare clematis. Wooden decking ran along the back of the house, and stepped up to a hot tub.

At the far boundary, he turned and faced the house. From there, he had a clear view of the upstairs rooms – curtains open, no lights on, no sign of activity.

Just then, Jessie walked into the back garden, shaking her head. 'You were right.' She handed his phone to him. 'I'd say the SIM card's been removed.'

He slipped his mobile into his jacket. 'Something doesn't fit here. Brand new Range Rover parked at the front, phone ringing out, no one answering the door.'

'He could've gone for a walk, or a jog. Who knows?'

'Maybe.' But that sixth sense of his was warning him that there was more to George Caithness's absence than a daily jog. He couldn't point to anything, just that niggling feeling that stirred when things didn't quite add up. 'Have Jackie check the Range Rover. It might not be his.' Then he pulled out his mobile, and walked to the middle of the lawn.

When Dunmore answered, he said, 'Your husband, George, isn't home.'

'I can't help you with that.'

'Any idea where he could be?'

'Have you tried his office, for God's sake?'

'He's not there, but his car's here. A black Range Rover. That's his, right?'

The sigh that swept down the line could have been a whispered curse. 'George could have gone out to buy a newspaper. He often does that. Or he could be at home watching TV, and not in the least interested in talking to the police. Which is something I have no interest in doing either. Good day.'

The line died.

Well, after her hissy-fit at the distillery, he supposed it was silly of him to expect her to welcome his line of questioning. But she shouldn't treat him with such disdain.

It only made him more determined.

CHAPTER 5

Back at the North Street Office, Gilchrist went looking for Jackie Canning – *best researcher in the world*, he called her – for the missing person's file on Hector Dunmore. As soon as he entered Jackie's office she held it up for him.

'This . . . this . . .' she tried, but her stammer stumped her every time.

'Hector Dunmore's file?' he said.

'Uh-huh.' Her mass of rust-coloured hair wobbled like an Afro. 'Two,' she said.

'You made a copy for Jessie?'

'Uh-huh.'

'Thanks, Jackie. You're a darling.' He took both files from her, and blew her a squelchy 'Mwah' in the process.

Jackie giggled, then shooed him away as if he were a naughty child.

Gilchrist dropped the original file on Jessie's desk, then headed to his own office. As he fingered the copies, he was surprised to see how sparse they were. It seemed that not much effort had gone into the investigation before the powers that be drew a line under it. A quick flip through confirmed Dunmore's Land Rover had been found on the outskirts of Mallaig on the west coast of Scotland, about two hundred miles due west of St Andrews, on 14 December. A well-worn black parka jacket with a fur-trimmed hood had been found in the rear seat, and a tattered briefcase that contained a notebook and paperwork was identified by Katherine Dunmore as belonging to her brother, Hector. As if for the avoidance of doubt, a couple of sheets of Gleneden letterhead were also recovered from the briefcase, with Hector Dunmore's name printed in the address.

It all seemed too convenient for Gilchrist's peace of mind.

Interestingly, no fingerprints had been lifted from the Land Rover, with a note from the SIO that *the steering wheel, handbrake and gear levers, seats – back and front – cabin and windscreen had all been wiped clean. Outside door handles, wing mirrors, and doors had been polished, too.* The Senior Investigating Officer was DI Tom Calish, whom Gilchrist had only the vaguest recollection of – white-haired, rubicund face, beer belly, smoked sixty a day, on the verge of retirement – which didn't bode well for Calish still being around. And twenty-five years ago, DNA was still in its infancy. So, with no fingerprints, and no mileage logbook – from what Gilchrist could tell – all Calish had to rely on for proof that the Land Rover had been driven there by Hector Dunmore in person, was the assumptive word of his sister, Katherine, and DVLA records for proof of company ownership. Despite suspicions surrounding the cleaning of the fingerprints, the Gleneden letterhead effectively closed the case in terms of identification, when Dunmore's disappearance from his home in St Andrews was confirmed.

No eyewitnesses in or around Mallaig had come forward, and the Mallaig Police received no reports of anything untoward, other than a couple of drunk and disorderlies that weekend. Search teams had been organised, and the local community came out in force to assist. But after six days the search was called off when a major snowstorm threatened to close all roads in and around the town. Besides, it was the festive season, and from the notes thereafter, it seemed to Gilchrist that everyone had gone home to celebrate Christmas and bring in the New Year.

January proved no better, with what Gilchrist could tell were half-hearted attempts to revitalise the investigation. Witness statements had been taken from people who knew Hector or worked with him. But as Gilchrist read them, he realised that the only statements of import were those of Dunmore's sister, Katherine, and her husband, George, the last people to see Hector alive. It seemed that Calish simply took their statements, then did little follow up. Hector had driven to Mallaig for reasons unknown, and abandoned his Land Rover.

And that was it.

Reading on, days passed with no additional entries recorded, then weeks, until the end of May when the case was finally assigned to cold storage. End of.

Not one of Fife Constabulary's better efforts, he had to say.

He pushed his fingers through his hair in frustration, and faced the window. Outside, winter was making its presence felt. The skies had cleared and the temperature had dropped to below freezing. Ice sparkled on frosted asphalt in the car park below. He found his gaze creeping over the boundary wall into the gardens beyond, his mind simmering away in the background, trying to make sense of what had happened all these years ago.

Hector Dunmore had been murdered and his body hidden in a cask in a distillery on the outskirts of St Andrews. Meanwhile, his

Land Rover had been driven to Mallaig for the sole purpose of faking his disappearance, by someone unknown, someone not sought by the police due to Calish's presumption that it could only have been Hector who'd driven it there in the first place.

Which was when another possibility flickered to life.

Gilchrist returned to the files, flipped through them until he found what he was looking for—

'Have you read the case files?' Jessie said.

Gilchrist looked up, and grimaced. 'I'm working through them.'

'Doesn't exactly show the Constabulary in the best light, does it?'

What could he say? It would be pointless trying to talk to Calish. Even if he were still alive, he would have to be in his eighties at least. 'There had to be two of them,' he said.

She nodded. 'One to drive the Land Rover to Mallaig, and one to drive him back.'

He smiled. Jessie had figured it out, too. 'But what if only one person was involved?'

'How would that work?'

'He drives the Land Rover there, parks it, cleans all the fingerprints off it, then takes the train back. Everyone thinks Hector's disappeared in Mallaig, so no one would've thought to check out the trains. Is there a railway station anywhere near?'

'That's where you're wrong,' she said. 'Someone did check train times. Even spent a couple of days reviewing CCTV footage in the station. But they got nowhere.' She flipped through the notes. 'That line of enquiry was stopped about the same time the snowstorm hit. If you think about it, they're looking for Hector in the area where they found his Land Rover, and not looking for someone who'd abandoned a car then hopped onto a train to St Andrews.'

'So they work on the theory that Hector drove to Mallaig then just disappeared?'

'Yeah.'

'What better way to do that, than to jump on a train?'

'Even if he did,' Jessie said, 'all we've got to go on now after twenty-five years are these files.'

Jessie had a point. Whatever CCTV footage and ticket records existed at the time of Hector's disappearance, were long gone—

'Maybe the killer lived in the Mallaig area,' Jessie said, 'and bumped off Hector in St Andrews for whatever reason, then drove the Land Rover home.'

Gilchrist shook his head. 'Good try. But I'd put my money on there being two people from Fife who collaborated in Hector's murder. Not just for the drive back from Mallaig, but to hide the body in the whisky cask in the first place. Did you know that sealant isn't used in whisky casks?'

'What do you mean?'

'Exactly that,' he said. 'The casks are made from wooden staves held together by steel hoops that go around them like metal belts, and pull the staves tight.'

'Don't they nail the lid on?'

'No. Nails rust and deteriorate. The lid fits into a rim formed in the top of the staves, and the pressure from the hoops being hammered into place holds the whole thing together, tight enough to make it watertight – even whisky-tight.'

'And where did you get your woodworking degree?'

'What I'm saying is, that it's not easy to dispose of a body in a whisky cask.'

'Humph it up and dump it in,' Jessie said. 'A bit awkward, maybe.'

'The body's not the problem,' he said. 'The cask is.'

She frowned. 'I don't get it.'

'Did you notice how the distillery staff had taken the lid off Hector's cask?'

'Can't say that I gave it much attention.'

'You remove the top pair of hoops, and slacken a few others. The staves that form the cask are bent into a curved shape, and held together by the hoops.' He held up both hands, fingertips to fingertips, as if praying with bent fingers. 'When you remove the hoops . . .' He straightened his fingers. 'The wooden staves slacken, and hey presto, you can remove the lid. After twenty-five years they would remain curved to some extent, but they would be slack enough to let the lid be pried off.'

Jessie let out a frustrated sigh. 'And the point of this wood-working lesson is . . .?'

'This,' he said, and turned the file so that she could read it.

'Duncan Milne?'

'Exactly. Twenty-five years ago Milne was Gleneden Distillery's manager. But in his statement – if you care to read it in detail – he says he worked his entire life in the whisky business, and started out at the age of fifteen as a cooper.'

Something shifted across Jessie's face, but she was still not seeing it.

'The only way to hide a body in a cask full of whisky,' he said, 'is to put the body into the cask *before* the whisky. And to do that, you have to dismantle the cask and slacken the hoops, then put the lot back together again. Once the body's inside and the cask's sealed, you fill it with whisky, then store it some place where you

40

know it's not going to be touched for twenty-five years, even longer.'

'Can anybody do that?' she said. 'Dismantle a cask and put it back together again?'

'And make sure it's secure and watertight for twenty-five years?' He shook his head. 'I'd say you'd need to have the skills of an experienced cooper.'

'So DI Calish would've been searching for a missing person in Mallaig, not realising that the body was under his bloody nose all the time.' She smacked her thigh. 'Do we have an address for this cooper guy?'

'Not yet. But Milne was nearing retirement, so he could be in his late eighties, early nineties, by now. If he's still alive, that is.'

'If your theory of two collaborators is correct, who do you have in mind as the other person? One of Milne's associates?'

'Too early to say.'

'In that case, it might be worth talking to Molly Havet.'

'Who's she?'

'Hector Dunmore's girlfriend.'

Gilchrist frowned. He hadn't come across that name in the files.

Had he missed something?

Jessie flipped open the original files. 'I found Post-its on the inside of the folder. One of them,' she said, peeling it from the page, 'gives Molly Havet's name and phone number.'

'How do you know she was Hector's girlfriend?'

'Because I phoned her.' She slapped the folder shut. 'You ready?'

CHAPTER 6

Before leaving, Gilchrist stuck his head into Jackie's office and returned the files. 'Find out what you can about Duncan Milne. He was the manager of Gleneden Distillery at the time of Hector Dunmore's disappearance. I'm looking for home address, phone number, if he's still alive, and if he isn't, is his wife alive? We may need to have a word with her.'

Jackie's hair wobbled with enthusiasm.

'And hand over to Mhairi whatever you find.'

By the time Gilchrist left, Jackie's keyboard was clattering like a machine gun.

It didn't take them long to find Molly Havet's home, a two-storey semi-detached on the northern outskirts of Ladybank, about thirteen miles west of St Andrews as the crow flies. Gilchrist pulled his BMW off the main road, worked his way down a narrow side track, and parked at the rear of the property.

Havet's address was the nicer of the two homes – tidied garden, bushes and hedge pruned tight for the winter. Windows sparkled in the January air. Wood glistened with fresh paint. A polished brass knocker in the shape of a bull's head centred a white door.

Jessie had phoned ahead, so Havet was expecting them.

A slim woman with grey hair worn far too long for middle age opened the door with a non-committal smile. She barely glanced at their warrant cards as she invited them in and led them through to the front lounge. She directed them to their seats – a soft-cushioned chair by the fireplace for Jessie, and a less inviting hard-backed chair for Gilchrist. She took her own cushioned chair opposite Jessie, picked up a poker from the grate, and stabbed it into the fire. Flames sparked. Wood crackled. She returned the poker to the grate, then stared at Jessie.

'Have you found him?' she asked her.

Jessie had told Gilchrist of her initial conversation with Havet, an exploratory phone call to introduce herself and, because she didn't know if the number was current or not, to say that they were trying to locate Molly Havet and would like to talk to her.

She'd made no mention of having found Hector's body.

Gilchrist said, 'Found who?'

'Hector Dunmore.'

'Why would you think that?'

'Why else would you be here?' She wrung her hands, and said, 'Well? Have you?'

Jessie said, 'Yes. We believe we've found him.'

'In St Andrews?'

'Yes.'

Havet closed her eyes and hung her head. She seemed to shrink into her chair as if her body had deflated. It took twenty seconds of silence before she lifted her head and stared into the fire as if she'd lost the will. 'I knew it,' she whispered.

'Knew what?' Gilchrist said.

43

'That Hector hadn't driven to Mallaig. Why would he drive all that way in weather like that?' She turned to face him, and he could read her pain from her eyes. 'And what was there in Mallaig for him to drive there?'

Jessie leaned forward. 'We found your name in the files,' she said. 'You didn't give a statement.'

'Because they didn't want me to give one.'

'What?' Gilchrist said, louder than intended.

'They told me I was of no interest to them. They didn't even bother to interview me. Just spoke to me over the phone.'

'Wait a minute,' Gilchrist said, struggling to hide his exasperation. 'No one had a face-to-face interview with you?'

'Not only that. I went to North Street Police Station in the first place, to tell them I was Hector's . . . I was . . .'

Gilchrist let several seconds pass, then said, 'We're listening.'

Havet shook her head, dabbed a finger to her eyes. 'Hector and I were going to get married the following year. A quiet wedding. No fuss. That was Hector. We'd told no one. We were just going to go away one week, and come back married.'

'I'm sorry,' Jessie said.

Gilchrist let a few more seconds pass. 'And when you went to the Police Station, what were you told?'

'That there was no one there, and someone would give me a phone call.'

'And did they?'

'Yes.'

'And?'

'And that was it. Nothing more. No interest. Exact words.'

Gilchrist frowned. What she was saying might have happened, but it didn't make any sense. 'Did they say why you were of no interest?'

44

'Because I'd been in England visiting my parents when Hector went missing. I'd been there a week, and didn't even know he'd disappeared until I phoned him, and his sister, Katherine, answered.'

'What number did you dial?'

'Hector's home number. What else?'

The distillery number, he thought. But he had his answer. 'Katherine was in Hector's home?'

'She must've been, to pick up the phone.'

'Was that not odd? Her being in his home?'

Havet scowled. 'I'd never really thought about it, but yes, I suppose it was.'

'Can you remember the name of the police officer who phoned you?'

'Detective Inspector Tom Calish.'

No hesitation. 'You have a good memory.'

'No. I just remember him being rude. I was Hector's fiancée, but that didn't seem to matter.' She let out a gush of breath. 'When I told him that, he said, Where did he buy your engagement ring? And when I said I didn't have one, he said, How can you be engaged if you don't have an engagement ring?' She picked up the poker again and stabbed the wooden logs. They could have been Calish's eyes. 'An engagement ring? What's that got to do with Hector's disappearance?'

'As a matter of interest,' Jessie said, 'why didn't you have an engagement ring?'

'Because we wanted to keep it quiet. I told DI Calish that we were going to buy rings for each other in the gold souk in Dubai, where we were planning to go for a short stay. But he just laughed at that.'

'He laughed?'

'I remember that. Because I felt hurt by it.'

'So he didn't believe you?' Gilchrist said.

'He told me that I was only trying to wheedle my way into Hector's will. But Hector didn't have a will, so I don't know how I could've wheedled into anything.'

'If they wouldn't take you seriously face to face,' Jessie said, 'did you try writing to them? Giving them a formal statement that way?'

'No. I called once more, and that's when DI Calish told me that I wasn't a person of interest, and they wouldn't be interviewing me.'

If not for that single Post-it in the files, with Havet's name and number on it, Gilchrist realised they might never have known of her existence. It struck him then that there might be others out there, people who knew something, whom Calish had decided were of no interest.

'Did Hector have friends who might have been told the same?' he said.

She gave the logs a half-hearted poke before shaking her head. 'No. Hector kept to himself. He was the quiet one of the family. Nothing at all like that Katherine.'

'And what's Katherine like?'

'Full of her own importance. She used to try to order Hector about, tell him that she wanted more of a say in running the family business. But Hector would have none of it. If you met him, you'd think he was a big softy, but he had a hard side to him, his business side that not a lot of people knew about.'

'So there was no love lost between brother and sister?' Jessie said.

Havet frowned at the logs. 'I think it was that husband of hers that was the root of all the trouble.'

'Trouble?'

'Arguments. Between Hector and Katherine. I never really knew George, but the few times I did meet him, I didn't like him. Hector once told me that George was the wrong man for Katherine, that he was a womaniser, and a misogynist. He even said George would shag a barber's floor given half a chance, excuse my French.

'I don't know what Katherine saw in him. And he was a bad influence. She would argue with Hector about something or other, and it would often turn into a screaming match. Well, the screaming would come from Katherine. Hector always stayed calm, at least on the outside, although he did tell me there were times he thought of just stuffing her into a cask of whisky and closing the lid.'

Gilchrist almost jolted. Jessie's widening eyes pulled her mouth open. But she pressed her lips tight, caught his eye, and gave the tiniest shake of her head – *No, I didn't tell her that Hector's body was found in a cask of whisky* . . .

'But he never did, of course,' Havet went on. 'Although, I notice that it's twenty-five years since he went missing. So, I presume you found his body in a cask of whisky?'

'That's quite the quantum leap,' Gilchrist said.

'Hardly,' she scoffed. 'You said you'd found his body in St Andrews. So where else would it have been all that time?'

Well, he supposed she had a point. 'How long have you had these thoughts?' he said. 'About Hector's body being hidden in a cask of whisky?'

'I mentioned it to DI Calish—'

'There's nothing in the files about that,' said Jessie.

'Of course there isn't. Haven't you been listening? DI Calish was a stupid little man whose only interest was to get to the end of the day so he could go to the pub. He laughed at me when I suggested that.' She slapped the poker against the logs. Sparks flew. She reached into a wicker basket at the side of her chair, and threw another log into the flames. 'Besides,' she said, 'every cask is stencilled with its batch number and date of filling, and the details entered into a logbook. Before computers, anyone could deliberately stencil the wrong date on a cask. So how would you really know what cask you're looking for?'

'But that didn't happen,' Jessie said. 'The cask was opened, as you said, twenty-five years since Hector's disappearance.'

Havet stared at Jessie for a long moment, before shifting her focus to Gilchrist. 'I'd say that was a mistake.'

'That they stencilled the date on the cask?'

'That they opened the cask after twenty-five years,' she said, which had Gilchrist's thoughts stalling for a moment. Then she helped him out with, 'I bet it wasn't supposed to be opened for another twenty-five years. By which time Hector's killer would be well gone.'

For Duncan Milne, Gilchrist thought, twenty-five years could have been more than enough. Fifty would be over the top. 'Did you know the distillery manager, Duncan Milne?'

Havet's eyes narrowed as she searched her memory. 'I've heard the name,' she said at length. 'But I never met him. Just have a vague memory about something Hector said to me, something about that man, Duncan, wanting more of a pension than he deserved.'

'More than he deserved? What did he mean?'

'I can't say for certain, but I know Hector was angry about it. Something about that man, Duncan – that's how he would always talk about him – that man, Duncan . . . wanting a gratuitous monthly stipend on top of his pension.'

'And what did Hector say about that?'

Havet fixed Gilchrist with a cold stare. 'Over my dead body.'

CHAPTER 7

On the drive back to St Andrews, Gilchrist phoned DC Mhairi McBride, and put the call through his car's speaker system. 'Did Jackie find anything on Duncan Milne?' he said.

'She did, sir. But it's not good. It seems he died twenty-four years ago.'

'The year after Hector's disappearance?'

'Yes, sir.'

Jessie raised an eyebrow at Gilchrist, and said, 'How long after exactly?'

'Hang on a sec.' It took a couple of beats for Mhairi to say, 'Eight months, three weeks, and two days.'

'So, sometime in August?'

'Yes.'

Gilchrist said, 'How did he die?'

'Drowned at the East Sands. A couple of newspaper reports said he'd had a few beers in the New Inn, and left the pub at closing time to walk home. They think he must've slipped on some rocks on the beach, and knocked himself out and drowned.'

'Where did he live?'

'Lamond Drive, sir.'

From the New Inn, Lamond Drive was in the opposite direction from the East Sands. So, why would Milne go for a walk on the beach? 'August, you said?'

'Yes, sir.'

'The nights would still be light when the pubs closed. Did no one see anything?'

'There were no witnesses, sir. His body wasn't discovered until the next morning by someone out jogging.'

'Didn't his wife report him missing?'

'No, sir.'

'Is she still alive?' Jessie asked.

'Died two years ago.'

Gilchrist hissed a curse. Well, there he had it. A line of enquiry that led to a dead end – literally. 'What about George Caithness?' he said. 'You found anything on him?'

'Yes, sir.'

Something in the tone of Mhairi's voice sounded hopeful. 'Let's have it.'

'He was born in Drumchapel, Glasgow, and spent his teenage years in trouble with the law – mild violations, petty theft, glue-sniffing, vandalism, that sort of thing. But in his late teens he was arrested three times. Two for breach of the peace at a football match, and once for serious assault after kicking someone unconscious outside a pub in the city centre.'

Jessie mouthed an Oh.

'He was fined for the first two,' Mhairi said, 'pleaded guilty to the third, and was given a suspended sentence.'

'Must've had a good lawyer,' Jessie said.

'Any history of drugs?' Gilchrist asked. 'Using? Selling?'

'Nothing that he was charged for.'

'When did he leave Glasgow?'

'He moved to Edinburgh after landing a job with Diageo in customer marketing, at the age of . . . hang on . . . twenty-one. There's no record of any law-breaking since then. Seems he turned into a model citizen. Not even a speeding or parking ticket. He rented for a while, then got onto the property ladder when he bought a semi-detached in Queensferry, just west of Edinburgh. He sold it two years later, and his name doesn't appear on any title deeds since then.'

It wouldn't have to, thought Gilchrist. Having found and married the eventual sole owner of a whisky distillery, Caithness had his very own sugar-mummy. 'So when did he move to St Andrews?'

'Don't have an exact date, but four years before Hector Dunmore's disappearance we have a record of him being paid through Gleneden Distillery. He could've been a salesman for them, travelling around, and not living in St Andrews.'

'So he was employed by Gleneden before he married Katherine Dunmore?'

'Yes, sir.'

'Right. We need to find Caithness as a matter of priority. He's not at home, and his office doesn't know when to expect him. His mobile's been powered off, or the SIM card's been removed. His car's parked at home, so we don't have a real-time number to run through the ANPR.'

The Automatic Number Plate Recognition system had become an indispensable tool in locating vehicles of interest. The ANPR used ordinary CCTV traffic cameras converted to read registration number plates in real time, with records stored for up to two years in the National ANPR Data Centre.

'Get onto the NADC, Mhairi, and find out when he last drove that Range Rover.'

'I'll need your authority to access their records, sir.'

'I'll take care of it. But start the ball rolling.'

'Will do, sir.'

When he ended the call, Jessie said, 'Any thoughts?'

'Plenty,' he said. 'For starters, why is George missing?'

'Because he knew Hector was about to turn up in a cask of whisky after twenty-five years, so decided to go on the run?'

'But why run at all? Why not stay and brave it out? Why not deny all knowledge of everything, swear on your mother's life that you know nothing about anything?' He flexed his grip on the steering wheel. 'By going on the run, he's now a person of real interest, and our prime suspect. But if he'd stayed put, we wouldn't have targeted him so readily.'

'Who ever said criminals were smart?' Jessie said.

Still, something niggled. 'I don't get it,' he said. 'Duncan Milne played a part in Hector's murder. I'm sure of that. But I'm also sure he didn't work alone. So what's the connection between Milne and Caithness? What did they have in common?'

'They worked in the same distillery?'

'And had the same boss, Hector, who didn't get on with George, according to Molly Havet. Sister and brother have a fight? So whose side would George take? His wife's?'

'You're beginning to confuse me.'

Truth be told, he was beginning to confuse himself. But the unfolding of recent events didn't sit right. Or maybe Molly Havet was right. Maybe the cask was opened by mistake. Maybe it was supposed to remain stored in some corner of the warehouse for another twenty-five years. That might help explain why Caithness went on the run. He'd been surprised. And with surprise comes fright.

Which brought Gilchrist full circle.

'Caithness is the key,' he said. 'In the meantime, we up our efforts to find him.'

Despite his enthusiasm at a possible break in his investigation, the rest of the day was a struggle. Obtaining permission to access NADC's records had taken much longer than anticipated, and Mhairi wouldn't be able to review recorded footage until the following morning. By six-thirty he was no further forward, and the thought of a pint in the Central Bar before heading home made up his mind for him.

Outside, winter seemed to have rejuvenated itself with a vengeance. Pavements shone with ice. He worked his way with care along North Street. A wind that could have blown in from the Arctic chased him into College Street.

Despite it being the first day of the week, when most regulars had spent their earnings over the weekend, the bar thrived with the full spectrum of students who nursed dwindling pints or ordered Tanqueray and Grey Goose martinis by the doubles. He managed to snatch a bar stool close to the Market Street entrance, and ordered a pint of Eighty Shilling, declined the menu, and phoned his daughter, Maureen.

'I'm in the Central,' he said. 'Like to join me for a bite and a chat?'

'Not tonight, Dad. I'm studying for an exam.'

'You've still got to eat, Mo.'

'I've already eaten.'

Which was how she should have answered his first question. But he didn't challenge her. With Maureen, doing so only pushed her farther away. Instead, he said, 'Have you heard from Jack?'

'He texted me over the weekend.'

Well, that was a start, he supposed. Since Jack moved to Edinburgh with Kristen, his girlfriend of the week – make that six months – Gilchrist could count on one finger how often they'd spoken on the phone. Even Jack's hasty departure from St Andrews had been done with some secrecy. One moment he was there, the next he was gone. A solitary Christmas card with *From Jack and Kristen* scrawled on it was all the written correspondence he'd received, although for Jack's generation, writing letters was about as obsolete as the fax machine. Less than half-a-dozen texts from father to son went unanswered, and over New Year, Jack's absence from Gilchrist's life seemed troubled by obstinacy.

Still, a text to Maureen was encouraging.

'So how is he?'

'Fine.'

'Still with Kristen?' he pried.

'He didn't say.'

'So we assume so?'

'I think so, yes.'

Gilchrist let silence fill the line as he sipped his beer. But by the time he returned the glass to the bar, Maureen hadn't offered anything more. For tuppence, he could tell both his kids that he'd had enough of their attitude, you're on your own, and contact me if you can ever be bothered. Instead, he said, 'Could you text him for me?'

'Have you tried texting him yourself?'

'He never gets back to me.'

'Well, that's Jack for you.'

'Mo. Listen. I don't know what's going on, but since he hooked up with Kristen, it seems like Jack wants nothing to do with me.'

'I wouldn't worry about it, Dad. It's a phase he's going through.'

He wanted to say, *Isn't he too old to be going through any kind of phase?* But instead said, 'So how are *you* keeping?'

'I'm fine. Yeah. Okay. Just plodding on. Studying away.' Then she surprised him with, 'Do you still have Blackie?'

'Not sure if *have* is the right word. But she's still around.'

'Would you be happy for me to take her?'

'If she'll have you, yes, of course,' he said, although he couldn't imagine how a cat that seemed terrified of her own shadow, and never let him within six feet of her, would allow herself to be looked after by someone living in a flat in South Street.

'What're you doing tomorrow night?'

'Probably working.'

'Can I swing by and pick her up?'

'You can try,' he said. 'If she'll let you near her. I'll even have some pizza in the oven if you'd like.'

'Thanks, Dad. That'll be great. I'll be in touch. Love you.'

He was about to say he'd be happy to give her a lift to Fisherman's Cottage, his home in Crail, but the line was already dead. He drew a mouthful of beer that almost drained the glass. Whatever hunger pangs he'd felt had disappeared. So he finished his pint, then texted Jack – Haven't heard from you lad. So sad. Your dad. He smiled as he sent it, then pushed from the bar and strode back to the Office for his car, and the drive home.

CHAPTER 8

8 a.m., Tuesday
North Street Police Station, St Andrews

Gilchrist followed Jessie into the small interview room, one of two that was accessed from the main entrance hallway. A narrow rectangular window high on the wall prevented passers-by from looking in, and interviewees from looking out. But at least it let in the grey winter sunlight.

Jessie took her seat with her back to the wall. Gilchrist sat next to her, and laid his notes on the desk, if it could be called that – nothing more than a coffee table. He slid two business cards across the table, one to Katherine Dunmore who ignored it, the other to her solicitor who slid it between the pages of her notebook without a glance.

Gilchrist had never met Eva Turnbull before, but she reminded him of so many young solicitors – black business suit, white blouse, short hair dyed blonde – eager to show her legal competence, and enthusiastic to the point of almost vibrating with energy. But a tattoo that crept from her collar and curled under her right ear spoiled the professional image.

Jessie switched on the recorder, stated date and time, gave her name and rank, and that of Gilchrist. 'Present also are Mrs Katherine Dunmore, and her solicitor . . .' She picked up the solicitor's card '. . . Ms Eva Turnbull of White De Bouchier Solicitors. Mrs Dunmore has agreed to assist in our enquiries concerning the disappearance and subsequent discovery of her brother, Hector Dunmore, and has been advised that her attendance is voluntary, and that she can leave any time.'

Gilchrist noted Dunmore's eyebrows lift at the mention of *voluntary*. Not quite how he'd presented it to her yesterday, but sometimes you just have to play the game. 'For the record,' he said, 'can you give us your full name and address?'

She did.

'And who do you share this address with?'

'My husband, George Caithness.'

'No children?'

She seemed to bristle at that question, and said, 'No.'

Gilchrist nodded. 'We were unable to talk to your husband yesterday. His car was parked at home, but he was out. Is he there this morning?'

'I'm sorry,' Turnbull interrupted, 'but I fail to see what my client's husband has to do with this *voluntary* interview.'

Gilchrist noted the emphasis, and said, 'Mr Caithness is a person of interest.'

'So my client can leave?'

He decided to change tack, and stared hard at Dunmore's blue eyes. 'Can you tell me the sequence of events yesterday morning after the discovery at the distillery of the body of your brother, Hector Dunmore?'

Neither he nor Jessie interrupted her as she recited almost verbatim everything she'd told them yesterday – the phone call from Marsh, the suspicion that the body might be that of her long-lost brother, Hector, the shock she felt when she eventually drove to the distillery and with a heavy heart identified his body.

When she finished, Gilchrist said, 'We would need to review your phone records—'

'Is my client under suspicion?' Turnbull snapped.

'Your client is free to leave anytime, but we would be grateful for her cooperation in helping us better understand the circumstances surrounding her brother's disappearance.'

'So what do my client's phone records have to do with anything?'

'We're trying to establish a time line leading to the—'

'You're fishing. Unless you intend to charge my client, I'm instructing her to answer only those questions regarding the discovery and identification of her brother's body.'

Dunmore raised her hand. 'I'm as desperate as anyone to find out what happened all these years ago.' She held her steady gaze on Gilchrist. 'I'm here to help in any way I can, Inspector. Ask me what you will.'

'For the record,' Turnbull said, 'my client is refusing to take my advice.' Then she reclined in her chair, eyes fixed on some point on the table, lips pressed to a scar. Her fingers, whitened at the knuckles, fidgeted with a biro as if trying to snap it.

Gilchrist ignored her, and focused on Dunmore. 'Can you explain why it took you so long to arrive at the distillery after Mr Marsh phoned you?'

'I spent some time with my husband, George, talking about the phone call. I can't explain it, but I always knew that one day

Hector would turn up. After Robbie called, I had this feeling of dread, which I couldn't shift. And then the reality of it all just hit me, and I broke down.'

Gilchrist let several seconds pass, then said, 'And what did George say?'

'He did what George is good at, which was to offer support and comfort, and console me. I was . . . I was quite distraught, as you can imagine.'

'Quite,' said Jessie, which received a narrow-eyed glare from Turnbull.

'And once you'd recovered your composure,' Gilchrist said, 'did George offer to accompany you to the distillery?'

'Of course, he did. But I wouldn't let him. I felt I had to be strong, that I had to do that by myself. Again, my need to do so was inexplicable.'

'And all of this happened *before* you'd seen the body?'

'Of course.'

'And what did George do after you left?'

'I've no idea. He said he was going to do a bit of catch-up in his study, then head off to the office.'

'Catch-up in his study? Work from home, you mean?'

'He often works for days at home, without going anywhere near his office.'

'What does he do?'

'He recently opened a marketing and publicity office. His intention was to promote Gleneden Distillery exclusively, but he's taken on more clients – local supermarkets, a couple of microbreweries, that sort of thing.'

'How recently?'

'Oh, last year. Spring, I believe.'

'But once you left for the distillery, George never went to his office, did he?'

She shook her head. 'No.'

'So where did he go?'

'I've no idea.'

Jessie said, 'Haven't you asked him?'

'I haven't heard from him since yesterday morning.'

'He never returned home last night?'

'No.'

'Do you have any idea where he is?'

'Not the faintest.'

'So he's disappeared?'

She scoffed. 'He's hardly disappeared, has he? He's just gone off on one of his romps again, to get away from the humdrum of everyday life. He'll probably come back today. If not, in a day or so.'

Gilchrist pushed himself from the table, his thoughts fluttering in a dozen directions. George would likely come back today? If not, then in a day or so? And his wife seemed not in the least troubled by that? If they weren't trying to find him, who would ever have known he'd left? Range Rover parked in the driveway to let neighbours know everything at home was nice and cosy. Perfect domesticity. Working from home. Nothing to worry about.

Except there was everything to worry about.

Now that Hector Dunmore's body had been discovered.

Gilchrist forced his thoughts back to the present. He stared at Dunmore. 'You said he's off on one of his romps *again*. So he's done this before?'

She let out a weary sigh, as if to give an explanation was too bothersome. 'Like any married couple,' she said, 'we've had our ups and downs. And several times in the past, George has felt the need of a few days by himself.'

'What d'you mean?' Jessie said. 'Like after an argument he just gets up and takes off, and you think nothing of it?'

'George doesn't handle stress well. So every now and then he needs to take a break, a breather if you like, to freshen up.'

'Is that why he's left this time?'

'I don't know. You'd need to ask him.'

Gilchrist raked his hair. 'I have to say that you appear completely unconcerned by your husband's inexplicable disappearance.'

'That's because he's not disappeared. He's only gone off for a day or so. And it's not inexplicable. It's stress relief.'

'Christ on a pole,' Jessie said. 'Are you for real?'

'I'd prefer if you didn't take the Lord's name in vain,' Dunmore said.

Turnbull pulled herself from her chair. 'I would remind you that my client is here of her own volition, and that if you continue to be rude to her, I'll terminate this interview.'

'Oh, piss off,' Jessie said, then turned her anger to Dunmore. 'Are you trying to tell me that this husband of yours, who comforts and consoles you, who gives you support when you most need it, has gone for walkies out the blue, and it doesn't bother you?'

'You don't know George,' she said. 'If you did, you'd understand.'

'Oh thanks for the psych evaluation.'

Gilchrist coughed to bring peace back to the meeting. 'In the past,' he said, 'when George felt the need to take a few days away, as you put it, where did he go?'

'Hah,' she said, and threw her head back and laughed. 'Once he ended up in Paris for a week. Another time he spent four days in London. But most of the time he's gone for a day or two in Scotland, walking some beach, fishing some river, drinking some whisky.'

Well, he thought, it takes all kinds. And who was he to argue what was right or wrong in a marriage? Look how his own had failed. As he held Dunmore's gaze, he thought another change in tack worth trying. 'Do you own any other property?' he asked. 'A holiday home, perhaps?'

'Don't answer that,' Turnbull said.

'Why not?' Jessie said.

'It's irrelevant. You're fishing again.'

Again, Dunmore raised her hand. 'It's all right, Eve. As I said, I've nothing to hide.'

Gilchrist waited while Turnbull settled into her seat, lips white, eyes on fire. Then he said, 'An address, or addresses, will do.'

Dunmore nodded and smiled. 'We have a country lodge that's been in my family for three generations. North of Perth. Dunmore Lodge, Perth, is sufficient for the Post Office to deliver mail.'

'Could George have gone there?'

'George hasn't been there for years,' she snapped. 'He's never liked it.'

'Do you rent it out?' Jessie asked.

She chuckled. 'You couldn't afford it,' she said, then when Jessie failed to see the funny side, added, 'No we don't. Family only.'

Gilchrist said, 'So, for the record, you don't want to report your husband missing?'

'Why should I?'

He could think of a dozen reasons. But one that jumped out at him was George's disappearance upon the discovery of Hector's body. Was that what this was about? If you killed someone, then hid their body in a whisky cask in a distillery, you would know it would be discovered at some point in the future. So, with Hector's body having been found, and Caithness out of reach, that definitely made him a person of interest. But now Gilchrist had Katherine Dunmore on side, at least for the time being, he needed to focus on events around the time of her brother's disappearance.

CHAPTER 9

Gilchrist pulled his chair closer to the table, and held Dunmore's cold gaze.

'Yesterday,' he said to her, 'you told me that you and George saw Hector on the night he disappeared. That was confirmed in your written statements twenty-five years ago. But when Hector's abandoned Land Rover was located on the outskirts of Mallaig, no one thought for a minute that he hadn't driven there—'

'Is this leading to a question any time soon?' Turnbull asked. 'My client doesn't need the details of such a personal and upsetting event read out to her so soon after what she's just been through.'

Jessie said, 'Not to mention that her husband's done a runner, too.'

'What is it with you?' Turnbull said.

'Why don't you shut up, and listen?'

Gilchrist cleared his throat. 'In your written statements, you both described what Hector was wearing that evening. What struck me was the detail you provided.' He gathered in his notes. 'This is from *your* written statement. Red and black checked

Marks and Sparks shirt. Burgundy woollen tie. Brown corduroy trousers, wide cord. And a Seiko watch with a black face and brown leather strap.'

'Surprised you didn't describe his underwear,' Jessie said.

Dunmore ignored Jessie's snipe. 'What can I say? That's what he was wearing.'

'Exactly,' Gilchrist said. 'And no socks or shoes? Not even a pair of slippers?'

'That's how Hector walked about his house. In bare feet. Ever since he was a little boy, he rarely wore shoes of any kind indoors.'

'Emphasis on the word *exactly*.'

She frowned. 'I don't understand.'

'Both you and George described what Hector was wearing in *exactly* the same words.'

He turned to Jessie.

'This is from George's written statement,' she said, and read out the same description. 'Odd, don't you think?'

'In what way?' Turnbull had pulled herself upright, preparing for an argument.

'It stinks of collusion. That's what way.'

Dunmore seemed unfazed. 'Well, I suggest you ask George when he returns.'

'According to your written statement, you left Hector's home at quarter to eleven that night. Not seven o'clock in the evening like you told me earlier.'

'It's been years since then. And my memory's not as good as it used to be—'

'Convenient that, isn't it?' Jessie said.

Turnbull interrupted with, 'If you have something to say, DS Janes, why don't you say it?' Anger rose off her like heat from rock.

'I don't believe a word of it.' Jessie eyed Dunmore. 'If I'd been on the investigation team back then, you wouldn't be sitting here right now.'

The hint of a smile cracked the edges of Dunmore's lips, giving Gilchrist the sense that they were being toyed with. A glance at Turnbull only added to his feelings, but had him thinking of something else. Why would someone as wealthy as Dunmore be represented by a junior solicitor? He would've expected her to hire a senior lawyer, someone who could stand up in court and speak on her behalf.

Of course, turning up with a junior solicitor could be Dunmore's way of minimising Gilchrist, letting him know that he wasn't worth spending the money on.

But he had one more angle to try. 'Was Hector married?'

'No.'

'Engaged?'

'No.'

Which confirmed what Havet had said. But he wanted to press harder. 'No wife, no fiancée, and no partner?'

'No.'

'Girlfriend?'

'No.'

He could sense Jessie's mounting tension, but he pushed on. 'So what happened to Hector's home? Was it put on the market?'

'George and I inherited it. *Eventually*. Without a death certificate, building societies and banks won't budge an inch.'

'Don't you mean, *you* inherited it?'

'Same difference. What's mine is George's. What's George's is mine.'

'Aw, how lovely,' Jessie said.

'Eventually,' Gilchrist said, 'you inherited it. The house and *everything* in it?'

She hesitated for a moment, as if suspecting a trap, then said, 'I think George may have returned some personal items to a number of Hector's friends.'

'I see. And what about Hector's share in the business? You inherit that, too?'

'It was a going concern, so we had to keep it running, although we always hoped that Hector would return, of course.'

'Of course.'

'But after seven years, we legally took ownership.'

'I hadn't realised Hector was so wealthy. Over three hundred thousand in stocks and shares at the time. Also a bachelor pad in the West End of Glasgow.'

For the first time that morning, cracks appeared in Dunmore's facade. Up until that moment, she'd acted as if she were in control. But £1 million in property, stocks and bonds – give or take a hundred thousand or two – plus the family distillery, was no piddling amount twenty-five years ago, or today for that matter.

'And your question is?' Turnbull again.

'No question. Just a statement of fact.' Gilchrist collected his notes together, a signal to Jessie that the interview was over.

Jessie said, 'Interview terminated at 08:51.'

Gilchrist stood. 'Thanks for your cooperation, Mrs Dunmore,' he said. 'You've been extremely helpful.' He was about to leave the room, when he said, 'I'd like to have a talk with your husband, George, when he returns home. Hopefully today?'

'Hopefully.' But her smile looked forced.

'Let me know the moment he returns, will you?'

'Of course.'

Back upstairs, Jessie said, 'She's talking utter crap. What wife would ever allow her husband to come and go as he pleases like that? Walks off for days at a time? Most husbands would be served their balls on a hot plate, sliced and diced, if they did that.'

'Ouch.'

'And she's not worried in the least?' She scowled in amazement. 'Well, here's what worries me. If George went walkies by himself for a few days, he would've taken his car. But he didn't. He just pissed off out of it on foot?'

'Or taxi?' Gilchrist said.

'Good point,' she said. 'Let me get onto that.'

'Before you do, this way.'

They found Mhairi in her office, but she'd had no luck locating Caithness's car from NADC records.

'Right,' Gilchrist said. 'If he took a taxi, find out where he went. If he didn't take a taxi, then I need the two of you to work on NADC records as a matter of priority. We need to find George, and establish what's going on.'

He left them to it, and returned to his office.

Seated at his desk, he checked his emails but found nothing from Cooper.

So he phoned her.

'Before you ask,' she said on answering, 'I haven't completed the PM report yet.'

'But you've determined cause of death?'

'I have indeed.'

Gilchrist pressed the phone to his ear, and waited.

'It appears that Hector Dunmore died from strangulation. Heavy bruising and ligature marks around the neck, hidden by his shirt collar. Skin wasn't broken, so a cord or a rope was likely used, rather than wire. His larynx was also damaged, which is more typical of manual strangulation than from a ligature.'

'Knotted rope?' Gilchrist offered.

'Possibly. But I'm unable to say conclusively.'

'Defence wounds?'

'No cuts or bruises on his wrists or arms. Nothing under his nails. If a knotted ligature was tightened so that the knot damaged his larynx, I'd say he would've been unconscious in fifteen seconds or so, and dead within a couple of minutes.'

'He could've been unconscious before he was strangled.'

'Then I'd expect to have seen little or no bruising around the neck, and more damage to the larynx. No, my guess is that he was alive and upright when his killer approached from behind, looped the cord over his neck and pulled it tight for all he was worth.'

'He?'

'There you go again, Andy, snatching at the smallest of clues.'

'From what you've told me, it would take considerable strength to strangle a man of Dunmore's size and build.'

'I wouldn't rule out a strong woman.'

'To damage the larynx as you've described,' he said, trying to remember what he'd learned during forensic courses he'd attended, 'it would take five or six times more pressure than it would to constrict the carotid arteries and jugular veins.'

'Good to see you pay attention from time to time.'

'So, I'm thinking male, as opposed to a strong female.'

'More than likely, yes,' she conceded.

'And how about toxicology results?'

'What about them?'

He knew from her tone that he was pushing too hard too fast. Toxicology tests could take days, weeks, even longer. And with death having occurred twenty-five years earlier, he knew Cooper didn't share his sense of urgency. Even so, he said, 'When can I get them?'

'I wouldn't hold your breath, Andy. After being immersed in whisky for twenty-five years, any toxicology results would likely be meaningless.'

Well, what had he expected? He'd been hoping that cause of death might help him visualise Hector's last moments. But what it hadn't done was give any credence to his theory that Milne had assistance in killing Hector. Even so, he was determined to carry on with his investigation on the basis that two men were indeed involved – Duncan Milne, deceased; and George Caithness, missing.

He ended the call, and went looking for Jackie.

CHAPTER 10

Jackie was seated at her desk, her crutches leaning against the wall. She looked up from her computer as Gilchrist entered, and smiled.

'What're you working on?' he asked her.

Rather than try to battle through her stammer, she tapped her computer screen.

He walked round her desk and saw that she was researching Duncan Milne's death. 'Do you mind?' he said, and took hold of her mouse. He scrolled down the screen, scanning the waterfall of sentences and paragraphs, and came upon a hand-drawn sketch of the East Sands. He zoomed in on the outlined shape of a body on a rock outcrop at the end of the beach farthest from the harbour.

He read the notes – measurements from body to sea, from rocks to sand, from beach to the pathway that formed part of the Fife Coastal Path. But they told him nothing new, and he closed the file.

From the bottom of the screen he expanded one of several minimised files – a scanned copy of a handwritten report, the penmanship so poor as to be almost illegible. He worked through it as best he could, but it told him nothing he didn't already know. He expanded another file, a copy of a fax report from PC Brian Marks to the SIO, DI Tom Calish – there was that name again. The report seemed to be nothing more than a list of files that had been removed, or were missing, from the filing system. From what Gilchrist had learned about Calish, he wasn't surprised the system was in a mess.

He pulled up the next file, and caught his breath.

Colour photographs of Duncan Milne lying on the beach filled the screen. His fully clothed body – dark-grey suit, white shirt collar, black shoes – lay face down, spread-eagled, arms and legs wide as if he'd been nailed to an imaginary cross on the rocks. His face lay in a pool of water trapped on the rocks by the outgoing tide. His hair was white, crewcut short and thin on top, almost bald. A blackened wound at the back of his head looked significant enough to be cause of death.

Gilchrist peeled through other photos, some close, some distant, but all of them taken by a police photographer who must have prowled around the body like a lion eyeing meat. It took another minute or two to find what he was looking for, three separate photographs that showed Milne's face.

If asked, he would have put Milne in his late seventies, not his early sixties as Mhairi had confirmed. Half-opened eyes peered up at him. Blue lips were pulled back to show teeth as black as tombstones, a sign that he might have smoked a pipe. A fine nose was flattened at the tip from lying face down in the rock pool.

Gilchrist pulled himself upright. 'Are these all the file photos?' he asked.

'Uh-huh.'

He thanked her, then walked from her office and found Mhairi on her computer, and Jessie on the phone. 'You got Duncan Milne's files?' he asked Mhairi.

Without taking her eyes from the screen, she removed a folder from a filing tray, and handed it to him. He found the PM report, and opened it. Twenty-four years ago, the forensic pathologist was Dr Bert Mackie, who had retired a couple of years earlier after a lifetime's service. His position was filled by Dr Rebecca Cooper, but the report Gilchrist was looking at had been signed off by Dr J. Sczabo, a name he'd never heard of. Or had he?

He searched his memory banks, and pulled up the vaguest recollection of a young fair-haired man – the police pathologist – fussing over some paperwork at a fatal car accident. Gilchrist had been in his twenties then, assigned to take witness state-ments, so wasn't closely involved in that investigation. But what he did remember – and it came back with clarity now – was that Dr Mackie had been on an indefinite leave of absence due to a family tragedy, an absence that extended to the best part of a year. Gilchrist hadn't known Mackie all that well back then, just knew him as an authoritative figure you didn't jerk around. It wasn't until Gilchrist was in his late twenties that he befriended Mackie, saw beyond the gruff manner that intimidated others, and came to value his worldly wisdom and forensic knowledge until the day he retired.

All of which explained the lack of substantive information in Duncan Milne's PM report. Without Mackie's oversight, Dr Sczabo's report was sketchy and inconclusive, and offered no professional comments or guidance as to the suspicious nature of Milne's death. And from what Gilchrist had deducted from the

74

photographs, Milne's death was far from accidental as Dr Sczabo would have you believe.

It seemed clear to Gilchrist that the wound had not been caused by Milne falling and knocking himself out on the rocks. Not at all. The only way to sustain a wound on the back of the head like that, from a fall onto rocks, would be to fall backwards, at which point the body might be spread-eagled and unconscious – but face-up, not face-down. You didn't hit the back of your head on rocks then roll over to lie spread-eagled with your face in a rock pool.

He gritted his teeth as he read through it.

The barest of forensic details were provided, and failed to be conclusive: *fracture at base of skull . . . non-penetrating trauma . . . consistent with fall on rocks . . . mild lividity on arms and face consistent with lying prostrate . . . minimal signs of fine froth in air passages . . . cause of death consistent with drowning . . . death accidental . . .*

Toxicology results confirmed Milne had indeed been drinking, but the level of alcohol in his body – 0.12 per cent – was not high enough to cause him to lose his balance, or forget which way was home and find himself lost on the East Sands.

Gilchrist slapped the file shut. He'd seen enough.

Milne had been assaulted from behind, suffered blunt-force trauma to the back of the head, and knocked unconscious. His assailant had then positioned his comatose body in such a way that his mouth and nose were submerged in a rock pool. For all anyone knew, the killer could have held Milne's head down in the pool to make sure he drowned, before leaving the crime scene to an incompetent investigative team. And as soon as the SIO, DI Calish, read the PM report, he would've been only too pleased to sign off on it at the end of the day, and head to the pub for a relaxing couple of drinks.

Christ, it didn't bear thinking about.

Notwithstanding the distinct possibility that Milne could have collaborated in Hector Dunmore's murder, where was the justice for the man's wife? How could the Constabulary have let her down so badly? And what of their children – if they had any – how would they have felt losing their father?

He walked to the window, pressed his hands flat against the glass, let its coldness seep into his skin, and temper the latent heat of his frustration. What had started out as a murder investigation had in turn resolved a twenty-five-year-old missing person's case, and opened up another murder – that of Duncan Milne who, along with a likely collaborator, was the prime suspect in the original murder investigation. And now, with the disappearance of Katherine Dunmore's husband, Gilchrist had only one endgame to pursue.

Find George Caithness.

And to do that, he would have to pull out all the stops.

CHAPTER 11

The question that troubled Gilchrist was – did he believe Dunmore when she said her husband, George, would return home in a day or so? But even if he did believe her, he came to understand that he was not prepared to sit back and do nothing. So, first thing he did was organise a search for an up-to-date photograph of Caithness.

'Get onto it,' he said to Jessie. 'Maybe his wife has one we can use.'

'If she has, it'll be riddled with dart holes,' she sniped.

'Well, let's try to work out how he left town without using his car.'

Jessie managed to obtain a high-resolution jpeg file from GC Publicity Ltd – George's embryonic marketing and publicity company – and emailed his image to every taxi company in and around St Andrews, asking if they made a pick-up call from the Dunmore residence in Hepburn Gardens on Monday between the hours of 9 a.m. and 1 p.m. – which was after Katherine Dunmore left for the distillery, and before Gilchrist and Jessie arrived at her house to talk to Caithness.

He also had Jackie email George's photograph to every police force in Scotland, and put a marker on the PNC with a note that he was wanted for questioning over the discovery of a man's body in Gleneden Distillery. The possibility that Caithness might also be involved in the death of Duncan Milne, Gilchrist decided not to make that public for the time being, as well as not putting out an appeal on national radio and TV until he first had some feedback – good or bad – on their efforts for that day.

He checked in again with Mhairi for progress on her review of the NADC's records. 'Anything?' he asked her.

'Nothing yet, sir. It's slow going. It's going to take a while.'

He then organised a pair of PCs to visit the local bus station on City Road, armed with a couple of dozen printouts of Caithness's photograph, and make enquiries, see if anyone recognised him boarding a bus on Monday, and if so, to confirm details of the route. Another couple of PCs were assigned a similar task to Leuchars railway station, and asked to obtain a list of passengers.

On his way back to his desk, he stuck his head into Jackie's office again. 'See if you can find anything on Caithness's Range Rover.' He rattled off the registration number, then said, 'And while you're at it, do a check on his driving licence. Let me know if he's been a bad boy or not. As soon as you can,' he added.

Jackie chuckled, and set about that task with fresh enthusiasm.

He also had two officers check activity on Caithness's mobile phone, and to start the ball rolling with the FIU – Financial Investigation Unit – by pulling his credit card and bank records. Better to be ahead than behind, he thought.

By late morning, all local cab company responses were in with an overwhelming no.

'Just from nine until one?' Gilchrist asked Jessie.

'That's what you wanted.'

'I'm now thinking he might've been home when we arrived,' he said, 'and refused to answer. So, change of plan. Get back onto the cab companies and have them go through their records for the entire day. And while you're at it, get them to contact all their drivers with a copy of that photograph. Maybe they didn't pick him up from home. Maybe our man walked into town and got a taxi there. If he's really done a runner, he'd want to cover his tracks.'

Word came back before midday that Caithness's mobile phone was dead, but more concerning was the discovery that no calls had been made from that number since Tuesday, the week before. GC Publicity confirmed that no one had heard from George for over a week, which according to them was not unusual. Sometimes they wouldn't hear from him for weeks at a time. So much for running your own business, Gilchrist thought.

But just as troubling, by mid-afternoon the results from the cab companies were in.

'Nada,' Jessie said. 'If our man, George, took a taxi, he didn't hire it from anywhere around here.'

Which was a worry for Gilchrist. How simple could it be to phone for an out-of-town taxi or mini-bus? And if George's mobile hadn't been used for a week, they would need to pull phone records for his landline, which would first need Katherine Dunmore's approval. He couldn't see her granting permission without an argument.

And, as if to keep the mood depressive, while Jessie had been following up on local taxis, Mhairi's review of NADC's records effectively led them to another dead-end – the black Range Rover parked on the driveway of the Dunmore home in Hepburn Gardens.

'The latest recording, sir, and the last time his Range Rover moved from the driveway was Sunday morning, the day before the discovery of Hector's body. The registration number was last captured on South Street heading west at 11:08, and before that, on Market Street heading east at 10:22.' She pulled her notes to her, and read from them.

'I reviewed more CCTV records around town, sir, and these show Caithness parking on Market Street, buying a newspaper in Tesco, crossing the road and entering Starbucks. At 11:02, he is seen exiting Starbucks, beeping his remote, climbing into his Range Rover, then driving east on Market Street, right into Church Street, and right again into South Street for the return journey home.'

'Anything before that?' he asked.

'Yes, sir. CCTV footage prior to Sunday, in reverse chronological order, show similar trips on Saturday, Friday, and Thursday, all around the same time, with him buying a paper in Tesco, followed by a visit to Starbucks. Wednesday's different, sir. His number plate wasn't captured on any ANPR cameras.'

'So he didn't go anywhere on Wednesday, it seems,' he said.

'No, sir. Would you like me to go back further?'

Gilchrist dragged his fingers through his hair. Something didn't seem right about the captured footage. George Caithness, owner of a new company, hardly sets foot in the place for weeks on end, and when he works from home, drives into St Andrews for a newspaper and a Starbucks? Why would he not spend enthusiastic hours in his new company? Why work from home at all? Why not be out on the road trying to drum up new business? Either he didn't need the money, couldn't care less, or was as lazy as a toad.

'Here's what I want you to do, Mhairi. Take the photographs and ask around in Tesco and Starbucks. What strikes me as odd about this, is that it's all like clockwork – same time, same shops, same routine, day in, day out.' He shook his head. 'It doesn't work for me.'

'I'm on it, sir.'

'And once you've done that, take the CCTV records back another week, and let's see if he's still doing the same routine then.'

He was walking along the corridor when Jessie caught up with him. 'Just in from Jackie.' She held up a printout, and tapped a paragraph that gave details of a claim against Caithness's motor insurance policy. 'Read that,' she said.

'Three thousand four hundred pounds damage?'

'Now have a look at the attached drawing.'

Gilchrist did – a simple hand-printed sketch that showed the positions of two cars, one marked *Range Rover*, the other *Ford Focus*, at a junction marked *A9* with a road leading off it and an arrow pointing to *Tullybelton*. 'If this is what I think it is,' he said, 'it looks like he was involved in an accident.' He couldn't fail to catch her smile, and said, 'So when did this happen?'

'Four months ago.'

But the significance still escaped him. 'Okay,' he said. 'Let's have it.'

She handed him a Google Maps printout with two areas circled and numbered in red. 'Number 1 is the location of the accident. And number 2 is Dunmore Lodge, the place where – Good Lord, no,' she said, affecting a posh accent. 'George hasn't been there for years.' She slapped the map, and snarled, 'The lying *bitch*.'

Gilchrist took a moment to stare out the window, then said, 'Someone else could've been driving his Range Rover that day.'

Jessie snatched the report from him, flipped a page, and stabbed a finger at it. 'Name of the driver,' she said. 'In black and white. George Caithness. It's even got his signature on it.' She held his gaze in a hard look. 'Are you thinking what I'm thinking?'

Well, he couldn't really think anything else, could he?

'Let's go,' he said.

CHAPTER 12

Gilchrist figured it would be quicker if he drove to Dundee, then took the A90 west to Perth, and from there north on the A9. His car's GPS system had the journey set at forty-six miles, and an estimated time of one hour ten minutes. But the January roads were slick and gritted, and heavy clouds pulled darkness down early. But even so, when he swung onto the country road towards Tullybelton – the exact spot where Dunmore had his accident – fifty-five minutes had passed.

Here, the roads had not been gritted. Shoulders of ploughed snow lined both sides. He kept his speed at a steady forty, his headlights on full beam. Pockets of ice glistened as he powered on. Trees and bushes swept past in the cold darkness. At one point, where the road opened up to a headlight-brightened tunnel that stretched to a dark horizon, he powered up to sixty. Three miles in, and his headlights shone on trees that bounded shallow curves, first one way, then the other, and he had to brake hard, slow to a sedate thirty as iced puddles cracked under his tyres.

A glance at his GPS console told him they were getting close. Only a few more bends to negotiate, and Dunmore Lodge should be on their left. He dipped his headlights, and night rushed towards them. He decelerated to twenty, and eased onwards, the speed slowing even more.

'Anything?' he said.

'Should be here.'

Off to their left, a stand of pine trees formed a visual barrier as good as any hedge. A glance at the GPS screen showed them at their destination. He crept forward another ten yards then saw a break in the shrubbery.

'Here we are.'

With all the mystery and subterfuge surrounding Caithness, Gilchrist felt it prudent to switch off the BMW's lights. Night smothered them like a black cloak. He eased off the road and drew to a halt. As his night vision settled, the outline of a narrow track, which formed a U-turn and doubled along the other side of the stand of pine trees, came into view. Dunmore Lodge should be off to his right now, but in the pitch black of a moonless night, he could be looking at the end of the world.

'Anything?' he asked Jessie.

'What do you think?'

He took his foot off the brake and let the car move forward. Tyres crunched gravel and stones. Winter grass brushed the underside. Black ice cracked as tyres rolled into and out of shallow potholes. A tight right-hand curve brought him to a wooden gate.

He stopped, and switched off the engine.

Ahead, nothing broke the black horizon. It could be an open field or a stone wall for all he could see.

'What now?' Jessie said.

'We have a look.'

'You do realise that if we find anything here without a warrant, it'll be inadmissible.'

'Well, let's hope we find nothing.'

'And the point of this exercise is . . .?'

'Reconnoitring.'

'Aye, right.'

'Grab a couple of torches from the glove compartment.'

Jessie clicked it open. 'Here we are,' she said, and handed him a small torch.

He pointed it to his feet, pressed the base, and a blue-white beam lit up the footwell. On the dash, he noted the outside temperature was two below, then removed the ignition key. 'Better wrap up.' He tightened his scarf, and zipped his leather jacket tight to his neck.

'Ready when you are,' she said, and stepped into the freezing night.

The gate was secured with a chain and padlock. Without heavy duty bolt cutters, or a key for the padlock, no one could drive in. But it was a simple matter of a quick up-and-over to gain access. On the other side, a scraped rut across the driveway gave Gilchrist the sense that the gate had been opened recently.

Strangely, that rekindled his doubts.

What if Dunmore had been telling the truth? Maybe Caithness *hadn't* set foot in this place for years. Maybe they'd had it wrong and Caithness was already home with his feet up, sorting through his latest apology for buggering off. Gilchrist forced all negative thoughts to the wind, put his head down and walked side by side with Jessie into the night, torch beams prodding the way ahead, picking up nothing but more darkness.

He knew they were close to the residence when the grass and gravel driveway changed to a loose pebbled parking area. The pebbles were the wrong shape, he thought, too large and too round for car tyres. But they did make reaching the house without a sound more or less impossible. Their shoes slipped and crunched stones as they approached the shadowed building that was Dunmore Lodge.

When they came across the Lodge – if that's what it could be called – the first thing that struck Gilchrist was its size. He'd had in his mind's eye a wooden cabin, a home from home with a bit of hardier living involved. But as he shone his torch up the stone wall, and over an upper window, the beam lost itself in the night air above.

'Bigger than I thought,' he said.

'What is this?' Jessie asked. 'Castle Dunmore?'

'Could be.'

'It doesn't look like anyone's here.'

At the front of the building, three levels of stone steps set out in a semi-circle led up and onto a flagstone entrance porch. A pair of sandstone pillars, more suited for the Coliseum than a Scottish country lodge, stood either side of a studded wooden door that looked as if it could withstand an onslaught from a battering ram.

'How old is this place?' Jessie said.

'Didn't she say it'd been in their family for generations?' His torch picked up a black-painted knob at the side of the door, and Jessie reached for it.

'Want me to ring it?' she said.

'Can do. But I don't think anyone's home.'

Undeterred, Jessie pressed the bell, and a distant metallic chime echoed back at them.

Gilchrist backed down the steps, onto the pebbled frontage, shone his torch over stone walls. Windows either side at ground level lay in darkness – no lights on inside. Windows on the upper level were just as dark. The light from his torch was not strong enough to reach any higher, but he had the feeling that the building had another storey hiding in the night sky.

He turned around and shone his beam beyond the pebbles, and onto a pair of stone flowerbeds either side of a set of steps that dropped down to what he thought was the front lawn. An image of tea parties, fluttering women in Victorian bustles laughing and flirting and playing croquet, rolling pétanque balls, flew into his mind unsummoned.

From behind, Jessie's footfall crunched pebbles as she made her way to the side of the house. He watched her go, torch beam dancing in front of her until she disappeared around the far corner. Alone at the front, he played his torchlight over the stone facade again, more out of interest than for investigatory purpose . . .

Which was when his heart fluttered.

Above him, on the corner of the building, the light from an infra-red CCTV camera stared down at him. A quick walk along the front of the building revealed the same set-up at the other corner. He wondered if the cameras had been installed as visual deterrents only, or if they actually recorded live footage – the former, his senses were telling him. He was about to follow Jessie when the far side of the house lit up like a disco kicking off. Another couple of spotlights, high up in the eaves, flickered on with a distinctive click, followed by two more on the front of the building. It seemed as if daylight had returned with a bang.

Talk about rabbits in headlights.

Jessie scurried towards him, head down, hand cupped against her forehead to shield her eyes. 'Bloody hell,' she said. 'I didn't touch anything.'

'Motion sensors,' he said. 'Probably round the back where there's no pebble moat.'

'Now you tell me. At least we didn't set off an alarm.'

'Hopefully,' he said. Some home alarms were linked to the local police station, but being this far from the nearest town or city – Perth, some ten miles south – he thought that unlikely. What was probably installed were wi-fi CCTV cameras that took a photograph then ran on video mode for twenty seconds, or a minute or so. They were too late to do anything about that now, so he said, 'Let's walk back to the car, and keep our heads down.'

'Should we report this?' Jessie said.

'I'm inclined not to, unless someone calls it in.' He turned off his torch, stuffed it into his jacket pocket, and walked towards the gate, out of the brightness, into the darkness. As if by magic, the spotlights switched off behind them, and darkness settled once more like a slap to the head.

Gilchrist strode on into the pitch black night, unable to shift the oddest feeling that somehow they'd missed something.

CHAPTER 13

By the time Gilchrist had driven back to St Andrews and dropped Jessie off at home, it was almost nine in the evening when he sat down at his desk. While he waited for his computer to come awake, he lifted several sheaths of paperwork from his in-tray and fingered his way through them. But in terms of moving his investigation forward, it was all depressing stuff.

No one had responded with positive sightings of Caithness, and enquiries at St Andrews bus station and Leuchars railway station offered nothing. No change of heart from any of the local cab companies, either. The only interesting find – if it could be called that – was further confirmation from GC Publicity Ltd that George hadn't been into the office since last Tuesday, a week ago, which tied up with his mobile phone records.

Which meant . . .?

Probably eff all, if he was being honest.

Still, something was niggling his subconscious, reminding him that Mhairi's ANPR footage showed Caithness going through the same mid-morning routine – a newspaper from Tesco, a coffee in

Starbucks – which gave him the answer to the square root of bugger all.

Mhairi's notes on her enquiries with Tesco and Starbucks staff had drawn a blank, too, with no one recognising Caithness from the headshot they'd been punting around. He studied the image again, and realised it had been taken by a professional photographer for use in GC Publicity's brochure, and if you looked closely enough, you could see it had been air-brushed. He jotted a note to Mhairi, telling her to visit Tesco and Starbucks first thing in the morning, but this time take an image from the ANPR footage, which might be recognised by staff. Even if it showed only the coat and hat Caithness had been wearing in these captured images, that might be sufficient to jog someone's memory.

He spent another half hour catching up on the day's reports, scribbling down thoughts on his next move. He'd just picked up a copy of Mhairi's reworked report when his mobile rang. He glanced at it – ID Mo – and took the call. 'Hi, princess.'

'You sound cheery,' she said.

'End of a long day, what can I tell you?'

'You still at the office?'

'Where else?'

'Jeezoh, Dad. Jack's right. You spend far too many hours working.'

'Keeps me out of trouble,' he said, and followed that with a short laugh.

'Well, if you're still in town, can you pick me up?'

He frowned, confused for a moment. 'Sure. Where are you going?'

'You've forgotten, haven't you?'

'Forgotten what?'

She chuckled, and said, 'See?'

He couldn't resist smiling. It had been weeks since he'd heard Maureen so cheerful.

'Blackie,' she said. 'I'm going to collect her tonight.'

Of course. How could he have forgotten? 'I can pick you up right now if you'd like.'

'I'll be downstairs.' And with that, the line died.

Gilchrist powered down his computer, lifted his jacket from the back of his chair, a bundle of printouts and files from his in-tray, then strode from his office.

The short walk across the car park was long enough to chill him to the bone, and he turned on the ignition, switched the fan up to high. By the time he turned into South Street, the cabin had heated up, and all traces of frost had vanished from the windscreen.

He pulled up to the kerb outside Maureen's, and a squint through the windscreen told him she was still in her flat – she never left lights on when she went out, just like her mother: something to do with having had miserly Presbyterians for parents. While he waited, he took the opportunity to phone Cooper.

'Have you been drinking again?' she said by way of introduction.

Something in the tone of her voice told him it might be the other way around, but rather than be pulled into an argument, he said, 'Following up on the PM report.'

'It'll be with you in the morning.'

'Anything you want to tell me over the phone?'

'Other than I don't take kindly to being called this late at night?'

He thought of reminding her that she'd once told him she seldom went to bed before midnight, but instead said, 'Yes.'

'Two stab wounds to his chest.'

A blast of cold air rushed in as the car door opened. 'Hi, Dad, can you pop the boot?'

He did, then took his mobile off the speaker system. 'He wasn't strangled to death?'

'I'm not saying that.'

'The chest wounds were superficial?'

'Both of them punctured the heart.'

He let out a rush of exasperation. 'Well, Becky, two stab wounds to the heart, on top of strangulation by knotted rope, sounds like overkill to me. Excuse the pun.'

The boot slammed shut.

'I've run tests on the liquid in the cask,' she said.

He knew Cooper well enough to know she was teasing. 'I'm listening.'

Another blast of wind as the door opened, and Maureen slid in beside him.

'Minimal traces of blood,' Cooper went on. 'Which suggest the chest wounds were inflicted after strangulation.'

He switched on the ignition, slipped into Drive, and eased into the sparse night traffic. He was conscious of Maureen listening in – excellent hearing, just like his own – and shifted his mobile to his right ear. 'So why the overkill?' he said.

'Any number of reasons. Anger. Frustration.' A pause, then, 'Jealousy.'

Jealousy didn't join the dots in his theory. Why would Caithness be jealous? Angry, maybe. Frustrated, another maybe. But why stab Dunmore in the heart after having gone to the trouble of strangling him? He powered through the mini-roundabout and accelerated down Abbey Walk.

'I've confiscated the entire batch,' she said. 'Not that they could do anything with what was left, anyway.'

Hearing Cooper say that brought to him with a jolt the revenue lost to the distillery. A reputable twenty-five-year-old single-cask whisky could fetch anywhere between £750 and £1000 a bottle. Multiply that by some three hundred and fifty bottles, and you weren't talking about an inconsiderable loss—

'We also found a key,' Cooper said.

'What kind of key?'

'A small key. Like a key to lock a window, or a jewellery box.'

'Why leave a key? Why not remove it before putting the body into the cask?'

'They never knew he had it, I'd say. It was in a pocket in the front of his trousers,' she said. 'Like the small pocket every pair of jeans has. If you didn't know it was there, it could be overlooked.'

He found himself fingering the pockets of his own jeans, and right enough, there it was, the small pocket that had survived the quibbles of the fashion industry for decades – a safe place to keep your pocket watch, he remembered someone telling him, when people used to carry pocket watches.

'Anything else?' he asked.

'That's it.'

'Thanks, Becky. I'll send someone over to collect the key in the morning.' He slipped his mobile into his pocket, then reached over and squeezed his daughter's knee. 'So how are you?'

'I wish you'd stop doing that.'

'It's good to see you.'

She grumbled something he failed to catch as the lights of St Andrews slipped behind them in his rear-view mirror. 'What did you put in the boot?' he said.

'A cage I borrowed from Jenny.'

'Do I know Jenny?'

'Probably not,' she said. 'So what happened to your plans to retire?'

'Put them on hold for the time being.'

'You showed me your resignation letter six months ago. I thought you were going to hand it in the next day.'

He flexed his grip on the steering wheel. She was right on one point, of course, and wrong on another. It had been *nine* months since he'd written his letter of resignation, not six. And he had indeed intended to hand it in the next day. But as it turned out, the case of the day became the case of the week, then the case of the month, until his investigation ended months later in an arrest and prosecution. Any and all thoughts he'd had of handing in his notice had been suffocated in the heat of it all.

'I've still got the letter,' he said. 'I can change the date.'

She tutted, but offered nothing more.

The remainder of the drive was done in silence until they reached Kingsbarns.

'Jack called tonight,' she said.

Gilchrist tried to keep his surprise hidden. 'As in, he spoke to you on the phone?'

'Instead of texting, you mean?'

He smiled to show he got her joke. 'How is he?'

'Okay, it seems.'

'Still with Kristen?'

She fell silent for several seconds, before saying, 'They're talking about spending the summer in Sweden.'

Gilchrist felt his heart slump. Kristen had been born in Sweden, so it wasn't beyond the realms of possibility that she would want to return there one day, maybe even settle down there – taking Jack with her. He tried to keep his tone level. 'For a holiday?'

'I guess.'

He stared at the road ahead, hoping Maureen would tell him more. But after a mile of silence, he said, 'So maybe a working holiday then?'

She shrugged. 'Didn't get any details. You know Jack.'

Well, that was the key to it all right there. He felt as if he didn't know Jack any more. And he certainly didn't know Kristen. Their rushed departure to Edinburgh last March had done little to improve their father–son relationship.

'So how's Jack's art coming along?' he tried.

'Good. Seems to be making half-decent money again.'

He said nothing more as he drove into Crail. He slowed down as he eased into Castle Street, and drew to a halt. He switched off the engine.

Maureen had a hand on the door handle when he reached for her arm. 'Tell me what's going on, Mo. With Jack, I mean.'

She shrugged her arm free. 'Nothing's going on, Dad. Jack's just fucked up, like he's always been fucked up.' She seemed to give her words some thought, then said, 'I believe he thinks he's in love.'

'With Kristen?'

'Who else?'

'Isn't she too old for him?' The words were out before he could stop himself.

'What's age got to do with anything?'

Her eyes challenged him, and he tried to smooth the moment with a smile. 'You're right,' he said. But as he stepped into a bitter winter wind, he couldn't shift the unsettling feeling that he was letting his children down – both of them.

CHAPTER 14

As if she'd been waiting for Gilchrist's return home, Blackie was on the outside sill of the dining-room window, pressing her whiskers and face to the glass, tail high as she strutted from end to end. Gilchrist had never understood it, but Blackie would let him 'stroke' her through the window, as if seeking the vicarious pleasure of human touch. But as soon as he opened the back door, she would leap to the ground and run for the safety of his garden shed.

Despite the lack of physical contact, Gilchrist fed and watered her as if she were a regular pet. But she'd never set foot – make that paw – inside his cottage, and never let him within six feet of her. Even when he filled her bowl with food – often done on impulse after he'd forgotten to do so for several days – she maintained her distance, eyeing him from the corner of his wooden shed, ready to slip into the tight space behind it if he even so much as contemplated chucking her chin. So, he was more than a little intrigued as to how Maureen intended to entice Blackie into the cage she'd brought with her.

'She's lovely, isn't she?' Maureen said, brushing her fingers over the window pane, and chuckling as Blackie arched her back, pressing her body against the glass.

Gilchrist had to agree. When he first found Blackie in his garden – a couple of years ago now? – she looked as if she'd gone a few rounds with a pack of dogs, and lost. With chunks of matted fur missing, an ear tattered and torn, ribs like a skiffle board, and a feline disposition as fearful as a fox being hounded, Gilchrist thought she wouldn't last that first night. Now here she was, black fur glistening with health, and a purr he could hear through the window.

'She's never let me near her,' he said.

'So you've told me.' She squatted, so that her eyes were level with Blackie's.

He watched in amazement as Blackie returned eye contact, and sat on the sill, then blinked in that slow-motion way cats do. And he swore, he really did, that Blackie smiled at Maureen. Of course, all of this was good and well through a pane of glass. Doing away with that invisible barrier would be a different matter.

'I think it's you she's scared of,' Maureen whispered.

'Don't know why,' he said. 'I've done nothing to frighten her.'

'You don't have to do anything. She senses your presence.'

'And where did you get your cat-whispering degree?'

'Why don't you move away from the window?'

'If she thinks I'm going to open the back door, she'll be off like a shot.'

'No. Don't do that. Just step away. Turn your back and walk into the living room.'

Gilchrist did as he was told, and settled into his chair in front of the TV, the window still in view, Maureen still squatting, facing

Blackie eye to eye. How on earth she was going to persuade Blackie to enter that pet cage, he had no idea.

As if to answer that question, Maureen lifted the cage from the floor, and held it up to the window. Blackie just sat there looking at her. Then, with movements as smooth and steady as a magician, Maureen slid the cage door open and held it close to the window pane. Blackie blinked, then pushed off her haunches, and pressed her body, tail held high, against the glass. Maureen moved the cage slowly to the right, then to the left, and Blackie followed, turning on the sill like a ballet dancer with perfect balance.

Without a word, Maureen stood and, cage in hand, walked into the kitchen.

Gilchrist watched Blackie's eyes follow her, as he heard the double click of the back door being unlocked. Any moment now, he thought, and she would be off like a rabbit. But to his surprise, when Maureen came into view and reached out to run her hand along Blackie's back, Blackie simply let her, arching her back on tiptoes, as if to gain maximum pleasure. To further confound Gilchrist, when Maureen opened the cage and held it up to the window sill, Blackie stepped into it without the slightest hesitation.

When Maureen returned inside, she placed the cage on the kitchen floor, then joined Gilchrist in the living room.

'I would never have believed it,' he said. 'Is it a female thing?'

'That's such a feminist remark, Dad, you have no idea.'

Her comment only added to his confusion. It seemed the world had become so PC in its consciousness now, that he often worried it would reach the stage when you couldn't say good morning to someone without being accused of some kind of

-ism. But he said nothing as she produced her mobile phone and spoke into it with some urgency.

When she ended the call, he said, 'You're not staying?'

'Jenny's picking me up.'

'Do you have time for a pizza? I could call one in.'

'No thanks. She's with her parents in the Golf Hotel round the corner. She's happy to give me a lift to St Andrews. Any excuse to get away from them.'

He thought of asking her if that was how she felt about him – any excuse to get away from him – but thankfully didn't. Instead he said, 'How about a drink?'

She glanced at her mobile. 'If you make it quick.'

Well, in one way, that was a surprise. In another, it wasn't. 'Wine? Beer? Spirits?'

'Wine would be lovely.'

'Red or clear?'

She smiled at that, a joke they shared after being served in a pub in Glasgow by an uneducated – for a purported sommelier, that is – waitress. 'You wouldn't have any Prosecco, would you?'

'You're right. I wouldn't.'

'In that case, I'll take any colour,' she said with a chuckle.

'Coming up.' In the kitchen, he walked around Blackie's cage with care, and opened his fridge. On the wine shelf, he found three bottles of white, one rosé, and a red – who said red wine shouldn't be chilled? He removed one of the whites, a Delle Venezie Pinot Grigio, and unscrewed the top – well, he'd never claimed to be a wine connoisseur. He retrieved two glasses from the cupboard, gave them a quick dust with a length of kitchen roll, then topped them up, making sure they were large measures, which seemed to be the only way Maureen drank wine.

He carried the glasses through, and said, 'A cheeky little Pinot Grigio.'

'Thanks, Dad.'

Wine was definitely not Gilchrist's go-to drink, but the chilled freshness of it pleased him as he took a modest sip. Maureen on the other hand, took hers past the halfway mark.

'How do you know Jenny?' he asked.

'Just a friend.'

'From school?'

'That's going back a few years, Dad.'

He waited for her to say more, but she took another sip of wine while reading a text message on her mobile. 'How's the studying coming on?' he tried.

'Okay.' She tutted at her mobile, then used both thumbs to tap a message at a hundred words a minute, it looked like. Message sent, she retrieved her wine and drained it.

'Like another one?'

'Can't, Dad. Jenny'll be here any second.'

She pushed to her feet and walked to the kitchen.

He followed her. 'I've got some cat food you can have. A couple of cartons, if you'd like.' He retrieved them from a cupboard, and pushed them into a plastic bag he recovered from a drawer next to the sink.

'Isn't she gorgeous?' Maureen said, cage on the kitchen work surface, Blackie purring away, rubbing her face against the wire door.

'Thanks for taking her, Mo. It's amazing.'

'No probs.'

'I really mean it. I can't believe she came to you like that.'

The doorbell rang, and Maureen lifted the cage. 'That's Jenny.'

100

He followed her along the entrance hallway, and when she stepped outside, handed her the bag with his now-surplus cat food. A Volkswagen parked at the end of Rose Wynd with its engine running suggested that was Maureen's lift.

'Can you manage?' he said.

'Sure, Dad.' She stretched up, gave him a quick peck on the cheek, then turned and trotted along the Wynd, cage swinging by her hip. She managed to open the car door without dropping anything, and placed the cage with care onto the back seat. Then she slid onto the front passenger seat. He gave her a wave as the car eased away. But she seemed to have lost all interest in him.

Back inside, he thought of finishing his glass of wine, but decided to have something more suited to his palate – beer was his style. He snecked the top off a bottle of Deuchars IPA from the fridge. A quick mouthful from the neck – now that was more like it – and he was ready to do a bit more work.

He returned to his chair in the lounge, switched on the TV, found the News channel and put it onto mute. Then he picked up the files he'd taken from his office, and turned the pages, one by one. He stopped when he came across a printout of phone records, Mhairi's tidy writing at the top of the page confirming the number was George Caithness's mobile. Some numbers were highlighted in yellow, some in pink, some underlined in red, but only one of them was underlined and boxed, with an asterisk beside it.

He noted the date – last Tuesday – and next to it – Avis Rent a Car.

Ah, he thought. Now they were getting somewhere.

CHAPTER 15

Wednesday morning started as the forecasters predicted – high winds and heavy rain – but not expected to last through the day. Surprisingly for that time of year the temperature was a relatively mild 7 °C, something to do with a warm front pushing up from the south. The trouble with Scottish weather forecasting was that high winds could be anything from stiff gusts to hurricane force gales that could raise evacuation warnings for the USA's eastern seaboard, but were business as usual in Scotland.

Gilchrist walked up Rose Wynd, wind in his face, collar against his neck, head tucked down. The sound of pounding waves and crashing surf sank behind him, carried seawards on a gusting wind that whistled between the buildings.

In his car, he phoned Jessie.

'Have you looked outside?' she said. 'I've just washed my hair.'

'Good morning to you, too.'

'It'll be a mess in an hour.'

'Wear a hat.'

'Don't suit them.'

'Headscarf, then?'

'Aye, right. Hankie tied at the four corners? Are you joking, or what?'

'I'll be with you in fifteen minutes.'

'Make it twenty, and bring the coffees.' She hung up before he could respond.

The drive to St Andrews took longer than intended, with traffic backed up from a tree that had been blown over. Its trunk crushed a hedgerow, and branches stretched across one lane of the road. The Council already had a team with chainsaws on the job, with cars being directed around it in single file.

By the time he arrived at Jessie's, it was almost half-past seven.

The passenger door opened to a blast of cold air. 'One of these days I'm going to immigrate.'

'Emigrate.'

'What's that?'

'*Emigrate*. You're going to leave Scotland. Not come to it.'

'You're bloody right, I'm not.' She lifted a coffee from the holder. 'Skinny latte?'

'Of course. Seatbelt?'

She clicked it on, and took a noisy slurp as he eased away from the kerb. 'Here's this morning's trick question,' he said. 'Why would Caithness phone Avis Rent a Car in Cupar last Tuesday?'

She took another sip, as if giving the question some thought, then said, 'Why didn't he phone Avis Rent a Car in St Andrews might be a better question.'

'Don't think there's an Avis in St Andrews. But why rent a car at all?'

'And what's so special about Tuesday?'

'That's what I want you to find out this morning.'

'Hold onto my knickers, and drop everything else?'

'That's what I'm looking for.'

The remainder of the drive to the Office was done in silence, Gilchrist fiddling with some possibilities, but coming up with not a lot. His email inbox and in-tray offered nothing new, and a brief chat with each of his team members did nothing to lift his mood. All radio and TV appeals were as good as dead ends. Fifteen calls from alleged sightings in England – from Newcastle to Southampton – only complicated his investigation, and removed critical manpower from where he believed he needed it most – locally. But each of these reports had to be looked into, and he assigned a couple of uniforms to follow up with local police forces on each call, cranks or not. Other than that, George Caithness could have ceased to exist in Scotland.

At 9.30, Gilchrist gathered his team together.

'Okay, somebody give me some good news,' he said. 'Mhairi? You first.'

'Yes, sir.' She removed a ten by eight photo from a file folder, and pinned it up on the corkboard. 'We have some images of Caithness visiting Starbucks and Tesco last week.'

CCTV footage was not known for its quality, and the image pinned on the board was a zoomed-in capture of a grainy figure walking across Market Street, paper tucked under his arm. Mhairi pinned up another photo – an even grainier image, and a more zoomed-in capture showing Caithness in hat and scarf and over-coat clicking his remote for his Range Rover.

Mhairi glanced at Gilchrist. 'Sorry, sir. These are the best we could come up with.'

He nodded. 'Go on.'

'We showed these to the staff of Starbucks and Tesco. Also the stores either side.' She shook her head. 'Only one person in

Starbucks could confirm seeing Caithness, but she couldn't help.'

'Did she serve him?' Gilchrist asked.

Again, Mhairi shook her head. 'She works as a barista. She focuses on making coffee, not eyeing up the customers, so she said.'

Gilchrist clenched his jaw. He'd hoped someone might have remembered speaking to Caithness, heard him say he was going somewhere, which might have given a lead of sorts. But if only one person recognised him, and hadn't paid attention, well . . .

That was that.

'What about NADC records?' he said.

'That, too, sir,' Mhairi said. 'We found no footage of the Range Rover at all last Tuesday, or before that on Monday or Sunday. It was picked up a week ago on the Saturday, in ALDI's car park, then later that day down by the East Sands.' She referred to her notes. 'I didn't know how far back you wanted me to take it, sir, but his car was seen in a number of locations about town the week before. But I don't think any of it helps us really, sir.'

Gilchrist thought not, too, but he nodded to Jessie. 'Find anything this morning?'

'Seems that Georgie boy hired a van last Tuesday from Avis Rent a Car in Cupar. A white Citroën.' She read out the registration number. 'Had it delivered to his home address Tuesday morning. Keys and contract dropped through the letterbox. Payment made by Visa debit card in the name of G. Caithness, for two days' hire.'

'Two days?' Gilchrist interrupted. 'What would he want with a van for two days?'

'Your guess is as good as mine.'

'Was it returned on time?'

'Dropped back off in Cupar on Wednesday night.'

'Did no one in Avis talk to him when he returned it to the depot?'

'The office was closed. The van was found the next morning, parked at the front door, keys in the ignition—'

'That's it,' he said. 'Mhairi. Get back onto the ANPR and track that van's movements from the moment it was delivered on Tuesday morning, until its return on Wednesday night. I want to find out why Caithness hired a van, and what he did with it.' Then to Jessie. 'Get back onto Avis, and tell them we're going to confiscate that van. We want to run a full forensic examination on it.'

'I've already tried to confiscate the van, sir. But it's out on loan again.'

'Who to?'

'A Mr Charles Smith,' she said. 'Who's moving home today.'

'Is that the van's first hire since Caithness returned it?'

'As far as I know.'

'Let's go,' he said.

As they drove from the car park, Jessie was on the phone to Avis, finding out where Mr Smith was moving from and to. 'Don't give me any of that data protection crap,' she said. 'I don't give a toss if it's protected by the Queen's knickers. If I have to come back with a warrant, all additional costs to our investigation as a result of your delay will be on your ticket.' She slapped her mobile on her thigh. 'Can you believe that?' she said. 'The bitch hung up.'

He accelerated down North Street. 'Phone Avis back, and tell them to call the North Street Police Station, and ask for DC Mhairi McBride. She'll confirm that you weren't some prankster. And make sure Mhairi knows what to ask for. We can't waste time waiting for a warrant.'

Jessie hissed a curse, but did as instructed. When finished, she said, 'See women at work? I tell you. Give them a bit of authority, and it's like they think they're the queen bee.'

'I'm not going to comment on that.'

They'd almost reached the Avis depot in Cupar by the time Mhairi called back with both addresses. It seemed that Mr Smith was moving from Guardbridge to Dundee. They'd driven through Guardbridge on their way to Cupar, and Gilchrist did a quick three-point turn and headed back.

As luck would have it, they found the van at the Guardbridge address, half-on half-off the pavement. A young woman in denim shorts, despite the strong wind and ice-cold weather, was manhandling a cardboard box into the back. She eyed them with suspicion as Gilchrist pulled up behind the van, stepped onto the pavement, and walked towards her.

'Can I help you?' she said.

Gilchrist held out his warrant card, and introduced himself.

Jessie did likewise, and said, 'We're confiscating this van.'

'What d'you mean?'

'What it says on the tin. You can't drive it.'

'You can't do that.'

'Just did.'

Relief spread over the woman's face when a voice shouted, 'Heh you, what the hell's going on?' A man in his twenties, shorn head and diamond earrings, dropped the box he was carrying and stomped down the garden path towards them like a front-row forward preparing for the tackle.

'Steady on, sonny,' Jessie said, warrant card held high. 'We're the polis.'

He seemed not in the least interested. 'Aye, well, fuck that.'

Gilchrist stepped onto the garden path to confront him before he did something he would regret. 'Charles Smith?' he said.

The man stopped, suspicion darkening his eyes. 'What d'you want?'

The woman said, 'They want to confiscate the van, Chuck.'

'What for?'

'It's involved in an ongoing investigation,' Gilchrist said to him. 'So best if you start unpacking, and we'll take it from there.'

'We've already put a fucking deposit down.'

'Phone Avis,' Jessie said. 'They'll help you out.'

He scowled at her, then removed a mobile phone from his back pocket. He jabbed at the screen with one finger, and walked back inside his house to make the call.

Gilchrist returned to the rear of the van, and nodded to the woman. 'When did you collect the van?' he asked.

'Chuck picked it up last night. Got to return it this afternoon, or else they'll charge us for another day. You know what the thieving bastards are like.'

Gilchrist took a look inside the back of the van. Four open-topped cardboard boxes had been pushed to the front. Clothes and coat hangers poked out the tops in a dishevelled array. The interior looked clean – in an unused sense, as opposed to having been power-washed – as if the van was less than a few months old.

'How many trips have you made?' he said.

'This is the first. We're just about to get started.'

'After you collected it last night, what did you do with it?'

She frowned at him. 'What do you mean?'

'Did you take it for a spin? Have a party in the back?'

'No, none of that. Chuck just drove it here, and parked it.'

Gilchrist almost let out a sigh of relief. Forensic evidence of whatever Caithness had put in the back of the van might not have been lost. Of course, if Avis had cleaned the van's interior in readiness for the next customer, they might already be too late. His thoughts were stalled by Chuck reappearing, face tight, eyes wild, no mobile in sight. He slammed the garden gate behind him, as he stomped up to the van.

'How'd you get on with Avis?' Jessie sniped at him.

'I'm not fucking happy about this,' he said.

'That's too bad.' Jessie again.

'Okay,' Gilchrist said, more to keep the peace than take control. 'I'm sorry, Mr Smith, but we're going to have to confiscate everything in the van for a day or so. You'll get it back once we've completed our examination.'

'Aye, that'll be fucking right,' he said, and went to reach inside the van.

Jessie stepped forward and shouted, '*Don't touch.*'

But he swung an arm to push her off, and grunted in disbelief as she grabbed his wrist and twisted it against the joint. A knee to the back of one leg, and another jerk of his arm, and all six foot two of Charles Smith landed on the pavement with a hard slap. A knee into his back with Jessie's weight behind it – boobs and all – had him gasping for breath. He barely resisted his other arm being tucked behind him, and it was all over and done when she slipped the handcuffs on, and snapped them tight.

Jessie jumped to her feet, barely out of breath. 'You're under arrest for assaulting a police officer,' she said to him, then turned to the woman. 'As the man said, we're going to confiscate your stuff for a day or two. And we're going to have to take samples from you and lover boy here.'

'What for?'

'For the purposes of elimination from our investigation. Are you happy to give a sample on that basis?'

'Do I have a choice?' she said.

'You've always got a choice.' She glanced at Charles, who'd made it to his knees and was struggling to pull himself upright. Then she jerked her lips in imitation of a smile, and said, 'Just choose more wisely than he did.'

CHAPTER 16

The key recovered from Hector Dunmore's pocket was disappointing.

Gilchrist had hoped it might have opened a railway or airport locker, or bank deposit box, in which Hector had stored the answer as to why someone would murder him. But as he turned it over in his hands, Gilchrist saw it could be a key for any one of a thousand locks.

He slipped it back into its evidence envelope, and pushed his fingers through his hair, troubled that his investigation was stalling, and by the unavoidable truth that he was no closer to finding Hector's killer than DI Calish had been to finding Hector all these years ago with his half-arsed investigation. Gilchrist had put all his hopes and resources into finding their prime suspect, George Caithness, and look what that had given him – diddly squat.

He pushed from his desk, walked to the window, wondering how the key could be significant at all. Christ, he was scraping at pickings, trying to find clues where none existed.

A fist rapped his office door.

'You got a minute?'

He turned in time to catch a glimpse of Chief Superintendent Diane Smiley as she returned to her office, footfall echoing along the hallway. He grimaced at her excuse for a question. Smiler didn't ask. She ordered. And in the relatively short time she'd been in charge of the St Andrews Office, Gilchrist had come to understand that being ordered to Smiler's office under the guise of a question meant he was in some sort of trouble.

Well, his day hadn't exactly been one of the best. Might as well pile it on.

He followed her tantalising trail of perfume. That was one thing he could say about Smiler – she was always immaculate, always manicured and coiffed to perfection, as if she were expecting an invitation to meet the Queen at any moment. Standing outside her office, he hesitated for a moment before knuckling the door with care, then easing it open.

'Come in, DCI Gilchrist.'

The formal address did nothing to change his concerns, and he entered the room to stand in front of her desk.

'Take a seat, Andy.'

Even though she hadn't lifted her head to acknowledge his presence – reviewing some report with what could be mistaken for concentration – he considered the informal address as a tad less worrying. He took one of two chairs that faced her desk, and sat. Then she pushed whatever report she'd been pretending to read to the side of her desk, and looked at him.

'How's your investigation coming along?'

'Which one?'

She glared at him over imaginary spectacles. 'The one that's going to make me less angry and less frustrated, DCI Gilchrist.'

There it was again; the formality. 'I don't have good news on either investigation, I'm sorry to say, ma'am.'

'Nothing?'

'We're looking into a few leads, but nothing definitive, ma'am. *Yet*,' he added, just to keep up his side of the argument.

She picked up a heap of papers, reports, articles, at the edge of her desk, and removed a letter from the bottom of the pile as slickly as any card sharp. She shoved it across the desk. 'This came in this morning. Couriered.'

'Which courier?' he said.

'Don't act smart with me. I'm not in the mood.'

Without a word, he took the letter from her. Even upside down, he could tell it was Gleneden Distillery letterhead, and didn't have to attempt to interpret the sprawling signature to know it was signed by Katherine Dunmore. The first initial – K – almost struck through the closing paragraph. The swirling D of her surname touched the second last paragraph. With writing like that, it could take her three pages to wish you a Merry Christmas.

He gave the letter a cursory read before pushing it back across the desk.

'Mrs Dunmore appears not to be happy,' he said.

'If you'd taken more than a nanosecond to read what it says, you would see that she intends to seek legal advice, and to write a formal letter of complaint to her local MP.'

'That's certainly her prerogative, ma'am.'

Smiler reclined in her seat and eyed him. 'I don't think you understand the gravity of the situation, Andy.'

'Which is?'

'God,' she gasped. 'You can be so infuriating.'

'Yes, ma'am.'

'You and DS Janes drove to Dunmore Lodge yesterday and entered the property without a search warrant.'

'We weren't searching.' Not exactly correct. 'We wanted to see if anyone was living there. So we rang the doorbell. There's nothing wrong with that.'

'You set off security cameras.'

'It's a big house. If anyone was in, they might not have heard the doorbell. We were trying to see if there was a light on in any of the rooms. There wasn't. So we left. But our presence was picked up by motion detectors. Which was inevitable.'

His story seemed to appease Smiler. She took a deep breath through tight lips, and said, 'We need to be careful.'

'We, ma'am?'

'Fife Constabulary. You. Me. We can't have Katherine Dunmore complaining about the police force willy-nilly, or sending in lawyer's letters *ad nauseum*.' She leaned forward, so that her elbows rested on her desk. 'She's a player, Andy. She has friends in high places. *High* places. You understand? She's a supporter of the local community. A businesswoman who has donated hundreds of thousands of pounds to local charities for years. She helped raise funds for the children's hospital, for crying out loud. She even donated twenty thousand pounds to the Police Federation as recently as last year.'

Ah, he thought. Now they were coming down to it. 'That's very noble of her.'

'I'm not sure *noble* is the right word.'

'How about ... *canny*?' he said, and watched Smiler's lips flicker a smile as his mind changed tack to scour other possibilities. It never failed to amaze him how the brain worked, how it locked on to some seemingly innocent comment and plugged it into an equation of sorts at the subconscious level. It was the mention of her donation to the Police Federation which triggered some neural reaction, and alerted him to what he thought was the obvious – you don't donate large sums of money to any organisation unless you're able to benefit from it in some way. And to do that, you had to have contacts. Personal contacts.

But if you pushed that aside, and considered the more basic elements of charitable donations, and focused on individuals rather than organisations, then threw in a bit of hanky-panky in the form of some criminal activity, then the donation might not be considered a gift, but a payment to silence a blackmailer. Which might . . . and again it was a huge might . . . explain why DI Calish's investigations of Hector Dunmore's disappearance and Duncan Milne's, quote unquote, accidental death were so incompetently handled.

What if Caithness had paid off DI Calish all these years ago?

What if—

'You're not listening, are you?'

Gilchrist came to with a jolt. 'What's that, ma'am?'

'I was saying that *canny* should be the operative word in any future dealings you may have with Mrs Dunmore.'

'I'll keep that in mind, ma'am.'

'I suggest you do more than just keep it in mind, DCI Gilchrist.'

He thought of coming back at her with some smart-mouthed comment, but decided against it. He had a double murder investigation to solve, and a missing person to find. And if you added blackmail to the list, the possibilities widened to an almost limitless horizon.

'Yes, ma'am,' he said.

115

'Yes, ma'am what?'

'I'll do more than just keep it in mind. Ma'am.'

She returned his gaze for several seconds as if calculating whether it was worth the effort to try to rein him in or not. Then she reached for her pen.

'That'll be all, DCI Gilchrist.'

'Thank you, ma'am.' He didn't look back as he left her office, or give her a parting glance as he closed the door. He was far too focused for that.

Now he knew what his next step was.

CHAPTER 17

He found Jackie seated at her computer, her attention so focused on the monitor that she didn't notice him enter. She jolted with surprise when he walked up to her, then her face broke into a smile that stretched her lips wide and creased her eyes.

'Happy to see me?' he said.

Her hair bounced as she nodded. 'Uh-huh.'

'Even if it means more work?'

She chuckled. 'Uh-huh.'

He stepped behind her desk, his gaze locking on to her crutches leaning against the wall. Something caught his throat. Here she was, a young woman in her early twenties who suffered from cerebral palsy, and a stutter so bad that she'd almost given up speaking. As for her mobility, Jackie refused to let her condition hold her back. He'd seen her on the move, crutches clicking forwards, sideways, backwards, any which way, as if her legs were more of a hindrance than a necessity. He used to joke with her that she'd beat him in a 100-metre dash. He put a hand on her shoulder, and squeezed. 'How're you holding up?'

She nodded. 'Oh . . . oh . . .'

'Okay?'

'Uh-huh.'

'That's great,' he said, and meant it.

Standing there, hand on her shoulder, he felt an overwhelming sense of sorrow. What kind of a life did she have? As best he knew, Jackie lived by herself in a one-bedroom flat in town, and had no intimate relationships with anyone, male or female. If living all by yourself had to be defined, then you would look no further than Jackie. It seemed to him that Jackie lived only to work in the Constabulary, year after year. And what an employee she was. Best researcher in the world he often called her. And by God did he mean it? And nothing he set her was ever too much trouble, each and every task tackled with a smile and an enthusiasm that seemed impossible to muster in someone so handicapped. He fought off the ridiculous urge to put his arm around her and give her a hug.

Instead, he said, 'When this investigation is done and dusted, I'm going to take you and the rest of the team out for a few beers and a bite in the Central Bar. And we can all have a wee catch-up chat about stuff.'

She burst out laughing at the thought of having a chat with anyone.

'Would you be up for that?' he said.

'Uh-huh.'

'Okay . . .' He leaned closer, so that his face was only inches from hers. 'I'd like you to keep this quiet. Between us. I want you to find out what you can on DI Tom Calish, formerly of St Andrews. He passed away some years ago, but he was the SIO in the investigation of Hector Dunmore's disappearance and Duncan Milne's death.'

She glanced at him, and he could read her question from her eyes.

'I'm not happy with the way Calish signed off on both investigations. I'm suspicious that he might have had an ulterior reason to do so.' He hated to use the word, but it seemed he had no choice. He grimaced, and said, 'He might have been involved in blackmail. But I don't know for sure.' He raised both hands in fake surrender. 'It's just conjecture at this stage, but I need to know a bit more about him so I can put this to bed.'

She nodded. 'Ba . . . ba . . .'

'Bank details?'

'Uh-huh.'

'If you can dig them up, that'd be great. But I don't know how far back you'll get as banks typically keep their records for seven years or so. If you come up with anything that needs digging deeper, we can always pass the case over to the FIU.'

Jackie nodded. The Financial Investigation Unit was a powerful investigative branch that could carry out forensic examinations of private and company bank accounts. But these accounts had to exist in the first instance. Again, another long shot. He pushed himself upright, and squeezed her shoulder again.

'Thanks, Jackie. And mum's the word. Okay?'

Back in his office, he worked through the rationale of why he was looking into DI Calish's past. When the idea, or rather, the suspicion of an idea, had first hit him, it made perfect logical sense. But now he'd pulled it from the darkness into the sunlight, it no longer had that criminal certainty he'd first felt. He'd taken Jackie off the Caithness case, at a time when he needed every hand on deck, and given her a half-arsed explanation. As he turned his attention to some unopened emails, he made up his mind that if Jackie turned up nothing by the end of the day, he would drop all interest in DI Calish.

Just then, Jessie entered his office. 'The SOCOs have found traces of blood in the back of the van.'

'Do they have a DNA match?'

'Bloody hell, it's only just in. Give us a break.'

'Well, let's get it analysed as a priority.'

'That's what we're trying to do,' she said. 'You need to come through and see what Mhairi's come up with,' she added, then walked from his office.

He found Jessie huddled over Mhairi's computer, peering hard at the monitor, taking notes. 'What've you got?' he asked.

Mhairi worked the mouse. The images on the screen jerked backwards. She clicked the cursor, and the screen stopped. Then she adjusted it a touch, and sat back.

Gilchrist leaned forward, not sure what he was looking for. The time at the top of the screen was just this side of midnight, and a quick calculation of the date put it at last Tuesday. A van then entered the screen and moved across it in staccato movements, until Mhairi froze the image.

'This is recorded ANPR footage,' Jessie said.

'Which road are we on?'

'The A90. On the eastern outskirts of Perth.'

Mhairi added, 'And heading west, sir.' She clicked the mouse, and the image shifted to another location. The screen held for a second, then blinked to reappear at another location. 'I first captured it south of Dundee, sir, crossing the Tay.'

'Nothing in St Andrews?' he asked.

'Odd, don't you think?' Jessie interrupted. 'From Hepburn Gardens, you can drive west to Strathkinness, wind your way through the country, and not a CCTV camera in sight.' She tapped a finger to the monitor. 'That sneaky bugger's trying to avoid being noticed.'

'Do we know where he's going?'

'I think so, sir. Give me a second.'

Gilchrist said nothing as Mhairi worked the mouse again, until the screen stopped at a grainy image of a van flashing past with its headlights on. 'This is the last sighting I can find of it, sir. Haven't been able to locate anything farther north of this location.'

'Which is where?'

'The A9,' Jessie announced. 'North of Perth. Any guesses where you think he might have turned off?'

Gilchrist pulled himself upright. 'He's taken the cut off to Tullybelton,' he said. 'He's driving to Dunmore Lodge.'

'Bingo,' Jessie said. 'But what's Georgie boy got in the back of the van? What's so big that he had to hire a van in the first place?' She tapped the monitor. 'We need a search warrant, and get our forensic boys to go through that lodge with a fine toothcomb. He's hidden something. And we need to know what it is.'

Gilchrist had to agree with her. But Smiler's words were still ringing in his ears, or at least one word in particular was – canny – her way of warning him to be careful. One breach of protocol, one step outside the box, and he could land himself in trouble, or more correctly, the Chief Superintendent could find her precious Office being landed with a lawsuit.

Shit and dammit.

If he and Jessie hadn't visited Dunmore Lodge yesterday, they could have marched up there today, warrant in hand, and sealed the place off. Whatever Caithness had taken with him in the back of that van had to have been hidden in the Lodge, or buried in the grounds.

But burying something would have taken time.

'Have you got any footage of the van heading back?' he asked.

'A moment, sir.' Mhairi fast-forwarded the screen, and images flickered past like a silent movie, then stopped. 'Here we are, sir. This is the first one on the way back.'

'How long between the last image heading to Tullybelton, and this one, the first one heading back?'

Silent, Mhairi worked the mouse again, jotting down the times. A quick calculation, and she said, 'Forty-eight minutes, sir. Give or take a few seconds.'

He faced Jessie. 'It took us what . . .? Fifteen, twenty minutes to reach the Lodge after turning off the A9?'

'Closer to twenty, I'd say.'

'Let's say thirty-five there and back. Which leaves thirteen minutes. So, whatever he had in the van, he must've dropped off at the Lodge. He didn't have time to dig a hole, bury it, and cover it back up, did he?'

'He could've had the hole already dug,' Jessie offered. 'All he'd have to do would be to fill it in.'

'Still too tight,' he said. 'And why risk a hole being found?'

'Maybe in the woods?'

'Maybe.'

Mhairi chipped in. 'Unless he didn't drive all the way to the Lodge. He could've buried it on the way there, sir.'

'Possible, Mhairi. But I don't think so. If he wanted to bury it at the side of the road, he could've done so on any number of country roads.' He pressed his lips tight. Too many possibilities. Not enough certainties. But the timing was something to go on.

All he had to do was make a decision. 'Whatever it is, he dumped it off in the Lodge. If we move forward with that, the Lodge is key.'

'Want me to start the ball on a search warrant?' Jessie said.

'It's not as straightforward as that,' he said.

'What're you not telling me?'

'Katherine Dunmore couriered a letter of complaint to Smiler this morning.'

'Aw, for crying out loud,' she said. 'Tell me you're joking.'

'Wish I could. I've already been warned to proceed with caution.'

'So . . .' Jessie held her hands out, palms up. 'That's it? We do nothing?'

'Not necessarily,' he said.

'I'm all ears.'

'Caithness seems to be slippery, and we need to be one step ahead of him.'

'You're forgetting he's missing,' Jessie said. 'And we don't know where he is.' She gave a derisive snort. 'So who's one step ahead of who here?'

Well, there was that, he supposed. 'I've no idea what was in that van, but we're going to find out, and I want to be prepared when we do. When we eventually find Caithness, he'll deny it was him driving the van. So let's catch him out.'

Mhairi said, 'How are we going to do that, sir?'

'We have the van. All we need is his DNA.'

'Hah,' said Jessie. 'I can't see Katherine the Great giving us his dirty undies.'

'Neither can I,' Gilchrist said. 'Let's go.'

CHAPTER 18

GC Publicity carried out its business from a converted barn in Kingsbarns. A pan-tiled roof that sported two attic windows topped a building that seemed to be built from more glass than stone. The original barn door had been replaced with a full-height glass panel through which employees on the ground and first floors could be seen, heads down at desks that looked more suited to an engineering office, although Gilchrist had to confess that he'd no idea what a publicity and marketing company should look like.

He parked his BMW between an Audi R8 and a Porsche 911 Turbo, making him think that maybe a publicist or a marketer was the up and coming profession to be in.

'Somebody's doing well,' he said, nodding to the Audi as he beeped his remote.

'Don't like the colour,' Jessie said.

The reception area was a spartan wooden-floored hallway. Tiny spotlights dangled from two rows of wires that ran from one end of the ceiling to the other. Two soft chairs with glistening steel frames faced a matching coffee table on which lay an array of magazines – *Brand Republic*, *Marketing Week*, *Campaign* – none of which Gilchrist had heard of, let alone read. The reception desk stationed a laptop computer, a jar of assorted pens and highlighters, a phone, and a young woman with short red hair, radiant eyes, and a smile that could front any dental magazine. And not a tattoo in sight.

Well, marketing and advertising was all about image, he supposed.

'Can I help you?' she said.

Gilchrist showed her his warrant card, introduced himself and Jessie. 'We're looking into the disappearance of George Caithness.'

A flicker of worry shifted across her face like a shadow. 'Mr Caithness hasn't been into the office for some time,' she said.

'Which is why we're here,' Jessie said. 'Who's in charge?'

'That would be Mr Lyons,' she said. 'But he's not in at the moment.'

'Second in charge, then?'

'Oh, I'm not sure. It's really Mr Lyons or Mr Caithness who are the bosses.'

Jessie nodded to the window. 'Who owns that orange thing out there?'

'The Audi?'

'We'll talk to him, then.'

'That's Charlotte's.'

'She'll do.'

'What did you say your names were again?'

Gilchrist told her, and added, 'St Andrews CID.'

She lifted the handset, pressed a button on the phone console, and said, 'Ms Ryan, I have a DCI Gilchrist at the front desk. He would like to talk to you about Mr Caithness.' She held onto the phone, nodding to commands that could be heard in a tinny echo. Then she replaced the phone. 'Ms Ryan will be down in a couple of minutes.'

While Jessie pulled up a seat at the coffee table, Gilchrist prowled the reception area studying framed photographs on the walls; advertising shots by a professional photographer of shop-fronts, delivery vans, forklift trucks, but none of Gleneden Distillery or any whisky-related products, which surprised him, he had to say—

'Can I help you?' The voice was distinctly English, with upper-class tones.

Gilchrist turned to face a woman he would place not only in her thirties, but in a model agency. Black high heels, tanned legs, short navy skirt, sky-blue blouse. The phrase *it's all about image* flashed through his mind, as he took hold of her hand.

'I'm Charlie Ryan, the de facto leader of the pack when every-one else is out.'

Close up, make-up dusted wrinkles that told him she was on the other side of forty.

Jessie scowled as she shook her hand. 'That orange thing yours?'

Ryan glanced outside, and smiled. 'My husband's. My Ford's in for a service.' She faced Gilchrist again. 'You wanted to talk about George?'

'We won't take up much of your time.'

'Follow me,' she said, and opened a door to a conference room large enough to sit ten people around an oval table. Ryan took a chair at the top. Gilchrist took the chair close to her, while Jessie sat opposite him. 'Can I get anyone a coffee?' Ryan said.

126

'Not for me,' he said. 'But thanks.'

Jessie ignored the question by removing a notepad from her bag.

Ryan clasped her hands. 'So,' she said, 'what do you want to know about George?'

Gilchrist said, 'His wife, Katherine, said that he'd started GC Publicity to promote Gleneden Distillery and its products mostly, then to branch into other areas. But I don't see any signs of the distillery.'

'Oh we have a small room upstairs dedicated exclusively to Gleneden.'

'Why not showcase it in the reception area? After all, it belongs to George's wife.'

'You'd have to ask George that.'

'So a decision was taken not to showcase Gleneden?'

Ryan crossed her legs as she shifted in her chair. 'I thought you wanted to ask about George,' she said. 'Not Gleneden Distillery.'

'It's all related.' He let a couple of beats pass. 'When did you last see him?'

'He was here just over a week ago. Last Monday.'

'I thought it was Tuesday.'

'No. I believe Monday. He might have phoned in on Tuesday.'

Gilchrist nodded, trying to recall Mhairi's ANPR footage. She'd had no recordings of George's Range Rover last Monday. He was sure of it. Which meant George had stayed at home, maybe even worked from home.

'Are you sure about that?' he said.

'I have minutes of a meeting he attended that day. In this very room.'

'May we see them?' Jessie said. 'The minutes.'

'Can I ask why?'

'You can.'

'Well?'

'The minutes.'

Something shifted across Ryan's face, like a ripple of energy that stiffened postures, tightened muscles, clenched jaws. 'When Mr Lyons returns to the office, I'll ask him if he's happy to let you see a copy.'

'We couldn't care less if he's happy or not,' Jessie said. 'We can get a warrant.'

'Do that.'

Gilchrist could not fail to catch the cold clip in Ryan's tone, so stepped in with, 'How did George get to the office last Monday? Our records show that his car didn't leave home.'

'I couldn't tell you,' she said. 'I mean, I didn't notice. Sometimes he drives his wife's car. He may have driven it that day. But I couldn't tell you with any certainty.'

Gilchrist could have sworn out loud. That comment had just created another shitload of ANPR footage for Mhairi to go through. 'I understand he works from home from time to time,' he said. 'How many days a week would he typically spend at the office?'

She shook her head. 'I couldn't say.'

'Don't you have timesheets?' Jessie snapped.

'We do,' she said with ice in her voice. 'For our staff's billable hours. But George is the owner of the company.'

'Which means what?'

'Which means that I don't get to see his timesheet, if or when he ever turns one in.'

'Somebody somewhere must have a record of the hours he keeps. Or is publicity and marketing one of these professions that you just turn up for whenever you feel like it?'

Ryan tutted, but offered nothing.

Gilchrist said, 'Could you show us George's office?'

'I take it he has an office,' Jessie sniped.

'This way.' Ryan pushed from the table, and walked to the door without a backward glance.

Upstairs, Ryan opened the door to an office with a sloped ceiling and wooden beams that split three skylight windows. The room felt stuffy and hot, and a tantalising fragrance of cinnamon tickled the throat. Gilchrist noticed a small vase of potpourri on the window sill. Open fields, grass bleached by winter, rose in a gradual slope to the dark wall of a pine forest.

'Nice view,' he said.

'Bit stuffy,' Jessie offered. 'Do you always have the heat up this high?'

'Mr Caithness prefers summer to winter,' Ryan said.

'So you're expecting him back?'

'Aren't you?'

Gilchrist said, 'I noticed his office was unlocked.'

'It always is.'

'So people can come in any time they like . . .' He opened a desk drawer '. . . and go through his files.'

'Of course. It's an office, not a private room.'

'It's been recently cleaned?' he asked.

'We have a cleaning contractor who comes in over the weekend.'

He closed the drawer, opened another one. 'Are the filing cabinets unlocked, too?'

129

'As I said, it's a working office.'

Next to the file cabinets stood an old-fashioned coat stand in the corner. No coats or jackets over it, but a woollen scarf had slipped off and lay on the floor. 'George's?' he said.

'More than likely, yes.'

'Looks like the cleaners missed that.'

Ryan tutted, picked the scarf up, and hung it over the coat stand.

Gilchrist closed the drawer, and returned to the front of the desk. 'I don't see any Gleneden products, or photographs,' he said. 'Not even one of his wife. It's like . . .' He took a three-sixty look around the room '. . . he never comes here.'

'Well, he does, I can assure you.'

'You got these minutes we can look at?' Jessie said.

'I'll have Mr Lyons call you.'

'Today, preferably.'

'You said you had a room for Gleneden,' Gilchrist said.

'We do, yes. Have you seen all you want to see here?'

'I'd say so.'

At the far end of the building, Ryan opened a door to a room that was not much larger than Gilchrist's bathroom in Fisherman's Cottage. Shelves lined with bric-a-brac ran along two walls: framed photographs stacked face down, piled one on top of the other; cardboard containers that announced Gleneden ten-year single malt, Gleneden fifteen-year Highland Blend, Gleneden Special Reserve, and others. He picked one up to make sure it was empty – it was. He flipped over one of the framed photographs – a coloured image of the old warehouse in the forefront, with the skeletal construction frame of the new warehouse in the back. Another showed the copper distilling vats, looking as inviting as the whisky itself. A coil of gleaming copper pipe stood next to a box of nosing glasses that competed with four stainless steel whisky measures.

'Why is none of this out on display?' he asked.

'You'd need to ask Mr Caithness,' Ryan said. 'It was his idea.'

'To store it away?' He failed to hide his surprise.

'Yes.'

He scanned the shelves again, ran a finger over the end of one of them – not a lot of dust. 'When did he instruct that?'

'A week or so before Christmas.'

'So they've been stored here for about a month?'

'About that.'

'Can you show me where they were displayed before then?'

'There was no one place,' she said. 'The photos were mounted throughout the offices. The bottle containers and other bits and bobs were here, there and everywhere.'

'So why pull them all together? And why just before Christmas?'

Ryan shrugged. 'Again, you'd need to ask Mr Caithness.'

Gilchrist nodded, puzzled by it all, as if everything that publicised Gleneden Distillery had been gathered in before Christmas. Had Caithness fallen out with his wife? Was this his way of preparing for a final departure? It seemed as if he knew he was about to go missing.

Had that been his plan?

'What do you intend to do with all this stuff?' he said.

'That'll be up to Mr Caithness,' she said. 'When he returns.'

Well, she might be waiting a long time, he thought. Still, he thanked her, and he and Jessie followed Ryan back to the reception. She shook his hand with polite professionalism, but ignored Jessie.

In the car, Gilchrist said, 'Penny for your thoughts?'

'You'd think if you had money to spend on a car like that,' she said, nodding to the Audi R8 at her side, 'you would choose a different colour.'

'It's her husband's.'

'You know what?' she said. 'We should've made some excuse about that scarf. It would've been perfect for a DNA sample. It wouldn't matter that we didn't have a warrant. We could get that later. All we're looking for is a sample for comparison.'

Gilchrist let his speed touch sixty, then slid his hand inside his jacket. He removed a pair of black leather gloves, and handed them to Jessie.

She stared at them, then said, 'You sneaky devil. Where did you find these?'

'Desk drawer.' He pulled out to overtake a car. 'Turn these inside out, and we've got George's DNA.'

'If they are George's,' she said.

Well, you could never be 100 per cent certain. But 99.9 was as good as. 'It's odd, don't you think, that there was nothing of Gleneden Distillery out on display. Nothing in reception. Nothing in his office. All stuffed on shelves in a cupboard with a closed door. Why do you think that is?'

'Getting ready for a change?' she said.

'Such as?'

'Painting and decorating? New client taking over? Planning to bring out some new marketing material for Gleneden? Or maybe he's lost interest in Gleneden? Who knows.'

Gilchrist held his speed at a steady eighty while his mind picked through Jessie's words and kept returning to one phrase in particular – *getting ready for a change*. But the reason for that change was not painting or decorating, or a new client, or new marketing material, nor even that George was no longer interested in Gleneden.

No, it was none of the above. But it had to be a change by George all right.

Or maybe the material had not been taken down to get *ready* for a change.

Maybe it had been moved in *response* to a change.

But if so, a change in what?

He tightened his grip on the steering wheel, and drove on.

CHAPTER 19

By 5 p.m., Gilchrist's investigation was no further forward.

He'd instructed Mhairi to check ANPR records for Katherine Dunmore's car last Monday, the day George had last gone to his office. But so far she'd come up with nothing, and he'd have to wait until the morning for a different result – if possible.

And his daily debriefing was disappointing, too. All leads on reported sightings of Caithness had been checked out and proven to be dead ends, and despite sustained national radio and TV appeals, no new leads had been forthcoming. But a flicker of some good news turned up late afternoon, when Jackie emailed Gilchrist with a report of her findings on DI Tom Calish.

To his surprise, the Royal Bank of Scotland – with whom Calish had two accounts – had provided copies of monthly statements for both accounts as far back as eighteen years, but regrettably six years after Calish's investigation into Duncan Milne's death. So the flicker expired, and he set the report aside, for all intents and purposes, another bloody dead end. By 7 p.m., his head was spinning, and he was about to call it a day when Mhairi rapped on his office door.

'Sir?' She slapped a handful of photographs onto his desk. 'You need to see these.'

The first photograph was an enlarged image of a CCTV footage clip of a parked car – Audi saloon, it looked like – in which a man was either emerging from, or getting into, the driver's seat.

'Is this Caithness?' he asked.

'No, sir. The car's registered owner is a Tony Maybury, with an address in Dundee,' she said. 'And we believe that's him.'

Gilchrist could tell from Mhairi's tone that she was telling him something important, but whatever it was, he wasn't seeing it.

'Have a look at the other photos, sir.'

He did. A series of a couple between two cars, standing in a lovers' clinch.

Mhairi tapped one of them. 'These were taken approximately ten minutes apart. And you can see the registration number plate here, sir. This is Katherine Dunmore's car, sir. And that's her with Tony Maybury.'

Gilchrist pulled the images closer. Dunmore had her back against her car, showing a bit of leg from her skirt riding high. It didn't take much imagination to work out what Maybury was up to.

'Check the dates, sir.'

He did. 'So these were taken last Tuesday night?'

'The day after Caithness was last seen at his office, sir.'

'And the day the van was hired from Avis.'

'Do you think George left because he knew his wife was having an affair? Or do you think they're celebrating knowing that George has left?'

And layer by layer the fog lifted to reveal another possibility. But he wasn't there yet. 'And this Tony Maybury,' he said. 'Who's he?'

'A businessman with form, sir.'

'I'm listening.'

'Twenty years ago, Maybury was charged with serious assault, but got away with it. Ten years ago, he was found guilty of a tax misdemeanour, and spent three months in HMP Castle Huntly.'

'Wasn't Caithness charged with serious assault, too?'

'He was, sir, yes. But they were in unrelated incidents. I checked it out.'

He smiled. Mhairi wasn't afraid to use her own initiative. 'Keep going,' he said.

'Since that jail term, Maybury's turned over a new leaf. But we know that people like him never change, sir. It's in their blood.'

'So what's his connection to Dunmore?'

'He's in the entertainment business. Sets up corporate marquees. Being hand in glove with a Scottish whisky distillery is good business for both parties. But what I'm thinking, sir, is that Dunmore's nowhere near as clean as she'd like us to think she is.'

'Because she's having an affair behind her husband's back?'

'No,' she said, with an emphatic snap. 'These photographs don't prove they're having an affair. Only that they're in close contact.' She paused, as if to collect her thoughts. 'What I believe, sir, is that the importance of these photos is the timing.'

'The timing?'

'I think so, sir. Yes.'

Gilchrist stared at the images, Smiler's word – canny – still echoing. He would have to speak to Dunmore again. But before doing so he needed to be well prepared.

'Does this Tony Maybury live close by?' he asked.

'I've got his home address, sir, yes.'

She read it out to him, an address in Dundee, a twenty-minute drive away. Jessie had asked to be excused from the Office, something to do with her son, Robert. So, he could go to Dundee alone, or . . .

'Grab your coat, Mhairi. Let's go.'

Jessie hadn't been altogether honest with her boss. She'd told Gilchrist that it was a special occasion for her son; a white lie about some publisher showing interest in his comedy book – he had indeed submitted his manuscript to several publishers, but hadn't heard back from any of them yet – and she'd promised to take him out for a meal.

But Robert wasn't into dining out. He preferred takeaways – curries, fish suppers, even a Greggs on the run – or on the rare occasion she had time to cook, Mum's steak pie served with a mountain of chips and beans – which she'd last cooked for him . . . oh my . . . August last year?

On the drive back from GC Publicity, she'd sensed Gilchrist's frustration with the progress of their investigation, and broached the subject about leaving early that night – *first time in ages that I've asked for an early bath* – and to her surprise, he'd agreed.

'Family's important,' he said. 'And you love your son.'

And now she was feeling guilty.

Almost 7.15 p.m., and Robert hadn't come home from work yet, and his steak pie and chips were beginning to dry up – in and out of the oven to keep them warm. Robert worked part-time as a joiner with Carson, Angie's brother, just weekends to begin with, but was now involved in larger projects. Jessie didn't understand all the construction terms, but Robert told her that they'd made a new-build wind and watertight over the weekend, and were now under the gun to finish the drywall by the end of the week. She'd texted him twice – once; to tell him she was home, and again; that his favourite dinner was in the oven.

But she hadn't heard back.

Even though Robert was now sixteen years old, and six foot one, with shoulders out to here and mature beyond his years, she couldn't help but worry about her wee boy. Her *wee boy*? How had he grown so quickly? Where had the years gone? It seemed like one minute he was learning to walk, the next he's starting work. And Robert had decided for himself that he wasn't going to go to university. Not that he wasn't bright, or because he was stone deaf with no chance of hearing – auditory nervous system never developed – but because he wanted to be a writer, and couldn't see how going through university was going to help him do that.

Jessie had suggested creative writing courses, but Robert had looked into a couple of these and again decided for himself. And it was these decisions of his, the fact that he could think his way through the process, then make a decision and stand by it, that convinced her that her wee boy was becoming a man, and would soon be able to stand on his own two feet – although he needed to make a living to do that. And again, Robert came up with a solution by working as a trainee joiner with Angie's brother.

Her heart swelled for her *wee boy*. She loved him to bits.

When Robert was younger, she'd worried that he would miss having a father, or even worse, would demand to meet his father when he was older – which would present all sorts of problems for Jessie, because she'd lost touch with his father, if losing touch was the right phrase: a drunken shag on the bedroom floor at some teenage party, and that was it, cock back into his trousers, then up and back to the party to continue getting pissed with his mates. Christ, she could barely remember his name. She'd tracked him down years later to tell him he had a son. Not that she was looking for maintenance or commitment or anything like that. Instead, she thought he had the right to know he was a father, and that he had a choice of having his son in his life, or not.

Not, was the quick answer in the form of a disconnected phone call.

She'd never heard from the bastard since.

And talking about never hearing from bastards, she tapped in her password and pulled up her last text – Dinners in oven yr fave steak pie see u soon luv mum xxx. She was about to tap in another text when she heard a car door slam. She peeked out the curtain in time to see a car drive off, and her son stride up the path.

She met him in the hallway, her emotions swinging from giving him a right telling-off for not answering her texts, to hugging him because he was home. But the latter won, and she pecked his cheek as he hugged her back. That close, she breathed in the sawdust smell and the manly sweat of a manual worker coming home from a hard day.

Sorry, mum, he signed. *Carson asked me to work late, and my phone needed charged.*

I thought you'd lost it, she signed back. She waited until he plugged in his charger, then signed, *You must be hungry.*

Starving.

Well, that was a relief. Sometimes Robert would come home having had an afternoon bridie from Greggs or a filled roll from Subway, and had no appetite. *Wash your hands while I get dinner ready.* She removed the steak pie ashet and tray of chips from the oven – not altogether ruined. The baked beans she switched to high on the top stove. They would be ready in seconds.

By the time Robert took his seat at the kitchen table, Jessie had a baguette cut and buttered, and the steak pie sliced and out on both plates. On Robert's plate, chips piled high competed with a swamp of baked beans. Her own plate looked empty by comparison. She'd lost two stones in weight since transferring to St Andrews, and even though she would like to lose another ten pounds or so, she was beginning to feel good about how she looked. Blouses no longer stretched around her waist like a stubby concertina, and trousers now hung loose enough to hitch up from time to time. Of course, she'd started looking in charity shops for the odd bargain, and last week had bought a wee sixty-quid plaid jacket for a tenner. Still the tiniest bit tight, but that would give her incentive to lose some more weight. She took a forkful of pie, and smiled as Robert piled three buttered slices of baguette onto his plate.

Thanks, Mum, he signed, then focused on cleaning his plate in silence. What was it about teenage boys and food? Or more to the point, with hardly a pick of fat on them, where did they put it?

When he started wiping the steak pie gravy from his plate with the bread, she signed, *Would you like some more?*

He shook his head. *Stuffed full.*

Do you want to watch telly with me, or are you going to write?

I'm going out tonight.

Where to?

Nowhere.

Who with?

A friend.

Jessie mouthed an Aahh, then signed, *Do I know her?*

Robert stared at his plate as his face flushed. He shook his head.

Jessie felt a sense of panic surge through her. Robert was only sixteen, for crying out loud. How old was this friend of his? She'd known this moment would come someday, but she hadn't expected it to hit her so soon, not for another year or two . . . at least. And now it was here, she felt as if she'd handled it wrong. Without meaning to, she'd put her son on the spot, embarrassed him with her careless questions. She found herself unable to think of what to say as he picked up his plate and her own and, without a word, slotted them into the dishwasher.

He was about to walk from the kitchen, when Jessie took hold of his arm. The trouble with signing was that you needed both hands, so she had to release her grip.

I'm sorry. I don't mean to question you. I'm happy that you have a girlfriend. Where did you meet her?

In the library.

She tried to be upbeat. *Does she know you want to be an author?*

He nodded, and whatever barrier she'd inadvertently erected between them dropped like a guillotine blade. *She wants to be an author, too.*

She beamed at him. *That's wonderful. Why don't you bring her home? Why don't you show her where you write?*

In my bedroom?

That's where your writing desk is. So why not?

He smiled at that, a wide grin that almost made it to a chuckle.

Do you need any money to go out?

I got a cash bonus for finishing the drywall ahead of schedule.

So you're rich now, are you? On the spur of the moment, she reached up and pulled him to her, and crushed him with a hug. When they parted, she signed, *I love you so much.*

I love you, too, Mum.

But you need to get showered and cleaned up if you're going out on a date. She gave him a gentle push on the back, and off he went, rushing upstairs. She opened the fridge and removed a bottle of white wine, some cheap plonk she'd got in for Angie – well, she does drink like a fish, and is just as fussy. She poured herself a large glass and, as she took that first sip, she smiled and thought – circle of life, right enough.

CHAPTER 20

After circling the city centre once, Gilchrist managed to find a parking spot on a spare meter. At that time of night, parking meters were free, but with the seemingly never-ending construction work going on in Dundee, spaces were few and far between.

'We don't have far to walk,' he said to Mhairi as he stepped into the cold night air.

Ten minutes later they stood at the entrance to a modernised tenement building. He eyed the list of names on the door, then pressed the button for Maybury. But after four more rings without an answer, he concluded that Maybury wasn't home.

'Been a bit of a wasted journey,' he said.

'You could try his mobile, sir.'

'You didn't tell me you had his number.'

'You didn't ask, sir.'

He forced himself to bite his tongue, and tapped in the number as she read it out to him. He put his mobile on speaker as the call was picked up on the third ring.

'Whatever you're selling, I'm not interested.'

The call disconnected.

Gilchrist tried again.

'Persistent bastard, aren't you? What the fuck d'you want?'

'Tony Maybury?'

A pause, then, 'Who's this?'

Amongst the background thrum, he caught the steady clicking of an indicator, which told him Maybury was in a car. 'Detective Chief Inspector Gilchrist of St Andrews CID,' he said. 'You got a minute?'

'And if I don't?'

'It'll take much longer than a minute in St Andrews Police Station tomorrow.'

Maybury coughed a short bark, then said, 'What's this about, then?'

'George Caithness,' he said, deciding it was better not to mention Katherine. At least from the get-go.

'That useless bastard.'

'You know him?'

'I know him, aye. He owes me money.'

'For doing what?'

'What the fuck's my business problems got to do with St Andrews CID?'

'You'd be surprised,' Gilchrist said. 'So what's he owe you money for?'

Maybury let out a sigh, as if he couldn't be bothered with the irritation of talking to the police, a mere Detective Chief Inspector no less. 'Done a number of photoshoots for him, and he hasn't paid me.'

'For Gleneden Distillery?' he asked, just to gauge the reaction.

'Naw. For his company, GC Publicity.' He laughed. 'Original, don't you think?'

'How much was the bill for?'

'Wait a fucking minute. What are you? Collections Unlimited?'

A pause, then, 'So how much?'

'Twenty large.'

'For a photoshoot?' Gilchrist said, unable to hide his surprise.

'Naw. I done a set of shoots for him. Like an idiot, I let the wanker rack up a bill.'

Gilchrist caught Mhairi raising her eyebrows. Twenty thousand pounds seemed a lot of money for photographs. But he had no idea what was involved – studio rentals, glamorous models, extravagant backdrops, or what?

'Is that all Caithness owes you?'

'Is that no fucking enough?'

'When did you last see him?'

'That bastard?' The line whined with what sounded like someone sucking air through their teeth. 'Not for a few weeks, I'd say. Well before Christmas.'

'About a month ago, then?'

'About that, aye.'

A thought struck Gilchrist. 'Do you know if he owed money elsewhere?'

'I'd heard he owed money all over the place,' Maybury said, although Gilchrist had a sense that the answer was a fraction too quick, an opportunity to seize something from the air, a bone to throw at chasing dogs, or irritating DCIs, to send them off track.

'Like who?'

'I couldn't tell you. Just heard it.'

Gilchrist let several seconds pass. 'Do you know his wife, Katherine Dunmore?'

'I know her well. She owns Gleneden Distillery. I do a fair bit of work for her.'

'Photoshoots?'

'Done a few of these over the years. Now it's mostly promotional stuff for Gleneden through corporate sponsors' events.'

Which tied in with what Mhairi had found. 'Did you ever engage George's publicity company for these corporate sponsors' events?'

'Now and again. We all mingle in the same business world.'

'Was there ever any conflict between George and Katherine?'

'What d'you mean?'

'Personal? Professional? Husband and wife working together in the same corporate world. Sometimes it's too much, the closeness. The lack of separation between personal and business lives often leads to strained relations.'

'Look,' Maybury said. 'What's this about?'

'George Caithness's disappearance. Has Katherine spoken to you about it?'

'No. Why would she?'

'Because you know her well.'

Silence.

'When did you last see her?'

Silence.

Gilchrist could hear the steady thrumming of traffic. The line was still live. 'And how well do you know her?'

The connection died.

He turned to Mhairi. 'Get onto Glenrothes HQ and get a marker put on the ANPR for Maybury's Audi. I want to find out where he is and where he goes.' Next, he phoned Jessie.

After six rings, it ditched him into voicemail.

'Mhairi's about to email you some stuff on a Tony Maybury. It looks like Katherine Dunmore and Maybury might be, for want of a better description, romantically involved. Have a look at it, and tell me what you think. We've got an early start tomorrow. I'll pick you up before six.'

Just then, Mhairi ended her call. 'Is there anything else I can do, sir?'

'Not tonight, Mhairi. But I want to have ANPR footage of Maybury's car to review, first thing in the Office at six.'

CHAPTER 21

5 a.m., Thursday
Fisherman's Cottage, Crail

Gilchrist was staring at the darkness of his bedroom ceiling when his alarm clicked on, a soft melody that increased in volume the longer it played. Nothing like the clockwork alarms of bygone days that could rattle slates off roofs. He felt exhausted. Sleep had eluded him as his mind scoured a subconscious overload of possibilities until his rationale arrived at the only logical conclusion – George Caithness hadn't disappeared of his own accord.

Because George Caithness was dead. He'd been murdered.

And somehow Tony Maybury was involved.

He had to be.

Gilchrist stripped off his shorts and T-shirt, and stepped into the shower. He lathered his body, shampooed his hair, and let the piping hot water work its magic. Ideas came to him, throwing up alternative answers to puzzling questions. Caithness being dead explained why he hadn't been seen since last Monday despite a nationwide hunt for him. Caithness being dead explained why no

148

one in GC Publicity had heard from him in over a week. Caithness being dead ticked all the boxes to the puzzling questions. But Caithness being dead also raised another set of questions, every bit as confounding as those before.

What was the motive for his murder? And why had he been killed *now*?

That last question caused Gilchrist to wonder if it was all about the timing. Was it coincidence that Caithness had vanished upon the discovery of Hector Dunmore's body? But if you didn't believe in coincidence, where did that put you? Which left him with the question he had to answer if he was to uncover the truth . . .

If Caithness was dead, where the hell was his body?

And with that, an image of Dunmore Lodge burst into his mind. Caithness's Range Rover in an accident on a road north of Perth was another that followed. The Avis van caught on CCTV on that same road was next. But if Caithness was dead, who'd been driving the van? Tony Maybury? Were the blood samples recovered from the van Caithness's? But if DNA results came back that morning and proved they were, then Gilchrist had another problem to overcome – inadmissible evidence. He'd removed a pair of leather gloves from Caithness's office without permission and, more significantly, without a warrant. If Smiler got wind of that, well . . . immediate suspension was a certainty, end of a career a possibility. His reasons for doing so wouldn't matter: an innocent search of Dunmore Lodge for clues to Caithness's disappearance now sounded implausible, even to his own ears; the removal of Caithness's gloves from his office for comparative DNA analysis sounded just as weak.

Why not apply for a warrant to search the man's home for evidence that might lead to discovering where he'd gone? That's what they would throw at him – standard protocol. But his argument that he would have done so if Dunmore hadn't couriered her letter of complaint to the St Andrews' Office, the day after he'd spoken to her, was so pathetic as to be laughable. No one in the police hierarchy would accept any such justification. He would be hung out to dry, kicked out to rot.

A glance outside to check the weather did nothing to cheer him up. Another winter's day in cloud-smothered Scotland. Who would have guessed? He grabbed his leather jacket from its hook in the hall, removed the scarf that he'd stuffed down its sleeve, and wrapped it around his neck. On the walk to his car, wind whistling, rain stinging, midnight-black to boot, for the umpteenth time that winter he struggled to shift the sense that it was time for a holiday in the sun, somewhere warm where the strongest winds were little more than balmy breezes, and the only thing he had to worry about was when to crack open that first beer – too early, or not soon enough?

He fired up his car, and slipped into gear. A glance at the dash told him it wasn't the hour to call. But he had work to get done that morning, damn it, and no time to waste.

Mhairi answered with, 'I'm on my way to the Office, sir.'

'Any luck with the ANPR footage?'

'I think so, sir. I'll have it set up for your arrival.'

'I'll be there at six.' He hung up, then phoned Jessie. 'You heard anything about the DNA results from the van?' he asked.

'Not yet. But I'm on it.'

'I'll be with you in ten minutes.'

'I suppose coffee's out of the question.'

He killed the call, then dialled Cooper.

'And to what do I owe this questionable pleasure?' she said.

'It just struck me,' he said without introduction, 'that these peculiar stab wounds in Hector Dunmore's body could have come from a cooper's driver.'

'A what?'

'It's what coopers use to hammer hoops onto whisky casks to make them watertight.'

'I haven't seen one. What does it look like?'

'I'll have one delivered to you this morning. But it's a shallow wedge-shaped tool, a bit like a chisel with a blunt point. A sharp point would slide under the hoops. The blunt point nudges the hoops along the cask. Slacken them in one direction, tighten them in the other.'

'So, being blunt, it would be difficult to stab someone to death?'

'Particularly if the victim was wearing clothes.'

'In that case, I'd say Hector Dunmore was strangled to death, then a cooper's driver hammered into his body post-mortem. But I'll reserve that conclusion until after I see this driver you're delivering to me.'

'Once you do, send me the report soonest.'

'As always.'

He ended the call, then phoned Mhairi again.

'Get hold of Gleneden Distillery, and tell them to courier a driver tool to Cooper. Make sure it reaches her by midday.' He ended the call, and drove into the rain.

At Jessie's he tooted his horn – not the most considerate thing to do before six in the morning – and was about to toot again when she bustled outside, hand on top of her head, and scurried down the driveway. He had the door open for her. When she slid inside, he drove off before she could clip her seatbelt on.

'Why are you going so slow?' she said.

He smiled to show her he got her joke, then accelerated into Bridge Street. 'I need you to collect a warrant this morning to search Dunmore Lodge. I've already set the ball rolling. It should be ready by ten.'

'Okay, Batman. What's your thinking behind this?'

'Caithness is dead—'

'What? They found his body?'

'No, but I'm sure of it.'

'How sure?'

So he rattled off his thoughts as he drove to the Office, barely slowing down at the Bridge Street mini-roundabout. To his right, the stone walls of the West Port looked like the entrance to some medieval castle. To his left, Argyle Street stretched westwards, where it branched off to Hepburn Gardens, and where the home of Katherine Dunmore was about to be rudely awakened.

But first things first. He had to check in at the Office.

Several minutes later, he swung off North Street, powered through the pend and slithered to a halt in the car park.

'If I'd known you were in such a rush, I would've brought a change of knickers.'

But he was already out the car and striding towards the rear entrance.

Upstairs, he found Mhairi at her desk. 'Let's see it,' he said.

Mhairi clicked through a series of CCTV images, starting in Dundee, crossing the Tay Road Bridge, following Maybury's car southwards, until it appeared in St Andrews, and was last seen heading in the direction of Hepburn Gardens. Despite the UK having more CCTV cameras than any other country in the world, they didn't catch everything, and Gilchrist hissed a curse at the loss of coverage.

'That's it, sir. But we pick up his car again going in the opposite direction.'

Gilchrist watched in silence as the screen shifted through a series of staccato images as Maybury's car retraced its earlier route. 'How long did he stay in St Andrews?' he asked.

'I've got it here, sir.' She flipped through her notes. 'He was last clocked at 10:25:14 then again at 11:49:40, which gives a blank period of one hour and twenty-five minutes give or take a few.'

'After the 10:25 image, how long would it take to reach Hepburn Gardens?'

'I've allowed a conservative ten minutes, sir.'

Gilchrist nodded. Once again, Mhairi was thinking ahead. He hadn't mentioned why he was interested in Maybury's car, but it really didn't take a genius to work it out. Still, it was good to see her working through the process, searching for evidence on her own. 'Ten minutes back for a total of twenty,' he said, 'leaves Maybury with at least a good hour to talk to Dunmore.'

'Why just talk?'

Both Mhairi and Gilchrist turned to the voice.

Jessie walked into the room. 'He could've given her one,' she said. 'And if memory serves me, he could've given her a few in that time.'

Gilchrist frowned. Jessie could be right. Maybe he had it all wrong, and Maybury had been driving to St Andrews for a late-night liaison with his lover. He clasped Mhairi's shoulder. 'See if you can find which way he was driving at the time of our call last night.'

'Already got it, sir.'

He leaned closer to the screen as Mhairi worked the images.

'Here it is, sir. He was driving towards Dundee at the time you spoke to him.'

'Heading home?'

'I believe so, sir.' She clicked the mouse, and the screen jumped. 'Two minutes later, he's heading in the opposite direction.'

'So, after my call, Maybury does a quick U-turn and drives to Dunmore's?' He pulled himself upright. 'That's no planned liaison,' he said. 'The call panicked him.'

'We should arrest that bitch right now,' Jessie said, 'before she gets out of bed.'

But it was too much of a quantum leap, not so much in logic, but in timing. The word *canny* still rankled. There could be no room for error. Whatever evidence they found to link Maybury and Katherine to George's murder had to be obtained under the correct protocol, as whisky-tight as an ageing cask, and able to withstand every legal argument thrown at it to the contrary.

And there was still the minor matter of a missing body, of course.

Christ. He grimaced, and gritted his teeth. 'We need to get our paperwork in order before we arrest anyone. We've got an hour at the most. I want to be knocking on Dunmore's door no later than seven-thirty. So let's get on with it.'

CHAPTER 22

Right on time, a minute before 7.30 a.m., Gilchrist parked half-on half-off the pavement outside the Dunmore residence. Both cars were parked in the driveway – Caithness's Range Rover Sport, and Dunmore's Jaguar XF. She was at home, which was a good start. Curtains were drawn on the upstairs windows. Morning dew covered the lawn in a wintry blanket. Whatever wind had threatened to turn into a gale had diminished to nothing more than a cold breath. If you didn't know better, you would think spring was around the corner.

Together, he and Jessie strode along the driveway to enter the front vestibule. Frosted glass panels that allowed a fogged view of a dimmed hallway provided no security against a determined burglar.

Jessie stretched her arm towards the doorbell. 'May I?' she said.

But Gilchrist had his mobile out. 'Let's try this first.'

From along the hall, he could hear the phone ringing – his own call – and imagined similar phones in various rooms throughout the house joining in. He stepped back from the door for a view of the upstairs windows as his call was shunted to voicemail.

He killed the call, and redialled the number.

Engaged.

He waited thirty seconds, and tried again.

The phone in the hall rang as he held his mobile to his ear. Both cars were here, and the curtains were closed, so it was only a matter of time before Dunmore answered. Again, his call was diverted to voicemail, and again he redialled after a thirty-second wait.

This time it was answered on the second ring.

'Who's this?'

'Katherine Dunmore?' he said, just to be sure.

'I said – who is this?'

'DCI Andy Gilchrist.'

'Oh for heaven's sake.' A heavy sigh, then, 'Is this how you spend your day? Going around waking people up in the morning?'

'I would've thought that someone in your position—'

'Don't try to lecture me,' she snapped. 'I'm not in the mood.'

'Let me put it another way. Your husband's missing, and hasn't been in contact with his office or his concerned wife for several days. But when you receive an unexpected call from the police at this hour in the morning, you don't think to ask if we have news on his whereabouts?'

The line fell silent for several seconds before she came back with, 'I'm not a morning person. I was sound asleep. I didn't know where I was when the phone rang.' She sighed, as if to remind him of *poor me*, then said, 'So you have some news about my George?'

'Can we come in?' He could almost hear her thought process, and he stepped onto the driveway, his gaze fixed on the upper windows in time to catch one of the curtains flicker.

'How dare you,' she said. 'How *dare* you.'

'How dare I what?' he said. 'We have information we need to share with you about your husband's disappearance.' He kept his voice level, his tone calm. 'It would be better if we conveyed this to you face to face.'

'I'll be down as soon as I can.'

The line died.

'What now?' Jessie said.

'We wait.'

'Can't imagine her appearing at the door in her dressing gown and curlers.'

'She'll be on the phone to her solicitor. Maybe even Smiler. Who knows?'

'Bloody hell,' Jessie said, rubbing her hands together. Then she cupped them and blew into them. 'So we could be waiting for a wee while, then?'

'Like a coffee to heat you up?'

'Thought you would never ask.'

'I'll stay here to tackle the onslaught.' He handed his car keys to her. 'Mine's a latte. Fatty. Not skinny.'

'I think they're all made with the same milk now.' She took his keys. 'You really want me to drive that thing of yours?'

'Why not? You have a valid driving licence, right?'

'You're such a plonker at times. Share a muffin?'

'Of course. Your choice.'

She nodded to the house behind him. 'There's no chance of her turning up before I'm back, is there?'

'I shouldn't think so. But you never know.'

'I'd hate to miss the fun.'

'Well, the sooner you get the coffees, the sooner you'll be back for the fun.'

'On my way,' she said, with a toodle-doo wave of the hand.

As it turned out, the muffin was scoffed, and coffees finished by the time a car pulled up behind Gilchrist's. In his rear-view mirror, Eva Turnbull emerged from the passenger seat, tugging her skirt halfway down her thighs. The driver emerged, elegantly dressed, with white hair and a blue pinstriped suit opened to reveal a yellow waistcoat. If Gilchrist was a betting man, he would put money on him being one of the partners of Ms Turnbull's firm, White De Bouchier Solicitors.

'That's us,' said Jessie, pressing the door handle. 'We're on.'

Gilchrist stepped out, too, and breathed in the chilled air. 'Ms Turnbull,' he said. 'Good to see you again.'

She glowered at him, but offered nothing. Her short blonde hair was slicked back as flat as a helmet, not wet from an early morning shower, but from too much hair gel.

The man by her side held out his hand. 'Peter White.'

Well, there you go, thought Gilchrist. He introduced himself, then Jessie, and held out his arm as an invitation for White and Turnbull to walk ahead of them.

'My client said you had some information you would like to share with her. About her missing husband, George,' White said.

'That's right,' Jessie said, then strode along the driveway.

Gilchrist followed her.

Jessie already had the doorbell pressed by the time Gilchrist and Turnbull arrived. White had held back, mobile to his ear. 'She should be down in a minute,' Jessie said to Turnbull. 'Your boss, is he?'

Turnbull replied with a crocodile grin.

'For a moment, I thought he was a model's dummy come to try out her ladyship.'

Turnbull frowned, and Gilchrist raised an eyebrow, a warning for Jessie to draw it in.

At length, White slipped his mobile into his pocket and walked towards them. At the door, he pressed the doorbell twice, then stood back.

'Secret code, is it?' Jessie said, as a shadow swelled on the frosted glass, and the door was unlocked with a clatter of metallic clicks.

Katherine Dunmore faced them. She'd been busy while waiting for her solicitors to arrive. Her brown hair was pulled off her face in a perfect coif, with just a few loose strands to give the impression that she'd rushed to get ready. A white blouse did nothing to hide her impressive cleavage, and matching trousers hugged her hips and thighs. Stiletto heels – no slippers for this lady of the manor – grey, to match her belt, finished the work of art.

'Good morning, Katherine,' White said, as he leaned forward to give her a pair of air kisses either side of her face.

Turnbull followed him inside, slipping past her with lowered eyes.

Jessie was next with, 'About time,' then Gilchrist who nodded in silence.

White seemed to know his way about the Dunmore mansion – for now he was inside, Gilchrist could see that's what it was, a mansion. Cornicing as intertwined as mating snakes ran around the hallway ceiling and up both sides of an open stairwell. Light from a domed skylight as long and wide as the first landing competed with a stained-glass window large enough to have been the main part of a church clerestory.

Gilchrist followed White to the end of the hallway, where White stepped back to let everyone enter, leaving himself and

159

Dunmore until the last, whereupon he held out his arm for her to enter first.

The room in which they now sat was less mansion-like, and reminded Gilchrist of an old smoking room he'd once been in as a boy with his father. Polished wooden wainscoting hugged all four walls, above which burgundy flocked wallpaper deepened the sombre setting. Wall lights did what they could to brighten a dark mahogany table that almost choked the room. White held out one of eight chairs for the lady of the house, not at the top of the table, Gilchrist noticed, which White reserved for himself. Turnbull was left to find a seat opposite, facing Dunmore. Gilchrist followed Jessie to the other end of the table where he sat facing White, with Jessie next to him. Not quite direct opposites, but good enough, with sufficient space apart to prohibit eye scratching.

White retrieved his mobile phone, and placed it with care on the table. 'I'd like to record this meeting,' he said.

Silent, Jessie unfolded her notebook, and licked the tip of her pen.

Turnbull had her own notebook out, and was already scribbling in it.

White began. 'My client, Katherine Dunmore, tells me that you woke her at seven o'clock this morning.'

'Seven-thirty,' Jessie corrected. 'It's almost nine now. Any later, and I thought we were going to have to call for a takeaway.'

'And that you had some information you wished to share with her with respect to the disappearance of her husband, George.'

'Is that a question?' Jessie said.

'My client also advised me that she wrote a letter to the Chief Constable complaining about the manner in which you'd previously interrogated her—'

'Interviewed,' Jessie said.

'And that she is still waiting for a reply to that letter.'

Well, Gilchrist thought. Dunmore's letter might have been couriered to Smiler at the St Andrews Office, but the original had been addressed to the Chief Constable – for greater effect, he was certain. Not that any of that mattered at that moment. What did, was how she was going to answer his questions. And from the tight set of her lips, *No comment* might be all he would receive.

'I was advised by Chief Superintendent Diane Smiley,' he said to White, 'that your client had written a letter of complaint. I'm sure she'll receive a formal response from the Chief Constable in due course.'

'And what information did you now want to convey?' White purred.

'We believe her husband, George, is dead.'

'That's preposterous,' Dunmore hissed.

'Have you heard from him?'

'I've already explained to you that he makes a habit of running off on his own for days at a time, even weeks.'

'And you expect me to believe that?'

'Why not?' she said. 'I can't find his passport.'

That almost took the wind from Gilchrist's sails. 'If you're so unconcerned, why look for his passport?'

'I'm not concerned. It's you who's concerned. I wanted to prove to you that he's just disappeared once again.'

'Not finding his passport proves nothing, and we're now treating his disappearance as a murder investigation.'

161

Gilchrist had taken a gamble suggesting her husband was dead, to gauge how she would react. But in that he was disappointed. For she clasped her hands together on the table, and now sat as still as stone, eyes fixed on some point before her, lips as tight as a scar.

White spoke first. 'You *believe* Mr Caithness is dead, you said. So you haven't found his body?'

'Not yet.'

'Well.' White looked surprised.

'Because your client lied to me.'

'Oh, really?' Dunmore said.

'You said George never visited Dunmore Lodge.'

'Well . . . that was in general terms. He's been there, of course. But not for as long as I can remember.'

'Four months ago?'

Her eyes burned. 'I shouldn't think so.'

Jessie slid a photograph across the table. 'That's him driving his Range Rover. On the road to the Lodge. He was involved in an accident there last October.'

'I know nothing about that.'

'That's convenient,' Jessie said.

White interrupted with, 'Are you accusing my client of any wrongdoing here? Are you suggesting that she's somehow involved in the disappearance of her husband? If my client says she knows nothing about an accident, then she knows nothing about it.'

Gilchrist placed both hands flat on the table, pulled himself closer. 'We can continue to have a nice friendly chat in comfortable surroundings,' he said. 'Or I can detain your client on suspicion of murder, then continue with a more formal chat in less pleasant surroundings.' He jerked a smile. 'Your choice.'

162

Dunmore leaned forward to whisper to White, who nodded, grim-faced.

Gilchrist glanced at Jessie who was glaring at Turnbull with all her firepower.

When Dunmore reclined in her chair, White said, 'My client has confirmed that she's willing to cooperate in any way she can. So, how can we help?'

CHAPTER 23

Gilchrist kept his smile hidden, and pressed his back into his chair.

Because of Dunmore's arrogance, his gamble had paid off. Here was a woman, born into money and land and business prosperity, who saw herself as someone whose breeding placed her higher in society than your everyday plebiscites. He'd taken a gamble on her being so conceited that she would brave it out and answer his questions with all the innocence of an ingénue, rather than resort to a string of no comments that could ultimately lead to her arrest on suspicion of murder. He could still detain her, of course, but as soon as he did, the clock started ticking – twelve hours to charge her or let her go.

No, he thought. There was more to be gained by playing along.

Again, the whispered echo of Smiler's voice stirred in his mind – *canny*. He would ca' canny all right. He would tread with care. He would dot a few more i's, cross a few more t's, before proceeding with formal charges. But if his convoluted logic was in any way close to being correct, Dunmore was a manipulative and dangerous woman. Even so, he'd never been known for pussyfooting around, and White had effectively given him carte blanche.

Might as well get on with it, then.

'Have you ever been unfaithful to your husband?' he asked her.

'I'm instructing my client not to answer that,' White said with thinly veiled outrage. 'That's nothing to do with an investigation into her husband's disappearance—'

'Murder,' Jessie said.

'—and I must object to your line of questioning in the strongest possible terms.'

'On the contrary,' Gilchrist said. 'It could provide motivation.'

'My client's having an affair would never provide motivation to . . . to . . .'

But Dunmore raised her hand to silence him. 'Yes,' she said. 'I've been unfaithful to George on a number of occasions.'

Gilchrist couldn't fail to catch Jessie's smirk, and he sat back to let her take over. His call to Tony Maybury had indeed forced the man to panic. Rather than make a phone call with the worry that his mobile might be tapped, he'd driven to St Andrews to talk to Dunmore face to face. Dunmore knew that Maybury was in their sights, so she couldn't begin by telling a lie that could be found out so easily.

'Recently?' Jessie said.

Dunmore inhaled through her nose, then closed her eyes and nodded.

'How recently?'

Gilchrist kept his eyes on Dunmore. When Jessie got her teeth into you, she could be the devil to shake loose.

Dunmore shook her head. 'I can't say exactly.'

'I don't believe you.'

'I don't keep a diary, you little—'

'This help you?' Jessie slapped another photograph onto the table, of Dunmore with her skirt riding high, Maybury with his back arched like a mating dog.

'What's the purpose of this?' White said, turning the photo face down on the table like the gentleman he purported to be.

Jessie raised an eyebrow. 'As DCI Gilchrist said, your client has been, and continues to be, economical with the truth.'

'I don't see what this has—'

'Motive,' she snapped. 'I thought we'd explained that.'

'I would like a moment in private with my client. So, if you don't mind . . .?'

'Tea-break.' Jessie pushed to her feet. 'Want to play Mum?' she said to Turnbull. 'Thought not.'

Outside, Jessie chased up the search warrant for Dunmore Lodge, while Gilchrist phoned Cooper.

'I'm busy,' Cooper said without introduction.

'You always are. But strictly off the record, any luck with the DNA?'

'Well, in that case, you'll be pleased to know that the results are back, and the DNA from the leather gloves is a perfect match.'

Gilchrist almost punched the air. Cooper had provided evidence that not only put George – or more likely, his body – in the back of the van, but also in proximity to Dunmore Lodge. But who'd been driving the van? Tony Maybury? He was getting close, but still had a long way to go.

'The DNA from the gloves is inadmissible as evidence, Becky, but I'll get something else up to you today.'

'One of these days, Andy, you're going to land yourself in trouble.'

Par for the course, he thought.

'Would you like me to return the gloves to you?'

'Hold onto them for the time being,' he said, and hung up.

Jessie caught his eye as she finished her call, and gave him the thumbs up. The search warrant had come through. When he told her about Cooper's call, she said, 'Well, that's it. Let's go inside and arrest the bitch.'

'Softly softly,' he said.

'Are you joking?'

He grimaced as Turnbull stepped outside, eyes squinting against the sunlight as she removed a packet of cigarettes from her pocket. Gilchrist watched her, mesmerised as she lit up, astonished by the almost irresistible pull of a cigarette. Twin plumes of smoke streamed from Turnbull's nostrils, and he turned and nodded at Jessie to follow him. Together they walked to his car – safer to watch someone smoking from a distance.

'We can arrest her for sure,' he said. 'But we're still missing critical evidence; the body for one. Who drove the van? Who ordered the van's rental? With George's DNA in the back of the van, how do we explain him being seen in Tesco and Starbucks from Wednesday to Sunday of last week? And why drive to Dunmore Lodge?' He glanced at the house, but Turnbull was still smoking. 'If we detain her,' he continued, 'she would clam up. All we'd get from her would be, No comment, *ad nauseum*.'

'Good. I'm sick of listening to her smarmy lies.'

'She doesn't know we've found Caithness's DNA in the van. All she knows is that we've spoken to Maybury, and know that she's having an affair. So, for the time being we have the upper hand. If we play to her ego, let her think we're miles away from solving it, I'm convinced she'll continue to give us answers.'

'That's if Waistcoat Willie's not already told her to shut it.' She tutted. 'What is it with plonkers like that? I bet he's got one of these pocket watches with the chain thingy.'

He watched Turnbull screw her shoe into the gravel, as if crushing a cockroach. Then she cleared her throat, spat into the flower beds, and returned inside.

'Let's go,' he said.

Seated at the table again, Gilchrist had the unsettling sense that White had instructed Dunmore not to answer any further questions until she was formally charged – which would mean no more consensual answers. In that case, maybe it was best to be more direct.

He eased into it with, 'We'd like your permission to remove some of your husband's personal effects for DNA purposes.'

'What for?' White said. 'You haven't found him.'

'For comparative purposes,' Gilchrist replied.

'Of what?'

Jessie slid her mobile to White. 'A warrant to search Dunmore Lodge.'

White glanced at Dunmore. 'You don't have to agree to the DNA samples.'

'It would help us in our search for her husband,' Gilchrist said. 'And we can always obtain a warrant if she objects.' He shrugged. 'Simpler just to agree.'

She let out a sigh as if to let them know how tired she was of all this petty police stuff, and said, 'Go ahead.'

Gilchrist nodded to Jessie, who said, 'Dirty undies in the laundry basket?'

Dunmore tutted.

'Bathroom upstairs?' Jessie said. 'Shaving brush? Toothbrush, that sort of thing?'

168

White nodded to Turnbull who slid off her chair and followed Jessie from the room.

'And it would be helpful,' Gilchrist said to Dunmore, 'if you volunteered a sample, too.'

'This forensic nonsense is becoming rather tedious,' she complained.

'I take it that's a yes?'

'Yes, damn it.'

'DS Janes will take a swab before we leave.'

'I will warn you,' White said, 'that Dunmore Lodge has many valuable pieces of art and is frequently used as a holiday home for my client. I would have to insist that any police intrusion in effecting a search of the premises must be carried out with the utmost care and with complete professionalism.'

'Noted,' he said, and waited until he caught Dunmore's eye. 'How well did you know Duncan Milne?'

'Who?'

'He was the distillery manager at Gleneden for over thirty years until he died the year after Hector.'

She made an issue of struggling to place the name. But she was no great actress. 'Oh, now I remember. He was quite a tall man. And not very pleasant. In mood and attire. He was always grubby. And grumpy.' She fixed her gaze on him. 'Why?'

'And how well do you know Molly Havet?'

'I'm afraid I've no recollection of Molly . . . Havet, did you say?'

'You said your brother, Hector, never had a girlfriend.'

'That's right.'

'But he was engaged to be married to Molly Havet when he died.'

She spluttered a laugh. 'That's utterly preposterous. Hector had no intention of ever marrying Molly Havet. Or anyone else for that matter. And that's a fact.'

'You seem so sure of that.'

A smile tickled the corners of her lips. 'I don't think much of your investigative skills.' She let out a quick laugh. 'Hector was gay. He was as bent as a five-bob note.'

CHAPTER 24

By the time Jessie and Turnbull returned from upstairs, Gilchrist had decided to end the interview. He worried that probing deeper could warn Dunmore that he knew more than he was letting on, or that at any moment White could advise her not to answer any further questions. Instead, he wanted to leave Dunmore with the impression that he and his team were flapping around in the dark, without a clue in sight.

Turnbull returned to her seat.

Jessie remained standing. 'Quite nice upstairs. His and her bathrooms.' She held up a couple of plastic bags. 'You said your husband often goes off on his own for a few days, and sometimes for a week or so.' She shook one of the bags. 'But he doesn't take his razor?'

Dunmore tutted. 'Oh for God's sake. He doesn't pack a bag. I told you that. He just buys whatever he needs when he's gone; razor, toothbrush, soap, even new clothes.'

Jessie looked deflated as she prepared to take a DNA swab from Dunmore's mouth.

Gilchrist left her to it, and walked back to his car.

He phoned the Office, and got through to Mhairi.

He explained that the DNA in the van was Caithness's, and said, 'Get hold of Colin and tell him to send a team of SOCOs to Dunmore Lodge as soon as. I'm willing to bet that's where we'll find his body.' But even as he said that, the unsettling thought that Dunmore was a cool customer niggled in his gut. He'd watched her when Jessie mentioned the search warrant. She hadn't so much as blinked. Still, he had to press on.

'And we obtained permission to take samples of Caithness's personal effects for DNA analysis. Jessie'll bring these to the Office. I need you to make sure they're treated as urgent.'

He ended the call as Jessie walked from the driveway.

She slid into the passenger seat, and clicked on her seatbelt. 'I think we should've just arrested that bitch. She's got such a fricking hit for herself that she wouldn't know how to say No comment.'

'Did something happen when I wasn't looking?'

'She changed her mind.'

'About what?'

'About willingly giving a DNA sample.' Jessie screwed up her face. 'You're not putting your dirty little fingers anywhere near my mouth,' she mimed. 'Cheeky bitch. So I took a sample of her hair instead.'

'Right. We need to talk to Molly Havet again.'

'How come?'

He switched on the engine, and eased off the pavement with a gentle bump. 'When you were upstairs, Dunmore told me that Hector was gay.'

'Ah . . . now I get it,' Jessie said.

'Get what?'

'That's why they planned to keep their wedding secret until they'd flown to Dubai and come back with wedding rings. He didn't want to upset any of his poofy friends.'

'Poofy friends?'

'His gay pals.'

'I know. But you can't say that.'

'Say what?'

But Gilchrist was already working through the logic of her words as he accelerated into the countryside.

At Molly Havet's, he parked in the same spot, and as they walked along the path to stand at the back door, he was taken by how tranquil the area was. At that location, trellised plants either side – clematis, honeysuckle, lavender – acted as a wind stop. The air felt warm in that suntrap, and seemed to chatter alive with birdsong. In the summer months, if you closed your eyes, he imagined you could believe you were in the Mediterranean.

Jessie clattered the knocker.

From within, he heard the shuffle of slippered feet on tiled flooring, the click of the handle turning. The door opened with a sticky slap, and Havet frowned at them.

'May we come in?' Gilchrist asked.

Without a word, Havet returned to her living room, leaving them to follow. Gilchrist closed the door behind him, and entered the lounge.

The fire was still on, the logs piled just as high. Havet had reclined in her favourite chair again, but this time didn't offer either of them seats. Gilchrist wasn't intending to stay long, so was happy to stand.

'We've had another chat with Katherine Dunmore,' he said.

Silent, Havet thrust a poker into the fire.

'She says she doesn't know you.'

'Well, she would, wouldn't she?'

'Why would she?'

'Because she doesn't. Not any more.'

'What do you mean? That she *used* to know you?'

She nodded. 'We went to school together, were even best friends for a number of years.' Her mouth purled. 'But we fell out after she killed my pet mouse.'

'Why would she do that?'

She looked at Gilchrist as if she'd never seen a man before. 'She has a psychopathic mentality.' She gripped the poker again, stabbed the logs. 'Cruelty to animals. Setting things on fire. Wetting the bed. The triad of psychopathic tendencies. Don't know if she ever wet the bed or not, but matches fascinated her, and she was cruel as could be.'

'Your pet mouse,' Jessie said. 'What did she do to it?'

'Threw it into the fire.'

'Alive?'

'She denied it, of course. But I knew it was her.'

'And where did you get your psychology degree?' Jessie sniped.

'I worked as a psychiatric nurse for twenty years. Does that help?'

Jessie lowered her eyes, scribbled into her notebook.

Gilchrist stepped closer. 'What school did you go to?'

'Madras in St Andrews.'

'A state school?'

'Oh, Katherine's father wouldn't waste money sending a lowly daughter to a private school like he did with Hector. The male heir perception. Pathetic, when you think about it.'

Gilchrist wanted to direct the conversation to his focal point. 'You said that Katherine didn't want you to marry Hector.'

'That's right.'

'Why would she say that?'

'Because she said that about every girlfriend Hector introduced her to.'

Rather than be led into a circular argument, he decided to go straight to the core. 'Did you know Hector was gay?'

'Of course I did. Everybody did.' She shook her head. 'But he wasn't always gay. He struggled with his sexual identity in his teens.'

'But he'd come out by the time you were engaged to be married to him?'

'What's wrong with that?' Another stab at the fire. Flames crackled and roared up the chimney, as if to emphasise her annoyance.

'Forgive me for being a tad obtuse,' Gilchrist said. 'But if you knew Hector was gay, why had you agreed to marry him?'

She looked at him, eyes narrow as if she'd been sworn at. 'What does any man marry a woman for?' she said. 'What does the good Bible say about it?'

Gilchrist nodded. Now he understood. 'Hector wanted to have a child of his own.'

'More than that,' Havet said. 'He wanted to have an heir to the Gleneden dynasty.'

Jessie guffawed. 'Dynasty? That's a bit much.'

'Hector's words,' Havet said, unperturbed by Jessie's outburst. 'Gleneden might not've been a dynasty at that point in time, but over the years, Hector used to say, in time it would, and he wanted to be the progenitor of it.'

'Which is why his sister, Katherine, didn't like you.'

'I never cared two hoots whether Katherine liked me or not. By that time, we had fallen out. And by that I mean never-speaking-to-each-other-ever-again falling out. I didn't like her, and she hated me, and that was that. But I had nothing to do with it. She didn't want Hector to get married at all. Period.'

'Do you know why?'

Again that narrow-eyed look. 'Hector ran Gleneden Distillery, and Katherine wanted a bigger say. She said she could make it more profitable. That's what she told Hector. But Hector wasn't stupid. He saw through her. She didn't want Hector to get married because he'd told her his son was going to take over the distillery when he died. She wanted to stamp her mark on the business before she was cut out of it. They argued like you wouldn't believe. But Hector refused to back down.' She leaned to the side, picked up a log and threw it into the fire.

'When Hector told his sister he was having none of it, what did she say?'

'What could she say? Nothing. She was a mere woman.'

'Tell me you're kidding,' Jessie said.

Havet shook her head. 'It was a generational thing back then. You have to understand that when Katherine was growing up, her father doted on Hector, his son, his heir, the one person who was left to carry on his name. He barely had time for Katherine. Hector said he never noticed it when he was younger; not until he was a teenager did he come to realise that his father hated Katherine.'

'Hate's a strong word,' Gilchrist said.

'Well, that's the word he used. Hate.' She poked at the log, and it turned over with a fiery crackle. 'Hector and I didn't go out with each other until I was in my twenties. But I'd seen his father, and knew what he was like. Dictatorial, is a word that springs to mind. Cruel, another. My mother worked in the distillery for a wee while, until she left. She said Hector's father was a creep, a sexual predator who took advantage of his position.' Another stab at the logs. 'We're going back thirty, forty years,' she said. 'The world was different then. Now, they'd charge the bastard with sexual harassment and hang his testicles out to dry.'

'Nice one,' Jessie said.

Havet cracked a smile.

Gilchrist said, 'So if old man Dunmore hated Katherine, but doted on Hector, he must have been sorely disappointed when he discovered Hector was gay.'

'Oh, they had rows about it, Hector said. His father threatened to disown him, throw him out of his home, and once actually fired him from the distillery—'

'He fired him?' Gilchrist said.

'Oh yes. It wasn't until his father died that Hector was pulled back into the distillery.'

'How old was Hector when this happened, his father dying?'

'Just turned twenty.'

He shuffled through the dates. 'So Hector couldn't have worked for any length of time in the distillery if he was fired then reinstated at twenty.'

'He'd worked in it as a teenager. Spent all his weekends and school holidays there. He even got up early in the mornings to take the spirit charge and reduce the alcohol strength in preparation for the bottling runs. He learned to drive in the distillery. Used to hurl that forklift truck about the yard like an expert. Moving crates. Stacking warehouses.' Havet slipped the poker onto its stand, unfolded a chain-link fireguard she'd kept by the side of her chair, and stood it in front of the fire. 'The distillery was in his blood from a young age, and when his father died, Hector took to running it as if he'd been born into it.' She showed some teeth again. 'Which in a way, he really was.'

Gilchrist paused to collect his thoughts. 'There seems to have been a lot of hatred in the family. Old man Dunmore hated his daughter, then his son, and when he died, Hector and Katherine seemed to carry on the legacy.'

'That's what some families were like back then. The man was the master of the house, and God forbid anyone who disagreed.'

'Where was Mrs Dunmore in all of this?'

'Alice? She was meek as a kitten, she was. Wouldn't say boo to a goose.'

'So both children were nothing like her. They took after their father?'

She gave his words some thought, then said, 'According to Hector, his mother wasn't always so meek and mild. She changed after Murdo died.'

'Murdo?'

'Murdo Dunmore. The first child. Hector's older brother. He died at twenty. Crushed by a whisky cask. Alice never recovered. She was a different woman after that.' Havet stared into the fireplace. 'Hector once told me that if Murdo had lived, his father would've treated him differently. Murdo's death tore the family apart. My mother said that Mr Dunmore took his son's death out on his workforce. Health and Safety were called in to investigate the accident and changes had to be made to the way casks were stacked and moved about in the warehouses.'

'So he was crushed in one of the warehouses.'

'Casks are stored two deep in the older warehouses.'

Gilchrist nodded. He'd taken note of that when he'd seen Hector's body.

'They're kept in place by wooden wedges. One of them slipped, or the wooden rail cracked, and the cask tilted and rolled off.'

Gilchrist flinched. What a way to die. Crushed to death. 'Were there any witnesses to the accident?' he asked.

'Just the one,' she said, reaching for the fireguard. 'Katherine.'

CHAPTER 25

On the drive back to the Office, Gilchrist said, 'There must be a report on Murdo's accident somewhere. I want to see a copy of it.' He squeezed the steering wheel. 'Christ all fucking mighty, why are we only finding out about this now? An older brother? Why didn't Dunmore mention that? Did she think we would never find out?'

Jessie said, 'Well, if we hadn't found out about Molly Havet, then, yes, she probably would've. We need to stop pussyfooting around that bitch, and head back to St Andrews and arrest her.'

Gilchrist almost agreed. But once again, his pragmatic side held him back. 'Let's see what the SOCOs come up with at the Lodge first.' He accelerated into the countryside, and phoned Mhairi. 'Any luck with the NADC records?'

'Not yet, sir. Still working on it.'

'The minute you find anything, let me know,' he said, and ended the call.

'Did you know she's finished with Colin?' Jessie said.

'Never even knew they'd started.' Which wasn't exactly true. He'd noticed the pair of them having a drink in the local bars, but had a sense that Mhairi was too God-fearing for Colin – or read that as, didn't like the amount of beer he consumed on their dates.

'Yeah,' Jessie said. 'Been going together for nine months or so.'

'And here was me asking her to get hold of Colin to send a team to Dunmore Lodge.'

'I'm sure she can separate her personal life from her professional life. Not like some of us.'

Gilchrist focused on the road ahead, aware of Jessie's eyes on him. He knew her well enough to pick up on her little digs, particularly where Cooper was involved. Which irked him, he had to say. But he'd fallen for Cooper, seen themselves as a compelling couple, even though their relationship could never have survived. He saw that now with a clarity that was almost as baffling as it was obvious. It had taken him several months to understand that he'd not been the cause of their break-up, that it wasn't he who was incapable of sustaining a meaningful relationship with the opposite sex. But even now, he still felt a longing for her, and that despite his best resolve knew she could bend his will like wind bends barley. He forced these thoughts away as he drove through the Office pend to the car park in the rear.

Upstairs, while Jessie and Mhairi logged in samples for DNA analysis, Gilchrist went to his desk. From his in-tray he removed two sets of paper-clipped copies of bank statements, one for an RBS account in the name of Mr and Mrs Duncan Graeme Milne, another in the name of Mrs Janet Milne, with a Post-it stuck to the top, initialled JC – Jackie Canning – and a smiley face beside it. He peeled off the statements for the joint account, and worked out that the dates covered the period from before Hector's death to six months after Duncan Milne's death. Each statement had a highlighted credit of £400 on the fifteenth of the month, except for the earliest two statements, which were both unmarked.

The second set of statements was much thicker, and was for the same account number now in the sole name of Janet Milne, for a period of some ten years. Again, each statement had a highlighted credit of £400, except for the latest three, which had regular credits of £800.

Gilchrist flipped through the statements, back and forth. Other than the highlighted credits, nothing jumped out at him. Both sets of accounts never amounted to anything earth shattering in value – the joint account maxed out one month at £3200 and change, and the single at £69 and some change. He noted regular debits from each account, which he assumed were for routine insurances and domestic bills. A couple of credits, other than those highlighted, were from the DHSS – Department of Health and Social Security – and what looked like two private pension schemes. Okay, he thought. Well done, Jackie. But what are you trying to tell me?

Because of Jackie's difficulty in communicating, they'd devised a scheme whereby whenever Jackie submitted hardcopies to Gilchrist, she would follow up with an email, just bullet points to explain what she'd given him. He opened his emails and, sure enough, there was one from Jackie. He ran his eyes down the bullet points.

Subject: Duncan Milne & Wife
- RBS provided records dating back 25 years. Wow!! Amazing!! Yippee!!
- RBS joint current account – DGM & JM
- 4 credits of £400 before H. Dunmore's death

- + 8 credits of £400 until DGM's death
- RBS current account – JM
- From the next month after DGM's death, 126 credits of £400
- + 3 credits of £800 until JM's death
- Will find bank details of where credits came from
- Will let you know asap. xxx

Gilchrist felt a smile tug his lips. Not the politically correct way to sign off an email to your boss, but what could he say? He read through the bullet points again until a memory of something spoken stirred in his mind. It had meant nothing to him at the time, but was now manifesting into echoing whispers that slipped away, came back . . . until . . . he had it – *that man, Duncan, wanting more of a pension than he deserved . . . a gratuitous monthly stipend on top of his pension.*

Gilchrist retrieved the bank statements and flipped through them again.

The regular payments on the fifteenth of each month and, if his convoluted logic was making any sense, for several months prior to Hector Dunmore's death, then every month thereafter. Until the demand – and that was how he read the credit history – a demand from Janet Milne for more money. A 100 per cent increase, from £400 to £800. Not an inconsiderable sum back then.

He read through Jackie's email again – Will find bank details of where credits came from – then pushed his seat back and walked from his room.

Mhairi was seated at her desk, on the phone.

He signalled to her to cut the call and come with him.

Jackie was seated behind her desk, focused on her computer screen. She looked up as he entered, her smile fading as Mhairi walked in after him. He strode around her desk, thrust the bank statements out to her, and slapped them with the back of his free hand.

'Brilliant, Jackie. Well done. Have you found out where the payments came from?'

She shook her head. 'Nuh-uh.'

He signalled Mhairi to come closer. 'Two things,' he said. 'First, I want you to get onto Harvey Kenn of the FIU. Tell him to look into Gleneden Distillery's financial records for the years covering these credits. And tell him it's urgent.'

Jackie's mouth opened in a silent Ah-hah, while Mhairi looked confused.

He handed Mhairi both sets of paper-clipped statements. 'Jackie, forward Mhairi a copy of that last email you sent me, to bring her up to speed. And second,' he said, 'I want the pair of you to find out how Duncan Milne's wife, Janet, died. Get me a copy of the death certificate if you can. Got it?'

They both nodded.

'Questions?'

'Just the one, sir. When do you need this for?'

'Yesterday,' he said, then walked from the room.

CHAPTER 26

Driving on the M90 Perth bypass, Gilchrist said, 'Fancy a coffee?'

'You must've been reading my mind,' Jessie said.

'And find out how Mhairi's getting on,' he said, indicating for the next exit.

Several minutes later, as he eased into town-bound traffic, Jessie brought him up to speed on her call to Mhairi. 'She's been onto Harvey Kenn, but he wanted to hear from you directly before he assigned resources to it.'

'Wanted?' he said. 'That's past tense.'

'Harvey must've pissed Mhairi off, because she went straight to Smiler and had her call the FIU and ream them all new arseholes. Exact words.'

Gilchrist felt his eyebrows rise. Mhairi was not only becoming one of his most astute detectives, but was finding her feet, not afraid to step on others' toes to get what she wanted.

'Harvey's since assigned one of his top staff onto it.'

'Anyone I know?' he asked.

'Viktoria – with a k – Walti. She's from Switzerland.'

'Is that significant? Being Swiss?'

'Maybe she'll do the job like clockwork.'

He chuckled. 'Which reminds me. How's Robert's writing coming along?'

'He's queried a couple of publishers, and hasn't heard anything positive back yet. But he came up with another knock-knock joke the other day. Do you want to hear it?'

'Sure.'

'You have to start it.'

'I do?'

'Yes, it's part of the joke.'

'Okay,' he said. 'Knock knock.'

'Come in,' she said, and burst out laughing.

Gilchrist found himself grinning, not at the joke, but at Jessie's irrepressible spirit. She loved her son as much as any mother could, and despite Robert's handicap she did what she could to help him make something of his life. Robert had never gone to a regular school because of his hearing. Jessie had tried it when Robert had been much younger, but the taunts he received from other children were more than she, and especially Robert, could bear. And after coming home from school one day in tears at the age of eight, she'd decided that was enough. She would pay for private tuition. So she did. It had cost her all of her savings, and every penny she earned went towards her son. When she'd told Gilchrist that Robert had decided not to go to university, but instead was offered a job as an assistant joiner to Angie's brother, Carson, he remembered thinking that Jessie's sense of relief was almost palpable. The lifelong pressure of earning money to pay never-ending private tuition fees was lifted overnight. Meanwhile, Robert was earning some money, while still chasing his dream of becoming a comedy writer.

As he drove on, his thoughts turned to his own son, Jack, who'd struggled to become a sculptor-artist. For years he'd barely scraped by, living on the edge in terms of earnings. But as recently as two years ago, Jack's paintings had begun to sell and, unaccustomed to having cash in his pocket, he squandered much of his newfound fortune in the local pubs on groups of people who'd all of a sudden become his friends.

But no drugs. Jack swore blind he never touched drugs.

And Jack was no longer in St Andrews, having moved to Edinburgh with the last of a long line of girlfriends of the month – this last one, Kristen, having become the girlfriend of the year. Gilchrist had met her only once, but regrettably hadn't hit it off with her. Or perhaps it would be more correct to say that Kristen hadn't hit it off with him, for within days of that first meeting, Jack and she skedaddled to Edinburgh to live in Kristen's flat. Since then, the number of times father and son had corresponded could be counted on the fingers of one hand. But it couldn't go on like that. Well, in reality, it could.

But only if both he and Jack allowed that to happen.

He glanced at Jessie, who was still smiling at the memory of her son's joke. Despite all she and Robert had suffered, they were as close as they'd ever been; unlike him and Jack. Not even a phone call at New Year to wish each other the best, or to remember old times, even rekindle lost feelings.

He gripped the steering wheel tighter, clenched his jaw, and drove on.

Dunmore Lodge looked more formidable in daylight, than it had at night.

Lodge was a misnomer. Castle would be more accurate. The main entrance was a heavy studded wooden door on black cast iron hinges, set into a corner turret that rose into the sky like some medieval tower. Overhead, a saltire hung as lifeless as a hanged body. Stone walls, three storeys high, were topped in crenellated parapets beneath which a row of six arrowslits striped the facade like exclamation marks. A shifting darkness in the rolling clouds gave the impression of soldiers gathering in the embrasures.

All that was missing was a moat and portcullis.

Two white SOCO Transit vans with opened doors and fully kitted interior spoiled the historical image. He gave them a wide berth as he drove past. At the end of the driveway, he completed a three-point turn, then pulled his BMW to a halt behind one of the vans.

'This looks different,' Jessie said, as she stepped outside. 'Didn't think this place was so big. Must've cost a fortune. Who would've thought there was so much money to be made from whisky?'

'Enough to kill for?' Gilchrist said.

He eyed a flat stretch of mowed grass that could be mistaken for a football pitch, which ended at a wall of trees, branches grey and bared for winter. Beyond the forest floor of oranges and browns, white dots shapeshifted in the distance. A discordant honking above and behind him had Gilchrist lifting his gaze to follow a skein of thirty or more geese as pointed as an arrowhead that floated and swayed in the cold air, sinking ever lower, and he realised that the white dots were swans swimming in a forest loch.

And with that came a lightning flash of an idea.

Where better to hide a body than weighted down in remote Scottish waters? Which could explain the Citroën van's short visit to the Lodge to dispose of Caithness's body. No burial at all, or hidden somewhere in the Lodge, but dumped into a remote loch.

'Can we find a map of the property boundary?' he said. 'Find out if that loch over there is part of the estate?'

While Jessie stepped away to make the call on her mobile, Gilchrist caught sight of Colin, the lead SOCO, who signalled to him that he wanted a word.

'You think the body's in here?' Colin said, nodding to the Lodge.

'If it is, it won't be lying on the living-room floor.' Conscious of the loch behind him, doubts clouded his mind. Why would anyone hide a body in a property owned by them, when they had the vast Scottish wilderness on their front doorstep? But even so, you might use the property as a stop-gap, a place to hide the body until you were ready to dispose of it. 'Nine days ago, last Tuesday,' he said, 'we believe the body was transported here by van.'

'What kind of van?'

'Citroën Nemo. You familiar with it?'

'I've seen them about. Small. Compact. Lightweight.'

Again, Gilchrist found the pull of the loch behind him distracting. You could drive a lightweight van over forest terrain without fear of becoming stuck in muddy spots – up to a point, anyway. He told Colin, 'I think what we're looking for are signs of a body having been brought here, but not necessarily disposed of here.'

'Okay. Got it.'

'And instruct your teams not to be disruptive.' Smiler's words still echoed. 'In and out as cleanly as you can.'

'What about access into locked rooms and cupboards?'

'If you can't open them, we'll get the owner to provide us with keys.'

'Got it.'

He thought of asking Colin to send a team to check out the loch, then decided against it. Resources were tight. Best to give the Lodge a once-over first. Just then, Jessie caught his eye, and walked towards him, holding out her mobile. 'Jackie's amazing,' she said. 'She's just emailed me the plan that's filed with the title deeds.'

'Is the loch on the estate?'

'Hang on a minute. I'm still pulling it up.' She busied herself with screen commands, then with her thumb and forefinger enlarged the image. 'Which way are we looking at?'

Gilchrist peered at the screen, then repositioned the mobile in her hand. 'That way,' he said. 'So, we're here, and the loch is . . .' He dragged the image westwards '. . . there.'

'Bloody hell,' Jessie said. 'How much land does that cow own anyway?'

Gilchrist adjusted the screen again. He wasn't interested in the size of the property, but in a pair of dotted lines that designated an unpaved track that led from the main road to the loch. From where they stood, he couldn't see the road, but estimated that the unpaved track had to be at least a couple of hundred yards long.

He glanced at the SOCOs making their way into the main building, and resisted the urge to follow them inside. Instead, he handed Jessie's mobile back to her.

'Let's go for a walk,' he said.

CHAPTER 27

Gilchrist found the unpaved track about four hundred yards along the road from the entrance to Dunmore Lodge. Rhododendron bushes either side of the entrance did what they could to hide it. In the summer months, tree copses on both sides of the road would make the entrance more or less invisible. You could drive past without noticing its existence.

The track was guarded by a moss-covered wooden gate set ten yards off the road. But what caught Gilchrist's attention was dead grass flattened by the passing of tyres. Rain over the last week had destroyed all print details, but you didn't have to be an Indian scout to know that a vehicle had driven over that spot recently.

'What do you think?' he asked Jessie.

'If you want me to play devil's advocate,' she said, 'these tyre tracks could be a few weeks old. They could also have been made by a car doing a U-turn, or someone just parking here for a wee nap, or a couple using it for lovers' lane at midnight.' She crouched, knees not quite touching the ground. 'In fact, I'd say there's been more than one vehicle in here. See that?' She pointed to another area of flattened grass by the wooden gate.

'One set going in, the other coming out?' he offered.

'Don't think so. There's more than two sets of tracks.'

Gilchrist stooped to take a closer look, and had to concede that Jessie had a point. He pulled himself to his feet, searched the fields beyond the gate. In softer spots of grass and ground, the unmistakable signs of a number of vehicles having driven along the track were obvious.

He eyed the wooden gate. 'That padlock's secure,' he said. 'Leave it that way. We'll have it dusted for prints.' They were unlikely to lift prints off the padlock after nine days of Scottish weather, and the likelihood that whoever had last opened it might have worn gloves. Still, he would be interested to find the key that fitted it.

'Shall we?' he said, putting one foot on the gate, and swinging his free leg over.

When he landed on the other side, Jessie reached for his outstretched hand, and pulled herself up with some effort. She lunged over the top rail to land with a heavy grunt. She patted herself down and looked at him. 'Don't say it,' she said.

'My lips are sealed.'

'It's not easy clambering over slippery gates when you've got this lot to deal with,' she said, hoisting her breasts, adjusting her jacket.

'Quite,' he said, and walked off along the grassy track.

The track followed a gentle curve that led them closer to the loch. At that location, the loch was out of sight, hidden by winter bushes and shrubs. But its presence was made known by the background sound of geese. Overhead, another skein floated in, wings arched wide as they negotiated a tight turn to drop close to the loch.

Gilchrist and Jessie were about two hundred yards along the track when they came upon a tree blown over by a storm. Its root clump rose from the ground like an earth wall, and its gnarled and rotted trunk lay split in several places. Dead branches littered the track, which Gilchrist came to see was a stroke of good luck. On the track itself, twin ruts, hardened by the passing of tyres over the years, defined where vehicles had gone. But a number of tyre tracks, clearer in the softer grass of the abutting field, identified where vehicles had driven around the fallen tree, then rejoined the track on the other side.

At first, he thought three or four vehicles had skirted around the tree. But, on a closer look, came to understand the forming of their pattern.

'Look at this,' he said. 'Tell me what you see.'

'One, two, three, four sets of tyre tracks,' she counted. 'Which ruins your theory of one set in, and one set out.'

'Does it?'

She frowned. 'Duh, Andy. Four sets mean two vans. Or cars. Or whatever. So it's two sets in, and two sets out. At least,' she said, just to add to his confusion.

But he walked off, staring at the ground as he traced the tyre tracks around the branches. In the soft ground, the tracks were deeper, clearer, and an expanse of shorter grass offered a set of prints that could have been prepared just for him. Where the tyre marks met up with the main track again, he stopped and eyed the scene. One set of tyre tracks formed a tight pair of curves that swept around the fallen tree. Another set formed a less tight pair that crossed the tight set in two places.

No doubts about it, or so he thought.

But the SOCOs would prove him right or wrong.

'Not two vans,' he said to Jessie. 'One van pulling a trailer.'

She scratched her head.

'Get Jackie to check the weather,' he said. 'But from memory, last Monday it rained in torrents across the whole of Scotland. You remember?'

'Par for the course, you mean?'

'So on Tuesday, the ground would've been sodden. Hence the tyre tracks.'

'Bloody hell, Andy. You'll be telling me you used to teach Aborigines how to track in the outback next.'

'I think I'm beginning to see possibilities,' he said.

'Want to share them?'

'Not yet,' he said, and set off along the track.

The ground around the loch was lined with reed grass that thrived close to the water's edge. Spiked clumps as thick and upright as porcupine spines made wading difficult – if you dared to step in. The loch itself was as long as it was wide, no more than four hundred yards in any one direction. How deep the waters were, he could only guess, but geese and swans congregated some fifty yards out, which suggested the water there was shallow enough to search for food on the bottom, and that beyond, the loch was much deeper.

It didn't take him long to find what he was searching for – tyre tracks at the water's edge, and flattened reed grass around which human disturbance was evident. 'Looks to me like someone's launched a boat here recently.'

'You're beginning to impress me,' Jessie said.

Truth be told, he was beginning to impress himself, but he'd been caught out too many times before to give a high-five there and then. He needed to be more certain before he placed his head on the block to be chopped off by those he'd pissed off – and he'd pissed off a lot. Your career didn't plateau at Detective Chief Inspector because you were everybody's favourite officer. No, sir. Over the years, his maverick style had not gone unnoticed, and any chance of promotion was a thing of the past. Early retirement was now a viable option.

And that would be it. Job over.

In theory, anyway, because his downfall to retirement had always been his innate curiosity, and the regrettable fact that crimes continued to happen, and needed to be solved. And once he'd been introduced to the puzzle of a crime, he couldn't let go. He had to solve it. He was driven to solve it. His life would never feel complete until he solved it. So, he would spend every hour of every day looking at clues, analysing reports, working through the case until he found the answer. And the closer he came to that answer, the more resolute his determination became.

As it was becoming right then.

He kneeled down on the grass, ignoring the dampness that seeped through his denim jeans. He brushed his hand over a clump of reed grass, then fingered several spines. They felt hard and firm to the touch. He did the same to a flattened clump, damaged from the weight of something being dragged over it – a boat, perhaps – which left the tell-tale signs of its passing on the tip of a reed. He scraped the residue off the reed with his fingernail, held it up to better light between thumb and forefinger.

A flake of paint – dark blue.

'What's that?' Jessie said.

He pushed himself to his feet. 'You got a tissue?'

'A used hankie?'

'That'll do.'

She removed a crumpled paper tissue from her pocket and, without a word, he folded the sliver of paint within it. He slipped it into his jacket pocket, stared off across the loch, his mind crackling with a myriad of questions, and turning up just as many possibilities.

One thing at a time, his inner sense was warning him.

Take that next step, and it will lead you to the next.

He turned to Jessie. 'We're heading back to the Lodge.'

CHAPTER 28

The walk to Dunmore Lodge across open fields, through bush-thickened woodland, gave Gilchrist one answer. The only way to drive from the Lodge to the loch was along the main road and onto the grass track. Other than the woodland being impenetrable by a vehicle, the soil in the fields was far too soft to bear the weight of a small van.

Back at the Lodge, SOCOs clad from head to toe in forensic suits padded in and out of the main door. Jessie walked towards the entrance steps, but Gilchrist said, 'This way,' and strode off along the front of the building.

Around the far corner, at the back of the Lodge, where Jessie had walked the other night in complete darkness, he found what he was looking for – a wooden shed, about twenty yards from the main building, much larger than a garden hut, but smaller than a barn. He'd first noticed it when he'd done a three-point turn earlier. He pulled on a pair of latex gloves and reached for the handle, a sliding pin and latch, padlocked secure.

'See if you can find the key for this,' he said. 'With all these padlocks, they must keep master keys somewhere. And we'll need to dust each padlock for prints.'

While Jessie went off to search for the key, Gilchrist took the opportunity to inspect the shed. He gripped the handle, rattled the door, but it stood firm. Stone gravel in front of the door offered no clue as to when it had last been opened. He scuffed his shoes through a patch of gravel, and came to see how easy it would be to hide your tracks, simply by shuffling or raking the stones.

He walked around the side, searching for a window through which he could look – none, as it turned out – and thumping the wooden planks with the heel of his hand. But if he was hoping for an easy way in, he was mistaken. The shed was a solid build. The planks had been coated with creosote, which gave off a tarry aroma that reminded him of the warehouses at Gleneden Distillery. He took a few steps away from the shed to have a look at the felt roof, only to confirm it was in good condition, and watertight.

As he continued to walk around the shed, he noticed that there were no weeds in the gravel at the base of the shed. Not what you would expect from a building that stood remote from a house that had no permanent residents. But it did give the suggestion that the shed might have been used more frequently than he'd first thought.

By the time he'd circumvented the shed, Jessie hadn't returned.

He faced the main building again, looking for the webcams that had alerted Dunmore to their presence the other day. He found them, mid-height on the three corners he could see. As his gaze ran down the back corner, it settled on a black metal tank – domestic heating oil – beside which stood a six-foot high pile of logs. He walked across the stones for a closer look, the smell of fresh pine thickening the air. He lifted one of the logs to his nose to confirm that they'd been recently cut and stacked there. He eyed the back of the building – no overgrown weeds or shrubs, no trash lying around. For a country home so remote, and rarely used, the grounds and outhouses had been kept in a profession-ally tidied condition—

'Got it,' shouted Jessie, waving a key in her gloved hand.

Gilchrist reached the shed as Jessie was slipping the padlock off. He opened the door, surprised by how smoothly it swung – no creaks, squeaks, or resistance from rusted hinges. The interior released a strangely pleasant aroma of tar, petrol, oil, dust. Despite the winter month, the shed possessed a latent warmth, as if it had trapped summer heat.

When he stepped inside, the first thing that struck him was the organised tidiness of the place. A host of garden tools – hoes, rakes, spades, saws, axes; some in duplicate – hung along one wall. Opposite, an array of electrical and mechanical equipment – chainsaws, lawn mowers, scarifiers, hedge strimmers – stood on the concrete floor or leaned against the wall. Four sets of extend-able ladders in various lengths, hung from hooks on the rafters. Every tool and machine looked in its place. All exposed blades glistened like sharpened steel as if they'd barely been used.

And, in the middle of the floor, was the second thing that struck him – a tarpaulin that covered either a low-slung sports car or a small boat. As he approached it, the raised tail-end told him it was a boat fitted with an outboard motor.

He gripped one corner of the tarpaulin and eased it up to expose an aluminium trailer on which rested the dark bow of a small wooden boat. Jessie took hold of the other corner, and together they walked the tarpaulin to the rear of the shed, where it folded over a 20 hp Evinrude two-stroke outboard, then slapped onto the concrete floor. Now that the boat was fully exposed, Gilchrist didn't need to compare the sliver of paint in his pocket with that of the hull. It was a perfect match. Plain as day.

'Get Colin over here,' he said to Jessie. 'Then get hold of the Dive and Marine Unit.'

As Jessie strode back to the house, Gilchrist noticed a tall white-haired man standing alone at the edge of the winter garden area, watching her. A heavy tweed jacket and thick corduroy trousers tucked into green Hunter wellingtons gave the impression of an outdoors man. All that was missing was the shotgun and a pair of Retrievers. But what he was doing there, and why he hadn't been ordered to leave, were two questions that needed answered.

As Gilchrist walked towards him, he had a growing sense of being sized up, as if in readiness of a physical challenge. The man didn't blink, didn't move, just stood there, poker-faced, staring at Gilchrist with a narrow-eyed look of contempt.

'What're you doing here?' Gilchrist said without introduction.

'I could ask you the same.' The voice was solid, with only a hint of a Scots dialect.

Face to face, Gilchrist's six-foot-one frame looked flimsy in comparison. He stood a good two inches shorter, his shoulders at least six inches narrower. He flashed his warrant card, but the man ignored it. 'I'll ask again. What're you doing here?'

'Watching.'

'Can I ask you to leave?'

'You can, aye.'

Just then, the lead SOCO, Colin, emerged from the front door with Jessie, pulling his forensic suit cover from his head. He made eye contact with Gilchrist, who signalled to meet him at the shed. Rather than come across heavy-handed with the man, Gilchrist said, 'We're conducting a police investigation. So I'll ask you once again to leave.'

'Are you that Gilchrist detective inspector?' the man said.

Gilchrist felt himself bristle. 'And you are?'

'Fraser Lindsay. I've been expecting you.'

'You maintain the house and gardens?'

'Come sun or snow.'

'Where did you cut the logs?'

Lindsay seemed unsurprised by the question, and lifted his chin as a silent nod to some spot beyond Gilchrist's line of sight. 'Over by the stream.'

'What stream?'

'Doesn't have a name.'

'So you live close by?'

'Not far.'

Gilchrist turned and waved a hand at Jessie to come over. When she reached them, he said, 'Detective Sergeant Janes will take your details and a brief statement.'

'Aye, Kate said you'd be right pushy.'

'Mrs Dunmore?'

Jessie tilted her head and grimaced as she flashed her warrant card. 'What are you? Clark Kent's brother?'

Lindsay looked down at her, as if she'd spoken a foreign language.

Gilchrist left Jessie to it, and headed off to meet Colin, his mind niggling him over his encounter with Lindsay. The man's presence explained the upkeep of the estate, but it was his use of the name Kate – not Katherine – that gave off all sorts of messages. And why had she failed to mention Fraser Lindsay, or that he looked after the estate? His name hadn't even been hinted at during any part of her interview.

There had to be a reason for that.

And he made a silent promise to himself to find out what it was.

CHAPTER 29

By five-thirty that evening, Gilchrist's frustration was reaching boiling point.

Every key and padlock for the shed, the main entrance to the Lodge, and the gate to the grass track to the loch, were devoid of fingerprints. The only prints the SOCOs managed to lift were those of Fraser Lindsay and Katherine Dunmore. Dunmore's were all from the inside of the house, while Lindsay's were found on tools and equipment in the shed, and on various pieces of furniture throughout the Lodge. Disappointingly, or perhaps more correctly, *unbelievably*, no fingerprints were found on the tarpaulin, the trailer, the boat, or on any part of the outboard motor itself. Everything about the boat sparkled – from the marine high gloss varnish on the inside of the hull, to the polished stainless steel clamps, and the cleaned and oiled propeller.

The SOCOs sprayed the inside of the boat with luminol, a chemical that reacts with the iron in blood haemoglobin to emit a blue glow that can be seen in a darkened room. As the glow lasts for less than a minute, Colin set up a digital camera on long-exposure. But it turned out to be a wasted effort. No traces of blood were found anywhere, not even on the varnished transom, the part of the boat on which fishermen typically kill hooked fish.

It seemed as if the boat had never left the shed.

To make matters worse, the SOCOs assigned to the loch reported no new findings. Casts were taken of the tyre tracks, but no one could say with any certainty that the tracks had been made by the trailer. Damaged reed grass at the loch edge, where Gilchrist had found that sliver of paint, was due to activity that could have been made by a boat being offloaded and launched, or by a group of people fishing from the water's edge, or even just standing there, birdwatching. Reed grass was tough and sturdy by nature, and clumped together close to the loch, they found no tyre tracks there.

With doubts now growing, Gilchrist removed the tissue from his pocket and held it out to Colin. 'See if this matches the paint on the boat,' he said, unfolding the tissue to reveal a flake of paint.

Colin studied it for a moment, then ran a hand over the boat's shallow keel, where damage was most likely to have occurred. 'Could be,' he said. 'But we'd need to scrape a sample from the keel, and compare both samples in the lab.' He scratched his head. 'Could take a day or two to get back to you.'

Gilchrist gritted his teeth. Talk about making things difficult. But he thanked Colin, then decided to drive back to the loch with Jessie.

On the way there, Jessie said, 'Jackie's got Janet Milne's death certificate. Eighty-seven when she died in her sleep. Heart failure. No suspicious circumstances.'

What had he been expecting? 'Was she buried?' he asked, just to keep hope alive. He could always have the body exhumed for drug tests.

'Cremated.'

Well, that was that. Another dead end. 'What about Gleneden's financial records? Anything on these, yet?'

'Afraid not.'

'All in all,' he said, 'not a great day.'

He parked off the road by the wooden gate. Night had fallen, and winter clouds hid the stars. From the glove compartment, Jessie removed a torch, and together they worked their way towards the loch, where the Dive and Marine Unit had set up Dragon lights. A team of five had arrived a couple of hours earlier, and Jessie had reported back to Gilchrist that due to early darkness the diving supervisor, Karen Gardner, had decided not to commence their search until the following morning. But Gilchrist wanted a first-hand update from Gardner, before driving back to St Andrews.

'We've probed parts of the loch,' she said, 'and its depth surprised us.' She nodded to the water. At night, nothing was visible on the black surface. 'It looks harmless, but it's thirty-feet deep in parts. Maybe deeper in others.'

Gilchrist felt his eyebrows lift. He hadn't expected waters that deep.

'But depth's not the problem,' she said. 'It's what's on the bottom that could be. So we're going to use the umbilical tomorrow. Just to be safe. That way, if anyone gets tangled, we can still supply them from a bank of air on the surface.'

They spent the next five minutes discussing how Gardner was planning to carry out the search, showing them an enlarged Ordnance Survey map of the loch and the surrounding area, marked up with arrowed lines indicating the proposed underwater search patterns.

'What about visibility?' Jessie said.

'Not good. A couple of small streams run into the loch, but there's not a great deal of through flow.' She pointed out the streams on the map. 'The subsoil is likely peaty gley, and the water will be rich in organic matter. Once it's disturbed, even just by swimming through it, visibility deteriorates rapidly. We're trained to carry out searches in zero visibility. But it makes searching more difficult, of course, and takes more time.'

Time, Gilchrist thought, was something he was running out of. And instructing an underwater search for a body based on the most tenuous of clues – a sliver of paint, for crying out loud – was not something he needed to burn up the hours. Christ, if Smiler got wind of this fuck-up and monumental waste of resources, she would give him his marching orders without a second thought.

Of course, he could always trump her with his letter of resignation.

On the walk back to his car, he said, 'I know it's getting late, but I'd like us to have a chat with someone before we head back.'

'Superman's brother?'

'Got it in one.'

They located Fraser Lindsay's home without difficulty, a sprawling architect-designed bungalow on the northern outskirts of Perth. Blinds were drawn on the lounge window, which cast a gentle light over a meticulous lawn. Garden edges were mulched for the winter months. A dark blue Land Rover Defender in immaculate condition – what else? – stood by itself on a spotless driveway.

Gilchrist was struck by the colour of the Land Rover, and the stainless steel ball and pin towing hitch fitted to the back. With the Dunmore Lodge boat in tow, they could be a matching pair. On the walk to the front door, he ran a hand over the towing hitch, his fingers coming away clean. No oil or grit or roughness that could suggest it had been used recently. The Land Rover's tyres, too, looked carwash-clean, and a quick feel under the wheel arch produced no dirt. The words *clean freak* sprang to mind.

At the door, Jessie rang the doorbell.

Five seconds later, the door opened on oiled hinges, without so much as a whisper.

Fraser Lindsay faced them, bare-footed, pyjama bottoms on, upper torso tanned and muscled, bath towel thrown over his shoulder like a shawl, hair glistening wet. A regimental tattoo with the motto *Who Dares Wins* stamped the centre of a chest shorn of hair, beneath which tight stomach muscles hinted of six-pack days of old – or maybe last month.

'Just out the shower,' Lindsay said. 'Come in.'

He turned and walked along the hallway, leaving Gilchrist to marvel at the muscles rippling on the man's back and shoulders as he thrashed his hair with the towel.

Gilchrist followed Jessie into an expansive living room redolent of campfire smoke and oil-based polish. A log fire crackled in a stone-built hearth seven feet tall, and pulsed out heat in almost overpowering waves. The room as a whole was sparsely furnished – wooden chairs with minimal cushioning around which side tables nestled in a casual fashion, each one unique. An oversized coffee table, at least six feet square, constructed from planks of wood as thick as railway sleepers, gave the impression that every piece of furniture had been created by an artisan carpenter.

In the uncomfortable warmth, Jessie undid her jacket. Gilchrist did likewise.

Framed photographs filled one wall from floor to ceiling, and showed a much younger Lindsay enjoying military life; a group of bearded soldiers in a rock-strewn desert, rifles held waist-high in a casual pose for the camera; a grim-faced soldier seated in the back of a jeep, wearing only shorts and an SAS beret, muscled body dripping with sweat as he sharpened a fine-pointed knife on a handheld whetting tool. It took Gilchrist a couple of beats to recognise Lindsay in his teens. Another showed a sniper stretched out on the ground, camouflaged like a jungle bush, trigger finger muscles taut and ready to fire—

'I'd offer you a cuppa,' Lindsay said, 'but I'm assuming you won't be staying long.'

'We'll see about that,' Gilchrist said.

CHAPTER 30

Lindsay now stood in the open doorway, fiddling with a cufflink on the left sleeve of a white laundered shirt. A tan leather belt matched tan brogues, which didn't quite match the navy-blue woollen trousers. 'I'm heading out for the evening. So you need to make it quick.'

'That depends,' Gilchrist said.

'On what?'

'On how well you answer our questions.'

Lindsay flickered a smile. 'You know, for all the years I've been doing this, I still struggle with that second cufflink.' He held his arm out to Jessie. 'Do you mind?'

Jessie obliged, pulling the cuff through, and fastening it. 'So who is she?'

'Who's who?'

'The woman you're going to meet.'

He gave a twisted smile. 'Not tonight. Interim planning meeting.'

'About?' Gilchrist said.

'Some proposed development that ignores the environment, which we're trying to halt. There's an osprey's nest in the Loch of the Lowes ten miles north of Dunmore Lodge, and we've been trying to encourage them to nest farther south. We also have plans to relocate the natterjack toad inland. We've found an ideal site, but if the developer's plans are approved, ospreys will never nest there, and we'll lose the ideal inland site for the natterjack.'

'Didn't know you were a nature lover,' Jessie said. 'You don't look the type. More like the kind who would shoot up the countryside with a shotgun.'

'Well, there you go. Can't tell a book by its cover.'

Gilchrist was aware of time passing, so said, 'We'd like to ask you a few questions about Dunmore Lodge.'

Lindsay's eyes narrowed. 'Get on with it, then.'

'You're the caretaker of Dunmore Lodge?'

'That's one way of looking at it.'

'And another way?'

'Minority partner.'

'Didn't know the Lodge was a business.'

'The estate is. We organise shoots, and have plans to develop a fish farm.'

'In Dunmore Loch?'

'Don't look so surprised. It's ideal for freshwater trout.'

Well, you learn something every day, Gilchrist thought. 'How often do you work at the Lodge?'

'Mondays, Wednesdays, Fridays, and weekends for catching up anything missed during the week.'

'Such as?'

'It takes a lot of effort to keep a place like Dunmore Lodge in good shape.'

'I'm sure it does.'

'So I don't accomplish everything I set out to do at the start of the week.'

'Why not hire someone else? I'm surprised there's only you.' Gilchrist didn't know that, but threw it out there just to gauge a reaction.

'Keeps me busy.'

'It must, with all these tools and pieces of machinery needing cleaned and oiled.'

'Well, there you go.' Lindsay faced a mirror in the hallway, flipped the tail of his tie over and under.

'And keeping that boat clean, too.' A pause, then, 'Do you fish?'

'Occasionally.'

'Ever take the boat out on the loch?'

'Rarely.'

'How rarely?'

'Once a year. Maybe more.' He studied himself in a mirror. 'Gives it an airing.'

'An airing?'

'It's not good to let engines lie unused for any length of time. I always drain the tank, dry the block off, oil it down, whenever I use it, of course.'

'Of course,' Gilchrist said. 'So when was it last out on the loch?'

Lindsay faced Jessie, fingers at his tie. 'How does that look?'

'Like you know how to tie a double Windsor,' she said.

'Right,' Lindsay said. 'I'm going to have to ask you to leave.'

'You haven't answered my question,' Gilchrist said.

'Which one?'

'When did you last take the boat out on the loch?'

'Last Tuesday.'

Gilchrist tried to keep his surprise hidden. 'To fish?' It was all he could think of.

'Fishing's not allowed. Kate won't grant a permit. I've tried to convince her there's money to be made. But she likes her privacy too much. Hence the plans for the fish farm.'

'So why did you take the boat out?'

'As I said, to give it an airing.' Lindsay glanced at his watch. 'You really do have to excuse me. I'm about to run late.'

'Take a seat,' Gilchrist said, his tone toughening.

'No.'

'We can continue this conversation at the station if you'd prefer.'

'If you're going to arrest me for God only knows what,' said Lindsay, 'then please get on with it. Otherwise, I'm leaving for my meeting. And you're leaving, too.'

Gilchrist glanced at the fireplace. Flames three feet high flickered and danced around logs that were beginning to catch. 'That looks like it's on for the night.'

'It keeps the place warm when I'm out. And it'll be on when I get back. Which is how I like it.' He strode to the fireplace and unfolded a fine-mesh metal fireguard at the side of the hearth, then stood it in front of the fire. The heat in the room lowered as if a switch had been clicked off. Then he held out an arm, an invitation to leave. 'After you.'

Jessie caught Gilchrist's eye, but he gave a quick shake of his head, then walked from the room. At the main door, he turned, and said, 'We may need to talk to you again.'

Lindsay smiled. 'Of course. Anytime.' He held out a business card that appeared in his hand as if by magic. 'Arrange it through that number.'

Not a request, but an instruction. Gilchrist took it – Peter White, White De Bouchier Solicitors; now why didn't that surprise him? – and slipped it into his pocket. Without a word, he stepped into the freezing night air, Jessie by his side.

As he eased away from Lindsay's house, Jessie said, 'I hate guys like that.'

'Like what?'

'Like they think they're God's gift to women. Did you see the way he looked at me?'

'No, I missed that.'

'*Can you do up my cuff?*' she mimicked, then snorted. 'Sure, I can. It was just a ploy to have a closer look at my boobs.'

'You're wearing a heavy jacket.'

'Yeah, but I could feel him staring, like I was supposed to look into his eyes and just swoon.' She hissed a curse, then turned away to stare out the passenger window.

Without warning, Gilchrist braked and took a sharp left into a darkened side street. A quick three-point turn, then he parked and doused the lights. Through the bare winter foliage, Lindsay's house stood silhouetted under a gibbous moon.

'You going to give me a hint?' Jessie said.

'Whatever meeting he's going to, it wasn't pre-planned. He'd just piled logs on the fire. He was in for the night, until we turned up.'

'So, you don't think he's going out at all?'

What could he say? That he was going with his gut? That if they waited five minutes, they could follow him? Or if he didn't leave, they could go back and interview him more thoroughly? Of course, the meeting could have been called off by then. In the end, he said, 'Let's give it five or ten minutes, and see what happens.'

But after ten minutes, Jessie said, 'Time's up. Now what?'

What indeed? But still that sixth sense of his niggled. 'Another five,' he said.

'And that's it?'

'Maybe.'

It took ten more minutes before Lindsay walked from his house and jumped behind the wheel of his Land Rover. A few moments later, he drove past them, oblivious to their presence.

'Maybe he's heading off to his planning meeting,' Jessie said.

'So why all the rush earlier?'

'Well, there is that.'

Gilchrist switched on the ignition, and eased onto the main road.

CHAPTER 31

Lindsay took the same road Gilchrist would've taken on his way back to St Andrews, east on the A90 to Dundee, which told him that Lindsay wasn't going to any meeting about natterjack toads or ospreys – why head east, when the ospreys were north?

Clouds had peeled back to reveal a moon that shone as bright as a beacon, forcing Gilchrist to stay well back from Lindsay's Land Rover. Ponds in adjacent fields, and puddles at the roadside, glowed like liquid gold. To the north, the Sidlaw Hills rose to a silhouetted ridge line. No one buys a Land Rover for its speed, and Gilchrist set his cruise control at a relatively sedate sixty, until Lindsay turned off the A90 into the village of Longforgan.

Once off the main highway, Lindsay might notice them following. So Gilchrist hung farther back, risking losing him altogether. But Longforgan consists of a single road less than a mile long that runs through the village to emerge at another junction onto the A90. Even so, he almost lost Lindsay, but managed to catch sight of him stepping out of his Land Rover in the Longforgan Coaching Inn car park.

'Did he see us?' Jessie asked, as Gilchrist drove by.

'Shouldn't think so.' In his mirror, he watched Lindsay walk along the pavement, and enter the lounge bar. At the far end of the village, Gilchrist pulled into a bus turning circle, drove around it and headed back. He turned left into a narrow street before the Coaching Inn, and parked his car off the road.

Together, he and Jessie walked along Main Street side by side, like tourists working up a thirst for a pint – although what there was to attract tourists to Longforgan was none too clear. As they neared the Coaching Inn, Jessie said, 'Don't think it's a good idea to step inside and have a pint.'

'Wasn't intending to.'

They walked past the inn and entered the car park. Even though it was poorly lighted, they found Lindsay's Land Rover with no difficulty. Parked next to it was a car Gilchrist recognised – Katherine Dunmore's Jaguar XF.

'Bingo,' he said.

Jessie shone her pencil torch through the Jaguar's windows. All seats were clear of personal belongings. 'Do you think it's just him and her?' she asked.

Four other cars were parked in the darkness. 'Take a note of the registration numbers and run them through the PNC. I'll be back in a tick.'

At the entrance to the Coaching Inn, Gilchrist eased the door open, and peered inside. Standing there, the only person who could see him was the receptionist.

'Good evening, sir. Do you have a booking?' Her smile evaporated as he held out his warrant card.

'A man came in here a few minutes ago,' he said. 'Is he dining, or having a drink at the bar?'

'Dining, sir. A table for two was reserved earlier this evening.'

'Can you tell me who made the reservation?'

She flipped through her notes. 'A Mrs Dunmore.'

'And when did she make that reservation?'

'Less than an hour ago, sir.'

He had his answer. No scheduled meeting to discuss natterjack toads or ospreys. Instead, a meeting called at short notice by Lindsay to discuss what he and Dunmore were going to do about that irritating team of detectives.

When he told Jessie, she said, 'We should go in and arrest the pair of them right now, the lying bastards.'

Which was tempting, he had to confess. But if experience had taught him anything, it was that in today's world, when guilty persons were arrested they lawyered up and clammed up. Any questions then put to them in a formal police setting were answered with grim-faced silence or No comment. Not to mention that he still had gnawing doubts about the Dive and Marine Unit's search of the loch in the morning. Should he call it off, or keep it going? Had Lindsay been telling the truth about taking the boat out for its biannual airing? Or had it been used to dump Caithness's body in the loch? No, he thought. Best to let Lindsay and Dunmore believe they were two steps ahead.

Meanwhile, he and his team would carry on behind the scenes.

'Want me to do anything with these other registration numbers?' Jessie asked.

'It's only the two of them,' he said. 'So don't waste any time on it. We need to focus our resources on establishing the relationship between Lindsay and Dunmore. There's more to Lindsay than being the estate manager.'

'Do you really think he's a minority partner?'

'Couldn't say. But I'll tell you this. By lunchtime tomorrow, we'll know for sure.'

By the time Gilchrist opened the door to Fisherman's Cottage, it was after ten-thirty. He hung his jacket on a hook in the hall, his keys on a hook in the kitchen. He had the back door open and was about to step outside when he remembered he was no longer a cat owner. Maureen was now looking after Blackie. He smiled at that, locked the back door and walked through to his lounge.

He flipped on the TV, searched for the *BBC News*, then clicked it to mute. He eyed his cocktail cabinet, nothing more than a trolley with an array of empty glasses and measures on the top, and an assortment of spirits, mostly whiskies – The Balvenie, Whyte & Mackay, Glenfiddich – on the bottom. Oftentimes, he would have a wee dram while he sat in front of the fire and read case files, or tried to make sense of investigation scribblings. But he felt as if his brain was on overload, facing too many questions, that he decided to sit down and try to clear his mind. Still, he was tempted to open the Drambuie that Maureen had given him for Christmas, then thankfully – at least he would be thankful in the morning – decided against that, too. Tucked in at the back of the trolley, behind the Tanqueray Ten he kept for Maureen, stood the smoked-glass bottle of Grey Goose he'd bought as a Christmas present for Jack. Somehow, just looking at it pulled up a wave of sadness. Was this the true depth of his relationship with his children, that for seasonal gifts they could come up with nothing more imaginative or meaningful than bottles of spirits or liqueurs to exchange with each other?

He remembered when each of his children had their first 'real' Christmas at the age of four, and of their mother, Gail, telling them all about Santa Claus. Even then, Maureen had listened to the magical tale of Christmas with a simmering sense of disbelief. Not until the following morning, when she found her presents under the tree as promised, did she buy into the story. Jack, on the other hand, swallowed the line for all it was worth, and barely slept that Christmas Eve, lying in bed with a handheld torch to catch Santa delivering his presents. Of course, he never did catch Santa, and in the early hours of Christmas morning, Maureen and Jack crept downstairs. By the time Gilchrist was ready to leave for work, their lounge was a mess of torn paper and ripped open cardboard boxes.

He found himself smiling at the memory. Since that 'first' Christmas, they'd never missed each other on Christmas Day, always staying in touch by popping round to deliver presents or, after Gail had left him and taken their children to live in Glasgow, by phoning on the day. Not once had a Christmas passed without them being in touch with each other, and where possible, even nipping out for a pint or two, or sharing a turkey and trimmings.

Until this most recent Christmas.

And why not include New Year, just for the hell of it?

Gilchrist grimaced stiff-jawed as he reached for his mobile. He checked his messages – nothing of interest, and no disasters at the Office – then dialled Jack's number. He listened to it ring out, expecting to be dumped into voicemail, or worse, for it to disconnect. Would Jack do that? Had their father–son relationship deteriorated to such a level that he could even contemplate his son cutting him off like—

'Hey, man. How's it going?'

Taken aback, Gilchrist quipped, 'Well, Happy New Year to you, too, Jack.'

'Oh, yeah. Sorry. Yeah. It's been a while. Happy New Year, Dad.'

'And Merry Christmas, too,' he added, just to make it more difficult for Jack to miss the point. How pitiful could a father be?

'Oh, yeah. Sorry. Merry belated Christmas, Dad.'

After a couple of silent beats, Gilchrist said, 'Are you still off the wagon?'

'Have the occasional relapse.'

He chuckled to show he didn't disapprove. 'You fancy a pint some time?'

'Sure. Why not?'

'My place, or yours?' He threw in another chuckle in an attempt to warm the chill, but felt as if he was failing. 'We could meet in St Andrews or Edinburgh. Or maybe somewhere in between. I don't mind. Your call.' God, he was gibbering.

'Let me think about it, Dad, and I'll get back to you.'

Well, there he had it. Jack refusing a pint was as good a way as any of telling him their relationship was done, or at least not as close as it had been. 'How's Kristen?' he tried, more in hope than concern.

'She's fine. Yeah. She's doing good.'

'Good. That's good.' Christ, this was worse than a string of No comments. 'Maureen said you'd called her.'

'Yeah. A week or so ago. Yeah. How is she?'

'She's good. She's now looking after Blackie.'

'Who?'

That answer reminded him not only of how long it had been since Jack was last in his home in Crail, but of how little he knew of his father's personal life. All of a sudden, he felt tired of it all. He was growing old, while Jack was growing up. He was ready to call it a day and retire, while Jack was striding out on ventures new. Maybe if he accepted that what was happening was the start of a new life for Jack, rather than the end of their father–son relationship, he might feel better about it.

'Listen, Jack,' he said. 'I've got another call on the line. I'll catch you later?'

'Okay. Yeah. Bye, Dad.'

But before he could wish Jack well, the line died. He held his mobile in his hand, as if waiting for Jack to call back and say that he and Kristen would drive over the next day to see him. He stared at the unopened Drambuie for a long moment, tempted just to slip off the cork and have a double – to hell, make it a treble.

Instead, he powered down his mobile, and went to bed.

CHAPTER 32

6.37 a.m., Friday
Fisherman's Cottage, Crail

Gilchrist wakened to a dull morning. His skylight windows could be black posters stuck to the ceiling. He heard no rain battering the slates, or wind rattling the windows, so maybe it was going to be a good day after all.

He reached out to his bedside table for his mobile phone then remembered he'd left it in the lounge. Duvet cover pulled back, and feet to the floor. A wide stretch of his arms and tightening of his shoulder muscles – stiff and painful – convinced him that he needed to get into shape. When had he last gone for an early morning run? When he lived in St Andrews, he used to jog along the West Sands. But since moving to Crail, morning runs seemed less appealing somehow, and he'd simply lost the desire to keep fit.

Or maybe it was just an age thing.

He found his mobile balanced on the arm of his sofa by the TV, and powered it up to a string of beeps from incoming messages. One missed call from Smiler before midnight, and

222

another after; a text from Cooper confirming that Hector Dunmore's toxicology report turned up nothing other than alcohol, and was effectively worthless; three texts from Mhairi fifteen minutes ago, bringing him current with the SOCOs search of Dunmore Lodge – no findings of any import, a discouraging start to his day; and five texts from Jackie with attachments – copies of bank statements of Gleneden's accounts – and a short message confirming the originals were already on his desk.

He set his mobile aside, walked to the kitchen, put on the kettle, trying to rid himself of an overwhelming feeling of failure. He opened the back door and breathed in the morning chill. The path to the shed where Blackie used to hide was dry – no rain overnight – the sky blushing pink to a clear morning. A run of frost lined the base of his garden wall, but with no wind to speak of, and the promise of a mild day ahead, that area would soon clear of ice.

The kettle clicked off, and he closed the door. Even the thought of a hot cup of tea did little to lift his mood. He wasn't hungry, couldn't face food, and wondered if he was hatching something. He dug around in the cupboards, then tried the fridge. But he was out of milk and, other than some chilled wines, the shelves were mostly bare. When had he last gone food shopping? He couldn't remember.

He dropped a couple of teabags into the teapot, then walked through to the bathroom, leaving the tea to infuse. A shave and a piping hot shower failed to work its magic, and as he towelled himself dry, he thought he could see what was troubling him.

A dream. It came back to him slowly, like steam emerging from mist, slipping away, then returning to manifest before him into a face, his son's face. Jack. But not Jack. A half-Jack that continued to shapeshift until it became two faces – Jack and Kristen.

Then it vanished.

He couldn't recall what happened next, or if that was the end of the dream, and for the life of him didn't understand what it meant – if dreams were supposed to mean anything. All he knew was that it had left him with an ominous sense of foreboding, a sense that something bad was about to happen – not to himself, but to Jack. As he dressed, he struggled to clear his mind of negative thoughts, force himself to think in the present and of today's problems.

But even so, a feeling of failure still hung around him.

In the kitchen, a cup of black tea helped revive him, but not enough to persuade him to put a couple of slices of bread in the toaster. Besides, he had no butter. Or marmalade. Or bananas. Or any other fruit, for that matter. Maybe he would shop later in town.

He picked up his car keys and was about to slip his mobile into his jacket pocket, when he stopped. He tapped out a text to Jack. Call me today it's important.

He read it over a couple of times, tempted to add more, then pressed send.

The wind was still, the sky clear, the temperature close to zero. He checked Smiler's missed calls – the first left no message, the second a curt *Call me when you receive this*. He shivered off a chill as he nestled behind the steering wheel, and fired up the ignition.

Beyond the town limits, he phoned Smiler.

'Returning your call, ma'am.'

'Yes, Andy, thank you.' A pause, then, 'This is a difficult one for me, Andy, and one I'm not happy about.'

'I'm listening, ma'am.'

'Do you know a Toni McManus?'

McManus? McManus? The name echoed the faintest of whispers. 'Can't say that I do, ma'am. Should I know him?'

'Her.'

'Oh.' He fell silent as his memory peeled back the years. McManus. Toni. 'Yes,' he said. 'Now I remember, ma'am. Wasn't she put away for supply and distribution of Class A drugs about six years ago?'

'Eight, to be exact.'

Well, there you go. How time flies. But Smiler's reference to *difficult* wasn't sitting well with him. 'So she's probably out and about by now, ma'am.'

'She is, and she's filed a complaint, Andy. Against you.'

'Why doesn't that surprise me?' The words slipped out before he'd thought them through.

'Are you implying there's an element of truth to the complaint?'

'No, ma'am. Sorry. Just a turn of phrase. Inappropriate in light of our discussion.' He could have kicked himself. 'I've no idea what her complaint's about.'

'She alleges that you sexually harassed her.'

He waited for Smiler to continue, then realised she wasn't going to say more. 'Well, that's ridiculous, of course. Did she say where this harassment allegedly took place?'

'Downstairs. In this Office. Interview room one.'

He cruised through Kingsbarns, trying to recall the details. Eight years ago, he was still in his forties, still struggling to come to terms with the demise of his marriage, why it had failed, and how he'd ended up as simply one more cuckold in a land of infidelity. And eight years ago, he still had aspirations to reach the top of his profession, maybe even make it to the Force HQ in

Glenrothes. But eight years ago, what he was not, was a shagger on the side. He'd been in a steady relationship with a girlfriend at the time – Beth – and had never been unfaithful to her. Even when married, despite the breakdown in sexual relations, he'd never had sex with anyone else until after his wife stomped from the marital home and took Jack and Maureen to Glasgow.

But eight years ago, the world was changing. What might have once been acceptable as casual banter in the pub, in the workplace, even in the passing, could now be challenged as harassment. What had once been considered jovial interaction between men and women was acceptable no more, and could be a chargeable offence under current laws.

Is that what had happened eight years ago?

Had he made some casual comment that had come back to bite him?

But even as his mind computed and analysed all these thoughts in the blink of an eye, he knew the answer was no – he'd not been party to sexual innuendo. He'd always taken care to ensure that any interviews in which he'd been involved had been carried out with utmost professionalism. He'd used foul language at a few interviewees in his time, but would like to believe that his words had fitted the context of that interview.

'So what was I alleged to have said or done, ma'am?'

'You allegedly made a pass at her as she was leaving the interview room.'

'A pass, ma'am?'

'A comment.'

'Which was?'

'Allegedly, you asked if she would like to meet up with you later.'

'And she has witnesses to this . . . this invitation?'

'No, she doesn't, Andy. Not to that.'

He jerked a glance at the phone. 'She has witnesses to something else?'

'In the Central Bar. That night. You propositioned her. Allegedly, of course.'

'Of course,' he said, as a memory came flooding back to him.

He saw Toni McManus now. After her interview, he'd left the Office around eight o'clock that night, and had a quick pint in the Central, before heading home. At that time of night, the Central was heaving, and as he was leaving he slid off his stool and accidentally bumped into a group of three women as he turned for the door. He'd apologised and smiled, and pushed past them, not noticing until he had that McManus was one of the group. But that was it. He never set eyes on her again, until two weeks later when she was formally arrested for supplying and distributing Class A drugs.

'How many witnesses, ma'am?'

'Two, Andy.'

Well, it seemed he was correct on the time and place. He braked hard as he entered a shallow bend, felt his tyres struggle for grip, and realised he'd not been focused on driving. At a more sedate fifty miles an hour, he said, 'Why did you call so late at night, ma'am?'

'I wanted to give you a heads-up.'

'No, I meant, how did you find out?'

'Phone call.'

'Anyone I know?'

'Peter White of White De Bouchier Solicitors.'

He might have known. 'It's a small world, ma'am.'

She cleared her throat. 'Did you authorise a Dive and Marine Unit to search some loch on Dunmore Estate?'

'I did, ma'am, yes.'

'Why wasn't I informed?'

'Didn't think it was necessary to do so.'

'Do you have good cause to carry out this search?'

Ah, bloody hell. The million-dollar question, with the ten-dollar answer. *Just a hunch* wasn't going to cut it, so he said, 'You sound concerned, ma'am. Can I ask why?'

'I asked – do you have good cause to carry out this search, DCI Gilchrist?'

Smiler wasn't known for being a pushover, but the change to formal address was a clear signal that he had to tread with care. 'I do, ma'am, yes. I believe George Caithness's body is—'

'Hold it right there, DCI Gilchrist.'

The snap in her tone did just that.

'Believe?' she said. 'Or have proof?'

'One second, ma'am.' He glanced in his rear-view mirror, and slammed on the brakes. Tyres slithered on the road surface, scattering gravel, as the car bumped onto the grass verge and slid to a halt. He disconnected his phone from the speaker system, and stepped outside. An onshore wind chilled by the North Sea freshened his mind. He gathered his thoughts, forced himself to concentrate. 'I've good reason to believe that George Caithness's body—'

'Let me try this one last time, DCI Gilchrist—'

'I heard you the first time—'

'Don't interrupt me, DCI—'

'Likewise, ma'am, I'm trying to explain—'

'I need *proof*, DCI Gilchrist. Do you understand that? *Proof*. Not beliefs. Not gut feelings. But cold, matter-of-fact proof—'

'Which I can't give you until I find the body.' He thought she cursed under her breath, but couldn't be sure. 'Therein lies the paradox, ma'am. I have clues and suspicions, which I believe are sufficient to authorise a Dive and Marine Unit search of the loch.'

'Such as?'

Bloody hell, if she only knew. But he was in so deep now, all he could do was wade on. 'Forensic evidence of Caithness's presence in the back of a van. *After* his disappearance, ma'am. CCTV footage of that same van en route to Dunmore Lodge. Credit card evidence linking the hiring of that van to Caithness.' He didn't want to mention the flake of blue paint he'd found at the water's edge, or Fraser Lindsay's comment that he'd taken the boat out that Tuesday for no other reason than a biannual airing.

'We also have circumstantial evidence that could link Hector Dunmore's murder to another historical murder, ma'am.' He paused for feedback, but she was leaving him to flap about on his own. Time to change tack. 'With all due respect, ma'am. Why the sudden concern after a solicitor's late night phone call?'

'I'm troubled, Andy. We have to go by the book on this one. Dunmore's established a golden reputation for herself over the years. She's well respected and highly thought of, with friends in high places. People of influence. Her reach is far. And deep.'

'It's amazing how many friends you can gather by gifting the odd case of whisky,' he said, in an attempt to lighten the mood.

'Exactly.' A pause, then, 'Have you heard of a Wildlife Trust project by the name of Scottish Stretch?'

He had, but didn't know much about it. 'Can't say that I have, ma'am.'

'It's a proposed development to link a series of Scottish lochs and rivers into a single combined stretch of waterways over a

229

hundred miles long for the purpose of relocating and protecting endangered wildlife species.'

'Such as ospreys and natterjack toads, ma'am?'

She paused, but only for a moment. 'So you've heard of it?'

'Indirectly.'

'Well, as you can imagine, with all the landowners, leaseholders, local councils, not to mention wildlife experts, conservationists, and a thousand other interested parties in over a hundred miles of waterway, obtaining planning permission for such an ambitious scheme is nothing short of a bloody nightmare.'

'And Dunmore Estate is one such landowner?'

'Precisely. And planning approval's at a tricky stage, so I'm told . . .' He was about to ask who told her. But he already knew the answer – Peter White. '. . . and they can't be seen to have Dive and Marine Units searching in one of their lochs unless we have . . . for want of a better word . . . *proof*, Andy.'

Well, there he had it. His very own catch-22. Without proof, he couldn't proceed to search for the body that would provide the proof he needed in the first place.

'Which means?' he asked.

'That the Dive and Marine Unit is to be pulled off site with immediate effect.'

'Ma'am, if I could make a suggestion—'

'No, DCI Gilchrist, you *cannot* make any suggestions. In light of the complaint about to be filed against you, I have no alternative but to remove you from the case.'

'Sorry, ma'am, I didn't catch any of that. Can you repeat it? I'm losing the—'

He killed the call.

CHAPTER 33

Back in his car, a plan of sorts formed in Gilchrist's mind. Smiler would put calls out for him. He was certain of that. So he had to make himself unreachable. At least for the time being. He stared off to the distance, trying to make sense of possibilities. Beyond the Castle Course, the white sands of Tentsmuir Beach bordered the Eden Estuary, blue and sparkling bright. He bumped back onto the road, and powered up to sixty in a matter of seconds.

Then he phoned Jessie.

'You're late,' she said. 'Sleep in?'

'Change of plan. Long story, but Smiler wants me off the case.'

'Say that again.'

'Dunmore's putting outside pressure on her.' He pulled out to overtake a van, zipping up to eighty before easing his foot off the accelerator. 'You didn't hear this from me, but she wants the Dive and Marine Unit pulled off the job.'

'What the hell for? That's bloody pointless.'

'So while I play hide and seek, I need you to follow up on a Toni McManus. That's Toni with an i. She was put away for supply and distribution of Class A drugs, and now she's out she's got it in for me, apparently. Get Jackie onto it. I want to know what she's done since being released – does she have a job, family, husband, partner, where's she living, how she earns her keep, the works. And I need it no later than midday today.'

'You're getting impatient in your old age.'

'I wish that's all it was.'

'So what's this Toni McManus got to do with the search for Caithness?'

'She's being used to get me pulled off the case. Maybe Lindsay knows her. Or maybe she works in the whisky industry. I don't know. But I need to find out.'

'If you're pulled off the investigation, another SIO will be assigned. Dunmore must know that, surely.'

Hearing Jessie argue that point had his rationale stumbling. It didn't matter which Senior Investigating Officer handled the case, the investigation would still proceed. But he found himself staring blindly through the windscreen as another possibility emerged, nothing to do with his being pulled off the case, but to do with delaying the investigation by calling off the underwater search. And if you asked why Dunmore was trying to do that, it had bugger all to do with the Scottish Stretch development being tainted.

It had to do with something else entirely. Which was what he needed to find out.

Which, in effect, brought him full circle. In order to find the proof Smiler wanted, he needed to carry on with the Dive and Marine Unit's search. But he didn't have it clear in his own mind, and could find no other way to explain it. All he knew was that he had no time, probably less than a few hours before the forensic search of Dunmore Estate was halted.

He had to move fast.

'Take a note of this,' he said. 'Scottish Stretch. It's some wild-life project to protect a stretch of lochs and rivers, one of which is Dunmore Loch. Find out what you can about it – who funds it, who heads it, what stage the planning's at, which government department is in charge of it. And if possible, see if you can get a copy of the plans that affect the estate. What the hell has Dunmore to gain by having Dunmore Loch included in the project? Money, tax relief, plain old brownie points, or what?'

'I'm on it,' she said. 'And if anybody asks about you?'

'You haven't heard from me this morning, and don't know where I am. And don't let on to Smiler that you've ever heard of Scottish Stretch.'

'Got it.'

He ended the call, then dialled another number.

It was answered on the first ring.

'Hey, Andy,' Dick said. 'What can I do you for?'

Dick was Gilchrist's go-to guy when he needed something done under the radar – an illegal search for a phone number here, a wire-tap recording of a call there. Whatever website or phone number or computer system Gilchrist needed hacked, Dick was the man to do it, the true definition of a computer nerd if ever there was one. Or maybe computer genius would be a more accurate description. Rumour had it that Dick had been on the verge of heading up a top-secret government cyber-defence agency, working under the auspices of MI6, but turned it down – *Money was shite, and why the hell would I ever want to work for a bunch of English wankers?* And from the outset of their relationship, Dick had never charged Gilchrist for any of his services – maybe something to do with the uncom-fortable fact that Gilchrist knew Dick was breaking the law, and vice versa. He had no idea where Dick's living came from, of course, and had made a decision, way back, never to ask.

What you didn't know, couldn't hurt you. In theory anyway.

'Need another favour,' Gilchrist said.

'Shoot.'

His mobile vibrated. He glanced at it, saw it was Smiler, and ignored it. She would receive the engaged tone, which might convince her that the signal was weak, and the reason they'd lost contact. But if he wanted to crawl out of the ever-deepening hole he was digging for himself, he had to move quickly.

'Take a note of these two numbers,' he said, and read them out – Fraser Lindsay's landline and mobile. 'I want a list of all the numbers he's called in the last forty-eight hours, including names and addresses.'

'Just as easy to give you a week's worth if you'd like.'

Sometimes Dick's information could be overwhelming, and Gilchrist didn't want to waste time going too far back. 'Not yet,' he said. 'I'll get back to you on that.'

'Sure. Anything else?'

'That's it.'

'How quickly do you need this?'

'Next ten seconds if you can.'

Dick tossed a chuckle down the line. 'Let me see what I come up with.'

The line died, and Gilchrist powered his mobile down in case Smiler continued to try to get through to him. Then he turned a hard left into Lamond Drive. He would hook up with Largo Road, and bypass the Office on his way to Dundee, and beyond to Perth and Dunmore Lodge.

* * *

By the time Gilchrist drove past the entrance to Dunmore Lodge, the sun was rising, the sky a curtain of burgundies, reds, pinks. He could kill for a coffee, but he'd hammered it along the A90, holding his speed at the ton for several stretches, and never dropping below seventy. Driving around Perth slowed him down, but on the road north again, he'd booted it.

When he arrived at the entrance gate to the loch, he was pleased to see the Dive and Marine Unit's van parked in the bushes. He pulled in behind it, and walked to the gate. The temperature felt five degrees colder, despite being inland. Hoar frost whitened the grass like laced cotton. In the distance, the rhythmic beating of a generator told him that the divers were already on the job, and using an airline for safety.

He leaped over the gate, and walked onwards, feet cracking iced puddles as he strode along the grass track. His breath clouded the air. Ice nipped his nostrils. He stuffed his hands deep into his pockets, thankful he'd at least had the common sense to grab a scarf on the way out. Three hundred yards to his left, Dunmore Lodge stood in the brightening sky like some pocket-castle, its silent presence ominous in the still winter setting.

He rounded the fallen tree, and heard voices talking, the sharp crackle of radio static competing with the high-revving clatter of an onsite generator. As the loch came into view, he caught the squat figure of Karen Gardner, thighs sturdy and muscular in wetsuit leggings as she stood close to the water's edge, worry etched on her brow. Even before he reached her, he could tell something was wrong. He followed her line of sight into the morning sun to an inflatable dinghy with an outboard motor, sixty to eighty yards out on the loch. A diver in full wetsuit gear was standing by the transom, looking over the side, holding a rope and a rubber airline that fed into black water.

Gilchrist's insides slapped over like a lump of lard. The thought of one of the divers being in trouble flashed into his mind and flew out a nanosecond later as a goggle-covered head broke the surface. Water splashed the dinghy as the diver reached for support.

Gardner noticed Gilchrist then, and gave a grim nod.

'Problems?' he said.

'They've found something.' She shook her head.

'Caithness?'

'Don't think so.'

He raised a hand to shield his eyes against the low morning sun. On either side of the loch, geese busied themselves around the water's edge, paddled through the white grass, as if maintaining a safe distance from the noisy intrusion. Overhead, an arrowhead skein came in low in a wide circle, floating lower and lower before sliding into the water one by one. His gaze returned to the dinghy, and he watched in silence as something was transferred from the diver in the water, to the diver in the dinghy; a bundle of some sort, small enough to be held in both hands; a clotted pile of vegetation, perhaps, or sodden sacking.

'What've they found?' he asked.

Gardner grimaced. 'They think they've found human bones.'

Gilchrist frowned. Human bones? How could they find bones? Caithness had been missing for only a week.

Gardner pressed a finger to her earpiece. 'You sure?' she said.

Gilchrist couldn't hear what was being said, but suspected from Gardner's deepening frown and silent nodding that it wasn't good.

Then she turned to him, face grim, lips tight. 'We need the pathologist to confirm it. But it looks like they've found the skeletal remains of a child.'

'A child? Are they sure?'

'It's a human skull,' she said. 'And it's badly cracked.'

Gilchrist let his gaze drift to the rolling hills beyond the loch, trying to work through the rationale. Child's bones? Cracked skull? A murder? Not what he'd expected at all. And for such deterioration to have taken place, the body must have been in the loch for a long time. Which opened up a myriad of questions.

How many years? Who would kill a child?

Or perhaps more importantly, *why* would someone kill a child?

To his side, Gardner spoke into her mouthpiece. Behind her, the generator powered on, oblivious to all that was happening in the human world. Gilchrist caught the wild flutter of blue tits darting through a cluster of bare branches. Off in the distance, the high-pitched call of birdsong chimed like music in the crystal clear air.

He turned to face Dunmore Lodge, his mind nosing through the logic.

Dunmore's attempts to halt the underwater search had a purpose now. The inclusion of Dunmore Loch in Scottish Stretch was necessary for some reason he couldn't see at that moment. But the memory of a flake of blue paint, the boat in the shed, the sudden appearance of Fraser Lindsay, his meeting with Dunmore last night, all seemed to be coming together to show him the answer to some question that had been created by that morning's discovery.

He turned his back to the loch, mobile in hand.

He got through right away.

'This is becoming a habit of yours,' Cooper said. 'One I'm beginning to like.'

He was in no mood for banter. 'You're needed,' he said.

'Give me the details.'

He did, and once Cooper hung up, he held onto his mobile. Should he phone Smiler and tell her of their findings? Doing so would keep the Dive and Marine Unit search alive and likely initiate warrants for the arrest of Katherine Dunmore and Fraser Lindsay. On the other hand, if Dunmore believed the underwater search had been delayed, she might let her defences down. Of course, Fraser Lindsay could turn up at the lochside any time and report to Dunmore that the search was proceeding despite her complaints. But as Gilchrist worked these thoughts through his mind, a plan of action unveiled itself.

He phoned Jessie.

'Thought you were hiding,' she said.

'Something's come up. Any luck with the Scottish Stretch plans?'

'Bloody hell, Andy, it's only the back of eight. But I've got Jackie working on them.'

'Good. Tell Mhairi to take another officer and bring Fraser Lindsay into the Office for questioning.'

'On what grounds?'

'On suspicion of perverting the course of justice.'

'You want me to go with Mhairi?'

'No. You're coming with me to give Dunmore a wake-up call.'

'This I like.'

'I'm on my way. I'll meet you outside her home. If she leaves before I get there, arrest her on the same grounds.'

'I love it.'

On his way to his car, his mobile rang – ID Dick.

'Got twenty-three calls in the last forty-eight hours,' Dick said. 'Would you like me to text them to you?'

Gilchrist didn't like the idea of having evidence of an illegal phone search stored on his mobile, so said, 'For the time being, just read off what you've got.'

'Anyone you're looking for in particular?'

'Yes and no,' he said, just to keep Dick honest.

'Okay, I'll read out the number first, including area code, then the name and address that number's assigned to. If you need time and length of call, I've got all that, too.'

Gilchrist stared off to the distant hills as Dick ran through his list. Third number in, he recognised Dunmore's mobile number before Dick followed on with her name. The names of people he didn't know followed numbers that meant nothing to him. One landline came up with a Dundee area code, and Dunmore's name came up three more times—

'Stop,' he snapped. 'Say that again.'

'Toni McManus,' Dick repeated. 'That who you're after?'

Gilchrist gathered himself. 'Keep going,' he said.

The very next number was Dunmore's, followed by three more numbers that were meaningless, before Dick said, 'And that's it.'

The tumblers in Gilchrist's mind were slotting into place. Lindsay had been in regular phone contact with Dunmore. But after the call to Toni McManus, he'd phoned Dunmore to tell her . . . what? That McManus was on board? That she'd agreed to fabricate a case against Gilchrist in an attempt to delay—

'Anything else?' Dick said.

'The call to McManus,' he said. 'When was that made?'

'Last night. Just before midnight.'

After Lindsay's meeting with Dunmore in Longforgan, to put into motion the scheme they'd devised to dump shit onto Gilchrist and have him removed from the case. 'Could you run one more number for me? Toni McManus,' he said. 'I'd be interested to know who she called after that call from Lindsay.'

'Let me get back to you,' Dick said, and the line died.

Gilchrist slid his mobile into his jacket, and walked to his car.

CHAPTER 34

On the drive to St Andrews, Gilchrist took another call from Dick.

'Nothing,' Dick said. 'This Toni's not been on the phone since.'

Gilchrist clenched his jaw. Maybe Lindsay's pre-midnight call was only to ensure McManus was up for it, after which she had nothing to do but wait, just leave it for Lindsay to call Peter White and start the ball rolling on her fabricated harassment claim – subsequent payment to McManus in a brown paper bag to be made in due course.

'I searched for other numbers,' Dick said. 'But there's none in her name. She could be using someone else's mobile – boyfriend, partner, whatever.' A pause, then, 'Want me to do anything more?'

'Just file that stuff somewhere, Dick. If I need copies I'll get back to you.'

The line died, and Gilchrist settled down for the remainder of the drive.

Katherine Dunmore hadn't tried to leave. A glance at the upstairs windows with its curtains still drawn told Gilchrist she hadn't even risen from bed. When he parked outside her home, Jessie was already standing on the pavement by the driveway entrance, the tip of her fine nose red from the cold.

He signalled her to join him in his car.

The passenger door opened to a wintry draught.

'What kept you? If I'd had balls they'd have dropped off by now.'

'Got you one of these,' he said, and handed her a Starbucks. 'Skinny latte. Just the way you like it.'

She pressed the carton to her lips. 'You're an angel.'

'And also one of these.' He dug into the bag and removed a blueberry muffin.

'What's this? My birthday?'

He passed her a handful of paper napkins. 'Drop any crumbs on the seat, and you'll soon find out if it's your birthday or not.'

She took care to place the muffin on the napkins, and said, 'Hang on a second, while I plug in my portable hoover.' She took a sip of coffee. 'You never heard of car valeting?'

'I'm told blueberry's difficult to get out of upholstery.'

'Not if it's leather.'

'Whatever.' He took a sip from his own carton, the coffee flavourful and refreshing.

She cast him a sideways glance, and said, 'Oh, this just in from Jackie.' She handed him her mobile. 'To do with Scottish Stretch.'

Gilchrist studied the screen, a plan of Dunmore Loch, as best he could tell, with some markings and measurements on it. He finger-thumbed the screen to enlarge it, and tried to work out what he was looking at. An area in the middle of the loch – noted as 2500 m² – had been hatched through with red lines, as if to define it as being prohibited from access. Around the edges of that area, ran a dotted line with green circles on it, noted as buoys. It didn't really tell him much, so he downsized the screen, and handed the mobile back to Jessie.

'How about Fraser Lindsay?' he said.

'Mhairi's on her way. So what's he done?'

Gilchrist let a couple of beats pass. This was where it could get tricky. 'I don't know if he's done anything at all. I'm trying to keep him away from the Lodge while the Dive and Marine Unit carry on with their search.'

'I thought Smiler ordered you to call it off.'

'She did.'

'This could land you in trouble,' Jessie said. 'Big time.'

'I don't think so. They found a body this morning.'

'Caithness?'

'The skeletal remains of a child.'

'*What?*' She splashed coffee onto a napkin. 'Oops,' then stared at him. 'In the loch?'

He nodded.

'Bloody hell. We've got that bitch good and proper now.'

'Not quite,' he said. 'We don't know anything about the remains yet. But Cooper's on her way. She might be able to extract DNA from the bones. But I don't know what condition the skeleton's in, or even if it's modern-day.' Now there was a thought. 'It might've been in the loch for centuries, for all anyone knows.' But even as the words left his mouth, he knew he was giving Dunmore the benefit of every doubt, and then some.

'So what're you saying?' Jessie asked.

'I don't want Dunmore to know about the skeletal remains yet. I want her to think we've called off the search, and that we've

243

found nothing to date. I want her to think she's still got the upper hand.'

'Why?'

Well, there he had it. Why indeed? But his gut was telling him there was more to be gained by interviewing Dunmore before she heard of the discovery of the skeletal remains. But more significantly, before she clamped up completely at the advice of her solicitor, Peter White, in a formal interview process.

He finished his coffee, nodded to Jessie's carton. 'You done with that?'

'Here. Have a piece of muffin,' she said, handing the napkin to him. 'You could do with putting on a few pounds.'

He stuffed it into the paper bag, while she drained her coffee.

'Ready?' he said.

'Into the breach, as they say. Whatever that means.'

At the front door, the house looked as if it had been locked up for the winter. But both cars were parked on the driveway, and Gilchrist thought he caught the curtains flicker when he closed his car door. Scuff marks on the frosted paving by the boot of the Jaguar had him thinking that Dunmore had already been out and about. But the place looked dead. He rang the bell, and from deep within a melodic chime echoed. He tried it again, then stepped onto the driveway to look at the upper windows. Curtains still closed.

Back to the doorbell, and the palm of his hand on it in earnest.

'She'll be filing a complaint for disturbance of the peace,' Jessie said.

He caught the faintest of sounds from deep inside. 'I think she's on her way.'

'What are you? Bat-ears-boy?'

Sure enough, the double clicks of locks being turned, and the sticky slap of the door being opened revealed Katherine Dunmore, fully dressed in burgundy and white pinstripe trouser suit, white shoes and belt, and white high-collared blouse. If he didn't know better, he would've said she was going for a job interview.

'For God's sake, I'm about to go out,' she snapped.

'We won't take long,' Gilchrist said.

'What's it about, then?'

'Might be best if we talk inside.'

'You can talk here.'

'We've arrested Fraser Lindsay on suspicion of perverting the course of justice.'

'You here to arrest me, too?' she said, without missing a beat.

'Why would you think that?'

She held his gaze in a dark look, thoughts shifting behind her eyes like shadows, then stepped aside to let them pass. 'First door on the left.'

As the front door closed behind them, Gilchrist entered a lounge redolent of varnish and flowers . . . and money – lots of it. A black grand piano sat in the corner farthest from the window. Three white fabric sofas – three- and two-seaters – with rope-edged armrests and brass feet, faced a red-patterned Persian rug large enough to carpet Gilchrist's entire cottage. A glass-topped coffee table – if it could be called that – seemed to have been carved from a solid lump of rosewood, inlaid with metal strips that might be mistaken for gold – or maybe were. Oil paintings in hand-carved wooden frames, so numerous it was difficult to make out the flocked wallpaper behind them, covered the walls like panelling. As he walked across the floor, he had the sense of every step taking him past thousands of pounds worth of furniture and décor.

'I'd offer you tea and biscuits,' Dunmore said, closing the lounge door. 'But you're not staying long.'

'Rushing out for a meeting, are you?' Jessie said.

She gave a knowing smirk. 'None of your business.'

'You think not?'

'If you must know, I have a meeting with my solicitor,' she said, and offered her a smile. 'Peter White. You've already met him.'

'Lovely man. Is he married?'

'You know, I really don't care for your attitude.'

Gilchrist stepped in. 'What can you tell us about Scottish Stretch?'

He thought he caught a shiver of uncertainty, as if she'd just heard the click of a trap being set, but didn't know where it had come from. Then she recovered. 'What's that got to do with anything?'

Silent, Gilchrist waited. Jessie had her notebook open, pen in hand.

'Very well,' she said. 'It's a project in the making for over twelve years now—'

'Yes, we know about that,' he lied. 'What I mean is, where does Dunmore Estate fit into the scheme of things?'

'If you knew all about it, you wouldn't be asking the question, would you?'

It seemed that Dunmore had a sharp mind to match her tongue. He would need to move forward with care. 'I'd like to hear it, in your own words.'

She took an impatient breath, then let it out. 'We have over two hundred acres of land which, under the auspices of Scottish Stretch, will be designated as greenspace for posterity. Land that will never be developed, but on which wildlife can live and roam without fear of ever being hunted.'

'So you won't be needing those, then,' he said, nodding to a glass-panelled display on the wall, which housed a trio of polished shotguns.

She followed his line of sight. 'Oh, these. These belong to George.'

'What's George's is mine. What's mine is George's. Is that not what you said?'

She tutted.

Jessie said, 'Do you have a licence for them?'

'They're collectors' items, for God's sake. You can't shoot with them.'

'Why the lock on the cabinet, then?'

'To prevent grubby little people like you from stealing them.'

Gilchrist shifted his stance, and said, 'We?'

'Excuse me?'

'You said *we* . . . have over two hundred acres.'

She tutted again. 'We, in the corporate sense of the word. Dunmore Estate.'

He nodded. 'Let's get back to Scottish Stretch,' he said, 'in the corporate sense.'

She blinked, as if trying to gather her thoughts, then said, 'Under the Scottish Stretch protectorate, Dunmore Estate has plans to rent out the grounds to interested parties.'

'Interested parties?'

'Visitors to the Highlands. Sightseers. Birdwatchers. Hill walkers. Land lovers.'

He waited, but it seemed that was all she was going to offer.

'Could these interested parties rent the Lodge?'

247

'The Lodge is private.'

'So that's a No. And the loch,' he said. 'What will become of that?'

She held his gaze as if sensing that the ice beneath her feet was suddenly in danger of cracking. 'What do you mean?'

'Would any of the parties be interested in fishing?'

'Fishing's a form of hunting,' she said, as if she'd rediscovered her voice. 'And all forms of hunting are banned under Scottish Stretch.'

'Really?' He tried to sound surprised.

Silent, she stared at him.

'It seems to me,' he said, 'that *you* . . . in the corporate sense of the word . . . would lose a potentially valuable income stream. You could rent out the Lodge, bed and breakfast if you liked. They charge a fortune for fishing permits these days. Do you know that? Money for nothing, it seems. Just take the cash then let them out on the loch on that wooden boat of yours, to dangle a line in the water and . . .' He gave a casual shrug. '. . . see what it pulls up.'

If he was hoping for some revealing look, he was disappointed. She simply smiled at him. 'Look around you,' she said. 'As you can see, I don't need money.'

'Everybody needs money,' Jessie said. 'Especially those who have it. They always want more. What they have is never enough.'

Dunmore looked at her as if she'd just crawled out of a sewer. 'What would you know about that?'

'Why are you involved in Scottish Stretch, then?' Jessie sniped.

'Have you never heard of philanthropy?'

Jessie pursed her lips, scribbled hard at her notepad.

Dunmore turned to Gilchrist. 'Are we through?'

The thought of arresting her and taking her to the Office flooded through him with a surge so strong he found himself struggling to bite his tongue. Instead, he said, 'You seem to be in a hurry to leave.'

'As I said, I'm meeting my solicitor.'

'Do you have any plans that show how Dunmore Loch fits in with the Scottish Stretch project?' he said, just to gauge a reaction.

'None that I intend to share with you.' She tugged the front of her jacket. 'Now, if you've nothing more, I'd be grateful if you left.'

As he followed Jessie to the front door, and was about to step outside, he turned to Dunmore. 'Do you think our search of the loch will turn up anything?'

She froze for an instant, her eyes as cold as steel. 'My solicitor should have delivered an injunction to your Office this morning, prohibiting disturbance of any kind on Dunmore Lodge and surrounding environs. Which by definition includes underwater searches.'

Gilchrist returned her ice-cold look with one of his own. 'And why is that?'

'To preserve the integrity of Scottish Stretch.'

Gilchrist felt confident the discovery of the remains of a child's body would trump any legal injunction to restrict investigation of the loch. But he'd come across the strength of conservation groups before, and their reach to the top of government branches could be nigh impossible to overturn – unless Cooper confirmed the child's skeleton was not centuries old, but only decades. His mobile rang at that moment – ID Mhairi – and he gave Dunmore a silent nod, then stepped outside, Jessie behind him.

'Sorry, sir. We're at Lindsay's home. But he's not in.'

Gilchrist was conscious of being within earshot of Dunmore, so he strode along the driveway. 'Is his Land Rover there?'

'No, sir.'

He glanced at his watch – not yet nine o'clock – and cursed at his own stupidity. Lindsay was an outdoors man, someone who probably revelled in early morning hikes over snow-covered hills. For all he knew, Lindsay could have put in half a day's work by nine in the morning. 'Get onto HQ,' he said, 'and put a marker on his Land Rover. We need to find out where he is. Then we need to bring him in.'

'I'm on it, sir.'

Jessie caught up with him as he ended the call. She scowled at Dunmore who was clambering into her Jaguar, mobile to her ear. 'That smug bitch. I tell you, just give me the word, and I'll slap cuffs on her so fast she won't know what's hit her.'

'Fraser Lindsay's not in.'

'He'll be at Dunmore Lodge,' she said, as if surprised he didn't know that.

'Hang on,' he said, as his mobile vibrated – ID Smiler. He blew out a lungful of air. Well, he had to speak to her some time. Might as well make it now. He pressed his mobile to his ear. 'Yes, ma'am.'

'Good to hear your phone's working again,' she said. 'Which is rather timely, because I've just taken a call from Chief Constable McVicar, who tells me that he's just off the phone with Ms Sandy Tennyson. You know her?'

For a moment, the name failed to register. Then it came to him. 'Isn't she a Member of the Scottish Parliament, ma'am?'

'Not just any member, DCI Gilchrist. She's the Minister for the Environment.'

He thought it odd how some people react to news, good or bad. It might have been the fact that he was in so deep that it didn't matter if he took one more step into the quagmire, or just leaped in headfirst and pulled himself to the bottom, but he found himself smiling – not because of the shit working its way down through the ranks to land on his head full dump, but because he saw the logical turn of events that convinced him that Fraser Lindsay was already at Dunmore Lodge.

Still, it seemed prudent to move forward with caution.

'Did she call to complain about something, ma'am?'

A hiss of breath down the line could have been a whispered curse. 'I thought I told you to stop all search activity on Dunmore Loch.'

'You did, ma'am, yes.'

'Well,' she said, and seemed to draw in her breath for the final onslaught, 'can you tell me why the Dive and Marine Unit are still operating as of twenty minutes ago?'

He stepped aside as Dunmore's Jaguar nosed from the driveway, then powered off along Hepburn Gardens with a blast of exhaust from its twin tailpipes, swirling in the cold morning air, his mind already working through the sequence of events that led to this call – Lindsay must have been at the Lodge and phoned Dunmore to tell her the Dive and Marine Unit were still there. Dunmore, with a Rolodex full of important contacts with far-reaching influence, must have then phoned MSP Sandy Tennyson, probably calling in a few favours, or asking for some more . . .

And now, here they were . . .

Smiler dressing him down . . .

Just what Dunmore wanted . . .

'DCI Gilchrist. Are you *listening* to me?'

Not what Dunmore *wanted*, but what she *needed* . . .

He eyed the departing Jaguar . . .

'DCI Gilchrist?'

'Yes, ma'am.'

'I'm waiting for your answer.'

He struggled to pull his thoughts together, some part of his mind churning over the rationale of something he didn't quite see at that moment, until . . .

All of a sudden, it hit him.

'*Shit*,' he shouted.

'I beg your pardon.'

He flapped his hand at Jessie, an urgent signal for her to get into his car. As he slid in behind the steering wheel and fired up the ignition, the tinny rattle of Smiler's voice railing against him boomed from the car's speaker system when he hooked up his mobile.

'. . . me, DCI Gilchrist. I *will not tolerate*—'

'We've found human bones, ma'am.'

Silence.

He pressed his foot to the floor, and the car bumped from the pavement, wheels spinning. 'The Dive and Marine Unit retrieved them from Dunmore Loch this morning.' He pulled out to overtake a slow-moving car, only to receive a blaring horn from a van speeding towards him. The near miss slipped into the distance, and he took a sharp right into Lawhead Road, and powered along the quiet street at fifty.

'To make matters clear, ma'am, the Dive and Marine Unit chose to commence their search in the small hours of this morning. Part of a training session for a new member of their team.' He was lying, saying the first thing that came to mind. But it

252

didn't matter any more. He tugged the wheel left, right, as he negotiated a pair of short, tight bends. 'Of which I was unaware.'

'Are you saying you've found George Caithness's body?'

'No, ma'am. Sadly, these bones are the remains of a child.'

'A child? Oh, dear God,' she gasped. 'But . . . does that . . .'

'I would like to instruct the Dive and Marine Unit to carry on with their underwater search, as I believe . . . although I have no clear proof yet, ma'am . . . that we might find George Caithness's body there, too.'

Smiler seemed lost for words, so he pressed on.

'If I could make a suggestion, ma'am, it would be that you advise Ms Tennyson that you understand her concerns, but that a murder investigation takes precedence over any and all conservation matters.'

'Yes . . . yes . . . I'll do that, Andy. Yes. Of course.'

'I've got to make a few calls, ma'am, so if you've no objection, I'll get back to you when I have some more information. Hopefully within the hour.'

'Do that, Andy.'

'Thank you, ma'am.'

He killed the call, turned a sharp right to the sound of horns tooting, booted it, then hammered the brakes as he skidded into Strathkinness High Road.

He gritted his teeth and powered up to eighty.

CHAPTER 35

'I thought I should ask,' Jessie said. 'Are you intending to arrest her?'

'Got it in one.'

'Now we're talking.'

'Phone Mhairi and tell her to contact Karen Gardner of the Dive and Marine Unit. Find out if Fraser Lindsay's there, and if he is, tell her to make a formal arrest.'

'Who? Gardner?'

'She's a policewoman, right? And while you're at it, tell Mhairi to find out if the Dunmores have registered firearm licences.'

While Jessie contacted Mhairi, Gilchrist reworked his rationale.

The scuff marks on the driveway at the Jaguar's boot had been the missing piece that clicked into place. And the fact that White De Bouchier Law Offices were in South Street, the opposite direction in which Dunmore was travelling. She never had any intention of meeting Peter White that morning. She had no solicitor's appointment. No, she was making a run for it, suitcases already packed and in the Jaguar's boot by the time Jessie arrived at her home.

As he approached the town of Strathkinness, he swerved left and right, working his way around a cluster of speed bumps, keeping his speed close to seventy. At the intersection with Main Street, he braked hard, tyres squealing into the tight right-hand turn.

'There she is,' Jessie said.

Ahead, on the downhill stretch to the A91 – the main road west from St Andrews – he could just make out Dunmore's silver Jaguar, brake lights flashing as it negotiated the bends with care. He powered on, almost hitting ninety at one point, and eased back as he entered the first of many bends as the country road wound its way towards the coast. He wondered what she would do if she recognised his BMW in her rear-view mirror. Try to outrun him? Ignore him? Drive on? Or wait for him to pull her over? He knew this road well, and had it in his mind to overtake her near Kincaple, make the arrest there.

When Jessie finished her call, he realised he'd been so focused on driving, and on his own thoughts, that he'd barely taken in a word she'd said.

'How did it go?' he asked.

'Mhairi's on it.'

He'd closed the gap to Dunmore's Jaguar to ten yards now. Even from that distance, he could see Dunmore's head move as she studied him in the rear-view mirror. She slowed down, and he took his chance.

He overtook her, then braked hard in front of her.

She slithered to a halt behind him.

'Take it easy,' he said to Jessie. 'We still need to be careful.'

'I'll do my best,' she said, then slapped the door open.

Dunmore had her window down. 'What on earth is it now?' she snapped at him.

He stood back from the opened window, Jessie by his side, her eagerness to handcuff Dunmore radiating from her like an electric charge looking for some place to earth. He gave a dry smile. 'You said you had a meeting with your solicitor.'

'I do, for heaven's sake.'

'Peter White?'

'Yes.'

He glanced uphill, then nodded to his left, at the grey silhouettes of St Andrews. 'His office is in South Street.'

'Oh for heaven's sake,' she snarled. 'I'm not going to his office. I'm meeting him at his home. In Cupar.'

For a fleeting moment, Gilchrist thought he had it all wrong, that his sense of logic on which he relied so heavily had let him down. But the memory of the scuff marks on the frosted driveway helped him keep his face straight. 'Address?'

'What?'

'Can you give me the address of Peter White's home in Cupar?'

A shadow sank deep behind Dunmore's eyes. Lips curled like a wild animal about to bare fangs. A tiny tremor shivered beneath eyelids that had taken on a kohl-like darkness. Then the scene rebooted, and she snarled, 'That's it. I've had it with you lot.' She reached for her mobile, tapped the screen, hissing under her breath like a tormented snake.

Gilchrist opened the driver's door. 'Step out of the car, please.'

She pressed her mobile to her left ear, to keep it from Gilchrist's reach, her other hand gripping the steering wheel to steady herself.

'Mrs Dunmore,' he said, his voice more firm. 'Please step out of the car. *Now.*'

'*Piss off,*' she shouted.

Gilchrist stepped aside, and nodded to Jessie who leaned inside, and snapped a handcuff onto Dunmore's free wrist and the steering wheel. 'I'm arresting you on suspicion of the murder of your husband, George Caithness. You do not have to say anything, but—'

'*Get your hands off me, you witch.*' Her mobile clattered to the floor as her free hand swiped like a cat's claw across Jessie's face.

Jessie's training kicked in. She pushed forward, took hold of Dunmore's free arm, twisted it and slapped it hard against her cuffed arm. 'I might be a witch,' she said, 'but you're under arrest.' She snapped on the other cuff.

'*You conniving little witch,*' Dunmore screamed, tugging at the cuffs, straining the steering wheel, bouncing on her seat as if to test the car's suspension.

'I'm also charging you for resisting arrest—'

'You have no fucking idea who you're dealing with—'

'—and assaulting a police officer—'

'Your career is over, you *bitch*—'

'You do not have to say anything, but anything you do say . . .'

Gilchrist waited until Jessie finished reading Dunmore her rights, then he leaned in and removed her keys from the ignition. He pressed the remote. The boot popped open, and he almost breathed a sigh of relief at the sight of two suitcases, packed for travel.

He pulled out his mobile, and dialled Mhairi.

'Where are you?' he asked.

'Almost at the loch, sir.'

'Can you see the Dive and Marine Unit?'

'Not yet, sir.'

'Get back to me as soon as you can.' He ended the call, and closed the boot. At the front of the car, Jessie had her mobile to her ear, calling in the arrest details. Dunmore sat silent, flush-faced, glaring through the windscreen. He opened the passenger door, reached in and retrieved her mobile phone from the footwell.

'I'm confiscating this,' he told her.

'Piss off.'

'Where were you flying to? The Mediterranean?'

Dunmore ignored him.

'Farther afield?' he said. 'The Far East?'

Silent, she shook her head.

'Running wouldn't have done you any good,' he said. 'We'd find you in the end. You must surely have known that.' He rested an arm on the car door and leaned closer. Her eyes sliced a sideways glance at him, before fixating on some point on the far horizon. But in that split second of eye contact, he read her anger, saw the darkness of her soul, and the words *raging psychopath* burst into his mind unsummoned.

'Where's George?' he asked.

Dunmore tutted.

'Did Fraser Lindsay help you dispose of his body?'

Her lips whitened, then she spat at him, a poor effort that left spittle dribbling down her chin. With her wrists cuffed to the steering wheel, she could do nothing other than let it drip onto her chest. 'You think you're so fucking smart,' she said. 'You're in for one hell of a surprise, a *huge* surprise, when George returns home. And when he does . . .?' She grimaced, her head nodding at the positive outcome. 'He's going to have your job, *and* your measly fucking pension. You'll spend the rest of your miserable fucking life *and* all your pathetic savings fighting us in court, day in, day out, never ending, until you're truly broken and homeless, you useless fucking heartless bastard. Believe you me.'

Gilchrist pulled himself upright, and stood facing the sea. The wind was picking up, stirring the dark waters into a galloping spread of white horses. Doubts flickered. Did he have it wrong? Had George Caithness really just stepped out of the room for a week or so, only to return and find his wife charged with his own murder? Dunmore's words cut like a knife into his thoughts. Not the reaction of someone who'd killed her husband and dumped his body in a loch. The venom in her voice, the defiance in her eyes, the resolute belief that she was right and he was wrong, oh so bloody wrong, had him swallowing a rising lump in his throat. He slammed the door shut and walked to the back of the car, out of Dunmore's line of sight.

Jessie was still on her mobile. A line of blood glistened on her cheek where Dunmore's fingernails had connected. It seemed cold all of a sudden. He shoved his hands into his jacket pockets, tried to shiver off a chilling wind. He wasn't wrong. He couldn't be. Surely. He eyed the Jaguar's boot. Inside were two suitcases. She was running away. She had to be. Plain and simple. No other reason for her bags to be packed. Or was there? For one confusing moment the idea that she was flying off to meet her husband, George, and catch up with him on some holiday resort in the sun, flew into his mind, then vanished as reality returned.

And with it, his sense of logic.

He retrieved Dunmore's mobile from his pocket, and tapped the screen. Locked. She could give them her password, or the IT whiz kids could open it up for him. Either way, it could provide him with much-needed information.

His own mobile rang at that moment – ID Mhairi.

He took the call. 'Anything?'

'Lindsay's not here,' Mhairi said.

'Been and gone?'

'According to Karen Gardner, she never saw him.'

Gilchrist stared at Dunmore, still seated in her car. She seemed to have settled down, but no doubt would spit venom again the instant he prodded. 'He might have gone home,' he said to Mhairi. 'If he's there, bring him in.'

He stuffed his mobile into his pocket, and walked towards Dunmore.

He opened the driver's door, and held out her mobile. 'Password?'

'Piss off.'

'With or without the password, our computer experts will access it anyway.'

Nothing.

'You're not doing yourself any favours, Katherine. If you're as innocent as you say you are, being unhelpful now could come back to hurt you.' He glanced at Jessie. 'It looks as if DS Janes might have cut her face pushing her way through some bushes.'

Something akin to animal cunning slid behind Dunmore's eyes. Then she looked up at him. 'How can I trust you?'

'You can't.' He shrugged. 'But it's up to you.'

'Gleneden,' she said.

'Pardon?'

'The password.'

Jessie had finished her call, and was slipping her mobile into her pocket when he caught her eye. 'Mrs Dunmore has given me permission to access her mobile phone,' he said to her. Then he faced Dunmore. 'Is that correct?'

She nodded.

'Please say it.'

'You have my permission to access my mobile phone.'

He stepped away, striding towards the boot, out of Dunmore's line of sight again, fingers tapping in her password. The phone opened to a wallpaper of a whisky still, copper polished and shining like new. He accessed her messages to find no names, only a string of initials – an unfaithful wife's coded list in case her cuckolded husband accessed her phone. He did a quick search for FL for Fraser Lindsay, but came up with nothing, then he opened the most recent message, a string of texts between KD – Katherine Dunmore – and SAS – whoever SAS was – the last of which was sent only twenty minutes earlier, about the time he and Jessie were arriving at Dunmore's home.

Omw xx

He thought it was an abbreviation for – on my way. Of course, it could be something completely different, but the preceding string of messages that ended with a text sent at 06:12 that morning, told him all he needed to know.

Srch still on
Pw will take care of xx
Worried!! Much action but in wrong place!!
Wdym?
They found smthng!!
What??

??
Planb?
Same place?
10?
☺ xx
Cu xx

Gilchrist was no expert in cryptology, or text messages for that matter, but you didn't have to be a genius to work out that the Dive and Marine Unit's activity in Dunmore Loch that morning had flushed out both Dunmore and her lover, SAS – Fraser Lindsay, ex-SAS soldier, of course – and forced them to adopt Plan B. Which might not be emigration, but definitely a break away from it all to see how the dust settled.

His gaze settled on one line – Same place?

Then the next – 10?

He checked the time on the mobile – 09:45 – then typed in another message.

Delayed. 10:15 ok? xx

Within thirty seconds, he received a reply.

Ok ☺ xx

CHAPTER 36

With Dunmore's mobile in his hand, Gilchrist returned to her Jaguar. 'SAS?' he said. 'Who's that?'

She closed her eyes, shook her head.

'You don't want to be unhelpful now, Katherine.'

'You do what you need to do. But I need to speak to my solicitor.'

'After you've been signed into custody.'

She hissed a curse.

Even though he knew he was likely on a loser, he thought it worth a shot regardless. He scrolled through the messages, and held her mobile out to her. 'Same place?' He waited a couple of beats. 'That's where you were driving to this morning. Not to your solicitor's home in Cupar, but the *same place* that you and Fraser Lindsay regularly meet. Correct?'

Her eyes darkened, and he had a sense that she would sink her fingernails into his face given half a chance.

'If George is going to come home, as you keep telling us, running off with Fraser Lindsay doesn't give the right impression.'

She tutted.

'Do you see the problem I have with that? Wife upset by husband missing, presumed dead. Then wife runs off with lover of the month.'

'He's not my lover,' she snapped.

'So it *is* Lindsay you're meeting.'

'I didn't say that.'

'You didn't need to.' He returned her fierce look with one of his own. 'Do yourself a favour, Katherine, and tell me where.'

She turned away, and stared off into the distance.

'Right,' he said. 'I'll talk to you later.' He walked back to his car. Jessie was sitting in the passenger seat, visor down, checking the cut on her face in the lighted mirror. 'How is it?' he asked.

'Probably contracted rabies from the heathen bitch.' She dabbed a tissue to her cheek, and pulled it away, blood speckled.

'Before you start frothing at the mouth, check this out.' He handed her Dunmore's mobile. 'I think SAS is Fraser Lindsay, but I need you to dig into it for me.'

Jessie took the phone. 'I've organised transport to Glenrothes, and a pickup to take her car to the pound.' She glanced at the Jaguar, Dunmore cuffed to the steering wheel. 'It shouldn't be long.'

'I don't have time.' He stepped back from the door, an invitation for Jessie to leave.

She slid her legs from the car. 'Where are you off to?'

'To give Lindsay a surprise.'

'Wish I could come with you.'

He nodded to Dunmore. 'Get her signed into custody. Make sure she's read her rights, and that she knows she has right of access to a solicitor—'

'The usual,' she said, cutting him short.

He held her gaze in a silent warning. He needed her to do it by the book. 'We're not out of the woods yet,' he said. 'Let's make sure she's locked down watertight.'

She caught his change in tone, and said, 'Got it, sir.'

He strode to the other side of his car, took his seat behind the wheel.

As he eased downhill, Jessie and Dunmore settling into the distance, he knew time was tight. Same place? He checked his GPS, and estimated he would arrive at the Coaching Inn around 09:20. He depressed the accelerator, and set off hard.

He was through Dundee and powering along the A90 when Mhairi phoned.

'I'm at Lindsay's home,' she said. 'Car's not in the drive. Could be in the garage, but I can't tell, sir.'

'Meet me at the Longforgan Coaching Inn,' he said. 'I think he's there.'

He made good time, and fifteen minutes later he was cruising along Main Street at twenty miles an hour. Ahead, the sign for the Coaching Inn shone white on black like a banner under the eaves. He drove past the restaurant and bar, then on beyond the accommodation building, the end of which defined the entrance to the car park. A quick glance left as he drifted past, and he clocked it.

Lindsay's Land Rover Defender was parked at the far end.

He passed a telephone kiosk, did a three-point turn, then bumped onto the pavement. He switched off his engine. From there he had a clear view of the car-park entrance, and was far enough back so that Lindsay wouldn't notice him. He dialled the number he'd memorised from Dunmore's mobile.

'Yup?' Lindsay's voice came over strong and deep.

'This is DCI Gilchrist of St Andrews CID. And I'd like to ask you about your relationship with Katherine Dunmore.'

'I told you to call my solicitor.'

'I'm afraid Peter White's tied up at the moment taking care of Katherine's problems.'

It took several beats before Lindsay hung up.

Gilchrist waited.

It didn't take long, one minute in fact, for Lindsay's Land Rover to nose into Main Street. Gilchrist didn't need to hide himself as Lindsay drove past. From the look on the man's face, he had more on his mind than checking out parked cars.

He waited until the Land Rover was out of sight, then fired up his car, swept onto the road, tyres squealing, and powered after him. At the west end of town, he had a choice of four exits. But it was a no-brainer – the A90 west to Perth, and the link south to Edinburgh or Glasgow Airports. Sure enough, as he entered the roundabout, he caught sight of Lindsay's Land Rover turning onto the westbound lane of the A90.

He phoned Mhairi. 'Where are you?'

'About four miles away, sir.'

What the hell was she driving? A golf cart? He couldn't afford to wait, so he said, 'Change of plan. Get onto HQ and put a marker on Lindsay's Land Rover. Then get back to North Street, and chase up Jackie.' He swung onto the ramp to the A90. 'You got a number for Karen Gardner?'

She read it out to him.

He ended the call, and dialled Gardner.

She answered with a curt, 'Gardner.'

The rattling noise of the generator had him turning down the volume on his speaker system. He introduced himself, and said, 'Have you found anything yet?'

'No, sir.'

266

Dunmore's string of text messages pushed into his mind – Worried!! Much action but in wrong place!! 'The body's in that loch,' he said. 'I'm sure of that. But I need you to focus on the middle of the lake.'

'Why, sir?'

Why indeed? Because if he had to dispose of a body from a boat, that's where he would dump it, as far from the shores as he could. But it was also the only spot on the loch hatched in red and surrounded by buoys, which he realised now was an area designated under Scottish Stretch which prohibited swimming, boating, fishing, or activity or disturbance of any kind – some 2500 m^2. In other words, the perfect place to hide a weighted-down body for posterity, and the reason Dunmore had backed the Scottish Stretch development so heavily, and pushed for an injunction against the underwater search, without which it was only a matter of time before they recovered the body.

He was certain of that.

But he chose not to explain his thoughts. Instead, he said, 'I'll have our Office send you a plan of the loch which shows where you need to concentrate your search.'

'Very well, sir. I'll let the crew know.'

He ended the call, and phoned Jackie. In their typical one-sided conversation, he told her what he wanted her to do, and to treat it with some urgency, then said, 'You got that?'

'Uh-huh.'

'You're a darling.' He sent a sloppy *Mwah* down the line, and hung up.

Next, he phoned Jessie.

'Did Dunmore's mobile receive a call from Lindsay?' he asked.

'Got another text from SAS about ten minutes ago, if that's what you mean.'

'What did it say?'

'Call me.'

'And did you?'

'Not yet. Should I?'

'No. Get Dunmore's phone to our IT guys, and tell them to dig deep into it.'

'I'm on it,' she said.

When he disconnected, he checked his speed – still sixty. About a hundred yards in the distance, the box-like shape of Lindsay's Land Rover trundled steadily ahead of him. For the time being, there wasn't much more he could do.

He shifted in his seat, and settled down for the drive.

CHAPTER 37

Gilchrist was proven right.

One hour and ten minutes after he'd started tailing Lindsay, the Land Rover swung into Edinburgh Airport's Long Stay Parking. He parked his own car some distance away, and waited until Lindsay boarded the courtesy bus. Once it set off on its stop-start route to the airport, he slipped out of his car, and strode towards the terminal building.

By the time he arrived, Lindsay was already inside.

The terminal buzzed with the late-morning throng. Suitcases wheeled past in every direction. Queues tailed back from check-in desks in ordered lines, some spilling beyond the barriers into haphazard scrums. The Tannoy system chimed in the background, a tinny sound that no one seemed to pay attention to. He kept to the window side of the terminal, away from the desks and lengthy queues, and edged towards International Departures. He could have made a formal arrest in the Long Stay car park, or even in Longforgan, and saved himself a drive, but he'd wanted to find out where Lindsay was running to, and if he was meeting anyone else before flying off.

He phoned Jessie again.

'Has Dunmore's mobile taken any more calls or texts from Lindsay?'

'Duh, Andy, I've already sent it to the IT guys.'

Of course she had. He changed tack. 'How about her personal effects? Did she have any airline tickets on her?'

'None. She swears blind she was going to meet Peter White in Cupar.'

'Without knowing the address?'

'Oh, she knew the address, all right,' Jessie said. 'She just didn't want to tell us.'

'*What?*'

'I've checked it out. And the address she gave me is correct.'

Gilchrist cast a panicked glance along the check-in desks. Did he have it wrong? Had he spent the morning following a man to the airport for no good reason? Had Dunmore really been driving to her solicitor's home? If Peter White was her long-standing solicitor, maybe it followed that she would indeed know where he lived. For several seconds his mind flooded with doubts. Then his sense of logic kicked in.

Why would Lindsay terminate Gilchrist's phone call, then drive off the way he had? Why would Dunmore allow herself to be arrested simply on the basis of not having given him her solicitor's address? The answer to both of these questions was one word – panic. He'd taken them both by surprise and, as his gaze found then locked onto Lindsay's tall figure stepping up to the Emirates check-in desk, he made his decision.

'She's bluffing,' he said. 'I'm at Edinburgh Airport, about to arrest Lindsay. He'll have her tickets.'

He ended the call and slipped his mobile into his pocket.

Rather than make a scene at the check-in desk, Gilchrist waited until Lindsay was issued his boarding pass and heading towards the escalators to the departure lounge before he walked up behind him and took hold of his arm.

'Let's do this quietly,' he said.

Lindsay's look of surprise turned to one of desperate calculation, as if he was trying to work out where Gilchrist had come from, and in which direction he could run to escape him.

Gilchrist pre-empted any rash decision by tightening his grip, and saying, 'This way.'

But Lindsay was having none of it. He took hold of Gilchrist's arm with a grip as hard and tight as a steel jaw, jerked it free, lunged at him with an old-fashioned forearm smash that caught Gilchrist high on his chest and sent him stumbling backwards. Lindsay stepped in, to follow up with another blow, the fierce look in his eyes telling Gilchrist that he was aiming for a killer punch to the head.

But Gilchrist was ready.

He grabbed hold of Lindsay's arm and pulled it into him, at the same time kicking out at the man's knee. But his kick was off target and failed to break the joint. Even so, Lindsay's momentum carried him forward. Together they tumbled to the tiled floor, Gilchrist already twisting his body and Lindsay's arm, so that when Lindsay hit the floor face-first, Gilchrist was already on top of him, forcing his arm high enough up the man's back to crunch gristle. Lindsay grunted in pain. A quick tug of the other arm, and before he had time to recover his senses, Lindsay was handcuffed and listening in stunned silence to Gilchrist arresting him on suspicion of complicity in the murder of George Caithness. He winced in pain from his arm as Gilchrist helped him to his feet, reading him his rights.

Twenty minutes later, Gilchrist was seated behind a grey desk in Lothian & Borders Police Unit's Airport Office south of the terminal building. He'd notified Airport Security of his formal arrest, and initiated the recovery of Lindsay's luggage and cancellation of his seat on the flight. Airport Security also confirmed that a Mrs Katherine Dunmore was a first-class passenger on the same flight, with a seat assigned next to her travelling companion, Mr Fraser Lindsay, who had made both reservations and paid for the flights on his personal Santander debit card.

Lindsay had now recovered from his shock at being arrested, and sat opposite, eyes cold and focused on Gilchrist in a hardman stare.

Gilchrist ignored Lindsay's look, switched on the office tape recorder, and went through the formalities of name and rank, date and time, and Lindsay's name, too. 'I've advised Mr Lindsay that he has the right to have a solicitor present. Which he has declined.' He eyed Lindsay. 'Is that correct?'

'I've done nothing wrong,' Lindsay replied. 'So I don't need a solicitor.'

Well, it looked like Dunmore's ignorant confidence was catching. For the record, he read out the charge against Lindsay, then held up a pair of boarding passes – one for the flight from Edinburgh to Dubai, the other for the connecting flight to Singapore. 'Two first-class tickets on today's Emirate flights to Singapore,' he said. 'Why Singapore?'

Lindsay shrugged. 'Why does anyone choose someplace for a holiday?'

'You and Katherine Dunmore were going on holiday?'

'Yes.'

'So how do you explain the one-way tickets?'

'We thought we might carry on, take a flight to Hawaii, do a round-the-world trip.' He shrugged again, an adventurous holidaymaker undecided where to go next. 'Or maybe south to Australia. Who knows? It makes it more exciting.'

'Expensive way to travel,' Gilchrist said. 'Buying airline tickets on the hoof, flying from one place to the next, with no destination in mind, so to speak.'

'Kate's loaded. So what does it matter?'

'It helps, of course, that her husband, George, has been murdered.'

'George hasn't been murdered. Kate's told you that time and again. He's alive and well. The drunken idiot does this several times a year. Just gets up and pisses off. That's why she's leaving him. She's had enough.'

'She's leaving George for you?'

Lindsay gave a twisted smile, one knowing womaniser to another. 'I'm happy to play along. Go with the flow. For the time being.'

'Then what?' Gilchrist leaned closer. 'Back to Dunmore Lodge to carry on doing her skivvy work, looking after the mansion, cutting the grass, polishing that boat of hers, while she gallivants around the world with her next man of the month?'

'Maybe I'll retire.'

'On an Army pension?'

Another shrug.

'Of course, with Katherine in tow, your monthly pension could be topped up with a tidy bonus for dumping George's body in the loch.'

Lindsay tried a scornful chuckle. But he was no actor. 'George'll be back next week to beg Kate's forgiveness. He always does. But he's too late this time.'

Gilchrist decided to edge closer. 'She's done this before, you know, given monthly stipends to others for helping her out.'

'Don't know what you're talking about.'

'Duncan Milne, former manager of Gleneden Distillery. And Janet Milne, Duncan's wife, or more correctly – widow.' He let a couple of beats pass. 'Duncan and Janet both died under suspicious circumstances.' He had no real proof of that, of course, but sometimes you just have to press. 'That's how you put an end to stipends.' He offered a dry smile, and drew a finger under his throat. 'Over and out.'

Silent, Lindsay stared at him.

Gilchrist pressed on. 'Did you know that Katherine arranged for her solicitor to file an injunction against us carrying out further searches on the loch? All to do with protecting a conservation area from unnecessary disturbance.'

'Really?'

'But the injunction won't be granted.'

Lindsay smirked. 'We'll see.'

Gilchrist focused on Lindsay's eyes, searching for the slightest sign of guilt over his next statement. 'It won't be granted,' he said, 'because they recovered a body from the loch this morning.'

Lindsay shrugged, raised his eyebrows, the text – Much action but in wrong place!! – no doubt granting him the strength to maintain his bluff.

'Skeletal remains,' Gilchrist said. 'Of a child. Cause of death appears to have been blunt force trauma to the skull, which resulted in us opening a fresh murder enquiry.'

The colour drained from Lindsay's face as the significance of what he was being told sank into his thoughts.

'So you see, no conservation agreement can take primacy over a murder investigation. Not even Scottish Stretch,' he added, just to make Lindsay aware that he knew what he was talking about. 'The entire loch will be searched from shore to shore. We'll even drain the bloody thing if we have to.' A pause, then, 'So what do you say to that?'

Lindsay scowled. 'I want to speak to my solicitor.'

Gilchrist looked at the time on the tape recorder. 'Interview terminated at 11:51.'

Then he pushed from the table, and walked from the room.

CHAPTER 38

6.48 p.m., Friday
North Street Police Station, St Andrews

By the end of the day, Gilchrist's investigation had taken two steps backwards, maybe three. With Lindsay and Dunmore in custody in Glenrothes Police Station, attempts to glean further information from either of them had resulted in a constant string of *No comments* at the instruction of their solicitors, Peter White and Eva Turnbull.

To make matters worse, White provided Dunmore with an alibi – she did indeed have a meeting scheduled at his home – and in light of the perceived police harassment against her, had decided to postpone her trip to Singapore to consult at length with White on her intention to file a lawsuit against Fife Constabulary.

Under pressure from Smiler, Gilchrist had no option but to release Dunmore.

But even more worrying, the Dive and Marine Unit had renewed their underwater search in the area defined by Gilchrist, and his last phone call to Karen Gardner half an hour ago

276

confirmed they'd found nothing. The loch was at its deepest, she'd said, with visibility close to zero. Although the going was slow, they weren't giving up.

Even so, Gilchrist sensed everything was about to grind to a halt.

He pushed to his feet and ran his hand down his face. He was tired, not just physically tired, but mentally tired, tired of the relentless battle against criminal suspects who sat stony-faced and silent, safe in the knowledge that they were taking advice from their solicitors and making it more difficult for the police to strengthen their case.

He pressed his forehead to the window, eyed the car park below. Pitch black. No sign of frost, just a thick blackness that reflected a cloud-laden sky. Rain was forecast for the next few days, which would turn to hail or snow if the temperature dropped a couple of degrees. How nice would it be to get away from it all, stretch out on some beach somewhere, and let time pass you by? As these thoughts of lazy days and summer months softened his mood, he puzzled over the way the mind worked, how some thought in one direction could open an alternate thought in another.

The spring-like warmth of Molly Havet's garden – that's where his thoughts had led him – and the realisation that he hadn't asked Molly if any personal belongings had been returned to her by George after Hector's disappearance, and if so, what had they been? Clothes? Books? Something more personal, perhaps – handwritten letters? Birthday or Christmas cards? And after twenty-five years, would any of it matter? He had a strong suspicion that it would lead him nowhere, but the fact that it was a box unticked had him dialling her number.

When Havet answered, he said, 'I'm sorry to bother you again, but I've just found out that George Caithness apparently returned some personal belongings to you after Hector disappeared all these years ago.'

'Personal belongings?' she said.

'Items of clothing or books perhaps, that you may have left in Hector's home.'

'Clothes?' she said, making the word sound like he'd sworn at her. 'And books? I don't know about any of that.'

Well, there he had his answer. Twenty-five years was a long time, too long for anyone to remember the minutiae of everyday life back then—

'But he did return what had been in my mother's family,' she said. 'After I kicked up a fuss about it.'

'And what was that?'

She told him, which had his mind firing with the unlikeliest of possibilities.

'Do you still have it?'

'Of course,' she said. 'I would never part with it.'

'I'd like to drive out and have a look, if I may.'

'Why would you do that?' she asked.

What could he tell her? That he had a niggling suspicion? That he needed to see it in person, so he could tick the box good and proper? Or that a change in tack from the confines of his investigation might help clear his mind?

'Let's just say that it's my innate curiosity.'

He arrived at Havet's home just before eight o'clock, and was let in without a smile.

She led him into the lounge, to her favourite chair in front of the fire, then nodded to a writing bureau in the corner by the front window.

'That's it there,' she said.

'Do you mind?' he asked, crossing the room.

The writing bureau was a sturdy piece of furniture, with curved continuous plinths in burled walnut, inset with filigrees of light and dark oak, squared off with strips of black teak. He ran his hand over the surface, the wood polished as smooth as glass. He was no expert in antiques, but his grandfather had one similar to it once – but nowhere near as magnificent – in the corner of his lounge. But this desk was more a work of art than a piece of furniture.

'A cylinder bureau,' he said, admiring the one-piece curved cover that opened like a roll-over shutter, hence the name. 'Is it Victorian?'

'It's mid-nineteenth century,' she said. 'But not English. German, I've been told.'

'Well, they certainly knew how to make them. It's beautiful.'

'It's been in my family for generations.'

Gilchrist stepped back to admire it. The writing desk stood on twin pedestals that each had three drawers. He took hold of the top drawer handle on the left pedestal, noting that each drawer had a keyhole. He suspected they were unlocked, and said, 'May I?'

'I don't use it any more.'

He pulled the drawer open with a firm tug to reveal miscellaneous cards, envelopes, old bank statements. He wasn't interested in any of that, and closed it again, marvelling at the way it slid in to a perfect fit, tight and flush with the face, no looseness, nothing like today's cheap assembly-manufactured crap. He tested a drawer on the right face, for the simple pleasure of admiring the workmanship.

Next, he turned his attention to the roll-top cover.

Again, a keyhole, but no key.

'You never lock it?' he asked.

'Key's in the inside top-right drawer.'

He took hold of both handles, then raised the cover. It slid up and over with perfect smoothness to reveal three tiers of small drawers left and right, separated by six pigeon-hole dockets between. Sure enough, in the top-right drawer he found the master key. He closed the drawer, again marvelling at the workmanship. He had a sense that this piece of furniture was worth several thousand pounds, maybe much more, and certainly worth making a fuss over. But it told him what kind of man Caithness had been, someone who'd seen its value and resisted returning it to Havet, even though it belonged to her.

'You said you had to kick up a fuss to have this returned to you,' Gilchrist said. 'I can see why George would want to keep it.'

'Oh it wasn't George who wanted to keep it. It was Katherine.'

'She thought it was Hector's?'

'No. She knew fine bloody well it was mine. She'd been there when it was delivered to Hector's. But when he died, she argued that everything in the house belonged to Hector's estate. I had to engage a solicitor to argue my case. Luckily I had the original paperwork.' She smiled at that, a sad shifting of her lips that spoke of bittersweet memories.

Back to the writing bureau.

He hooked a finger from each hand into a pair of holes on the top surface, and pulled it towards him. A four-inch thick panel slid out to form the writing desk, on which a trio of dark-grained leather skivers were inset. Interestingly, or so he thought, pulling out the panel also pulled out four additional smaller drawers fixed to the back of the panel, which lined up with perfect craftsmanship to give four drawers left and right, and two narrower drawers beneath the pigeon-hole dockets. Small pull-handles, inset at the edge of each skiver, let him lift them up to reveal an additional space underneath. All in all, it was an incredible display of nineteenth-century craftsmanship, a piece of furniture fit to be the centrepiece of any home. In days gone by, with the cylinder cover rolled down and locked, it was as safe a place as any in which to keep personal and important papers.

But he still hadn't found what he was looking for.

And now he had the writing desk open, he realised he'd made a wasted trip.

Still, it had been worth a shot. He fiddled with this drawer and that, pulling them out, lifting them up, running his hand along the panels, shaking his head in wonder at the level of skill these Victorian-era craftsmen must have had. He was about to close the skiver lids when he noticed that the storage space beneath the middle skiver was less than that of the other two – by a good half-inch, he figured. Now why was that? Why make that space less deep than the others when the skill in constructing these desks was to provide as much storage and filing space as possible?

He dropped to his knees and looked under the pull-out desk panel. Solid.

He ran his fingers over the edge of the flat panel. Nothing.

He checked the sides. Again, nothing.

Now he was puzzled. He pressed down on the centre skiver drawer, ran his hand around the edges. Still, nothing—

'Is there a problem?'

Havet's voice pulled him back to the present. 'I was wondering if there was another drawer here.'

Havet pushed to her feet, and walked up to him. 'Hector showed me once,' she said. 'But I've never used it.' She gripped both ends of the pull-out panel, and tugged. 'It's stiff.' She gave a firmer tug, and the front of the panel fell open on a row of tiny hinges that could be seen only when the panel was open.

And there, in the centre of the inner face, was a small keyhole. 'What's this for?' he said.

She shook her head. 'I don't know. I've never opened it.'

Gilchrist slipped his hand into his jacket pocket, and removed the key they'd found in Hector's corduroy trouser pocket. It looked the right size, but the odds of it being the key that would open that hidden slotted drawer were astronomical. He held his breath as he slid it in, then twisted it to give off the tiniest of clicks.

Had he unlocked it?

There were no handles or finger-pulls to be found, so he eased a fingernail into what looked like the edge of the sliding panel, and pressed it one way, then the other. Each wiggle drew the hidden drawer out millimetre by millimetre, until he had enough of it exposed to clasp the end with his fingers, and pull it open. Although it was a tight fit, the drawer slid out like the first piece of a Chinese puzzle.

The storage it provided was no more than ten inches wide by eighteen inches long, but only a quarter of an inch deep – sufficient in which to secrete a dozen or so foolscap pages. He removed the contents, a single sheet of paper, creased from being previously folded. He pressed it flat on the central skiver.

'A birth certificate?' Havet said.

The document appeared genuine, with inked entries written in neat handwriting which identified the newborn as Jane McEntegart Milne, born in St Andrews Memorial Hospital, and the mother as Gina Milne. The father wasn't named – hence the child's surname, Milne – and told him that the child was illegitimate.

'Who's Gina Milne?' he said.

'Never heard of her.'

Gilchrist eyed the dates, and did a quick mental calculation. The Milnes that sprang to mind were Duncan and Janet, who would've been in their fifties when baby Jane was born, making them the likely candidates to be Gina Milne's parents. But no one had mentioned that the Milnes had *any* children, let alone a daughter called Gina.

He checked the birth certificate for the mother's address. And there it was. The same address that Janet Milne lived in all these years through her marriage to Duncan, ex-manager of Gleneden Distillery.

Gina Milne had to be their daughter.

Molly Havet had said she'd never used that secret drawer, so it didn't take a nuclear physicist to work out that the birth certificate must have been put there by Hector Dunmore – who'd carried the key to the drawer on his person, until the day he was murdered.

But why would he have kept this birth certificate? What was so important about Gina Milne's illegitimate daughter that he had to keep her birth certificate hidden? But if you eyed it from a more devious angle, and asked the question – *why* would Hector show Molly the hidden drawer in the first place? – the logical answer came back – because he wanted her to know how to access it in case anything happened to him.

But which still didn't answer the question – *why hide a birth certificate?*

Gilchrist walked to the front window. Outside, he could be looking at the dark side of the moon – black as a coal face. Nothing stirred. No stars, no lights of any kind could pierce a cloud-like fog that had silenced the night. He could be looking at his own investigation, the blind leading the blind. Because that's how he felt.

Unable to see the significance of that birth certificate.

Was this child the reason Duncan Milne, and subsequently his wife, Janet, had been able to sustain a blackmailing campaign against the Dunmores for a monthly stipend of £400 in addition to his pension?

Too many questions, and not enough answers.

But whatever the reason, Gilchrist was sure of one thing.

Come hell or high water, he was going to find out.

CHAPTER 39

Saturday morning
Fisherman's Cottage, Crail

The call came in at 05:34, wakening Gilchrist from a deep sleep. He reached for his mobile, and mumbled into it, his tongue struggling with the command from a sleeping brain.

'Sorry to trouble you, sir,' a woman's voice said, 'but I thought you should be the first to know.'

The voice resonated with a hint of familiarity. But for the life of him, he couldn't pull up a face. 'I'm listening,' he said, slipping his legs from bed, pushing himself to his feet.

'We've found a body, sir.'

Wide awake now. Karen Gardner. 'Whereabouts in the loch, Karen?'

'About twenty feet from where you said it might be, sir. With visibility as bad as it was, it took us longer to locate it. Wrapped in black plastic bin liner didn't help, but we've got it on board now, and are in the process of bringing it ashore.'

Crail was over fifty miles from Dunmore Lodge, but he said, 'I'm on my way. I'll be with you in an hour.'

In the bathroom, he turned on the shower, and let the water run hot while he phoned Jessie. 'Bloody hell, Andy. It's still pitch black. What time is it?'

'They've pulled a body from the loch. I'll pick you up in fifteen minutes.'

He hung up, checked his mobile for messages – none – then stepped into the shower cubicle. He soaped himself from head to toes, scrubbed his skin hard and fast, while the piping hot water fired his thoughts into gear. He'd texted Jackie on the drive back from Havet's last night, and instructed her to find out everything she could about Duncan and Janet Milne's daughter, Gina, and her illegitimate child, Jane McEntegart Milne. He gave the child's place and date of birth, and told Jackie he wanted addresses, phone numbers, place of work, marital status – the works – for both Gina and Jane, with emphasis on the need to talk to one or both of them today, as a matter of urgency.

He'd then phoned Mhairi, and instructed her to drop whatever she was working on and to assist Jackie as soon as she got into the Office in the morning. He needed them to find Gina and Jane Milne, and get back to him the instant, the *very instant*, they found anything.

Shower over, and clear in his own mind how he was going to proceed, he towelled himself dry. He didn't bother shaving, or eating breakfast, and by the time he fired up his BMW, eleven minutes had passed since Karen Gardner's call.

As he left Crail and powered into the dark countryside, he was running late. His place to Jessie's was just over ten miles, which he couldn't cover in four minutes, no matter how fast he drove. So he gave her a call.

'Running a tad late,' he said.

'So I've got time to pull on my knickers, then?'

'Oh, definitely.'

'We'd better be stopping for you to buy coffee,' she said, and hung up.

Next he phoned Cooper.

She answered right away, voice brisk and assured, as if she'd been awake for hours. 'You know, Andy, you could save your-self the trouble of all these early morning calls if we lived together.'

Her comment was so unexpected that he was lost for words. He stared at the tunnel of light ahead, and struggled to think of how to respond.

Cooper chuckled, and said, 'As that's gone down like the *Titanic*, I suppose I should ask why you're phoning at such an early hour.'

'They've found a body,' he said. 'In the loch. This morning.'

'Caithness?'

'Too soon to say, but we're thinking it is. I'm on my way to the loch right now. How quickly can you get there?'

A pause, then, 'I'll be there no later than eight.'

'Good.'

'Before you hang up, Andy—'

'Look, Becky, I really don't need this . . . this innuendo—'

'Ah,' she said. 'I was about to tell you that I've got a match on the DNA.'

What? On full alert now. 'Whose DNA?'

'The child's remains recovered from the loch yesterday.'

He wanted to ask how she'd managed to turn it around so quickly, but it didn't matter, she had a match. 'I'm listening,' was all he dared say.

'The skeleton is mostly in reasonable condition. But the good news is that mittens and bootees protected the hands and feet, so the fingernails and toenails have been well preserved. Based on the bootees, my thoughts are that the child died about thirty years ago, so I've sent samples off for carbon-14 dating, particularly effective for bones of that age. If you can come back with a date range for the mittens or bootees, I feel confident we can pin the year of death down to plus or minus five years. And knowing how pushy you are, I've asked for the results for Monday.'

He would have liked the results today, but being the weekend, there wasn't much he could do to expedite that. 'And the DNA results?' he said.

She tutted, as if irked by his impatience. 'I can say with ninety-nine point nine per cent certainty, that the child's father is Hector Dunmore.'

Gilchrist removed his foot from the accelerator. The countryside, and the world with it, seemed to slow down. Hector Dunmore? The father of a murdered child? But who was the child? And with that thought came a possibility, the odds of which were astronomical. Had they recovered the remains of Jane McEntegart Milne? But the date on the birth certificate snuffed that out of the equation. Hector would still have been in primary school when Jane McEntegart Milne was born.

So if the remains were not baby Jane Milne's, then whose were they?

And who had killed the child? And why hide her body in a loch? Why not bury it instead? Throughout the hills and dales of Great Britain, the countryside had to be riddled with the unfound remains of bodies unknown.

But one question that reared up above all others was –

'Do you know who the mother is?' he asked.

'Don't have a match yet, Andy. I'll leave it at that for the time being.'

Not like Cooper to be cagey in her answers. But her canny phrasing told him more than she wanted him to know. 'Which means you have your suspicions?' he pried.

'This is the problem I have with you. You're always jumping to conclusions, looking for evidence where there's none. I repeat – I don't have a match.'

'*Yet*,' he emphasised. 'Which suggests—'

'You don't listen, do you?'

'Right,' he said, louder than intended. 'When you find out who the mother is . . .'

But she'd already hung up.

He gripped the steering wheel, and gritted his teeth. Christ Almighty. This was what he disliked most about Cooper – no, what he *hated* about Cooper – her ability to swing from one end of the emotional spectrum to the other in the space of a nano-second. But despite that, he could not prevent a smile from tugging his lips at the thought that Cooper and he might some-how resurrect their relationship.

Then, just as quickly, the smile vanished.

No way. Absolutely not. Underlined.

If ever there was a couple as emotionally and socially dispa-rate, and a sure-fire recipe for disaster, he and Cooper were it. He would have to remind her that their interaction now was purely professional, and that their past relationship – albeit a memorably libidinous one – was most definitely behind them.

When he pulled into Canongate, Jessie was standing at the bottom of the hill. 'What kept you,' she said, as she jumped inside.

'Came as fast as I could.'

'Well, maybe you can carry on driving like Lewis Hamilton and take me to Starbucks. I need my morning fix.'

'Too early,' he said. 'Won't be open.'

'Drop the negative attitude. You can drive by and see if it's open.'

But Starbucks on Market Street was closed, as was Costa Coffee.

'Shall we try Dundee?' he said.

'Better make it Perth. I don't want to be disappointed again.'

By the time they'd driven through Guardbridge, Gilchrist had brought her up to speed with his call from Gardner, and his thoughts on Cooper's findings. But when he mentioned the birth certificate in Molly Havet's writing bureau, she slapped her hand on her knee.

'That Dunmore bitch is in it up to her ears,' she said.

Silent, he accelerated to seventy.

'Two bodies dumped in the loch? And Hector Dunmore's the father of one of them? I'd put money on that bitch having dumped George in the loch. It makes sense now, doesn't it? She might've known about the baby, so would know where to dump George.'

But Gilchrist couldn't agree. 'Too much of a quantum leap,' he said. 'It could've been their father who put the child in the loch. Then maybe Hector got someone pregnant and his father didn't want him to bring disgrace to the family.'

'So he murders the child, rather than lose face?' she gasped. 'That's a stretch and a half, I have to say.'

'But the point I'm making, is that you can't finger Katherine Dunmore just because you don't like her. And we don't know for sure yet, that this morning's body is George.'

'Well . . .'

'And if the skeletal remains are thirty years old, there could be other players in the mix. Gina Milne for one. Duncan Milne for another. The Milnes were devout Catholics by all accounts, and there's that unanswered question of what's behind the monthly stipend. And was Duncan Milne murdered to keep his silence? And his wife, too?'

'Whoah, there. Talking about quantum leaps? Janet Milne died of old age.'

'But within three months of the stipend being doubled?'

Jessie stared off at the passing countryside. 'There is that,' she conceded.

'Of course, the skeletal remains being of baby Jane Milne just can't be. Hector would still have been a child himself when she was born.'

'And he wasn't around to dump George Caithness's body in the loch. Therefore . . .?'

'We're back at the beginning,' he said.

He drove on in silence, both he and Jessie lost in their own thoughts. It wasn't until he'd crossed the Tay Road Bridge and had accelerated on the A90 when he phoned Jackie. It was still too early to have found anything on Gina Milne, but Jackie lived alone, and was known to live for her work, every second of every minute focused on some police-related enquiry.

She answered right away, and Gilchrist said, 'Morning, Jackie. I didn't wake you up, did I?'

'Nuh-uh.'

'You been busy?'

'Uh-huh.'

'Anything on Gina Milne yet?'

'Uh-huh.'

He glanced at Jessie, who looked just as surprised. 'Can you email it to me?'

'Nuh-uh. S . . . s . . . scan.'

'You need to scan it at the Office?'

'Uh-huh.'

'Okay, Jackie. That's terrific. But I need you to scarper into the Office as soon as you can, and get that off to me. And I've told Mhairi to assist you with anything you need done this morning. That's how important this is. Okay?'

'Uh-huh.'

When he hung up, it took him a couple of moments to gather his thoughts.

'Look,' he said. 'Think of this logically. Hector might be dead, but we now have two links to his past – one, that he's the father of the child recovered from the loch, and two, he hid baby Jane Milne's birth certificate in a writing bureau. There had to be a reason for him doing that, and maybe they're connected in some way. But the only person who can help us get to the bottom of it all, is Gina Milne. She's the answer. She has to be.'

'If she's still alive.'

His enthusiasm plummeted, then recovered. 'And if she is, she'll know who baby Jane's father is.'

'You hope,' Jessie said.

Gilchrist glowered in silence. They had no way of knowing if Gina had been overly promiscuous or not, although he suspected that having devout Catholics for parents, Gina would have been well brought up. Of course, you could never tell.

'Bloody hell, Andy. My head's spinning. Can we stop for a coffee soon?'

292

'I thought you said Perth.'

'That was before you bombarded me with a gazillion possibilities.'

'We're nearly there,' he said. 'If you see a roadside coffee shop, shout it out.'

But Jessie failed to spot any, and Gilchrist drove into Perth and pulled up outside the same Costa Coffee shop they'd stopped at last time. He handed Jessie a tenner.

She reached for the door handle, and said, 'You're becoming a man of habit.'

'Then you'll know I like a fatty latte.'

As he watched Jessie enter Costa Coffee, his mobile rang – ID Mhairi.

'What've you got?' he said.

'Gina Milne, sir. Although she's now Gina McQueen, and has been for twenty-nine years.'

'She's still alive and well?'

'She is, sir, and living with her husband, Angus, in the village of Morar. Been there since she moved away from Fife.'

Morar? Morar? The name tickled some distant memory, but he couldn't pull it up. 'Any details on her family?'

'Highland Council records have only her and her husband at their home address, sir.'

'Were you able to uncover anything on Gina's daughter, Jane?'

'Not yet, sir. Jackie's still working on it.'

It was more than likely that Jane had moved away from home, maybe even married and had kids of her own. But if she was an illegitimate child, had Angus McQueen stepped up and taken her on as his own daughter? Some men might find that hard to swallow.

'Text me Gina's address and phone number, and I'll give her a call.'

'Will do, sir.'

He was about to hang up, when he said, 'I have a vague memory of Morar being some village on the west coast. What's the closest town?'

'It's about three miles south of Mallaig, sir.'

Ice brushed Gilchrist's spine. The outskirts of Mallaig was where Hector Dunmore's Land Rover had been abandoned twenty-five years earlier. The name Milne wouldn't have registered on anyone's radar back then, because Gina had changed her name to McQueen. But if Duncan Milne had abandoned Hector's Land Rover, he only had a three-mile walk to his daughter's home, where he could lie low until the search for Hector was abandoned.

Bloody hell, it was all beginning to slot into place.

CHAPTER 40

When Jessie handed him his coffee, she said, 'I forgot to tell you, but I ran a check on Dunmore's precious shotguns, and they're all licensed, even if they are only for display. But you'll never guess. She once had licences for four handguns.'

'Which would've been turned in after Dunblane. Right?'

'I guess so.'

Gilchrist gave that some thought. After the Dunblane Primary School massacre in 1996, over one hundred and sixty thousand handguns were surrendered to the police under new legislation that banned private ownership of handguns. Of course, if you hadn't licensed your handgun in the first place, you might not want to turn it in – which might explain why so many guns were still on the street. Still, if Dunmore's handguns had indeed been licensed, she would have been legally compelled to surrender them.

He took a sip of his coffee, then said, 'I'm about to give Gina McQueen a call.'

'It's a bit early, is it not?'

'Might be an early riser.' He pulled into traffic as the call was connected.

After a couple of rings a man's rough voice, said, 'Who's this?'

'Angus McQueen?' Gilchrist said.

'Aye.'

'Is your wife, Gina, available?'

'Who wants to speak to her?'

'DCI Gilchrist of St Andrews CID.'

Silence for a couple of beats, then, 'What d'you want to speak to her about?'

He glanced at Jessie, who shook her head. Angus might know nothing about Gina's illegitimate child, so he had to tread with care. 'It's a personal matter,' he said. 'Is she available? We won't keep her.'

'Aye, well, let me go and get her then.'

The phone clattered as if it had been dropped into a bin. In the background they could hear him calling out to his wife in a gruff manner. Somewhere a door closed, then a woman's voice shouted out. The sound of footsteps, then some more clattering.

'Hello?'

'Gina McQueen?'

'Yes?'

'Formerly Gina Milne?'

A pause, then, 'Yes?' A bit unsure of herself.

Gilchrist introduced himself and told her that he had DS Janes on speaker.

'Good morning, Gina,' Jessie said.

'Good morning.' She seemed cheered by Jessie's upbeat tone.

'We're looking for your help,' Jessie said. 'If you can.'

'What about?'

'We're trying to locate Jane McEntegart Milne, and we were hoping you could give us an address for her. Or a telephone number, perhaps.'

'Oh . . . oh . . .' she said, her voice high as if distressed. 'I don't think I can do that.'

'Why not?' Jessie asked.

'I can't . . . it's not . . . I . . . I . . . just can't.'

'We have a copy of her birth certificate,' Gilchrist said.

Silence.

'And the father's name's not on it.' He listened to the electronic hiss of silence, then pressed on. 'I need to know who the father is, Gina. It's important.'

But Gina had lost her voice, or was about to hang up.

Jessie leaned forward, and said, 'Gina, we wouldn't want you to get into any trouble with your husband if he doesn't know anything about Jane. If you haven't told him about her, I mean.'

'No . . . no . . . yes . . . no, I see.'

'But if you don't know where Jane is, or you don't want to tell us, that's okay,' she said. 'We don't need to know. But it would be helpful if you told us who the father is.'

Silence.

'You do know who the father is, don't you?' Jessie said.

Gilchrist felt himself cringe – one second nice and gentle, the next in with the toe-capped boot.

'Of course, I do,' Gina said. 'What're you implying?'

'I'm only making sure that you know the father's name, so that when we come out to your home in Morar to have a chat with you, you'll be able to—'

'No,' she said. 'You can't do that.'

Gilchrist caught her sense of panic, but Jessie said, 'We can, Gina. And we will.'

Gilchrist decided to step in. 'Would it be easier, Gina, if we met some place away from Morar? Say, Mallaig Police Station? Or some other place of your choosing?'

It took a couple of beats before she said, 'I'm driving to Fort William tomorrow, to the library.'

'We can't wait until tomorrow,' he said. 'We need to meet today.'

'Well . . . I . . . I suppose I could go there today.'

'We'll be coming from Perth. So it would take us some time to drive there. How about one o'clock?'

'The library shuts at one on a Saturday.'

'We could make it for twelve-thirty?'

Again, some hesitation, as if she was trying to work out how she could drive to Fort William without her husband knowing. 'Okay,' she said at length. 'I'll see you then.'

The line died.

Jessie looked at Gilchrist, and raised her eyebrows. 'Is she shitting it, or what?'

'I expect her husband doesn't know about her illegitimate child.'

'I didn't like him,' Jessie said. 'Too authoritarian for me.'

'Authoritarian?'

'And as rough as a badger's arse.'

'Having never touched a badger's arse, I'm afraid you've got me there.'

Jessie chuckled for a moment, then her face turned serious. 'D'you think she might've been raped? That'd definitely be something she wouldn't want to share with her husband.'

'That's a possibility. But there could be any number of reasons for her husband not knowing, if indeed he doesn't know.'

'Of course he doesn't know. That's what the caginess was all about.'

Well, he wasn't going to argue with her over that. Over the years, he'd met some well-to-do women who sounded and looked as if they'd been steeped in money from the day they were born – silver spoon in mouth, and all that. But the secret many carried throughout their lives told a different story, a story of tough upbringings, of sexual abuse, of incest and rape, and oftentimes worse – having to do whatever they had to do to pay the bills. So what if Gina kept the secret of her illegitimate child from her husband. It was her life, and she was entitled to live it the best way she could. He just hoped that when she finally spoke to them, that her past was nowhere near as bad as some of the other women he'd come across.

He set his cruise control at seventy-five, and drove on towards Dunmore Lodge.

They arrived at the lochside before 7.45 a.m., the Dive and Marine Unit's Dragon lights lighting up the scene like some witches' party. The sun wouldn't rise for another forty-five minutes, and the grass pathway crackled with frost underfoot as they picked their way to the water's edge where a man-sized bundle lay on the ground wrapped in black plastic bin liner. Duct tape that had held the package together had been sliced open and pulled apart to reveal the bloated body of a naked man lying on his back, alabaster skin blue with decay where putrefaction had already set in.

Karen Gardner nodded to them as they approached, and held up Mhairi's headshot photo of Caithness. 'I'd say he's your man.'

Gilchrist pulled on a pair of latex gloves, and crouched down by the body. That close, the corpse gave off an unpleasant whiff of rotting flesh, which almost had him gagging.

Jessie joined him. 'You think you'd get used to it,' she said. 'But you never do.'

He placed a hand to his nose, cocked his head for a better angle, and studied the dead man's face. He'd seen enough images of Caithness over the past week to recognise that here he was indeed, dead and dumped in a loch, and now brought back to dry land.

The body showed no signs of distress, although the swelling of the stomach suggested that putrefaction was well under way on its inners. As if to prove that point, Jessie took hold of the body's right hand, which stirred the corpse, and a rotten guff wafted into the air.

Gilchrist pushed to his feet, and walked off, sucking in fresh air.

Jessie seemed oblivious, and was examining the body's fingers with care.

Gilchrist caught up with Gardner. 'It's Caithness,' he said, and stared over the loch, inhaling clean, country air. A marker buoy with a white light floated on the surface. 'Is that where you found it?'

'Yes, sir.'

One thing troubled him – other than the fact that they'd recovered a man's body from the loch – that without the corpse being weighted down in some fashion, it could have floated to the surface eventually, due to the build-up of gases of putrefaction. In earlier times, when bodies were dumped in deep waters, the disposer often sliced the stomach, removed the guts, and inserted a heavy rock into the stomach cavity to ensure the body could not resurface.

'The body's a week old,' he said. 'It could've floated to the surface given time.'

300

Gardner shook her head. 'Over here, sir.'

He followed her to the back of the Unit's Transit van, where she opened the rear door. 'This was wrapped around it.'

Gilchrist took hold of an anchor with a length of chain threaded through a number of circular weights – ten in total – the kind used as dumbbells. A quick calculation put the overall weight in the order of 60 kilogrammes. Caithness's body was never intended to be seen again.

'We had to unthread the weights before we could bring him to the surface. Another reason why it took us so long to bring the body ashore, sir.'

Gilchrist nodded. The divers would likely have had to carry the weights to the surface one at a time, too. He looked up at the sound of footsteps approaching through the gloom, and recognised Cooper as she headed straight for the body, pulling on latex gloves.

He excused himself from Gardner.

Without introduction, he said, 'No markings anywhere that I can see. So I'm keen to know cause of death.'

'You always are,' she said.

Jessie said, 'A couple of broken fingernails on the right hand, but that's about it.'

'Thanks for your detailed report,' Cooper said, granting her a thin smile.

Jessie drilled her with a dark look, then walked away.

'She's an excellent detective,' Gilchrist said. 'You shouldn't be so offhand.'

'I'll try to remember that next time.' She leaned forward and turned Caithness's head so that it was facing her. Then she pried open the eyelids, shone a torch into each eye, and closed them.

She inspected both nostrils by torchlight, pushed her fingers into the mouth to open it.

'Anything?' he said.

'He didn't drown.'

'So he was dead before being dumped in the loch?'

'I'd say so. But I'll know for sure once I carry out the PM.'

'You see anything that might suggest cause of death?'

She ignored him as she pressed down on the tongue and thrust her fingers as far into his throat as she could, as if she were trying to force the body to gag – something Gilchrist was struggling to avoid doing. Then, seemingly satisfied, she turned her attention to the neck and throat, pressing her hand into the skin, working her way down and over the chest to the bloated stomach. A gentle touch was all that was needed to cause a rift of flatulence, which could have been a mild waft of perfume for all the consideration Cooper was giving it.

'Anything?' he asked again.

'Impatience is your biggest failing, Andy. You need to learn to curb it.'

He thought of mentioning he was about to interview Fraser Lindsay that afternoon, and it would be good to know cause of death before doing so. But when she rolled the body onto its side, and reached for her thermometer, he knew it was time to leave. 'Get back to me as soon as you can,' he said.

'Don't I always?'

But he wasn't listening, more intent on distancing himself from the rotting stench. He found Jessie with Gardner, who handed him a packet of Polo mints. 'These'll help, sir.'

'Just what the doctor ordered.' He popped two into his mouth.

'Would you like us to continue searching the loch, sir?'

Having now recovered Caithness's body, he found himself struggling to answer her. Two bodies recovered, one unexpected, so perhaps there was every reason to continue with the search. Of course, the cost of resources was always a touchy subject, and with the added attention being drawn to Dunmore Loch due to Scottish Stretch, maybe it was best to pack up and head home.

'Considering only that area close to the middle of the loch I showed you,' he said, 'how long would it take you to complete it?'

'Couple of days, sir, provided we don't find any more bodies.'

For all anyone knew, the loch could have been a dumping ground for the Dunmore family through generations. But as it stood, he knew he was pushing it to the limit. Still, it wouldn't be the first time he'd butted heads with the hierarchy. 'Give it another day,' he said, 'then get back to me. We've got a suspect in custody, and how he responds to some serious interrogation might make me decide to drain the whole bloody thing if we have to.'

Gardner feigned shock, and chuckled. 'Will do, sir.' Then she strode off to her team, and ordered them into action.

'Find anything else on the body?' he asked Jessie.

'I can't stand that stuck-up bitch,' Jessie said. 'And what's with the new hairdo?'

'That aside,' he said.

'No defensive wounds, and no bruises or cuts that I could see. I'd be betting on a drug overdose – sleeping pills, painkillers, something like that. Easy to administer when you're not looking, or had a few wines too many.'

Gilchrist felt inclined to agree. He looked at Cooper who was running her hands down Caithness's legs, squeezing the calf muscles as if checking for cramp. Despite her haughty manner, Cooper was excellent at what she did, and he knew she would get back to him as soon as she had answers.

In the meantime, he needed to check something out at the Lodge.

CHAPTER 41

The door to the wooden shed was unlocked, but sealed with police tape.

Gilchrist eased up the tape, opened the door without breaking the seal, and squeezed inside. He switched on the light, and closed the door behind him, once again struck by how quiet and dry it was inside. He ran his eyes along both sides of the shed, trying to remember what had been stored there when he'd first entered, but having a sense that nothing was missing. It all looked in order.

What he did suspect was missing, or to be more correct, what he now realised that he hadn't seen on his earlier inspection, was a boat's anchor. No matter how small the boat, out on the loch you would want to anchor it if you were going to do a spot of fishing. Of course, Dunmore Loch was going to prohibit fishing once Scottish Stretch was approved, so maybe it was a moot point. But still, you would have an anchor in the boat whether or not you needed it. At least, that's what Gilchrist would expect if the boat was his.

He peeled back the boat's tarpaulin, let it drop to the concrete floor like an oversized blanket. The sweet smell of oil rose off the

305

wood as if it had been varnished the day before. He pulled himself up and over and into the boat, which barely rocked on the trailer's stiff suspension. He eased back seat covers either side, but found nothing. He did the same with a loose panel under the transom, but that space was empty, too. These were the only storage spaces he could find on board and he leaped back over the side, and took care to replace the heavy tarpaulin.

Next, he checked the cupboards and shelves at the end of the storage shed, but again found nothing. If Dunmore Lodge had a boat laid up in the boatshed, it definitely didn't have an anchor assigned to it. He wasn't sure how the SOCOs could match the chain and anchor that had secured Caithness's body to that of the boat, but he felt confident they might find evidence of the dumbbell weights having come from Fraser Lindsay's home.

On his way back to the lochside to collect Jessie, he phoned Mhairi again.

'Anything new?' he asked.

'We're still working on it, sir.'

Well, what had he expected? He'd hoped that they might uncover something that would avoid the need to drive to Fort William and meet with Gina McQueen.

But now it seemed that Gina could be key.

Fort William Library was an unattractive one-storey building at the end of the town shopping centre accessed by a pedestrianised walkway. Grey cobblestones inset in a series of fan-like patterns spread away from a slabbed pavement. Shrubs and bushes in the Parade – an expansive grass area that overlooked the refurbished street – had been trimmed for the winter months. Outside the library, a solitary ski-lift cable car dangled from a steel pole as if to ward off evil mountain spirits.

Inside, the library was like most other council concerns whose budgets had been cut to the core by a belt-tightening government. Space that had once housed shelves of books had been replaced by shelves on wheels, a cafeteria, tables, chairs. Natural sunlight brightened the space through a glass-panelled roof.

Jessie and Gilchrist found Gina McQueen seated by herself, sipping a coffee, leafing through a magazine. She almost jumped to attention when she saw Gilchrist and Jessie bearing down on her – police the world over are easy to spot.

She slapped her magazine onto the table as Gilchrist approached, as if to suggest they should move to another place in the library for their meeting.

'Here's fine,' he said, giving her a brief glimpse of his warrant card. He pulled a soft-backed chair out, and sat. Jessie did likewise. The library wasn't busy, but public spaces were not the best place in which to convene an interview. He said nothing while Jessie removed her notebook and pen from her pocket, then pressed the pages flat.

Just that action had Gina fingering her throat, only to end up clutching a crucifix necklace. 'I didn't expect you would take notes.'

'In case we forget anything,' Jessie said.

'Oh . . .'

'Is there a problem?' Gilchrist said.

'Well . . . I . . .'

'It's much less formal than having you travel all the way to the St Andrews Office for a recorded interview.' He kept his tone light, his smile in place. It was important they gained Gina's trust.

After all, they were about to confront her with personal – and possibly intimate – questions about her illegitimate daughter, questions she probably never imagined she would be asked. Softly-softly was a good way to start. Then he eased into it with, 'Did you tell your husband, Angus, that you're meeting us?'

Her lips whitened as she shook her head. 'No.'

'I see,' he said. 'So we'll do what we can to keep him out of it. Okay?'

She tried a smile, fingers at the crucifix.

'We have to ask,' he went on, 'but are we correct in understanding that Angus doesn't know about your daughter, Jane?'

'Yes.'

'And that you don't want him to find out—'

'Oh, dear God, no, he mustn't, he mustn't find out.'

'That's all right. What you tell us today will remain between us.' He wasn't sure if he could do that – depending on what this interview uncovered – but he had to start somewhere. He reclined in his chair. 'Why don't you tell us what happened? From the start.'

She closed her eyes and pressed both hands to her chest as if to catch her breath. But he saw she was giving a silent prayer to God – for the strength to tell the truth? For divine guidance on how to keep her long-held secret from her husband? Or perhaps how to tell a convincing lie? Who could tell?

Then she opened her eyes. 'I was fifteen,' she said, her voice low and whispery. 'Just turned fifteen.' As if that made any difference. 'My dad got me a weekend job.'

'Your father. Duncan Milne?' he said, to avoid any misunderstanding.

She nodded. 'He got me this job in Gleneden Distillery, serving in the shop, cleaning the floors, dusting the shelves and the display cabinets, all the simple stuff that anybody can do. I was still at school, so it was a blessing to earn some money.' She stared at the table for a moment. 'I never had any money before that. My parents didn't want to spoil me.'

'When you served in the shop,' Jessie interrupted, 'did you sell bottles of whisky?'

'Yes.'

'You have to be eighteen to serve alcohol in Scotland. So that's a lie.'

'It's not a lie,' Gina said. 'They knew how old I was, but I was big for my age.'

'You don't look that big.'

'No, not that type of big. You know, I had big . . . you know . . .'

'Big tits?' Jessie stared hard at her.

Gilchrist helped out with, 'You're saying you looked older than fifteen?'

'Aye, I did. Much older.'

He smiled. 'Keep going.'

'The job started off with Saturday mornings, four hours only. Sometimes I'd finish by ten o'clock, and they'd let me go home early, and still pay me for four hours.'

'Why would they do that?' Jessie again.

'Because of my dad. He was friendly with Mr Dunmore.'

Gilchrist glanced at Jessie at the first mention of the family name. 'Was that Edwin Dunmore, the owner of the Distillery?' he asked, again to avoid any doubt.

'Aye.'

'And if you were working for a couple of hours and being paid for four, did you think Mr Dunmore hired you just so you would have some pocket money?'

'I think so, aye. There was never much to do.'

'You said the job started *off* with Saturday mornings. Did it progress beyond that?'

'Aye, it did. After a couple of months, Mr Dunmore asked if I wanted to come in on Sundays for a couple of hours. He said my dad told him that I was good at school, and he'd like me to help him with keeping the books. He said of all the jobs in the whisky business, book-keeping was the one he disliked the most.'

'Didn't he already have a book-keeper?' Jessie said.

'He said she'd left for another job and that he was a couple of weeks behind.'

Gilchrist knew with dreadful certainty where this was going. 'So after working in the shop on Saturday mornings, you worked in Mr Dunmore's office on Sundays.'

'Aye. But only after midday mass.'

'And you worked alone with Mr Dunmore?'

She hung her head.

He didn't need the details, just the end result. 'And during your Sunday work in Mr Dunmore's office, did he make any . . . any unwanted advances towards you?'

'He did, aye.'

'Of a sexual nature?'

Again, she nodded.

'And in the end . . . did you fall pregnant?'

Gina closed her eyes, squeezing out tears that spilled down her cheek.

Jessie rummaged in her pockets, and removed a crumpled tissue. 'Here,' she said. 'It's not been used.'

Gina dabbed her eyes, ran it under her nose, then crushed it in her hand. 'I'm sorry,' she said. 'I haven't thought about it all these years. I've confessed my sin I don't know how many times, but it doesn't make any difference. I still feel so much guilt.'

Gilchrist felt his heart go out to her. Here was a woman who'd been sexually abused as a fifteen-year-old child, taken advantage of by a perverted employer under the pretence of work. And after all these years, she still felt shame and guilt, even though she had nothing to feel shameful or guilty about. Of course, this was the hallmark of paedophiles, their ability to turn the tables, shift the blame, make the person they'd raped or abused feel as if it was their fault – if only they'd put up greater resistance; if only they'd been more firm in their voice. For a God-fearing fifteen-year-old girl, the mental strength or the wherewithal to withstand the sexual advances of an adult man of seemingly good standing, a successful businessman, no less, no doubt a pillar of the local community, her employer who was giving her a job for pocket money, would be beyond her—

'Did your father know you were pregnant?' Jessie asked.

'Not at first.'

'Until you started to show?'

'Aye.'

'Then what happened?'

'I was taken out of school, and sent away to a convent to have the child.'

The child. Not *my* child. But Gilchrist caught Jessie's eye, and nodded. Convent of Holy Hope was noted on the birth certificate as place of birth. 'Did you report Mr Dunmore to the police?' he asked.

Her head jerked with surprise. Fear flashed behind her eyes. 'I would never do that,' she said. 'No one knew he was the father.'

'What?' Jessie again.

'He made me swear,' she said. 'Swear on the Bible that I wouldn't tell anyone, that I would blame it on some boy I'd met in town, and that I didn't know his name.'

'Did your father not report *that* to the police?'

'Mum didn't want him to. She said once it was reported to the police, everyone would know. And what would the neighbours think? It was more than she could stand.'

'So you went ahead and had the child in the convent,' Gilchrist said.

'Aye.'

'And nobody knew about it? Not even any of your friends?'

'No.'

'You must have felt so lonely,' he said.

'I've never felt so alone in all my life. It was awful. And the nuns weren't kind. They said I would burn in hell for infinity for what I'd done.' She gave an involuntary sob, and said, 'One nun, I'll never forget her, Mother Helen, she was, she asked if I knew what infinity was, and I said I did, because we learned it in maths in school. But she told me to imagine one grain of sand as being the longest time ever, and if I multiplied that by every other grain of sand on every beach in every country in the world, that was what infinity was. I was utterly terrified.'

Gilchrist shook his head. Well done, Catholicism. Divine devotion drilled into young minds by the fear of God, or in this case, Hell.

'So after you gave birth,' Jessie said. 'What happened?'

Gina closed her eyes again, fingers clutching the crucifix as if her life depended on it. 'I had no say in the matter. My parents were adamant about that. I was told I couldn't keep the child, that I would have to give her up.'

'So you knew you had a daughter,' Gilchrist said.

'I looked after her for almost four weeks.' She stared at him through tear-filled eyes, an almost beatific look on her face. 'She was the most beautiful baby I've ever seen.'

Gilchrist knew that in that time the bond between mother and daughter would have grown. Losing her daughter then must have been heart-breaking, unbearable.

'Then two nuns came to my room and told me it was time.' Her voice dropped to a whisper. Tears trailed down her cheeks. 'I begged them not to take my baby. But they wouldn't listen. It was God's will, they said. I cried and shouted and wouldn't let her go, but it was no use. I tried to hold onto her, I tried. But I . . . I just couldn't . . .'

Silent, Gilchrist and Jessie gave her time to recover.

When he thought she had, Gilchrist said, 'Did you ever see your daughter again?'

'No.'

'Do you know who adopted her?'

She shook her head. 'No.'

'Who gave her the name Jane McEntegart Milne?'

'I did. McEntegart was my mother's maiden name.'

'And Jane?'

'After my grandmother.'

Gilchrist pushed his chair back. There wasn't much more Gina could tell them. She'd given birth to her daughter, who'd then been taken away from her and adopted, so there was nothing to be gained by searching for the adoptive parents. It seemed that all the hopes he'd pinned on that avenue had slipped away. But if it all meant nothing, why had Hector secreted the birth certificate in Molly Havet's writing bureau? It made no sense.

But there had to be a reason for Hector doing that.

There just had to be.

'Did you ever try to find your daughter again?' he asked.

'No. Never. It's best that I leave well alone. All I know is that she's living a better life than I could ever have given her.'

Gilchrist frowned. 'How do you know that?'

'Because I looked out the window.'

'I don't understand,' he said, even as the tumblers of his mind fell into place.

'I wanted to have just one last look as she was carried away. I couldn't see who they were, but they drove off in a big expensive car.' She smiled at that memory. 'So I know she would have had a better life with them, than she would ever have had with me.' She stretched her lips into a pained smile.

'And that's how I want to remember her.'

CHAPTER 42

On the drive back from Fort William, Gilchrist phoned Cooper. 'Have you been able to identify the cause of death?'

Cooper let out a heavy sigh, as if exhausted by his persistence. 'Despite the body being wrapped in plastic and weighted down with an anchor chain, I can't rule out the possibility of drowning . . .'

Gilchrist shook his head at the hopelessness of it all, and the unimaginable cruelty of humankind. Only once in his career had he come across a body pulled from the sea, hands and feet tied, and covered from head to toe in hessian sacking. Old Bert Mackie, the forensic pathologist at the time, had confirmed that the poor soul had been alive and in good health when he'd been hogtied, sacked, and thrown overboard to drown—

'Because of the length of time the body was submerged – ten days you estimate. No froth in the mouth or nostrils, usually the most obvious sign of death by drowning. No water in the respiratory bronchioles and alveoli, which would normally indicate body immersion as opposed to body *sub*mersion, meaning that he was dead before he was put into the loch.'

'Normally?' he asked.

Cooper chuckled. 'You never miss a trick, do you?'

'Go on.'

'At this time of year, with water temperatures close to freezing, being immersed while still alive could cause cardiac reflex arrest, and death from laryngospasm without actually aspirating any fluids.'

'So what're you saying? That he wasn't dead when he was dumped in the loch?'

'I'm saying that he *appears* not to have drowned, but until I receive the biochemical and toxicology results, I can't say with certainty that he did not die by drowning.'

'But you're ninety-nine per cent sure.'

'Oh, for God's sake, Andy. If it's any consolation, I've requested these tests to be treated with the utmost urgency.'

'Okay, Becky. Thanks for that.'

She tutted, and hung up.

'Doesn't suffer fools, does she?' Jessie said.

'Are you saying I'm a fool?'

'In Queen Becky's eyes, most of us are fools.'

Well, there he had it, his own thoughts on Cooper's imperious manner confirmed.

8.12 p.m., Saturday
Glenrothes Police Station

Rather than wait until the following morning, Gilchrist decided to interview Fraser Lindsay that night. When he entered the interview room, Jessie was already seated there, tape recorder in place, notebook opened on the table, Lindsay opposite. Where he'd expected Peter White to represent Lindsay, he was surprised to find a gaunt-faced woman seated next to him, who looked old enough to be his mother. Her shock of unruly hair was so white it could have been dipped in emulsion. The stench of cigarette ash that hung around her had Gilchrist clearing his throat and wondering what on earth he'd ever found pleasing about smoking.

She glanced up as he entered, and slid a card across the table. 'Maggie Barden,' she said, as if that explained all.

Gilchrist eyed the card – Margaret Barden LLB of Margaret K. Barden & Associates, with an office in George Street, Edinburgh. He'd somehow expected the law firm of White De Bouchier to use all of its collective legal muscle to represent both Lindsay and Dunmore, but now Peter White was out of the picture, Gilchrist sensed a seismic shift in party interests – a conflict between Dunmore and Lindsay? – which could work to his advantage. Where he'd once seen the difficulty being White consolidating defence arguments for Lindsay *and* Dunmore, he now sensed an opportunity. If he'd read the situation correctly, and a falling out had indeed taken place, then this interview with Lindsay could be crucial to the successful interrogation of Katherine Dunmore.

Barden wore a navy-blue jacket several sizes too large for her bony shoulders. A blue blouse opened far too deep at the neck revealed scrawny cleavage wrinkled and tanned. Dark shadows under bloodshot eyes spoke of too much work and not enough sleep.

Gilchrist took his seat, and Jessie introduced everyone present, noting date and time of interview. Then she sat back to let Gilchrist take over. He placed both hands on the table, looked

Lindsay in the eye, and reminded him – for the record – that he'd been arrested under Section 14 of the Criminal Justice Scotland Act and charged with complicity in the murder of George Caithness.

'Before we begin the interview,' he added, 'is there anything you'd like to say?'

Lindsay glanced at Barden, who nodded. 'My client is asking for all charges to be dropped in exchange for his turning witness for the Crown.'

Gilchrist smiled inwardly. He'd been correct. It would be up to the Crown Office or Procurator Fiscal to make that call, of course, but for the time being, he would be happy to play along, see what was on offer.

Barden pushed a single sheet of paper across the table to him, and another to Jessie. 'My client's statement,' she said, 'which confirms that he was not complicit in George Caithness's murder—'

'Of course, he wasn't,' Jessie snapped. 'Prisons the length and breadth of the country are filled with prisoners who . . .' She clawed the air. '. . . didn't do it.'

Barden fixed a red-rimmed gaze on Jessie with an intensity that warned Gilchrist to tread with care. 'If you take the time to read my client's statement,' she said, 'you'll see that my client admits only to knowing about the disposal of the body, and that the only crime he's committed was in not reporting what he knew to the police.'

'That makes him an accomplice,' Jessie said.

'Arguably. Hence the request for all charges to be dropped in an exchange.'

'And tell me, why would we believe him now?'

'Because my client is here to tell the truth.'

'Or to save his own arse.'

Gilchrist stepped in. 'You're asking for a lot.'

Barden's thin lips parted to reveal grey teeth in an imitation of a smile that failed to materialise. 'If you want to prosecute Katherine Dunmore to the full extent of the law, I would urge you to listen to what my client has to say.'

Gilchrist most certainly did want to nail Dunmore to the criminal mast, but not at the expense of letting another killer walk free. 'We would need evidence,' he said. 'Evidence that would stand up in a court of law.'

Barden nodded, then turned to Lindsay. 'Tell him.'

Lindsay took a deep breath, and said, 'I've known Kate Dunmore as long as anyone. I probably know her *better* than anyone. And one thing I can tell you about Kate is that she's cruel. She uses people for her own needs. She's done so all of her life. I first met her when I was ten. Her family would spend a couple of months every summer in Dunmore Lodge. Many weekends, too. And always Christmas and New Year.'

'How do you know that?' Jessie again. 'She tell you?'

'My father used to run the estate until he passed away. Then I took over.'

'Keep going,' Gilchrist said.

'I was ages with Kate. At first I thought she was really nice. Her brother, Hector, too. But Kate had a real wicked side to her.' He narrowed his eyes, fixed his gaze on something beyond the confines of the room. 'I'll give you an example. When we were kids, the Lodge was home to families of cats that roamed around the place, never real pets, but never wild either. But they were really useful for keeping vermin under control.' He closed his eyes for a moment, and when he opened them, said, 'One time, one of the cats had a litter of ten kittens, and Kate and I would play with them and feed them scraps.

'Well, one morning, I arrived at the Lodge. It was the day after a family barbecue, and Kate had lit a fire in the barbecue pit, and was stoking it with twigs and branches and dousing it with lighter fluid. At first I thought she was preparing another barbecue, until I heard the screams.' Lindsay stared at Jessie, and gave a dead-eyed smile. 'Have you ever heard kittens scream?'

'And the point of this story is . . .?' Jessie said.

'Cruelty to animals is one of the three traits that define psychopathy.'

Jessie leaned forward. 'You were a sniper in the Army.'

Lindsay frowned.

'Have you ever seen someone's head exploding? Bits of brain and bone everywhere.' She sat back. 'Why don't you cut the poor me from the story? Kate this, Kate that. I'll tell you what I think. I think you're every bit a murdering psychopath as she is. And if you think this poor-me spiel is going to get you off the hook, you'd better think again.' She slapped her hands on the table. 'Are we done here?'

Gilchrist shrugged his shoulders at Barden. 'DS Janes has a point.'

Barden was reading her notes, as if she was detached from what was happening in the interview. Then she looked at Gilchrist. 'My client was giving an insight into the mindset of Katherine Dunmore, a woman he has known closely—'

'Try intimately,' Jessie said.

Barden flickered a dry smile, then pressed on. 'A woman he has known closely for some forty years.'

320

'And for twenty of these forty years, your client was a sniper in the SAS,' Jessie said, then folded her arms, and glared at him.

'We kept in touch over the years,' Lindsay said.

'An on-again-off-again relationship? That kind of thing?'

'You could say.'

'I just did.' Jessie smirked for a moment, then said, 'So just how close were the two of you? Screwing each other senseless every time you came back on leave?'

'I have to object,' Barden interrupted. 'My client's personal—'

'Object all you like,' Jessie snapped. 'But if your client's jerking us about, he can kiss goodbye to any kind of deal.' She cocked her head at Lindsay. 'Well?'

Lindsay wrung his hands, and nodded. 'Yes,' he said. 'I would often come back on leave, and Kate and I would have . . . would have an intense relationship.'

'Oh I'm sure you did,' Jessie quipped.

Gilchrist and Jessie had discussed their interview strategy, with Jessie trying to rile Lindsay into saying something he might not otherwise say. But that was before he knew that White De Bouchier were no longer involved. He lifted a hand from the table, only an inch or so, a subtle signal to Jessie to rein it in, let him proceed until further notice.

'Okay,' he said. 'Let's say that we know Katherine Dunmore is as cruel as you say she is, and has mental health issues, even that she's a full-blown psychopath. What evidence can your client provide that would justify granting him immunity from prosecution?'

Barden eyed Lindsay over imaginary spectacles, a silent instruction to get on with it.

'Robbie Marsh,' Lindsay said.

'Excuse me?' Gilchrist said, the name fluttering in the confusion of his memory.

'Current manager of Gleneden Distillery?' Jessie said. 'That Robbie Marsh?'

'Yes.'

'And . . .?'

Lindsay almost smiled. His chest swelled as if with pride. 'Every police force in Scotland and beyond has been looking for George Caithness for over a week—'

'No thanks to you,' Jessie snapped.

Gilchrist raised his hand off the table again, and cocked his head in the smallest of instructions to quit interrupting. 'Keep going.'

'And you've been reviewing CCTV footage about town and everywhere else, trying to track his last movements before he disappeared. Right?'

Gilchrist said nothing. You didn't have to be an investigative expert to know that's what they'd been doing. It was standard operating procedure, and CCTV footage of George Caithness on one of his daily trips to Tesco and Starbucks in St Andrews had been posted on national television for days. Of course, with Caithness bagged and anchored thirty-feet deep at the bottom of Dunmore Loch, Gilchrist thought he knew what was coming.

He was not disappointed.

'Robbie Marsh played the part of George Caithness for five days,' Lindsay said.

'Why would he do that?'

'Because he knew he was already dead.'

'That doesn't explain why he played George's part for five days.'

322

'Because he was going to get a chunk of money for doing that.'

'And how do you know all this?'

'Kate told me.'

'And you believed her?'

'Yes.'

Gilchrist stared at Lindsay, as if seeing him for the first time – a man who could lie in wait for hours on end, hidden, camouflaged, in perfect stillness, long-range sniper rifle loaded and primed, waiting for just that right moment to squeeze the trigger and take someone's life. And here he was, trying to wriggle out of being charged as an accomplice in the murder of an innocent man, by pointing the finger of blame at someone else.

That is, if Gilchrist believed what he was being told, that Lindsay only knew about the disposal of Dunmore's body in the loch. But if you believed that Lindsay participated in the disposal of the body, where did that put you? And why would he now implicate Marsh, when it might be the simplest thing for Marsh to do likewise with Lindsay? To add credence to his claim that Katherine Dunmore *used* people for her own needs? Gilchrist didn't think so. But there was another possibility, which he was only now beginning to contemplate.

He focused all of his attention on Lindsay, and asked a question that took care of a quantum leap in logic. 'If Robbie knew that Caithness was dead, did he know where the body had been dumped?'

Lindsay smiled. 'He dumped it.'

Gilchrist almost rocked back from the table. 'So you're saying that you knew Robbie Marsh disposed of George Caithness's body in the loch at Dunmore Lodge?'

'Yes.'

'And you openly admit to that?'

'Yes.'

'Did Robbie Marsh dispose of the body by himself?'

'Yes.'

'I don't believe you.'

Lindsay shook his head, clenched his jaw. 'I didn't dump the body in the loch.'

'Just stood back and did nothing? Just watched it all happen? Over the side . . . plonk . . . and in he went?'

'Well . . .' A nervous glance at Barden for support, or advice. Lindsay might have been a top-notch sniper in the SAS, killing people under licence of the British government, but being an accomplice in the murder of an innocent British citizen, the penalty for which was incarceration at Her Majesty's pleasure, was another thing entirely.

Surprisingly, Barden said, 'In order to make a fair exchange, Fraser, you should tell the truth.' She turned her pained gaze to Gilchrist, held his eyes in a hostile look that asked the question – deal, or no deal?

Perhaps it was Barden's use of the word *truth* that had taken Gilchrist aback – an *honest* solicitor? Had he ever come across one? If he had, he couldn't recall. But he held her look as his mind wrestled with it all. He could always renege later on any deal he cut, but somehow that seemed to go against the grain of Barden's inexplicable attempt at honesty.

He nodded his silent agreement.

Jessie twitched with impatience, or maybe disbelief.

Barden turned to Lindsay. 'Carry on.'

Lindsay stared at his hands on the table, lips pressed into a white scar, as if in one last attempt to prevent the truth from spilling free. Then he looked up, and said, 'I helped with the boat. I provided it, I mean.'

'You drove it from the boatshed, to the loch?' Gilchrist said.

'Yes, sir.'

Lindsay's sudden deference warned Gilchrist that he was about to hear a series of lies. 'And did you take the boat out on the loch?'

'No, sir. I left it by the lochside for Robbie to use.'

'Why?' Gilchrist asked. 'Who told you to do that?'

'Kate.'

'Did you go out on the loch with Robbie?'

'No, sir.'

'Just watched Robbie from afar?'

'Yes, sir.'

'With George Caithness's body in it?'

'Yes, sir.'

'Where did the anchor and chain come from?' Gilchrist knew Lindsay's answer could incriminate him once and for all – if they chose to renege on their deal, that is.

'The boatshed,' Lindsay said.

'And you gave it to Robbie Marsh to wrap around the body?'

'Yes, sir.'

'Did you assist in wrapping the anchor around the body?'

'Hold on, hold on,' Barden interrupted. 'My client has admitted that he brought the boat to the loch, and that the boat had an anchor. I don't think my client would have assisted in wrapping the body in the anchor chain, prior to its disposal in the loch. Nor would he have helped Mr Marsh drop the body into the loch.' She looked at Gilchrist again, eyes bloodshot and raw.

Gilchrist had listened to countless solicitors give sound legal advice to their client, but never before had he heard one direct her client with such specific instruction – putting words into mouths, sprang to mind. 'Well,' he said, 'for the time being let's say that you provided the boat, then witnessed Marsh dump the body into the loch.'

He could sense Jessie's unease at his side.

Christ, if Smiler ever got hold of a recording of this interview, he was in for it. For a moment, he thought of switching it off, then decided that the damage was done, that it was best just to press on. He struggled to gather his thoughts, line up his next question, then came up with one that now seemed to beg to be asked.

'How did Robbie Marsh get to Dunmore Lodge?'

'He hired a van, and drove up.'

'A white Citroën van, from Avis. That the one?'

'Yes, sir.'

Gilchrist smiled. Now they were back on track. 'And where was Katherine Dunmore when all of this was going on?'

'At home. About town. I don't know. Just making sure she had an alibi.'

'But she didn't count on you dobbing her in, did she?'

'No, sir,' he said, and something passed behind his eyes that told Gilchrist there was more to come. Much more.

CHAPTER 43

'Keep going,' Gilchrist said.

'Kate and Hector had an older brother,' Lindsay said.

'Murdo,' Gilchrist said.

'Yes, sir. Murdo.'

Silent, Gilchrist waited.

'Murdo was killed in an accident at the distillery.'

'Crushed to death by a cask of whisky,' Gilchrist said.

'Everyone *thought* it was an accident. But it wasn't. Kate killed him.'

'Do you have proof of that?'

'Kate told me.'

Jessie gasped, then said, 'How do we know you didn't kill him, and you're now trying to pass it on to her?' She leaned forward. 'How did she tell you? Oh, Fraser, my dear friend I've known all these years,' she mocked, 'I've just gone and killed Murdo. I've made it look like an accident. But please don't tell anyone.' She sat back in her chair. 'Get real, for crying out loud.'

Gilchrist waited until he caught Lindsay's eye. 'We can't simply take your word for it. We need proof. Hard evidence. Which I'm assuming you can't provide. Is that correct?'

Lindsay shook his head. 'No, I don't have any evidence. I can only tell you what she told me, how she planned it, and how she did it.'

'So how did she do it?'

'It happened in the old warehouse, where the ageing casks are rolled onto two wooden planks and kept in place by wooden wedges. The larger casks are never stacked higher than two layers. In one way, it's all ramshackle, but in another the casks are left untouched for years, so nothing's going to move them.' Lindsay shrugged, as if it was all so simple. 'She told me that she used a four by two to lever the cask back, just a touch, enough to take the weight off the wedge. Then before its weight settled back onto the wedge, she nudged the wedge closer to the edge. She set it up so that the slightest push would send the cask to the floor. She said she'd told Murdo that one of the casks looked unsafe, that he should have a look at it. When he did, she tapped the wedge, and the cask rolled onto Murdo and crushed him.'

If what Lindsay was telling them was correct, then Katherine Dunmore was one cold-hearted human being. 'How heavy are these casks?' he asked.

'Enough to crush a man to death in an instant,' Lindsay said.

'I was thinking more along the lines of how heavy they were for a young woman to move using only a piece of wood.'

'With the right length of wood for a lever, it would be easy enough to shift the weight off the wedges. After that, you just nudge the wedge forward.'

'Did Katherine have any help?'

'No.'

Gilchrist thought the answer too quick, too definitive, leaving him with the sense that Lindsay was explaining something he'd watched play out. Regardless, without evidence it would be impossible to prove now that Dunmore had murdered her brother. Or even that she had Lindsay as an accomplice. Even so, he made a note to review the accident report again. But if Dunmore, as a young woman – a teenager – had the guile and the wherewithal to kill her older brother and make it look like an accident, the next question was obvious.

'Did Katherine kill Hector?'

'I don't think so,' Lindsay said. 'She never told me anything about that.'

Which was what he'd expected. She might have been able to use a length of wood to lever casks off wooden wedges, but removing and replacing metal hoops on an ageing cask would require the skill and expertise of someone in the business – the perfect candidate being the late Duncan Milne, former cooper and distillery manager at the time.

But that still left the question of why? Why would Duncan Milne, a devout Catholic and a man of modest means in a salaried position of responsibility, murder Hector Dunmore then stuff his body into a whisky cask? What was his motive? And again the questions – did someone assist him in Hector's murder, and if so, who? – remained just as troubling. Cooper's confirmation that the DNA of the child's skeletal remains pulled from Dunmore Loch put Hector Dunmore as the indisputable father. Was the solution to the entire puzzle the answer to the question – who was the child's mother? He scribbled a note to phone Cooper after Lindsay's interview.

'When Hector disappeared,' he said, 'how did Katherine take it?'

'By that time, I'd joined the Army, so I don't know.'

Jessie said, 'Thought you kept in contact with her all these years.'

'Only when I was back in the country.'

Gilchrist needed to steer the interview back to the focal point – who murdered George Caithness? And why? 'Let's go back to this van,' he said, 'and the delivery of the body to the lochside.' He kept his eyes on Lindsay. 'Did Robbie Marsh kill George Caithness?'

Lindsay frowned. 'No. Kate did. She said George had a prescription for sleeping pills, and that she must have slipped one too many into his drink. She said it was an accident.'

'An *accident*?' Jessie slapped both hands on the table. 'Does she think our heads zip up the back?' She hissed something that could have been a curse, then said, 'She knew fine well what she was doing. Murdering poor old hubby George so she didn't have to give him half of everything in a divorce.'

Gilchrist decided to slip in a change of tack. 'How do you know Toni McManus?'

'I don't.'

'Your mobile records show a call to her around midnight from Longforgan.'

'That was Kate. She asked to use my phone.'

'So you gave it to her, and she called McManus?'

'Yes.'

Which helped show that Katherine Dunmore was a master at covering her tracks before she'd even set off – a phone call here, a car hire there, each simple act distancing herself, bit by innocent bit, from direct implication in any criminal activity.

'What about Edwin Dunmore?' Gilchrist tried. 'What can you tell us about him?'

'He could be pretty scary. He never looked happy, always seemed to be in a mood.'

'Any reason for that? I mean he had a flourishing whisky business, a Highland estate, acres of land, big house. He must've been raking it in. Why would he never look happy?'

Lindsay's eyes narrowed, as if at the recall of some distant memory. 'I don't think he got on well with his wife.'

Jessie tutted, pushed back her chair. 'I need a breath of fresh air from all this shite.'

Gilchrist noted the time of Jessie's departure for the record, then said, 'Why would you say that?'

'Because I heard them arguing. Constantly. Then old man Dunmore would drive off in a temper and make a mess of the gravel driveway. Used to drive my father wild, having to rake all the stones back into place.' He shrugged. 'Kate told me that when she was lying in bed at night, she often heard her mother crying.'

Gilchrist listened in silence. Katherine's mother could have known of her husband's paedophilic tendencies, or at least suspected them. No man could live closely with his wife without her knowing his most intimate and private thoughts and feelings. Men might think they were holding secrets from their wives, but it was only the rare few who succeeded in doing so. He didn't think Lindsay would know the answer to his next question, but in light of what Gina Milne had told them, he thought it worth a try.

'Was Katherine ever sexually abused by her father?'

Lindsay gave the tiniest of nods as he said, 'You know . . . I've always suspected that.'

'Why?'

'I'd seen the way he looked at her. Even as a young boy, I always thought there was something not right about it. Not the way you would expect a father to look at his daughter. More . . . how would you say . . . *predatory*, than fatherly.' He seemed pleased with his choice of words.

'But Katherine never admitted to you that she'd been sexually abused by her father?'

'No.'

'Just your presumption that she might have been?'

'Yes.'

'How about verbal abuse?'

Lindsay shook his head. 'Old man Dunmore was always shouting at someone. Used to give my father a lot of grief. *One of these days*, my father used to say, *that man's going to hear a piece of my mind*. But he never did. So nobody thought anything about him shouting at his wife or children. He shouted at Murdo and Hector just as much as he did at Katherine,' he said, as if that made it all acceptable.

Gilchrist gritted his teeth at the mental image of a man who bullied all around him, who went through life without regard to other's feelings, who gave constant verbal abuse but never took any in return, who used people – wife, children, employees, anyone and everyone – for his own benefit as if it were his God-given right, an ugly excuse for a man whose family lived in fear and silent tolerance and, in all likelihood, utter dysfunction. He forced the image away, and said, 'How about physical abuse?'

'Didn't need to. When old man Dunmore shouted, that was enough.'

Yes, Gilchrist thought. It was indeed enough.

He terminated the interview and went looking for Jessie.

CHAPTER 44

'What a prick,' Jessie said when he caught up with her in her office. 'Surprised you could stand it as long as you did.'

'You don't believe him, is what you're saying?'

She looked at him, eyes wide with surprise. 'Do you?'

'Some of it.' As they walked down the stairs, he said, 'What do you think Dunmore was like as a young woman?'

'Just as bitchy then as she is now.'

'In terms of strength, I mean.'

'You've got me there.'

'She's not particularly well built, is she? I mean she's just your normal woman.'

Jessie opened the door and stepped into the car park at the rear of the Office. 'If killing your husband makes you normal, then yes, she's just your normal woman.'

'Where's the nearest joiners?' he asked.

'Jesus, Andy. You're beginning to worry me.'

They found Robbie Marsh at the back of Warehouse 3, watching a man with a toolkit belted to his jeans trying to manoeuvre an extendable ladder against the rear wall. A quick glance as they approached, then Marsh gripped the ladder as the man scaled the rungs.

Gilchrist walked up to Marsh. 'Problems?'

Marsh shook his head. 'Routine maintenance. Damaged gutter.' Only then did he notice the length of wood in Gilchrist's hand. 'Looks like you're getting ready to build yourself a fence.'

Gilchrist had purchased the wooden fence post from an eclectic hardware store on South Street. He thought it might be a tad short, but it seemed as good a way as any to test his theory. He smiled at Marsh, and said, 'Got a minute?' leaving Marsh in no doubt that he wasn't being asked.

Even so, Marsh said, 'Health and Safety would have my guts if I left Tam up there by himself.'

Gilchrist cocked his head, and shouted, 'Hey, Tam. Get down. Right now.'

Tam glared at Marsh, who nodded his head with some reluctance. Even before Tam's feet touched the ground, Gilchrist said, 'This way,' and strode off towards Warehouse 1.

'Want to tell me what this is about?' Marsh asked.

'Once we're inside.' At the warehouse door, he said, 'Open it.'

Marsh fiddled with his jailer's set of keys, and unlocked both top and bottom locks. He pulled the door open to reveal a dark interior and, without a word, stepped inside.

Again, the dry mustiness of the warehouse struck Gilchrist. It seemed as if years of silence were simply lying in darkness, just waiting for someone to enter. The warehouse had sealed light fixtures, a safeguard against an electrical fault sparking an explosion in the whisky-fuelled atmosphere. He walked past a row of casks, oak wood dark and dry and dusty, and turned along a concrete pathway that ran between rows of casks stacked two-high. When he reached what he thought was a likely spot, he stopped.

'How heavy are these casks?' he asked.

'Depends on how old they are. The more mature, the greater the angel's share, hence the lighter they are.'

Gilchrist noted the date on an end cask on the top row – twelve years old – then stretched up and knuckled the wood. A few taps around the rim suggested that the cask was well over half full. Perfect. He pressed both hands on the wood, put his weight behind it and gave a hard push. But the cask was solid, held in position by wedges where it rested on wooden rails, nothing more elaborate than four-by-four lengths of wood.

'I want to try an experiment,' Gilchrist said, at which Jessie stepped forward and slid the fence post under the cask, into the gap between the wooden rails.

'Hey, what's going on?' Marsh objected.

'We told you,' she said. 'An experiment.'

Gilchrist said, 'I want to see how easy it is for a woman to move one of these.'

Marsh's mouth formed the shape of an Ah, but he didn't try to stop them.

'You ready?' Gilchrist asked Jessie.

She nodded, then put her shoulder under the post and pushed upwards.

The cask rocked, but didn't budge.

'It's heavy,' she gasped. 'But not impossible.'

Gilchrist nodded, then said, 'Push it high enough to take the weight off that front wedge. Then hold that position and reach over and move the wedge.'

'Whoah,' Marsh said. 'What're you up to?'

'You'll see,' Gilchrist said, as Jessie's face reddened, and she shifted the weight onto one shoulder, then reached for the wedge.

'Shit,' she groaned. 'I can't reach it.'

'Okay. Let it down. We'll try a shorter length.'

Jessie relaxed, and the cask settled with silent weight back into its position.

Gilchrist held the post at Jessie's shoulder. 'Shuffle forward until you're at a position where you can lever up at the same time as reaching for the wedge.'

Jessie edged forward, rested the post on her shoulder and reached for the wedge. 'That's about it,' she said.

'Okay.' Gilchrist stepped back. 'Try it now.'

'She gritted her teeth and heaved upwards. 'Bloody hell,' she gasped. 'I can't move it.'

'The lever's too short, right?'

'Right.'

'So you need a longer lever to shift the weight, but doing so puts you too far away to reach the wedge to nudge it forward a touch.'

Jessie's face shifted from puzzlement to understanding as her lips broke into a tight grin. 'That conniving bastard,' she hissed.

Gilchrist nodded. 'There had to have been two people involved. One to take the weight of the cask, and one to move the wedge.' He turned to Marsh. 'Experiment over.'

Silent, Marsh scratched his head.

'You got a minute for a chat in the canteen?' Gilchrist said.

That late in the day, the canteen was quiet. Gilchrist carried two mugs of coffee to the table, and sat next to Jessie. Marsh sat opposite, looking perplexed.

'So what was that all about?' he said.

'An experiment,' Jessie repeated. 'And now we're about to try another one.' She slid a photograph across the table to him.

Marsh stared at it, a deepening frown creasing his forehead.

'Recognise anyone?'

Marsh pulled the photo closer, shook his head. 'No.'

'It's supposedly you.'

'What?' Marsh took a closer look at the CCTV image of Market Street showing a man in an overcoat entering Starbucks.

'The quality's not great,' Jessie said. 'But we have it on good authority that it's you. All dressed up to look like George Caithness.'

Marsh's head jerked in alarm, mouth agape. Then his head shook, gently at first, until his lips whitened in defiance. He shoved the photo back at Jessie. 'No fucking way,' he growled. 'There's no fucking way that's me.'

'Well, it's certainly not George Caithness,' Jessie said. 'Because poor old George was already dead and dumped in Dunmore Loch by then.'

Marsh's face paled as if his body had drained of blood. 'You . . . you found him?'

'You didn't think we would?'

'No . . . I . . .'

She shoved another photo across the table to him – a white Citroën van. At that angle, the driver could be seen as little more than a grainy shadow. 'I take it that's you as well.'

Marsh shook his head, either in disbelief or denial, Gilchrist couldn't tell.

'We've spoken to Fraser Lindsay,' Jessie said. 'And he's agreed to turn witness for the Crown in exchange for a mitigated sentence.'

White-eyed, Marsh stared at them. 'I had nothing to do with it,' he said. 'I swear on my mother's grave, I had nothing to do with any of it.'

Well, not strictly correct, Gilchrist thought. Transporting, then disposing of a body by dumping it into a loch, was not exactly nothing. But what worried him was that the evidence they'd uncovered so far did not exactly point in the direction of Katherine Dunmore. Any decent lawyer – and Gilchrist was in no doubt that Peter White was just such a man – could pass her husband's murder onto Fraser *and* Marsh, arguing that they were nothing more than foolish men who let their desire for an attractive woman and a life of wealth blind them to reality. So, he still had work to do.

Edwin Harold Dunmore – landowner, businessman, misogynist, paedophile, bully, and master of a dysfunctional household – had a great deal to answer for.

With that in mind, Gilchrist phoned Cooper.

CHAPTER 45

While Jessie arrested and charged Marsh, Gilchrist toyed with the idea of bringing Katherine Dunmore into the St Andrews Office for an interview, maybe even holding it in the Glenrothes Office, within walking distance of Glenrothes HQ, and a much more intimidating setting, or so he believed. But after giving it some thought, he'd decided against rushing into any interview. They still had too many unanswered questions to be in any position to confront Dunmore with sufficient evidence to charge her with the murder of her husband. So he made a list of questions, trying to cross-reference them and link them to others. After all, Dunmore was the common factor, the focal point of the entire investigation. But he remained convinced that arresting her would only force her to clam up and answer nothing, or answer everything with a frustrating and unhelpful No comment – witness how Peter White had instructed her to do just that during her earlier abbreviated spell in custody.

He didn't want his investigation to end up in a long and expensive trial, the outcome of which could go any way. So, he decided to in-gather as much evidence as they could, then confront her in one final onslaught.

Two days later, Gilchrist was ready for the final interview. Dunmore had formally identified the body pulled from the loch as that of her husband, George Caithness. She'd put on a plausible display of grief; no crocodile tears, just a handkerchief held tight to her mouth, and dark sunglasses – despite the dull weather – behind which she could hide dry eyes.

With the interview set up in the offices of White De Bouchier in South Street, he still believed there was more to gain by letting Dunmore think she had the upper hand. And what better way to portray that than her being interviewed in the safe and familiar surroundings of White De Bouchier's conference room, her trusted solicitor and managing partner of the law firm, Peter White, by her side.

The meeting was set for 4.30 p.m., which gave them the early part of that afternoon to run through their interview strategy together, practise their lines, but also give the impression of being so late in the day that the meeting would be short, and they'd all be home for dinner by five-thirty.

With files and notepads tucked into folders, Gilchrist and Jessie left the North Street Office at 4.10 p.m. and walked the short distance to White's law firm. As anticipated, Peter White, the perfect gentleman, led them into his firm's conference room overlooking South Street. Katherine Dunmore was already seated, but didn't look up as they entered. Instead, she glared at a printout of something that White clearly wanted her to make herself familiar with before the interview.

'Tea? Coffee? Biscuits?' White said, sweeping an arm towards a silver tray on top of a washed-oak credenza that matched the conference table, and on which sat a percolator and a small plate of biscuits. The offer was *help yourself*, but Gilchrist shook his head.

'We won't be long,' he said, and pulled out a chair for Jessie to sit next to him.

Jessie opened her notebook, then once again noted the time and place and introduced all four present, adding, 'Mrs Dunmore's attendance is voluntary, and she's free to leave anytime.' Which was what they'd agreed – let Dunmore believe she had the upper hand.

Gilchrist kept his focus on Dunmore, one part surprised that she didn't simply just rise from the table and walk from the room – after all, she was free to leave – while another part knew she was too arrogant to believe a pair of local detectives could find evidence sufficient to charge her with so much as a minor crime, let alone the murder of her husband.

It took several seconds of silence before he managed to engage Dunmore's gaze. As he returned her cold look, he had the strangest sense of something evil shifting around her, like a wind chilling the air. If blue eyes were the colour of a heartless soul, he was looking into the core of one. He shivered off icy fingers at the nape of his neck, focused his thoughts on the interview.

'Thank you for agreeing to this meeting,' he began.

She tutted.

'We'll try not to take up too much of your valuable time,' Jessie said, which earned her a hateful grimace from Dunmore, and a raised eyebrow from White, about as good a start to the meeting as Gilchrist could have hoped for.

He slid a photograph across the table. 'We believe this is Robbie Marsh disguised as your late husband, George, entering Starbucks coffee shop in Market Street—'

'Excuse me,' White interrupted. 'Who's Robbie Marsh?'

'The manager of Gleneden Distillery.'

White glanced at Dunmore, who gave a curt nod of annoyance.

Gilchrist slid another photograph across the table. 'And this is Robbie Marsh driving to Dunmore Lodge with, we believe, George's body in the back, wrapped in black bin liner, ready to be dumped in Dunmore Loch.'

Dunmore stared at the photograph without so much as a blink or twitch of a muscle. Not even the thought of her late husband being so heartlessly disposed of seemed sufficient to generate an emotional response.

White pulled the photo to him, then almost smiled. 'I'm assuming you have stronger evidence than this . . .' He studied the image for a moment. '. . . this featureless photograph of a man you purport to be Mr Marsh allegedly on his way to dispose of the body of my client's late husband.'

'Oh, yes, we do,' Jessie said. 'The caretaker of Dunmore Lodge, Fraser Lindsay, whom your client knows intimately, is currently in custody and has agreed to turn witness for the Crown.'

Not a flicker.

'Your client knows Robbie Marsh intimately, too.'

'That's nonsense,' Dunmore snapped.

'I'm pleased to see that something gets your attention,' Jessie said. 'You couldn't care less that your hubby's been murdered and his body dumped in a loch. But God forbid you've been shagging your distillery manager.'

Without a word, Dunmore pulled her papers to her, as if preparing to stomp off in a how-dare-you hissy fit.

But now they were here, Gilchrist didn't want to miss the chance of trying to break her. 'You're free to leave,' he said. 'But if you do, we'd have no option but to arrest you on suspicion of *complicity* in the murder of your husband.'

A look of animal cunning shifted behind her eyes as her body stilled.

Gilchrist felt himself tense. She'd caught his deliberate emphasis, and understood the meaning of his words. Being arrested on suspicion of complicity, as opposed to suspicion of murder, could be difficult to prove without incriminating evidence, which would reassure her that the lowly pair seated at the table were nowhere near as clever detectives as they thought they were.

So far, so good.

She leaned to the side, whispered to White who listened in silence, lips tightening as he took her instruction. An eye-widening look of worry was followed by a firm shake of his head and reciprocal whispering that ended with her unmistakable hiss of, 'Shut up.'

Then Dunmore pulled herself upright, gave a cold-eyed smile that barely parted her lips, and said, 'I might have wished my husband dead from time to time, but that doesn't make me complicit in his murder.'

White raised a hand. 'For the record,' he said. 'I have advised my client not to offer any information freely, but to answer only those questions asked of her. Furthermore, I have reminded her that she is free to leave anytime she—'

'Whereupon she'll be arrested,' Jessie snapped.

'Upon which event I have advised my client in the strongest terms to make no further comment.' He shook his head again. 'But my client has declined to accept my advice—'

'There's the door,' Jessie said.

'Ultimately, it'll be in my client's best interests that I stay and witness this interview, even though I've been instructed not to interfere.'

Well, Gilchrist thought, that just about covered every eventuality to avoid White being reported to the Law Society for failing to serve his client with professional integrity. On the other hand, Dunmore looked like she'd already fired him and was warming to the legal challenge.

'Tell me about your father,' Gilchrist said.

'What's my father got to do with anything?'

'How friendly was he with Duncan Milne?'

'Who?'

'You know perfectly well who Duncan Milne is.'

She pursed her lips, as if taken aback by the hardening of Gilchrist's tone. 'Oh, yes,' she said. 'Duncan, who used to be the manager of the distillery.'

'More than just the manager,' Gilchrist said. 'He was a cooper to trade, a man who could dismantle and reconstruct whisky casks.'

Jessie said, 'We believe Duncan Milne was involved in Hector's murder.'

'What?'

Gilchrist kept his attention on Dunmore's eyes while Jessie pressed on as they'd agreed. Good cop bad cop routine sprang to mind, but it was more like firing at her from all angles, keeping her confused, not knowing in which direction the interview was heading, or what question to expect next, or from whom.

'The cask had to be partially dismantled to remove the top,' Jessie said, 'in order to put poor old Hector's body inside. Then it had to be professionally repaired, with the hoops hammered back into place, tight as you like, to make sure it was completely watertight. Then it was topped up with whisky, and stored in the warehouse to lie there for twenty-five years. Which was a mistake,' Jessie pressed on. 'Molly Havet thought it should have been stencilled and stored as a fifty-year batch. That way, we wouldn't be talking about it now, would we?'

Gilchrist noticed a shimmering of Dunmore's jaw at the mention of Havet's name, but she said, 'Well, thank God for that.'

'For what?' Jessie said.

'For finding out who killed Hector, even though you can never bring his killer to justice.'

'Why not?'

A flicker of doubt, as if she sensed the snare tightening. 'Because Duncan Milne's dead.'

'I thought you didn't know him.'

'I couldn't recall his name at first. But now you've mentioned him, it's all coming back to me.'

'I see,' Jessie said. 'But Duncan didn't murder Hector all by himself. He needed help. Inside help.'

Silence.

Gilchrist said, 'Did you know Duncan Milne's daughter, Gina?'

Dunmore stilled, as if time had stopped for a heartbeat. 'No. Should I?'

'I think you do know her.'

She frowned, shook her head. 'I don't know her at all.'

Without a word, he slid a copy of the birth certificate across the table to her.

She stared at the certificate, eyes tight, face pale, body locked in time and space.

'You can pick it up,' Jessie said. 'It won't bite.'

Then Dunmore's world rebooted. 'Don't be so bloody insolent,' she snapped, and grabbed the certificate as if to shred it into pieces. She slapped the back of her hand against the paper. 'I don't know this . . . this Gina Milne,' she said, and slid the certificate to White by her side.

White spent several seconds reviewing it. 'I don't see the significance of this birth certificate,' he said at length, then looked at Gilchrist. 'What has Jane McEntegart Milne to do with my client?'

'You'll note that the father's name has been omitted,' Gilchrist said.

'I still fail to see what any of this has to do with my client.'

Jessie said, 'It's amazing the progress in DNA over the years. It can tell you all these secrets that would otherwise have gone undiscovered.'

White pushed his chair back, raised his voice. 'Will someone please tell me what this birth certificate has to do with my client?'

Gilchrist took over. 'The father's name was withheld,' he said, 'because he didn't want his family name soiled. But in the end, he wasn't completely heartless. An arrangement of sorts was reached.'

'An arrangement?' White asked.

'A monthly stipend was paid to Gina's father, Duncan Milne, to ensure his silence over the years.' The room stilled, as if the air itself had frozen. Dunmore's face could have been carved in stone. 'And the child, Jane McEntegart Milne, was adopted,' he said. 'By her biological father.'

Jessie opened her file, and removed a report. 'These DNA results confirm that the child's biological father was Edwin Harold Dunmore. And these copies from the adoption agency,' she said, removing a batch of copied handwritten notes, 'confirm that Jane McEntegart Milne had her birthname changed to Katherine Elizabeth Dunmore.'

CHAPTER 46

It didn't take Dunmore long to recover. 'Is this why you've asked me to this meeting? To tell me I'm adopted? To try to shame me? To tell me that my family name is not mine by birthright?' She breathed in through her nose, nostrils pinching from the effort. 'If you make this information public, I swear I will sue you for every penny you have, and the skin off your back.'

The venom in her voice left Gilchrist under no illusion of the sincerity of her threat. Of course, cornered snakes were always the most dangerous, and Dunmore was being nudged inch by inch, word by word, into an inescapable corner of her own making.

White said, 'Forgive me, but I fail to see the relevance of any of this.'

Without a word, Jessie slid two more photographs across the table.

White shuffled through them, and frowned. 'What are these?'

'Crime scene photographs,' she said. 'East Sands, St Andrews. Although at the time of Duncan Milne's death, it was written off as an accident. Slipped on wet rocks, knocked himself out, and drowned.' She glared at Dunmore. 'But it wasn't an accident at all. Was it?'

Dunmore had settled once more into an almost petrified state, and her serpentine gaze slid lifeless from Jessie to Gilchrist, and back again.

'What're you implying?' White said. 'That my client was somehow responsible for that poor man's accident?'

This was the problem, Gilchrist knew, that without hard evidence linking Dunmore to historical deaths, all they could go on was conjecture. But he and Jessie had agreed just to nip and bite and push and press and hope they got a result, good or bad.

Jessie glared at Dunmore. 'You were there that night. You'd driven Duncan to the pub. You'd even shared a drink with him. Here,' she said, and slid over a printed copy. 'It's in your written statement.'

Dunmore scowled at the copy, but didn't touch it.

'So we're thinking that it wasn't any accident at all. We're thinking that you did it, you killed Duncan. Maybe you told him you wanted to take a walk along the East Sands, and Duncan obliged. But then in an unguarded moment, you hit him over the head with a rock you'd picked up off the beach, and left him to drown.'

Dunmore's face broke into a genuine smile, and she gave an almost imperceptible shake of her head. This was the reaction Gilchrist was waiting for. After the shock of being faced with her adoption papers and the revelation that they all knew she was a bastard child, she believed she was now back in control. These idiot detectives had no proof of anything. They were making it up as they went along. They were fishing. They had to be. The snake shifted on its seat, preparing to slither from the corner.

348

Not so fast.

'We're also now investigating the circumstances of your father's death,' Gilchrist said. Not exactly true. But with all they'd uncovered in the last couple of days, he wasn't willing to strike it off the list just yet.

Jessie pushed another photocopied record across the table. 'Edwin Harold Dunmore,' she said. 'His death certificate. Heart failure due to alcohol poisoning.' She shot a smile across the table. 'Someone in the distillery business? Surrounded by gallons of high-proof distillate? Easy to access? Despite the taxman's strict recording requirements, who could possibly miss a litre or two of the stuff? And pouring a hefty measure of seventy-five per cent proof into your father's nightcap when he'd had a few drinks too many anyway would be a simple task. The next morning, he could either have one hell of a hangover, or be lying in bed, dead from heart failure brought on by alcohol poisoning.' She retrieved the death certificate. 'I'd say you killed him—'

'This is preposterous,' White snarled.

'—to inherit the business. Plain and simple. It's what you wanted, wasn't it? You were on the bottom rung of a tall business ladder, a mere woman who was next to nothing in the eyes of a bully of a father who ran the business like a dictator. Two older brothers, both lined up to take over when the old man eventually passed away? Mother too weak to stand up for herself? Then along you come, the bastard child of an underage affair for which old man Dunmore should've been jailed, and you're slotted right into the family, secret and all, as if everything is hunky dory in the world of the Dunmores.'

But Dunmore eyed Jessie as if she were no more troublesome than a fruit fly.

'Did old man Dunmore try it on with you?' Jessie said. 'I bet he did. He'd creep into your bedroom at night when you were little. Was that why he wanted a daughter? Fresh flesh to have at his leisure? It's what he liked. Your biological mother, Gina, had only just turned fifteen when she had you. Did you know that?' She flashed a smile. 'Of course, you did. You'd seen your birth certificate. Hector showed it to you, way back then. But he kept the original. And you never did find out where he'd hidden it, did you?'

During Jessie's tirade, Gilchrist hadn't taken his eyes off Dunmore. But throughout it all, not once had she shown any signs of emotion. To anyone watching, they could be talking to a cardboard replica. But he knew Jessie wasn't finished.

Far from it.

She pressed closer to the table. 'So you had to get rid of them,' she said. 'Didn't you? One by one. And you'd already started, hadn't you? First, Murdo, accidentally crushed by a cask of whisky.'

White grunted, face reddening. The fact that he'd stayed silent during Jessie's rant was a wonder in itself. But there was only so much the man could take. And at that moment, he'd had enough. He slapped a hand on the table, lips forming an ugly grimace, as if about to splutter objection.

'Stay out of it,' Jessie snapped at him.

'This is preposterous.'

'It certainly is. Your client's a psychopathic serial killer.'

'I must advise my client to terminate this meeting.'

'Whereupon I'll arrest her for murder.'

Something changed in White's manner at that, as if he'd seen through their charade, that Gilchrist and Jessie had no hard evidence to link his client to historical deaths. Witness how they'd mentioned being arrested only on suspicion of being *complicit* in her husband's murder. So, with that in mind, he seemed to conclude they could bleat as loud as they wanted in an attempt to harass his client, try to trick her into incriminating herself with the slip of a tongue. But he knew his client, and knew it would never succeed.

He reached for Dunmore's hand and gave a fatherly squeeze.

Dunmore pulled her hand free, and glared at Jessie in molten silence.

Jessie gave her a look as good as she got. 'And what a way for poor Murdo to go,' she said. 'Crushed to death. That must have hurt. I mean, when you think about it, there must've been a moment just before he died when he cried out in utter agony.' She riffled through her notes, then said, 'His head wasn't crushed. But his chest was. Ten broken ribs.' She pouted her lips. 'Ouch. That must've been painful.' Then she looked at her. 'Did he scream? I bet he screamed. Did he shout out your name? Did he cry for help?' She shook her head. 'No, you wouldn't help him. Even though you were there when he died, you wouldn't help him. But neither would Fraser Lindsay. He was there, too. He had to be, because you couldn't move the cask by yourself, could you?'

Gilchrist caught the tiny movement, the slightest curl at the corner of Dunmore's lips, and felt the first stirrings of doubt. He'd missed something. They both had. Then the answer came to him. Lindsay hadn't been with Dunmore at the time of Murdo's death, because the cask had already been moved to nudge the wedge closer to the edge – maybe a day or so earlier. Alone, and with Murdo standing on the right spot, it wouldn't have taken

351

much for Dunmore as a young woman to remove the wedge by herself by giving it a sudden blow.

'And after you'd killed Murdo,' Jessie continued, 'you then killed your father. I bet you enjoyed that one, didn't you? The miserable old bastard taking his last drink, a cocktail of high-proof alcohol that was as good as a dose of arsenic. And once he was out of the way, it was an easy step to break your mother – your *adoptive* mother – and convince her to go into a care home. Not forever. Just for a short while, you would've told her. That way, you could get her to agree, couldn't you?' She rummaged through her notes again. 'We've got the records here. Let's work out the dates.' She scribbled numbers on the back of the file folder, then said, 'Looks like she was admitted six months after Dunmore senior's death, and only a matter of a few weeks later until . . .' She pulled out another certificate, and smiled at it. 'Now, would you look at that?' She pushed it across the table. 'Died during her sleep. An accidental over-dose, aided by . . . you've guessed it first time . . . too much alcohol.'

Jessie rested her elbows on the table, and said, 'But what I don't get is . . . why kill her at all? She was no threat to you.' Then her face broke into a smile. 'But you wanted it all to yourself, didn't you? The whole shooting match. The distillery business. The country lodge. The house in St Andrews. And then . . .' She paused, as if for dramatic effect. '. . . you saw one more opportunity to increase your portfolio, as well as getting rid of that last obstacle to it all . . . Hector. The sole surviving male heir of the Dunmore dynasty. But the plan you came up with didn't allow you to do it alone, did it? You needed the expertise of a man like Duncan Milne to help you hide Hector's body in a cask of whisky.'

Dunmore had reverted to staring with cold hatred at Gilchrist, as if it was more simple to face him than to look at Jessie.

'Then along came George,' Jessie said, 'who fell in love with you, won over by your money, or by dropping your knickers. Either way, it didn't matter. George was smitten. And by all accounts, he was leading an honest life until you convinced him that Hector had to go. But he needed help to dispose of the body, and the distillery was already paying Duncan Milne a monthly stipend to keep old man Dunmore's criminal affairs from the public domain. But with the boss having kicked the bucket, Duncan feared he was going to lose his stipend.

'So . . . and I'm guessing here, because both people are dead . . . but one night not long before Christmas twenty-five years ago, Duncan and George took care of Hector. It took two of them to kill him, stuff his body into a cask, and store it in the warehouse. Then Duncan drove Hector's Land Rover to Mallaig where his daughter, Gina, your mother, lived.'

Still no response.

'And with Hector out of the way, Duncan Milne would continue to receive a stipend, while you inherited Hector's estate. After which, you and George could live happily ever after in your big house, driving fancy cars, investing in art and jewellery, holidaying in the most exclusive resorts. Oh yes,' she said. 'We know all about the Caribbean investments, an island here, a resort there.' Jessie jerked a grimace for a smile. 'You've built up quite an investment portfolio for a woman who started off as a mere bastard in a man's world.'

Even that failed to generate a reaction.

Gilchrist leaned forward. 'At first I thought your mistake was assigning the cask to a twenty-five-year batch. That's what troubled me. I couldn't understand why you wouldn't just reassign the cask to a fifty-year batch when the date for opening was drawing near, and you knew that Hector's body would be discovered. After all, it would've been easy enough to revise the records. So why not do that? Why not just keep the body hidden in the warehouse for another twenty-five years?'

A reaction at last, nothing more than a raising of her eyebrows, as if marvelling at the ingenuity of the question.

'And then it struck me,' he said. 'It's what you wanted. Of course it was. Because by that time, you'd tired of George. Your marriage was failing. It was over. George had outlived his usefulness. You had to turn to younger men to believe you were still young and attractive. But divorcing George would be expensive, and God help anyone who stood between you and your money. But importantly, and this is the key,' he said, 'George was the only person living who could connect you to Hector's murder. Which brings us to your final mistake. Your plans for Scottish Stretch.'

Gilchrist allowed himself an easy smile as he stared into Dunmore's eyes. He'd seen many a cold-hearted killer during his time in the Constabulary, but Dunmore had to be the most cold-hearted of all. 'Would you like me to continue?' he asked her.

'Oh, please do. I'm sure you're going to enthral us all with your detective skills.' She glanced at White, tutted, and shook her head.

But White seemed less confident. His thin lips had taken on a downturned scowl, and he seemed far from happy as he shifted in his seat. Still, give him his due, for he turned to her, and said, 'I should remind you that your attendance at this meeting is voluntary, Katherine, and that you can leave anytime—'

'And be arrested,' Jessie chipped in.

But White turned on her. 'You've neither shown nor provided me with any evidence that is nothing other than circumstantial. My client will take her chance.' He pushed his chair back and held out his hand to help Dunmore to her feet.

'We're almost finished,' Gilchrist said, cursing at himself for not continuing to press while they had the interview in full flow. 'Five more minutes and we'll be out of your hair.' He tried a smile, but wasn't sure he pulled it off. 'Unless you'd rather we call you in for a formal interview tomorrow morning and continue from where we left off.'

That did the trick. Dunmore tutted again, and said, 'Get on with it, then.'

It took Gilchrist a few seconds to gather his thoughts, try to find some way to cut the meeting short. They still had a number of questions to ask, but he decided against these, and said, 'On the one hand, you have such an ambitious conservation project, while on the other you fail to take advantage of Scottish Stretch within your own property. Seems to me like that's a contradiction.'

Dunmore frowned at him, a surprise in itself. 'I don't understand.'

'Neither could I,' he said. 'For someone whose driving force in life seems to be the accrual of money, I couldn't fathom why you didn't want to charge fishing rights on the loch, or rent out the Lodge to visiting parties. Hill walks. Shooting parties. Whisky sampling. That sort of thing. They all tie together. You might not make enough to retire on, but it's money for nothing.'

Jessie said, 'But with George's body anchored to the bottom, you wouldn't want anyone to accidentally snag a fishing hook to him, would you?'

'Which seems the obvious answer,' Gilchrist said. 'But Scottish Stretch has been in the making for over twelve years. And the idea of getting rid of George was a recent event. So there had to be some other reason you didn't want the loch disturbed, *something* that happened much earlier.'

Jessie slid another photograph across the table. 'And hey presto, here it is.'

White frowned as he leaned forward and stared at the image, struggling to make out what it was. Then he gasped, pulled himself upright, and said, 'Good God, is that . . .?'

'It is,' Gilchrist said. 'The skeletal remains of a child.'

'Not just any child,' Jessie said, sliding another set of reports across the table. 'But another Dunmore, I'm afraid to say.'

White's face had paled. 'Are you implying that Edwin Dunmore fathered another child and . . . and . . .'

'Not this time,' Gilchrist said.

'Try Hector,' Jessie added, digging out more paperwork and pushing it over to White. 'These DNA results confirm that Hector Dunmore is the biological father of that unfortunate child. And this set of DNA results,' she said, tapping another report that Cooper had sent them after Gilchrist's phone call to her, 'confirms that the biological mother is his half-sister, Katherine Elizabeth Dunmore.'

Gilchrist flashed a smile. 'Your client.'

CHAPTER 47

'Of course,' Jessie pressed on, 'these results are in the region of ninety-nine point nine nine per cent accurate, so there is some degree of uncertainty. Let me see.' She scribbled on the back of a folder, and said, 'Oh, look at that. Point zero one per cent.' Then she stared at Dunmore, and it took Gilchrist a moment to realise that if he didn't step in, Jessie was going to reach across the table and strangle her.

'Do you have anything to say?' Gilchrist asked her.

But Dunmore said nothing. Her neck seemed to lose the power of its muscles as she hung her head, and fingered inside her bag for a handkerchief.

Gilchrist nodded to Jessie who was already walking around the table, handcuffs in her hand. 'Katherine Elizabeth Dunmore,' she said, 'I'm arresting you on suspicion of the murder of . . .'

Gilchrist looked up, and froze as his blood chilled. A Glock was his first thought, or maybe a Sig Sauer; but he'd never been good at identifying guns. Nowadays, they all looked same. His second thought was a silent curse that he hadn't followed up on Dunmore's surrendering her handguns. 'Don't, Katherine,' he said. 'You'll only make matters worse.'

She turned to face him, and surprised him by smiling, at long last an uninhibited smile that reached her eyes and stretched her lips. The years seemed to slide from her like water off varnished wood, letting him see another side to her, a side she kept only for those she cared about. Not that she cared about him at that moment, he thought he understood that much, but it did strike him as strange – wildly so if you thought about it – that she would smile at him during what had to be her most painful moment.

'How can I make matters worse?' she asked him.

He found himself turning his head away from the barrel of the gun, a black hole that seemed to follow the movement of his eyes. At any moment, she could squeeze the trigger and end his life right there, although it did strike him that the gun never so much as wavered in her grip. Of course, it wouldn't, he realised. Growing up with the likes of Fraser Lindsay, learning to shoot on expansive lands owned by her father – deer, rabbits, hare, or anything else that moved, come to think of it – would make her a marksman in her own right. Not that there was any chance of her missing from three feet. You didn't need high scores in marksmanship for that.

He was conscious of a silent stillness in the room, of the other two – White locked to his chair; Jessie standing stock still – as if aware that their slightest breath could be the noise that sent her over the edge, and heralded the end of them all.

'You'll get a fair trial,' he tried. God, he sounded pathetic.

Her smile widened, and again he was struck by her beauty, but also by something else, a glint in her eyes that seemed not altogether from this world. 'Scottish Stretch,' she said to him. 'Was that really what got you thinking?'

He would have nodded in agreement, but worried that any movement might cause her to squeeze the trigger. 'One of them,' he said.

'What else?'

He lowered his gaze until it settled on the photograph of the skeletal remains, and moved his fingers, ever so carefully, to tap the image. 'When the DNA results came back, it was more or less a given.'

'Why didn't you arrest me then?'

'Because you would've clammed up.' He gave a wry smile at White. 'I'm sure that's the advice your solicitor would've given you.' He held her eyes, still intrigued by her smile. 'I needed to hear your confession, your admission of guilt, or to see signs of guilt, as it turned out. I didn't think you would've enjoyed a lengthy court battle.'

'No,' she said. 'I wouldn't have allowed it.'

He thought it odd, her choice of words, as if she would have any control over the due process of the law. 'What I don't understand,' he said, 'is that you had everything, Katherine. You have a life that others can only dream of. Why risk it all by killing George? Why not set him up for life somewhere, then get on with your own? After all, you can afford it.'

She shook her head, and her smile failed her. 'Not everything,' she said, and let her gaze shift to the skeletal remains. 'It was quite extraordinary,' she said, lifting the photo with her free hand, although if Gilchrist had any thoughts on the matter, it would have been how extraordinary it was that the gun never wavered. Not even the slightest tremor. 'Listening to your rationale,' she went on, 'and how you worked through the logic.'

'But I didn't get it all correct, did I?'

She gave the tiniest of shakes. 'No. You didn't.'

Silent, he waited for her to tell him.

'Robbie Marsh is innocent,' she said. 'Tony Maybury wore George's clothes and made the daily trips to Tesco and Starbucks.'

'And he drove the van to Dunmore Lodge?'

She nodded.

'And dumped George's body into the loch?'

Another nod.

'And Fraser Lindsay supplied the boat, had it all ready at the edge of the loch,' he said, more statement of fact than question.

She nodded again, but something in the way she looked at him told him he still didn't have answers to it all. He thought he knew what it was, but he still had to ask.

'You said – not everything. What did you mean?'

Her smile warmed the room once again. 'Always the detective. Always one more question.' All of a sudden, White moved his chair by her side. '*Don't*,' she snapped, and stretched her arm so that the muzzle of the gun was no more than two feet from Gilchrist's face. On instinct, he squeezed his eyes shut, waiting for the shot that would end his life, and had the disorienting sense of the room settling into stillness once more.

'It's okay,' White whispered. 'It's okay, Katherine. Nobody's going to move.'

'Why don't you give me the gun?' Jessie said, although Gilchrist sensed no real conviction in her tone.

'Why don't I give you more than the gun?' Dunmore replied.

'You said – not everything,' Gilchrist repeated, eyes now wide with the realisation that not only his life was in grave danger. He'd faced down the odd killer or three over the years, but never before had he come face to face with such a callous one. 'Not everything. What do you mean?'

'What do you think I mean?'

He tapped the photograph of the child's remains. 'I'd say it's to do with that.'

She let her gaze drift to the image of the skeletal remains, then she nodded. 'After Lizzie, I was told I couldn't have any more children.'

'Lizzie?' he said.

She turned the photograph towards him. 'Elizabeth Dunmore,' she said. 'Although by that time I'd grown to hate the surname.'

'Why?'

'Why do you think?'

He watched the fire go out of her eyes, and sensed the final truth was close. 'I was right about your father? Taking advantage of you as a child?'

She flinched.

Dear God. Like father, like son. It didn't bear thinking about. He shook his head, kept his tone level, his voice low. 'I'm so sorry, Katherine, I'm so, so sorry.'

She tutted.

'Why didn't you report the old bastard to the police?' Jessie said. 'He would've been arrested and charged. He would've been sent to prison. You would've been free from him.'

'Because he said he would tell them about Annette. That he would blame it all on me. That he would make sure I would go to hell for what I'd done.'

Gilchrist's thoughts stumbled. Annette? Who was Annette? Then he thought he saw it. 'Annette was Lizzie's sister?'

She nodded. 'Older sister.'

'The result of an incestuous relationship with your father?'

She closed her eyes at that, and a tear ran down her cheek. For one confusing moment he thought of rushing her, just swiping the gun from her. But then she stared at him, and the moment passed.

'And what happened to Annette?' he said, although he knew the answer.

'She's in the loch.'

'And your father knew?'

She smiled at him again, but that time there was no warmth in it. 'He placed her in the loch. He told me he'd heard stories about water nymphs being immortalised and looking after the souls of the dead.' She shook her head. 'I was young. Only thirteen. I had no idea.'

Gilchrist noted the change in tone, sensed the shift in her thinking.

'Katherine. *No*,' he shouted, and reached across the table.

'God forgive me,' she said, and pressed the gun under her chin.

CHAPTER 48

By the end of the following day, Tony Maybury had been arrested and charged with complicity in the murder of George Caithness, unlawful burial of a body, and for attempting to pervert the course of justice. Maybury admitted having been paid £30,000 by Katherine Dunmore to impersonate Caithness in the days following his disappearance in an attempt to fool the Constabulary into thinking her husband had been alive for five days after he'd been killed and his body dumped in Dunmore Loch.

Robbie Marsh was released, and promptly resigned from his position as manager of Gleneden Distillery. All it took was a phone call. It hadn't mattered that he was completely innocent, only that he'd been mistrusted in the first place. Two days later, he moved to Islay where his brother worked as a brand heritage manager with one of the island's distilleries.

The Law Offices of White De Bouchier were closed for four days while the SOCOs carried out a forensic examination of Katherine Dunmore's suicide. The conference room walls were then stripped and repainted, and the ceiling pulled down and repanelled. New furniture and hardwood flooring to match had the whole place smelling and looking like a new build.

But Peter White wasn't around to see it. After being questioned for six straight hours by a team of detectives pulled in from Tayside Police as overload relief, he admitted to giving Dunmore an alibi on the day she'd been arrested with packed suitcases in the boot. He hadn't arranged to meet Dunmore in his home office in Cupar, and was charged with attempting to pervert the course of justice. He also admitted to offering to represent Toni McManus *pro bono* in exchange for her falsified testimony against Gilchrist. When released on bail, he took himself and his wife off to the Caribbean for a four-week holiday. The firm's lead partner, Alexandre De Bouchier, confirmed that White was not expected to return to the firm that once bore his name.

Two separate teams from the Dive and Marine Unit were assigned to Dunmore Loch to scour its depths for baby Annette. But the search was called off after five days without success. With the loch being at the farthest point inland of Scottish Stretch, and the media splashing headlines of children's bodies being dumped in it, a group of councillors lobbied Holyrood for Dunmore Estate to be excluded from the project on the grounds that Scottish Stretch in its entirety could be irreparably tainted by such horrific historical events.

Fraser Lindsay was charged with being complicit in the illegal disposal of Caithness's body. But he retained a formidable solicitor who argued that all evidence against him was circumstantial, and could not be proven in court. Despite Gilchrist's best efforts to find more compelling evidence, the Crown Office agreed, and the case was dropped a week later.

On hearing that news, and at the end of another long day, Gilchrist decided there was nothing he could do about it. Despite a body count that put Katherine Dunmore in the top echelons of Scottish serial killers – George Caithness; Murdo and Hector Dunmore; Edwin and Alice Dunmore; Duncan and Janet Milne; and newborn children, Annette and Lizzie – once she took her own life, there was nothing more for Gilchrist to do except close his investigation and archive the files.

With no accused to stand trial, Gilchrist struggled to find satisfaction in the result and, in a strange way, felt responsible for allowing Dunmore to kill herself in the manner she had. He should have been more aware of her mental instability, paid more attention to her interest in guns, ticked every box associated with the surrender of her four handguns. But worst of all, if he hadn't played her, hadn't led her to believe she was one step ahead of them, but arrested her instead, in all likelihood she would still be alive, albeit he'd be exhausted from hearing a spate of No comments.

He ran his hand down his face, felt the skin beneath his eyes sag. Under his chin it felt as loose as chicken wattle. God, he was getting old, but almost as bad, he was tired of the job, tired of searching for clues, tired of chasing down leads, and just dog-tired of the pointless loss of life and family misery suffered at the hands of the criminally insane. He powered down his computer, lifted his jacket from the back of his chair, and left the Office intent on driving home, and stopping in at the Golf Hotel for a quick pint, and maybe a bite to eat, if his appetite inspired him.

He had his car door open and was about to slide inside, when he decided to phone Maureen. After all, with the case now closed, he had one of those rarest of rare events – at least for him – a free night.

Maureen answered with, 'Hi, Dad, I was just thinking about you.'

'I thought I felt my ears burning.' Her chuckle pulled a smile to his lips, and he said, 'I'm about to have a pint in the Central. Care to join me for a few?'

'Hang on,' she said, and the line dulled to the sound of whispered chatting. Then she came back with, 'We'll meet you there in five minutes. See you.'

The call ended before he could ask who her companion was. But it didn't matter. He was just pleased that she'd sounded so upbeat, and it'd been over a week since he'd last had a chat with her, and longer since they'd had an evening out together.

In College Street, his footfall echoed off the stone walls either side. The temperature hung around the freezing mark, and cobblestones covered by frost glittered in the light of a full moon. The sky sparkled, and he tugged his scarf around his neck. Despite the short walk to the pub's side entrance, when he pushed through the door he was relieved to step out of the winter chill and into the murmuring din and ambient warmth of a busy pub.

He was searching for a gap to push through to the bar to place his order, when he noticed Maureen waving at him as she entered from Market Street. He squeezed his way through the early evening throng, to be greeted by a tight hug.

'Hi, Dad.'

He hugged her back, pecked her cheek, then glanced over her shoulder expecting to see her companion. 'I thought you weren't coming alone.'

'They're on their way,' she said.

'How many?'

'Two. We should grab a table.'

A party of four at a corner table were gathering their jackets, and a short exchange confirmed they were leaving. 'This do?' he said, pulling out a chair to let Maureen slide into the back.

Once seated, he thought Maureen seemed breathless, upbeat, as if excited about his spur-of-the-moment invitation for a few drinks. 'So how's the studying coming on?'

'Getting there. Slowly.'

'And Blackie?' he asked, expecting to hear she'd run off and never been seen again.

'She's fine,' she said, and let out a childlike giggle. 'She's lovely. And so friendly. I've made a bed for her in the corner next to the kitchen. A basket filled with old cushions. And her water and food bowls are close by.'

'I didn't know you were a cat whisperer.'

'There's a lot you don't know about me, Dad.'

Right. Best not to go there. 'So, what're you having? My treat.'

'Sauvignon, please.'

'And the others?'

'Probably best to wait until they get here.'

At the bar, he thought of buying a bottle of wine – Maureen had been known to finish one off in fifteen minutes. But he didn't want to encourage her, especially now she seemed more settled. Instead, he ordered a large Sauvignon, and a pint of Eighty for himself. He was about to carry the drinks to the table when a voice by his shoulder said, 'That pint looks good enough to eat. Better make it two.'

Gilchrist thought Jack looked thinner than normal, but somehow vibrant and fit. Gone was the pallid ghostlike expression, and in its place clean-shaven skin that glowed with a hint of days in the sun. And no paint-spattered T-shirt or tattered jeans that hung below his waist and defied gravity. Instead, dark-blue designer jeans and a white open-necked shirt under a pricey-looking black leather jacket gave the impression of a well-to-do young man.

A short exchange of 'Hey, Andy, looking good, Jack,' had Gilchrist struggling not to spill either drink.

'Here,' Jack said, removing them from his grip. 'I'll carry this lot to the table while you order another pint. And a dirty gin Martini. Dry. Single. Not a double.'

In a bit of a daze, Gilchrist had to say, he turned to the bar and placed the order. He had no idea what a dirty gin Martini was, and thought he might have misheard Jack. But the barman didn't bat an eyelid.

Jack returned to the bar, and put an arm around Gilchrist's shoulder. 'Sorry I haven't been in touch, Andy, but we've been busy.'

'That'll keep you out of trouble,' Gilchrist said, and almost cursed at his innuendo.

But Jack didn't pick up on it. 'We haven't stopped,' he said. 'But it's been worth it.'

'*It* being?'

'We'll tell you once you bring the drinks over.'

And with that, Jack returned to sit next to a woman who, seated with her back to the bar, looked nothing like how Gilchrist remembered Kristen. Where her hair had once been spiky and jet-black, hair so blonde it was white fell almost to her shoulders.

He placed the drinks on the table, and eased past Jack to take a seat next to Maureen, by which time Jack had his pint in his hand, and was holding it up in the generic invitation to wish each other well.

They all chinked glasses to a mixture of, 'Cheers, sláinte, good to see you again,' and Gilchrist took strange comfort in the fact that Jack pulled his pint down to the halfway mark. His son might be better dressed, but he was still the same Jack. Well, without the vodka shooters. But the night was still young.

'Andy,' Jack said, 'you remember Kristen.'

'I do, yes.' He offered her a smile. 'Your hair. It's different. It suits you.'

She responded with a vague smile of her own, which failed to reach her eyes, leaving him with a sense that she'd come along that evening only at Jack's insistence. He'd met her once before, but despite her surprising frank and open honesty he'd soured her feelings for him with his suspicions of her criminal past.

As if sensing the awkwardness in the moment, Jack put an arm around Kristen and kissed the side of her head. Then he sat back. 'We've set up our own studio.'

'That's impressive,' Gilchrist said, and meant it. 'What's it called?'

Jack slid a business card across the table. 'Hedström.'

Gilchrist glanced at Kristen. Hedström was her surname – Swedish – and all of a sudden he had the disconcerting feeling that Jack had been pulled into something not of his own making. He picked up the business card, turned it over, and could tell from its stiffness that it was printed on quality paper. 'Nice,' he said. 'And the name's definitely different.' He slipped the card into his pocket, and took a mouthful of beer.

'It's got a real sound of artistic panache to it, doesn't it?' Jack said.

'But the studio's not extravagant at all,' Maureen said. 'Is it?'

Gilchrist said, 'What? You've seen it?'

'Just seen photos of it, Dad. Settle down.'

Gilchrist jerked a smile, took a sip of beer, annoyed at his rush of emotion.

Jack took another sip of beer that almost drained it. 'We agreed to keep it simple,' he said. 'Nothing fancy. Just the basics. And we've got over three thousand square feet of old warehouse space that we've just finished converting. And we're working on a sculpture together.' He slid his mobile to Gilchrist. 'What do you think?'

Gilchrist would be the first to admit he wasn't artistically inclined, but a first glance had him enlarging the image. Gleaming strips of metal twisted and spiralled from a plinth of sorts into the contorted shape of what might be mistaken for someone's face; a Picasso painting constructed in 3D.

'I'm impressed,' he said, and meant it.

'Already got some interest from the States,' Jack said, retrieving his mobile.

The difference between *some interest from* and *sold it to* was vast enough to have Gilchrist's cynical side on edge. He didn't know how best to ask what was troubling him, but in the end, said, 'So you've started up a new business?'

'Yeah, man.' Jack grinned at Kristen. 'Best partner I could've asked for.'

Well, there he had it. A partnership. The phrase *jointly and severally liable* flapped through his mind like a warning banner. The words sounded innocent enough, but carried with them a financial sting if the business failed, which many start-ups unfortunately did. He only hoped that Jack hadn't invested too heavily—

'And . . .' Jack said, eyes focused on Gilchrist. 'We have more news.'

At that, Kristen smiled, and said, 'I'm pregnant.'

Several thoughts flashed through Gilchrist's mind in snapshots – You shouldn't be drinking alcohol if you're pregnant. You don't look pregnant. When are you due? Are you and Jack going to get married? And, regrettably, just as cynical as ever, are you sure?

But thankfully he said, 'That's wonderful news—'

'A toast,' Maureen interrupted, and raised her glass. From the glow in her face, he realised that Jack and Kristen's news had been the real reason for her upbeat mood, and not her father's invitation for a few drinks. 'I'm going to be an aunt,' she said. 'Can you believe that?' Which sounded more statement than toast. Then she surprised him again, by saying, 'To family.'

Gilchrist raised his pint and joined in with, 'To family,' then chinked his glass against each of the others, one at a time. In doing so, he made eye contact with Kristen, and in that moment, something passed between them, some unspoken acknowledgement that she knew she was not the kind of person he would have wanted his son to live with, have a family with, be the mother of his grandchildren. But don't worry, Jack and I love each other, and I'll look after him.

He smiled at her then, and she smiled back, an open smile that peeled years off her. He took another sip of beer, and sat back, listening to the chatter between the three of them, the excited enthusiasm of youth, the blind faith that they couldn't fail, that everything would turn out well, that this was the start of their adult lives, with the future ahead of them, bright and clear and full of hope and promise, and the world theirs for the taking.

When the conversation faded into the background, and the words seemed to slow down as if someone had adjusted the recording speed, he didn't pay any attention to it, just revelled in the warm ambience of a family gathering, enjoying his pint and the mental release from the pressures of his job, pleased to see his children together and enjoying one another's company.

Not until Jack looked at him and frowned and mouthed in silence did he realise all was not well. Then Maureen's hand gripped his arm and shook it, as her voice came at him as if from a distance. Someone's seat toppled with a hard clatter that vibrated in his head, and a smile stretched his lips. And the last thought that came to him, even as his peripheral vision darkened, was – it's good to see that it's all worked out well in the end, my family.

ACKNOWLEDGEMENTS

Writing is often a lonely affair, but this book could not have been published without help from the following: Jon Miller, formerly of Tayside Police; Kenny Cameron (retired), Police Scotland; and Alan Gall, retired Chief Superintendent, Strathclyde Police, all for police procedure; Professor Dame Sue Black, for the gory stuff; Robbie Hughes, Group Distilleries and Estates Manager, and Stephanie McIntyre, Production Support Assistant, Glengoyne Distillery – well worth a visit – for inside information on the whisky distilling process; Peggy Boulos Smith and Al Zuckerman of Writers House for advice and encouragement when it was needed most; Howard Watson, for professional copyediting to the [n]th degree; Rebecca Sheppard, Senior Desk Editor, Sean Garrehy, Art Director, Brionee Fenlon, Marketing Coordinator, and John Fairweather, Senior Production Controller, for working hard behind the scenes at Little, Brown to give this novel the best possible start; and in particular Krystyna Green, Publishing Director, Constable, for once again placing her trust in me and encouraging me with her enthusiastic praise for this novel. And finally, Anna, for putting up with me, believing in me, and loving me all the way.

Enjoyed *Dead Still*?

Read on for a special taster of the next book in T. F. Muir's

DCI Gilchrist series . . .

The Murder List

CHAPTER 1

DCI Andy Gilchrist's breath fogged the air in thick clouds that burst from his lungs in painful gasps. A quick glance at his Fitbit monitor showed a pulse rate of 112 – higher than he would've liked. But he gritted his teeth and pressed on. About 800 metres to go, as best he estimated – half a mile in old money. He concentrated his gaze on the Macdonald Rusacks Hotel in the distance or, more correctly, a patio window that overlooked the balcony above the Rocca Restaurant, glowing yellow from a bedroom lamp within—

His mobile vibrated. He pulled it from his pocket – ID Jessie – slowed down as he made the connection, his logic warning him that Jessie wouldn't call at that hour in the morning unless it was serious. He drew to a halt, and gasped, 'Yeah?'

'We've got another one,' she said, without introduction.

Gilchrist sucked in lungfuls of air, unable to speak.

'You all right?'

'Yeah,' he managed. Two more deep breaths settled the pounding in his chest enough for him to say, 'Another . . . as in . . . you think it's . . . the same killer?'

'Yes. No doubts. None at all.'

He'd never known Detective Sergeant Jessie Janes to be indirect, but something in the rush of her voice warned him that this recent murder was one of the worst she'd seen. 'I'm listening,' he said.

'Margaret Rickard. Sixty-three. Employed with Santander for fifteen years as an HRD assistant. Retired two years ago. Lived alone. Never married. One brother. Older. Tom. He called it in.'

'Tom found her?'

'Took his dogs for a walk this morning. Popped into her home in Kincaple to make her a cup of tea. Said he and Margaret have been early risers their whole lives. Said they were close and kept in touch mostly every other day. He's a wreck, the poor sod.' She let out a pained sigh. 'No bloody wonder.'

Gilchrist felt that familiar frisson shiver his spine, a sensation he always felt at the start of an investigation. Of course, as he was presently signed off from work, this wasn't his investigation *per se*. Still, he and Jessie had kept in contact over the last four weeks, she on the pretext of asking how he was keeping; he to keep up with Office matters – you could only take so much of not being part of a working unit—

'It's early days,' she said, 'but as best we can tell there's no connection between Rickard and Soutar.'

Adam Soutar, this killer's first victim. 'Was Soutar a customer of her bank?'

'No. RBS.'

'How about Tom? Maybe he knew Soutar?'

'No. According to Tom, the name Adam Soutar means nothing to him.'

Gilchrist didn't want to give up on the idea that Rickard and Soutar somehow knew each other, but his team would uncover a connection if one existed. His breath had settled, his thoughts seemed clearer. 'Where did he find his sister?'

'In the living room.'

'So how did he get in? Does he have a key?'

'He does. Said he rang the bell, but Margaret didn't answer. She's usually up and about at that time. So he let himself in.'

'When did he last speak to her? Did he say?'

'Saturday afternoon. Last time he visited.'

'He hadn't phoned her since?'

'Haven't checked that yet. But there's no reason for him to lie.'

Probably not, although Gilchrist knew from experience that you never could tell. 'Any sign of forced entry?'

'None.'

'So how did the killer get in?'

'Maybe he knew her?'

He pressed the phone to his ear, preparing for the brutal stuff. 'Okay,' he said. 'Let's have the details.'

'Tom found her on her back, on the living-room floor. Naked. Spread-eagled. Hands and feet nailed through the carpet.'

'Post mortem?' he asked, more in hope than curiosity.

'Too much blood. She was definitely alive when the nails were hammered in.'

'Dear God.' He closed his eyes. How anyone could do that to another human being didn't compute. He didn't think that nailing someone to the floor in a crucifixion-like form was intended to send any kind of anti-religious message. No, not at all. He thought he knew the psychopathic mindset well enough to know that this MO was the work of someone who needed to experience ultimate domination, control of life over death, and to inflict unbearable pain – and humiliation, of course. Let's not forget humiliation.

He opened his eyes. 'She was naked. Where were her clothes?'

'On the settee.'

'Neatly folded?'

'Yes.'

Well, there he had it. If ever he had doubts that it was not the same killer, they were quashed right there. And in his mind's eye, he ran through the scenario preceding this latest killing: Margaret Rickard, a retired woman in her sixties, shaking with mind-numbing fear as she is instructed to strip naked – *Take them off. The lot. That's it. To the buff* – her killer-to-be gloating with psychopathic satisfaction as she peels off her bra with hesitant shame, then with a final shiver of resignation steps out of her underwear to stand before him . . .

Now why him? Why not her?

But he cast off that thought. Too much strength needed to overpower a man as big and as fit as Adam Soutar – six two, eighteen stone, known to be a serious hill climber, someone who would not be overpowered by gentle force. No, this killer was male. Strong. And fit. He had to be. So . . .

He pulled his thoughts back . . . she stands before *him*.

Naked. Trembling. Terrified of what is about to happen.

Then what?

Her soon-to-be killer watches with grim-faced impatience, eager now to get on with his murderous task, as she follows his next instruction. Struggling in vain to hide her nudity, she folds her clothes one by one, piece by piece, taking care to press each garment flat – just as Soutar had done – before placing them on the settee in a neat pile.

Then came the part that Gilchrist struggled to comprehend.

'Any signs of resistance?' he asked.

'None.'

'So she lies down on the floor, stretches her arms and legs wide, and lets herself be nailed to the floor?'

'That's what it looks like.'

Just like Soutar, a powerful man who appeared to have simply spread himself out on his bedroom carpet without objection, and let himself be nailed to the floor. It didn't make sense. Doctor Rebecca Cooper, Fife's foremost forensic pathologist, confirmed no drugs in Soutar's system, other than a mild level of alcohol equivalent to a couple of glasses of wine, which Soutar had been known to favour, more or less on a daily basis.

'I don't get it,' he said.

'That makes two of us.'

'Where's Soutar's body now?'

'Still at Bell Street with her Royal Highness.'

Bell Street Mortuary was where Cooper performed post-mortem examinations. If she had unresolved concerns over cause of death, she wouldn't release the body until she'd ticked all the boxes. On hearing about Soutar's murder on the news, then phoning Jessie for details, Gilchrist had resisted the urge to visit the mortuary – after all, he'd only been signed off that week. But he made a mental note to talk to Cooper later that morning, and felt a bitter wave of resolve sweep through him as he prepared for the question he barely had the nerve to ask.

He faced the sea, focused on a light on the horizon, and steeled himself. 'Any other injuries to the body?'

'Her tongue's been cut out.'

'Oh for God's sake.' He emptied his lungs, then sucked in air for all he was worth. He struggled to block out the horrifying image, shifted his gaze to the Eden Estuary, and forced his mind to recall a recent photograph he'd taken from the West Sands – black sea lightening under a heavy-clouded dawn sky, Tentsmuir Beach a sliver of white on the other side of the estuary. It looked as if he'd printed the photo in black and white, but that February morning had been so dull the world could have been devoid of colour.

But it was no use.

Unsummoned images flickered into his mind in blood-red flashes. You couldn't pull out a tongue with your fingers – too slippery – and the body's natural reaction would retract it into the mouth. No, you needed some tool to grip it and stretch it long enough to remove it with a scalpel. He felt certain it had to be a spiked tool of sorts to pierce the tongue and grip it with no fear of slipping – like a carpet fitter's knee kicker. But knee kickers were hefty pieces of equipment, and too big to squeeze into—

'You still there?'

'Yeah, I'm just . . .' He shook his head and turned from the estuary, found his gaze returning to the Rusacks as his fear of the next question grew. Even so, he had to ask. 'Was she alive when her tongue was cut out?'

'Looks that way. Fair amount of blood on her face, neck, and carpet.'

'And the tape?'

'Yes.' Jessie let out a sigh. 'Mouth taped. Nose, too.'

Just like Soutar.

He closed his eyes, squeezed the bridge of his nose until he felt pain. Nailed to the floor, staked out naked and helpless, unable to breathe, the stump of your tongue bleeding profusely, it would take less than a few minutes to drown in your blood – not to mention the pain that would surely push you to the brink of unconsciousness as your body writhed in agony against the nails in a futile struggle to stay alive . . .

He opened his eyes, and realised he hadn't asked the obvious.

Soutar's body had gone through one final act of humiliation – a single vertical cut through his left nipple, confirmed by Cooper to have been done post mortem. No one could explain why the killer had cut through Soutar's nipple, other than to suggest it was some act of depravity from which he took sickening satisfaction, God only knew why.

'Any post-mortem cuts?' he asked.

'Yes,' Jessie said.

Her hesitancy had him asking, 'Through her nipple?'

She let out a heavy sigh, warning him that worse was yet to come. 'Again, it's early days, Andy, but I don't think Soutar's nipple was cut just for the hell of it. The killer was leaving us a message.'

'A message? What sort of message could a sliced nipple leave?'

'He was cutting a number.'

'Ah,' he said, as his sense of logic gave him the answer. The single slice through Soutar's nipple could mean only one thing. Number one. Soutar was his first victim. 'And you know that now,' he said, 'because the number two was cut into—'

'No, Andy. Try *four*.'

His breath clogged in his throat. Four could mean only one thing. Dear God, surely never. 'So there are two more victims—'

'Correct—'

'Nailed to some floor in some building—'

'Correct—'

'And no one has a bloody clue where.'

'None whatsoever,' she added.

The difficulty facing the investigation team struck him with such overwhelming force that his immediate thoughts were of certain failure. Victims one and four had been found in the Kingdom of Fife; Adam Soutar in his home in Cupar, Margaret Rickard in her home in Kincaple on the outskirts of St Andrews. But it didn't necessarily follow that victims two and three had also been killed in Fife – provided, of course, that one and four referred to the order of the killings, and not to some obscure numerical code known only to the killer. But with nothing to go on, he said, 'I need to see Soutar's files.'

'Already on your desk. As soon as I saw the number four, I knew you couldn't resist. Besides,' she added, 'we could really use some help.' A pause, then, 'Where are you? Want me to pick you up?'

'How soon can you get to the Office?'

'Fifteen minutes, give or take.'

'Make it twenty, and bring the coffees.'

She chuckled. 'Want to share a muffin?'

But Gilchrist had already ended the call, and was jogging back to his car.

CHAPTER 2

When Gilchrist entered the North Street Police Station for the first time in four weeks, it felt surreal, as if he wasn't there at all, but was recalling memories through anxious dreams while he convalesced at home like Dr McAuley – his local GP – insisted he should. *Take it easy, and put your feet up for once in your life.* But being signed off for eight weeks due to ill health – even though he had the toughest time acknowledging that exhaustion could in any way be termed *ill health* – was more than he could be expected to handle.

Upstairs, he entered his office and was overcome by the oddest sense of stepping into the room for the first time, or perhaps more correctly, the uneasy feeling that his position of Detective Chief Inspector of St Andrews CID had long been forgotten. Gone were walls that once held tattered corkboards crammed with highlighted memos, dog-eared reports, scribbled Post-its, spiked to the cork with more pins than a hedgehog has spines. Gone, too, was his whiteboard that traced a history of past investigations, older case notes visible only as wiped-out ghostly images over which more recent timelines, places, names of suspects, had been circled, boxed or linked with arrowed lines that swept with investigative certainty from one to the other. Instead, in their place hung two whiteboards, pristine clean, magnetic markers and a row of coloured pens neatly positioned in the boards' trays.

The wall by the side of his desk, on which he'd Sellotaped handwritten to-do lists or blue-tacked crime scene photographs, had been stripped clean, too, patched up and painted. In fact, as he took his seat at his desk he saw that the entire room had been painted. He tried to remember what shade of cream the walls had been – lighter or darker? – but his thoughts were distracted by a loose-leafed folder that sat squarely on his uncluttered desk.

He opened it and forced himself to study the crime scene photographs.

Adam Soutar's unseeing eyes stared out at him, wide and petrified, as if he'd peered over his taped nose and died from shock. Gilchrist flipped onto the next image – another of Soutar's face, not as close-up – which showed trails of blood over his bare chest. He flipped to the next image – more of the same – then the next, and the next, and again until he was turning over the photos like a card shark searching for a missing ace.

Even so, it was no use. He pushed to his feet, reached for the window, and opened it wide. He sucked in clean, cold air. His head spun, his peripheral vision darkened, and for one moment he wasn't sure if he was having a panic attack, or suffering from the exertion of his early morning jog. He found himself placing both hands on the window sill, closing his eyes, and lowering his head until the dizziness passed—

'Got a blueberry muffin to share,' Jessie said. 'Your favourite.'

He turned from the window, tried to give her a smile, but failed.

Jessie frowned for a moment, then caught sight of the opened folder. 'Bloody horrific, isn't it?' She held out his Starbucks. 'Your usual latte. That'll get rid of the foul taste in your mouth.'

'Thanks,' he said, and took a welcoming sip.

She grimaced, nodded to the crime scene photographs. 'I won't challenge you with details of where I've just come from. But I'm sorry to say it's more of the same.' She tore off a chunk of muffin, threw it into her mouth, and downed it with a slug of coffee. 'I was doing well with my diet until this morning. No chocolate. No muffins. Now I know you're to blame.' Another sip, then, 'You not having any?'

He shook his head. 'I'll stick with this for the time being.'

'Are you sure?' Her hand hovered over the muffin.

'Positive.'

'Your choice.' It didn't take her long to devour the rest of the muffin, three bites as it turned out. She dabbed a tissue at her lips, then grinned. 'I'd forgotten how good these are.' She nodded to the folder again. 'You get a chance to read any of that?'

He shook his head. 'Just the photographs.'

She reached for the folder, flipped through the photos one by one. She stopped at a close-up of Soutar's bare chest, then pulled the image closer. 'You know, I hadn't noticed until now, but that cut's sliced right through the centre of his nipple as if he's measured it precisely.'

Intrigued, Gilchrist leaned forward and, with a sense of purpose that time, managed to study the image with professional dispassion. Sure enough, the skin above and beneath the nipple appeared to have been sliced in equal lengths. The open cut went through the centre of the nipple with almost surgical precision. He thought it odd, but said nothing.

'Now I've noticed that,' Jessie said, 'it makes sense of the mess this morning.'

'What do you mean?' It was all he could think to ask.

Jessie removed a pen from her pocket and opened her notebook. She drew a small circle, and crossed two lines through it – left to right, and top to bottom – forming the shape of a cross. Then she drew a diagonal line to create the number four. She held the notebook out to him. 'That's how Margaret Rickard's nipple was cut,' she said. 'With precision.'

'And equally spaced?'

'As if he's measured it.'

'So we're looking for a psychopathic killer with OCD tendencies?'

Jessie shrugged her shoulders. 'All I'm saying is, that it's odd. Don't you think? But now I think about it . . .' She flicked through more images of Soutar's body until she found what she was looking for. 'Here,' she said. 'Take a look.'

Gilchrist stared at Soutar's face, his mouth taped with duct tape, his nose, too. It took several seconds before he thought he saw what Jessie seemed excited about. 'It's as if he's placed the duct tape across his mouth and nose with care,' he said.

'Try precision,' she said. 'See? The tape's been cut with scissors, not ripped.'

'It's duct tape. You can't tear it off like masking tape. You *have* to cut it.'

'But do you have to line it up?' She pulled the photo closer. 'He puts the tape over the mouth first, then stretches another strip over the nose, so that the ends match up.'

Gilchrist had to agree. Soutar's nose had been flattened to one side by the tape being stretched to line up the ends. But something still wasn't right. 'He couldn't do that.'

'Why not?'

'Think about it. He's cut the tongue out. Soutar's alive and kicking, about to drown in his own blood, and the killer takes time to place the tape over his nose and mouth with precision? I don't see how that's possible.'

Jessie stared at the image, as if seeing it for the first time. 'You have a point.'

He took the photo from her, and pulled it close. He studied the image and came to see what he thought everyone, including himself, appeared to have missed. 'Have another look at Soutar's face,' he said. 'And tell me what you see.'

Jessie eyed the photo for a few seconds. 'He looks terrified?'

'Other than that.'

It took five more seconds before she squinted a look at him. 'Is this you back to your old tricks, or what?'

'Your tongue's just been cut out, and you're drowning in your own blood. You'd be coughing and spluttering and spattering blood all over the place.'

She frowned at the photo. 'You're right. There's some blood, but not a lot.'

'Cooper's PM report concluded that Soutar died by drowning in his own blood. So was the tape placed there post mortem? Or not?'

'Post mortem, I'd say. It's too precise to be done when he's alive.'

'Agreed.'

'So he waits until he's dead, then tapes him up with precision.'

Gilchrist nodded, as other thoughts filtered through his mind. 'I'm assuming we still have the tape,' he said.

'We do.'

'If both strips of tape were placed post mortem, then I'd imagine the other side would show minimal blood, rather than being awash in the stuff.'

'I'll get onto that,' Jessie said, then smiled up at him. 'It's good to have you back, Andy.'

He gave a wry smile, and closed Soutar's folder with a finality he longed for. Then he walked from his desk to the window, all of a sudden overwhelmed by his return to the Office. Until that moment, he'd thought he'd been more than ready to get back to work, that he was taking unfair advantage of being signed off for eight weeks, being paid for taking the time to get into shape again; change of diet – less of the starchy stuff, and more fish and chicken; and a composite fitness regimen – light weights, take it easy with the trunk curls, timed jogs along the West Sands. But now he was back at the Office, looking at images that would be cut from triple X-rated horror movies, was he really ready for it?

He let his gaze drift over the old familiar scene below.

Beyond the boundary walls, to the backs of the buildings on Market Street, in winter window boxes that sat on kitchen sills, he could just make out the faintest hints of colour – hyacinths, crocuses, winter aconites, past their best. In drab back lawns, daffodil stems poked through frosted soil as if to insist that winter really had passed, and spring was here at last. He found his thoughts drifting to his garden in Windmill Road, before his late wife, Gail, had left St Andrews and pissed off to Glasgow, both kids in tow, before he sold up and bought a cottage in Crail. He remembered how Gail used to spend hours tending bulbs in readiness for spring – one of the many things he liked about her – which had his thoughts returning to Margaret Rickard, retired, living in her cottage on her own, lonely, harmless, her life snuffed out for seemingly no reason. What had her thoughts been that morning? Now they were gone. She would never again see the heart-warming colours of spring, or smell the promise of summer on westerly breezes—

'What're you thinking, Andy?'

He kept his back to Jessie, and said, 'Can you give me a few minutes?'

'Everything all right?'

'Just a few minutes, please.'

Without a word, she left the room.

He waited until he heard the lock click before he lifted a hand to his face and wiped it dry.